SHIVER ME

SHIVER ME

Book one of the Wretched Lady Series

VERMILLION

To anyone who feels Fate has forgotten them. Worry not.
She'll be knocking again shortly.

And to my Js, who believed in Shiver Me before I ever did.

This romance contains explicit content and is not suitable for young readers.

Full list of content warnings can be found at Readvermillion.com

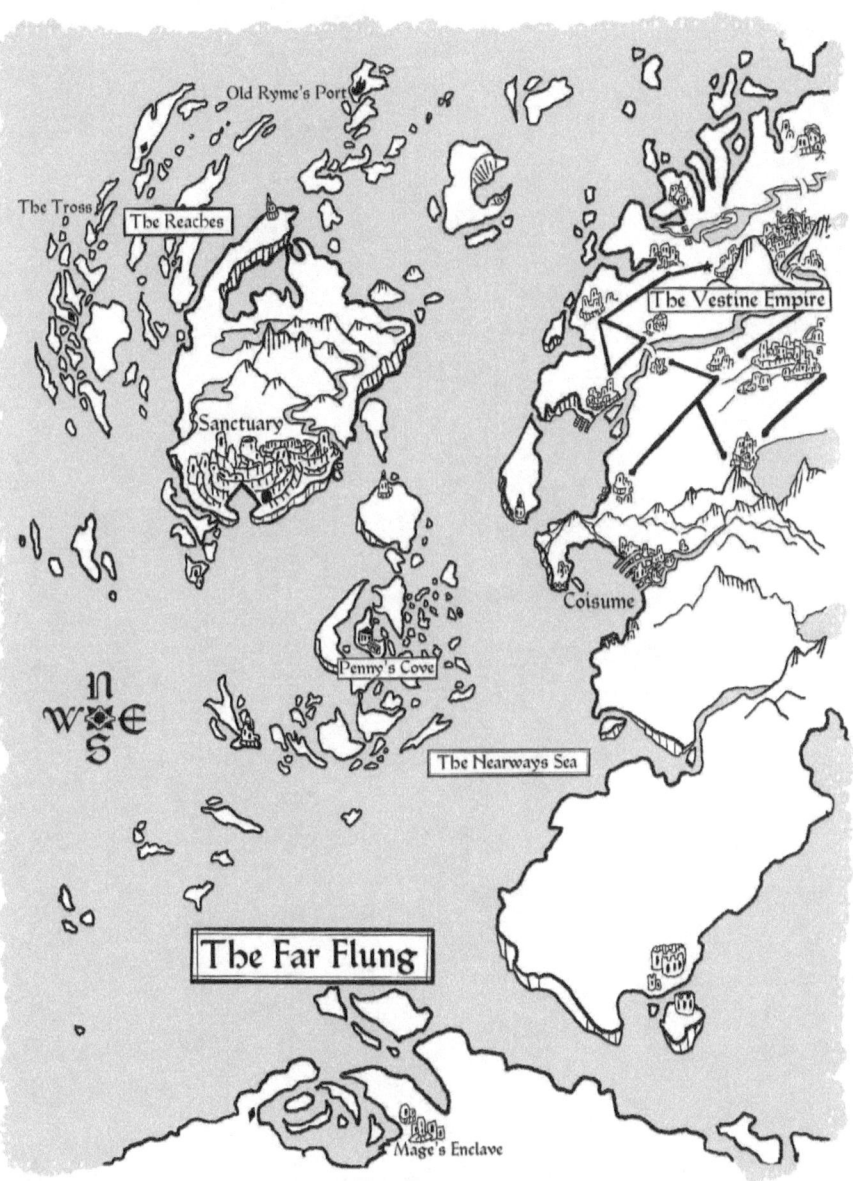

1

CONNOR

The *Wretched Lady* rolled under my boots, her decks held together with pitch and the last of my crew's goodwill. Her hull sliced through the waves toward a curious prize. Another ship. A merchantman, almost unheard of in these parts. She was small but polished, with crisp new sails and shining wood. Fat as an anchovy, I guessed, with a belly full of riches.

Suspicious.

Perhaps I should have left the strange ship to the wind and water. As it was, I had little choice in the matter. Here we would fight. My ship had spent too long waiting around, hidden outside Sanctuary's forbidding port in case the damned gates opened and we had a chance to get our captain back. We'd missed it—if the scant opportunity to breach its well-guarded walls had ever appeared—forfeiting our usual summertime raiding and trading.

The *Wretched Lady* was desperate. Salivating. Starving.

And what had we run across? A meal. The only such morsel in these waters for ages. Twenty years at least since Sanctuary had slammed its gates shut against the seas and its neighbors, choosing to speak with galleons full of guns instead.

White canvas fluttered ahead of me, tempting. Sailors scrambled on the little ship's ropes, trying to catch the wind we rode so sweetly toward her and run.

Our luck must finally have been turning, for these waters had teeth. Ships did not slip from the gates of the city on the great isle, they charged, heavy with shot, ready to blast pirates from the water. Sanctuary, its citizens called it. A city hidden behind ever-growing battlements of stone. Sanctimonious, more like.

Hard to believe in peaceful intentions when their gates remained locked tight, but their influence left bloody footprints across the islands. We pirates had seen enough of their mercy. The rest of the Reaches, too.

We had no need of Sanctuary.

This ship though, was a gift. No matter her purpose.

If I could take her.

The *Wretched Lady* needed whatever was in her hold. Whatever was valuable enough to risk these treacherous waters.

On the foredeck, with my blade at the ready and a foot primed on the salted wood of the railing, there was no room for hesitation.

I shouted our advance, my bellow catching nothing but air. Trenna, a deck above me, already pressed the *Wretched Lady* toward its quarry, careful not to lose the wind that filled our sails. The navigator was worth far more than her weight in salt, and the *Wretched Lady* was more than happy to do her bidding.

Trenna set her shoulder into the steering wheel and slowly, sweet seas, so slowly, our ship slid starboard, menacing the prow of the fancy skiff. Our crafts were of a size, but any good seaman knows the boat barely matters when you're fresh to the water. Just the same as his ship, the captain looked the part of a regular mariner in an oversized great-coat, though he seemed as uncomfortable on the great blue beneath us as I would be baking a loaf of bread.

Convincing, if he was truly lost in unfamiliar waters. Either that, or his mission was complicating his sailing. I could see the man, the halfhearted sweep of his arm, the fully trained turn of his heel. What was he playing at? If I slid my knife up his buttons, would his merchant's browns give way to Sanctuary blue?

I'll know soon enough.

I cared more about the shine on the boat beside us. Her stores. Her cargo. I wanted to get my feet on this ship more than I wanted breakfast. We'd been putting off repairs on the *Wretched Lady* for two months now, letting barnacles languish on our hull and our fastenings rust into bloody crusts that hurt to look upon. It was a wonder there was any white in our sails with all the patching we'd done. I was grateful my crew hadn't mutinied from the poor provisions in our rapidly emptying larder. I tested the weight of my cutlass, its worn pommel reassurance enough.

This prize would be ours.

The *Wretched Lady* would sing, her crew too, and I'd set aside my worries for a whole week, maybe two.

I was captain now, even if I hated the thought. I was ready to lead the crash of men into ship.

Some pirates had learned too much from Sanctuary. Sending their greenest men out as cannon fodder, just like the city did unfortunates from their most recent walls.

Not the *Wretched Lady*. Our captain was always the first over the side. Stakes were high and prizes were sweet, or, well, they had been until Griffin had disappeared into Sanctuary's dungeons.

My captain.

I hadn't replaced him. I was only holding his place.

I recalled his bloodied grin, the lazy swipe of his cuff over his brow, the weight of his hand on my shoulder at the beginning of a battle much like this one, urging me on. Griffin would have been the first over, alright.

I readied myself to fly over the side. I'd fill his boots as best I could.

Sanctuary's dungeons would crack. They had to.

We'd get Griffin out. We'd get him back. It was all the better that I was moments from a fight. I could burn off some fury over the fact that they'd gotten their silky, unsullied hands on him at all.

If there were bluecoats down there under all the homespun, I'd take a chunk out of Sanctuary's navy in his honor.

Clang!

Our figurehead, a buxom lass with the head of a boar, glanced off their prow with a crackle of splitting wood, her iron capped tits striking jagged gashes into the other boat's generous front end. Lucky for the little ship, her bones missed the tusks, which we'd sharpened like spears. I'd seen them punch a hole straight through the bow of a taller vessel.

I reached down, trying to free the nearest grappling hook from its iron fixture. It wouldn't budge, not even when I grunted at the rusty metal. *Great.*

I gave it a kick. Satisfaction rushed through me as the hook lifted up and into my waiting hand. The feeling fled as soon as I noticed the added weight of the clasp itself. I'd jerked the blasted thing out, nails and all, the missing apparatus exposing an empty circle where an aiming charm would have sat if we had any money to get one secondhand on the continent. Hiring a mage outright would take more coin than I'd seen in my whole life.

Cursing, I shoved the whole thing into a nearby crate, careful to keep the hooks away from my flesh. The *Wretched Lady* might be falling to shit but her prongs were still sharp. I couldn't afford to leave it lying about and I couldn't afford to lose it, not until our reward was a sure thing.

I gazed down the deck. My crew was there, ready at stations. They hadn't signed on with me, and we all knew it, but they still showed up. They trusted the *Wretched Lady*. I did too.

I'd been raised in the ropes of this same vessel, climbing the ladder from ship's boy to runner to, well, Captain. Didn't stop me from getting a little teary when I saw my fellow pirates lined up, armed to the teeth, ready to face death and worse for our *Lady*.

Tide almighty, let there be something good in the larder down there. Geese or honeyed ham or … anything that might soothe our aching bellies. My crew deserved better than old, hard biscuits and the bottom of the jam barrel. Anything would do.

"Captain!"

I jolted from my worries, caught drooling on the edge of a fight.

A stout man peered over the gun that separated us, all piercing blue eyes, white skin, and red beard. The butt of a gun swung against his chest in the wind. I knew there were two others primed at his back.

"Aye, Rory?"

He thrust another hook, this one firmly attached to the side, into my hand.

"They're up to something."

He didn't bother with my title again. I followed his gaze to the deck of our prize. A moment ago there had been a fair showing of a merchant crew, scrambling to ready themselves for our boarding. Now the deck lay quiet. Empty.

Men still perched in the rigging, but their hands had slowed on the winches, their heads bent, eyes glued to something below. Was it some trick? Magery?

Alarm bells rang in my ears, quieting only when I reminded myself that even the richest merchants couldn't afford to waste a mage on one tiny ship.

Sanctuary, on the other hand, had the gold, but not the goodwill.

They'd shut their gates to the mages, casting them out just like the rest of us. Those that had not fled back to their secret enclave in the south had been snapped up by the Vestine Empire and the free cities of the continent. I hadn't seen one of their gray cloaks on the seas since I was a kid.

Magic or not, these sailors were making my skin crawl.

Something was wrong.

Then I saw it. A bubbling of bluecoats at the entrance to the quarter deck.

Hah! Mystery solved.

They'd discarded the merchants' brown at last. With their disguises gone, even I could recognize a Sanctuary ship on the edge of Sanctuary's seas.

We'd have a better fight, then. They must have left their heavy guns at home or else they'd have put a hole through the *Wretched Lady* already. In fact, they seemed to have dropped the entirety of their fighting spirit. I watched the trickle of bright blue sailors become a ribbon and then a knot at the edge of their fair ship. They didn't shoot, or goad us, or even wave their shiny swords.

Always Sanctuary, never surrender.

The navy didn't give up, not without a fight.

From what I could see, the only one of them with a lick of sense was the helmsman, who was still trying to turn the ship away. It was futile. We were so close.

I should jump, rather than worry about all the blue below me. Take the prize.

Still, I waited.

Sailors filled the deck. I expected their challenge. Nothing came. More flooded out of the hatch, jerking wooden chests back and forth between them.

The captain strode forward, shoulders thrown back, as pompous as could be. Not a coward now, then.

The air hummed with the pent-up desire of my crew, our prize caught, straining against barely held control. I raised a hand, securing the other on the throwing hook. Rory, Trenna, everyone. All waiting. All holding.

A gaggle of men flanked the captain, looking for all the world like they were arguing among themselves. Those in the front had their backs turned to us, their attention on their fellows. A bit insulting to our pirate dignity, that.

Was it mutiny? Surrender? Some other foul trick? Nothing mattered but the brand new fixtures and full stores aboard that sweet little ship. They were as good as mine. I swung myself up onto the rail.

A scream whipped through the air. I was fast, faster than any of my crew, and I was only halfway to leaping. It didn't sound like one of ours.

The bluecoats parted, revealing the source of the screaming.

The men escorted—well, that was a pretty word for it—passengers. These were no sailors, not with their skirts buffeted by the sea air. I'd never seen a woman, let alone two, aboard one of Sanctuary's warships.

I froze.

They couldn't mean to—

"Is this what you want, marauders? Take them then, and leave us be!" the captain screamed up at us, not knowing which dirty pirate deserved his ire.

One of the women, a smear of cream against naval blue, was putting up a mighty struggle. She managed to bite the hand away from her mouth and let out another shriek.

That was enough for me.

I steadied myself and leaped, the thrill of wind and the churning of the waves accompanying me. My mates would follow.

I hit the prize's deck, far enough from the crowd of bluecoats, my crew a moment behind, their shouts adding to the chaos. From the corner of my eye, I saw Rory smash down in the midst of our enemies, who were only now packing pistols and elbowing each other in an attempt to spread out and fight. I did not see the women. That was all the better. I was loath to kill anyone, much less a lady.

I caught one of the bluecoats over the head with the hilt of my cutlass, sending him to his knees. Another ran at me, one of the lucky few who'd cleared the cluster of terrified men. These sailors did not hold a candle to the regimented troops we usually encountered on a Sanctuary ship, but I was hardly privy to the navy's plans.

A whistle cut through the fighting—a crow's nest signal, mostly reserved for tricky sailing. Pella, up in the ropes, trying to get my attention. She usually camped out in our rigging, picking men off with her guns. I clobbered another soldier and searched her out.

She found me before I found her, waving a hand toward the water, legs anchored in the ropes.

"They've dropped them! Captain, look!" Her voice had a touch of frenzy to it. I peered over the railing, my blade at the ready while I followed her pointing finger.

In the space between the boats, a wooden chest floated, and a few more were sinking fast. Little to merit the visible whites of Pella's eyes, nor her coming all the way down here.

"The women, Connor! They dumped them!" Spit flew as she yelled, still pointing.

Two bluecoats brushed past me, busy fending off Rory's attack. I stuck a foot out, sending one of them sprawling into the other and grabbed Rory, drawing him to the side with me.

There. A white splotch of skirt and skin just under the surface.

Wash it all, the cruelty of this. A ship might be taken, and she might be sunk, but never were her passengers used as ballast to drop.

My hand tightened on Rory's arm, the only place I dared show my horror.

"We can get them, you and I. It means losing this prize," he said, calm in the midst of it all.

"Aye."

I needed this ship. We all did. But the sea herself would have our heads if we let innocents drown. She, and she alone, chose who lived and died in her waters.

One of the women had gotten an arm over a floating chest, and was fighting against the churning waves. *Good.* She might stand a chance if we got her out of the cold water. The other had disappeared. Sunk. Lost.

Not if I had anything to say about it.

Behind me, the deck was a slaughter.

What a prize the *Wretched Lady* would have had.

2

CONNOR

Alas, it wasn't to be.

"Wretches, to the sea!" My cry rippled over the scattered pirates.

Without waiting, Rory tossed his pistols up to our ship and dove into the roiling water below.

A laugh billowed out behind me.

I turned and found the other captain picking his way through the nearly beaten bluecoats, already celebrating the success of his twisted gambit. He was an everyman of the worst kind, and I set myself to memorizing his face. Beneath the gold of his hair, hard eyes gleamed, blue as the coat he'd spent so much time hiding.

"I knew you pirates would be desperate for a woman." His words turned my stomach. With my crew safely returned to our ship, or to the water to dive for the women he'd thrown over the side, I was the only one left to hear him. Curses clawed behind my teeth. I wanted to rail at him. I wanted to slit his throat.

The wind betrayed me, sails lifting above us. He would get away with it.

"Go on! I gave you two, boy. Be sure to share them good."

I pressed his face between the pages of my mind. There would be no forgetting the satisfied curl of his lip as he spilled his bile. The prize shifted below my feet. The ship was pulling away. Already, the Sanctuary men were rushing to unfurl sails and further her speed.

Without giving the sailors my back, I shoved my cutlass into my belt and took to the railing, my eyes still locked on the captain. I risked a glance at the water to gauge my jump, then flashed him a grin fit to scare even the hardest of naval men.

"Be assured, we will meet again." The threat hung between us.

Then I launched myself from the beautiful ship that should have been mine.

As I fell, I sucked in as much air as I could, time speeding feverishly around me as the hulls of both ships rushed past. Hitting the freezing crush of water, body straight as I could make it, I prayed the height of my leap would send me down like a cannonball and that the sea would guide me. The drowning woman had sunk farther with each drop of the captain's drivel, and I could only hope I had not let him speak too long.

My eyes opened, stinging with salt as I felt myself pushed down and down, under the shadow of the ships. All vibrancy was lost here, leaving me in the sort of darkness that swallowed other darknesses.

The sea was a kinder mistress than the Sanctuary's navy, certainly. Eerie as she was, the ocean was only as cruel as an innocent could be. As the power of my dive dissipated, my body begged me to swim back up, to give up. Against my better judgment, I continued down. Deeper, deeper. I searched for any sign of the woman's passing.

There. A smudge. I kicked toward it. No blood had been spilled in the water, so there was only the regular danger of sharks, and besides, this was man-made, square. A chest, one side dancing down faster than the other. I got a hand on it, less to capture it than to use its descent as a guide. I was in the right place. I had to be.

My brain had not given up protesting, and now my lungs

joined in, screaming. I was no trained diver, and my body knew it.

Another few seconds, I promised the beat of my own heart.

I reached as far as I could past the chest, letting it slip away. I could barely focus my eyes.

Nothing.

I couldn't stay down here.

I wanted so badly to breathe again.

I twisted, ready to ascend.

And there, a little to my left and not so very far down, I saw her. A cloud lighter than the rest of the muddle. A mess of skirts.

Thank the seas.

I resealed my lips and strengthened my resolve, swimming toward the woman. I was rewarded with the drift of an other-worldly white hand up from the depths of her clothing. It was enough to remind my body of my promise, and me of my purpose.

We weren't meant to be down here. *Not for long*, I whispered to my straining lungs.

I wasn't prepared for the scratch of fabric, even in the water, when I circled her body with an arm. She wasn't some stick, and I dreaded losing her as I kicked up. I slipped my hand through the sturdy buckles at her waist and wove my fingers into the gaps between her buttons. If she was dead, then she wouldn't mind, and if she wasn't, she had other things to worry about.

My chest was near bursting. Would my legs give out? I kicked again and again. I could not shake the desire to leave her and fly up. My free arm cut through the water. Would anyone question me if I said I'd found nothing? No one would ever know.

Kick.

I wanted to breathe. I needed to.

Kick.

I couldn't do it. I was too far down.

Kick.

The woman's dress alone weighed as much as a hundred of me.

Kick.

I gave up.

I wriggled my hand out of her underpinnings. I dragged the other down, hoping to propel myself that much quicker to the surface.

My wrist caught in the woman's sash, and I pulled against it, trying to free myself. We would both have watery graves.

Kick.

No! I wanted to scream. I could barely think. My head ached from the cold. I sent my hand down again, pushing the water back. I had to make it to the surface, if only to chase down the laughing bastard who'd kept me from my prize: a hold full of new fastenings, enough hardwood to patch the *Wretched Lady*'s many scrapes, and a belly stuffed with better food. That captain seemed like the type to force starving men to watch him pick delicacies off his plate.

Kick.

Was that the shadow of the ship?

Kick.

Kick.

I only had a few more in me before we were lost.

Kick.

Pressure against my back.

A hand in my shirt and another on my arm, pulling me up. The woman and her thousand-pound dress too, suddenly as light as a feather.

Was this the end? Would the sea lay us so gently to rest?

But this was the surface, not the depths, and suddenly I was gasping, my eyes streaming, body assured of life again. I sucked down salted air, choking on the sea where she lapped at my mouth, as if to remind me of where I had just been and who had granted me passage.

I was more spit than man, but I was alive.

A rope was pressed into my face, and behind it… Alecto, hair slicked midnight over his sun-browned face. He must have been freezing in the water.

"Climb, Connor." My head spun at the instruction. I found Rory at my back, face bobbing just above the surface of the sea, a great wash of skirt over his shoulder. Farther on was Billy, the eerie green streaks in her eyes somehow stronger down here, against the water, her freckled cheeks split in a grin. She pressed the drowned girl's head up out of the waves.

"Her first. There's water in her lungs. I can…" I reached for the body. I could help.

Another head popped up. Silver, the hair he was named for plastered to his head, molten metal against his dark skin. He tugged at something under the surface. More rope, which he'd secured around the woman and anchored to himself. He would guide her up.

I sighed in relief, though my limbs burned from the strain of keeping my head out of the water.

"Captain, can you climb?" Alecto again, his tone too gentle for our present circumstances. If I couldn't, he would haul me up too.

"Her first," I insisted. I had to see this through. "And the rest of you, get out of the water!"

"We have more than enough line, Captain." Alecto waggled the rope in my face one more time, and gave me a push that might have been playful if not for the concern rolling off him, off each floating member of my crew. I was hardly their captain, no matter what they called me as a courtesy.

I'd lost our prize, half my crew were tempting fate in the freezing water, and I'd nearly killed myself searching for what might be a corpse.

I took up the rope, the siren song of a warm, dry deck louder than the ache in my muscles or the argument in my head, and began to climb.

3

CONNOR

I cleared the railing of the *Wretched Lady*, my hands swiftly becoming a mess from the salt and rope. My eyes swept the deck. My crew was standing around, their attention split between the retreating prize and our new passenger. A woman— well and whole from what I could see—sitting up on the deck, being fussed over by Pipes and Pella. I hoped she would be willing to trade her wet clothes for a blanket.

My elation at the stranger's rescue was short lived.

"Devils!"

The girl thrashed against the weight of her soggy gown, forcing the pirates around her to step back or risk a wounding from her nails.

"Where is she?! Drowned? Dead?!" Accusations leaped from her mouth like mullet from the sea. Her white hands slapped down on the splintery planks when she found no one within range of her fury.

I thanked the water that still clung to those skirts, for if she could have stood she would surely have struck someone. My crew had endured enough today.

This lady had every right to her anger, but it was unfair to direct it at us pirates, who'd just risked our lives and our prospects for her comfort. If her companion was drowned, it was no fault of ours.

"Where is she? What have you done to her?! You brutes!" the lass cried.

"The question isn't what we've done to her, but what we'll do with you." I wanted my words to sting, to cut through whatever panicked story she'd built in her head. Cruel of me, maybe. I was still a little shaky from my own brush with the deep. Her head slowly turned, eyes wide for an instant before her brows crashed down and her mouth opened in a rage. I didn't give her time to unleash it.

"If I'm not mistaken, you need a berth." I pretended I wasn't doing my best impression of a drowned rat. This was still my ship, and she was still my problem. "I cannot promise you any destination in particular, but surely the next town or two will have a situation suitable for a lady."

It was far from our most pressing concern. We both needed to shed our wet clothes, or else risk even this mild weather killing us where we stood.

"A berth? You must be a fool, for I would rather die in the water than beg passage on this tub." She managed to flip herself over, hands bunched in her heavy skirts and knees tucked. "Pirates..." she muttered, trying to rise.

"I don't see that you have much choice, lass. You were forcibly expelled from your most recent accommodations." She blanched, as much as someone who'd only just gained their color back could.

"As if you rogues weren't the reason for it! Chasing us across the sea!" She'd recruited a barrel for leverage, and was pulling herself up.

We were spared her continued violence when a great yell went up from the side. The lady and I slipped into silence as a slack body was towed onto the deck by the remainder of my crew. I caught Alecto's gaze as he slid his hands from under her sodden shoulders. The young man shrugged and stepped away.

Silver was preoccupied, undoing the rope around his middle, but I guessed he wouldn't grace us with a smile.

Only the sea had any say in who'd live or die this day.

"Get back, you louts. We haven't much time."

Trenna cut through the commotion to kneel beside the prone woman, her coat pooling around her heels. She bent to listen at the woman's chest, her black hair slipping from its unruly braid. The stranger was deathly pale even against her light clothing. If all went poorly, it would be her burial shroud. Trenna began to fiddle with the many straps involved in the removal of the woman's seas-cursed dress.

I stepped in, ready to help.

"Oh, you absolute beasts! You've killed her!" The girl started back up again, hobbling past me, her blond brow drawn down and pretty face twisted in anguish. "You've killed her," she screeched again, though the sound drained away as she was confronted with her friend's limp and bloodless body.

I didn't envy her. We'd tried, but there was an old saying: a drowned man becomes the ocean himself, and this girl was bluer than the calm seas. I watched as Billy, still wet from the rescue, offered the angry young woman a steadying hand. The newcomer hissed at the pirate, but curled her fingers around her arm anyway.

The distinct sound of ripping buttons dragged me back to the body on our deck.

"Connor, can you breathe for her?" Trenna looked up at me, her jaw set and eyes dark with the weight of the day. She hadn't made much headway on the tight neck of the dress. "Water in the lungs," she whispered when I knelt at her side, gesturing at the woman's partially rent bodice. "I can't get this off."

I took in the many buckles and straps and felt bile rise in my throat. She needed room to breathe, if we could help her start again. I drew my cutlass. There was no way I could open one of her fastenings with my hands half frozen, much less all of them.

Her friend began screaming in earnest as I slid the blade

down the drowned woman's chest, sawing at the cloth that caged her.

"He's not—" Billy tried to calm the woman, grabbing at her arms when she struck out again.

"I'm trying to save her life," I growled at the girl, slicing her friend's dress to her navel. The fabric split under my knife, revealing a map of veins over the woman's breast.

A sob leached out behind me.

It was never pleasant, hoping my hands could do what her body wouldn't. I focused down, layering all the power in my body over her heart, forcing it to beat, willing her breath back into her body.

Trenna had the woman's mouth open, and was checking for a blockage. I pumped and released. Again and again.

The woman's body jerked. Water cascaded from her lungs with a vengeance, leaving her sputtering and miserable. But then it was only spit spilling out, not ocean, and she was sucking in breaths like there was no better medicine.

Trenna didn't sit back in time to avoid the torrent. I only caught a splatter, my hands hovering, not trusting that her chest was really rising.

She was alive.

The sobbing grew louder, her friend's tears turning to joy. I spied the girl from the corner of my eye, catching the suffering on Billy's face as the stranger wrung her arm like a washday rag.

"It's alright, it's alright," Trenna murmured to the drowned woman.

"Alright?" The woman took in a ragged mouthful of air, the subtle lines around her eyes and between her brows deepening. "It's very much not. Which of you ruffians ripped my bodice?" She struggled up from the deck, wedging an elbow behind her so her other arm could clutch at the two halves of her dress, and glared at Trenna.

Deeming the pirate more of a curiosity than a threat, her gaze soon lit upon the rest of us. The stranger wasn't on the verge of tantrum, like her friend. Instead, she radiated the frustration of someone recently interrupted during an important task. As if she had been busy drowning and we were in the wrong for bringing her up.

"We only meant to help, lady. You'd swallowed half the sea," I said, hoping to ease her confusion. That drew her attention, but not quickly, not like my words mattered. I could almost see the wheels turning behind her sharp brown eyes.

"Indeed."

She took me in, from the puddles around my boots to my drenched hair and long-broken nose. I wouldn't have known what to think of me, or of any of us, if I hadn't been raised on the *Wretched Lady*. Pirates wore no uniform, and unlike Sanctuary where citizens were confined to their walls, the sea called to folks of all creeds and cities and races.

"I thank you for your care, then." Her tone was hard as stone, and it took the lazy movement of her hand across her chest for the wry humor of her words to reach me. She was no longer a corpse, and her breasts were still mostly exposed to the whole crew. Was she in danger of a faint or was I? An embarrassed blush rose up my neck at the speed of a winter storm.

"The fault is mine." I attempted to belay any ill feeling. "Your dress was so tight. The straps... We thought you deserved the best chance." I wouldn't apologize for saving her life. If she was a delicate from the city who would rather drown, I would not bother to dissuade her. In fact, she could leap into the sea anytime it pleased her.

My discomfort was alleviated by her peaky companion. The girl had managed to divest Billy of her jacket—the only dry thing on her—and was advancing with the much patched and filigreed thing.

"They saved you..." She tucked the crimson coat around her friend, fingers pecking like hens. "Oh, oh, I'm so glad. You... Well, to be completely honest, I thought you'd drowned."

"I did" came the matter-of-fact answer.

I wondered if I should let them fawn over each other for a time, but thought better of it. The naval captain's laughter was fresh in my mind. I wanted the man's blood and I needed his fixtures. There would be time enough for the women to take each other's measure once the *Wretched Lady* had her heading.

My crew watched us quietly, but I imagined what was running through Trenna's head, and Rory's, and Alecto's. If I didn't find another prize, their bellies would speak for them.

"Ladies, it is our great pleasure to welcome you aboard the *Wretched Lady*." I was in possession of at least one winning smile, and I turned it on them, hoping to convince them to make our life easy. "Call me Comely Connor." I paused for the inevitable round of snorts, then continued once the crew had themselves under control. "The captain of this humble vessel."

The women were not impressed. In fact, the girl curled her lip and tightened her arm around her nearly drowned friend.

"We will do our best to find you safe harbor, but if you'd prefer, you're welcome to shimmy right back down those ropes and see what the old sea hag has in store for you." Both women fixed me with matching glares.

"No? Well then, I recommend we all—" I jutted my chin at the wet Wretches. "—get out of our soaking clothes and get somewhere warmer." The pirates did not need a second warning to make themselves scarce. We knew the dangers of the cold and the wet.

Though the elder hid it well, and the younger stoked only the fires of rage, a shadow of fear crept in behind the women's eyes. As one, they clutched their dresses closer.

"You've caught us in the middle of—" I was cut off.

"Ransacking and harrying our boat!" the young woman bit out. Her companion's fingers found her sleeve and squeezed in silent reproach.

I could only nod. If they needed us to be mindless loot seekers, hell-bent on treasure and its companion, pleasure, that was a part we were born to play. Many pirates did. Not every ship was like ours, and these women would do well to fear most. Better if they were to trust none.

"Aye, we eat just like other men and our coffers don't fill by magic." I looked at them sidelong, as if nothing were riding on my next question. "You see, on a pirate ship, only cheats, murderers, and sundry dangerous characters get thrown off. I'm wondering which we have here in front of us." I let the words hang, eyes dancing between them, satisfied by their gasps as the women took my meaning.

They could not know how desperate I was to learn more about their ship. Sanctuary's navy masquerading as traders on a voyage too important to be disturbed by us pirates? With women on their ships? It would be the talk of the islands. Whether these city dwellers knew anything about it was still to be seen, but I couldn't question them while they shook to death in the wind. We'd only just saved them. It was better to leave them to stew while everyone dried out.

The crowd around us had thinned a little, but every ear was angled our way. The *Wretched Lady* hated Sanctuary, and their navy even more.

None of us had ever seen the bluecoats sacrifice passengers to the waves, but the cruelty of the act was familiar.

"It is a rather unfortunate situation we find ourselves in. You may call me Reg—" the drowned woman began, her face resigned.

"Oh no! You won't get us that way." The younger one spoke over her, her blue eyes burning. "I've read the papers! I know how names work on these repugnant ships." She turned to her friend. "Don't tell them, whatever you do. They'll take your name and toss it in with the rats! They'll tie it to the anchor and drag it against the bottom!" Her companion must have been in possession of a calming charm because one look from her had the girl trailing off.

In a way, the stranger was right. Names were complicated for pirates, but there was no reason to inform her of the intricacies of such things. Not when she believed us all ruffians.

"Why then, what does one go by on a pirate ship?" the drowned woman asked, with no sign that she believed her friend.

"A pirate name, of course," the younger said. "They all have one. Jim O'Bones, or Ninetails Nina."

I could not contain the laugh that her butchered exclamation conjured in my head. I'd never heard anyone mention the cat-o'-nine-tails with such enthusiasm.

The drowned woman thought on that a moment, then addressed me with complete confidence. "Comely Connor, I request a pirate name, and I believe my charge will need one too if we are to be your guests."

The girl nodded, blessedly silent.

"I'd be happy to oblige, ladies, but pirates choose their own names, just as soon as they join a crew of their own free will." The women's eyes went big as matching moons.

"Besides, names don't matter so much if you die out here. Which you will if you don't strip off those clothes. We have plenty of blankets, or you can borrow aught else from the crew. Don't want to lose you to the wet after we worked so hard to fish you from the sea." This did not land well with the women. They seemed bent on their own destruction. So be it.

"If that won't do for you, we'd all be happy to share a little body heat. Get you warmed up quick enough, that." I winked, wondering if they'd faint. Suddenly, our pirate blankets weren't looking so bad, I reckoned.

They looked at each other, their shivering apparent. After some silent debate, they nodded.

"Blankets are fine, if... if we are not bothered in them," the drowned woman replied for both of them.

Thank the seas. I was halfway to my own death out in the cold. "Done."

4

REGULA

We surveyed the captain's cabin, Odette and I.

It was the best the ship had to offer, but it paled in comparison to Odette's quarters in the city and even our berth on the *Edgewater*. The furnishings had passed shabby and were headed toward falling apart. The once proud wood needed a serious polishing, the iron fastenings of the window and doors were hanging on by their very last nails, and the upholstery was worn where it had once been lush.

It hardly mattered. We were safe and relatively warm, wrapped in blankets pulled from gods knew where and bundled well away from the cracks in the windows.

Odette took my hand, startling me from my inventory of the room. She rubbed it briskly, as if to reassure herself of my continued existence.

"Regula, I thought you lost," she whispered, still cautious not to name me before the pirates. Odette peered up at me even as she let my hand drop. Either I'd reassured her I was well enough, despite the events of the day, or I'd shaken her beyond what good manners she had. I was sure neither feeling would stick for long. I was mightily thankful for the friendship we'd built out of my employ. It was a comfort to have her with me after my brush with death.

The only daughter of one of the oldest Sanctuary families, Odette was a tempest, very little concerned with the hows or whys or whats of things. Spoiled as the worst pet. At the tender age of eighteen, she'd put her foot down and dispensed with her multitude of nannies, causing her parents another in a long string of headaches. I'd been their compromise: an older woman with little connection, a spotless reputation, and much comportment to recommend me. We'd spent the last few years together, with me as some muddle of companion, chaperone, and nursemaid.

For all our adventures, I'd never imagined we'd find ourselves on a pirate ship. It was just the sort of predicament that came naturally to Odette, and one that I'd been hired to avoid. Not that I minded. Odette was all lightness and ease, everything that I wasn't. In care of her, I'd lived more than I ever would have without.

We'd been bound for Coisume, the channel city across the Nearways Sea, on an errand of no small importance. After requests had turned to suggestions, and suggestions to demands, Odette had finally bowed to her parents' will, agreeing to wed the beau of their choice. They picked a husband from the Vestine Empire, shocking all of us who did not keep track of the wall's politicking. He was a son of the Ocuis, an immense merchant family from the continent rumored to be very close to the emperor. I had not even known the two parties were in conversation, since Sanctuary had been closed to outsiders for so long.

Odette had agreed to the marriage, as she always did things, on her own terms, chiding and cajoling until they'd agreed to let her source her own trousseau just as they'd sourced her new life. If Sanctuary was truly to be allied with the empire and through it, the continent, then she would be the laughingstock of his people in her dusty old fashions. She'd put her foot down. Her betrothed was foreign, and so too would be her trunks when she married him.

I'd kept out of it, mostly. Odette liked nice things and Coisume had them. The city of channels sat happily in the middle of the continent, protected from Vestine by a range of impassable mountains and a supposed monster in its bay. A crossroads for luxury, linked to the whole of the Far Flung by sea, with fabrics and jewels Sanctuary could only dream of. The perfect place to source a trousseau without owing the Ocuis, or worse, the empire, a favor. How Odette had managed it, I didn't know, but her family sent a petition all the way to the First for approval and we'd been booked on the *Edgewater* the next day.

As a married woman, she would have little need of a companion, and I'd planned to leave her in Coisume. The city was, if rumor could be trusted, a haven of sorts for women without title or fortune. Women like me.

I watched as Odette skipped around the room, pulling books from an overstuffed shelf and leafing through the papers on the captain's desk. Her curiosities were simple things, easily satisfied. Nothing compared to the intrigues she'd weave when she was not allowed them.

We were really nothing alike. I'd be the first to admit to being quieter, harder, and less willing to reach for the zest of the everyday. In the glass over the washing basin, my clouded reflection was all dark hair, pale skin, and melancholy compared to her fresh golden self. I was a good head taller too, and at least a few stone heavier.

It made sense that I was the one who'd nearly drowned. I was glad of it. Odette would live for both of us, if it came to it.

The sea had changed me. There had been things down there that I simply couldn't understand. The irrepressible cold. The struggle against the water, against my own body. A great shadow. The swish of scales against my legs. I closed my eyes against the memory.

I was here. Safe. Alive.

Nothing had taken a bite out of me.

Even if the ocean wasn't to be my grave, Odette was in the midst of losing me. It had been in her eyes, somewhere behind the dramatics, these last few weeks. She may have even orchestrated this whole trip so that we could spend a little more time together outside of her father's fine apartments. In the inner walls of Sanctuary, wealth didn't do much more than stifle pleasantly. That said, it was infinitely more enjoyable than working to death along the outer walls or sinking so deep in the ocean that the fish couldn't even find you.

No matter how sad it made my charge, we both knew I would leave her in Coisume, if we ever reached it.

The pirates hadn't been part of my plan. I doubted very much that they'd deliver us perfectly to our chosen port. Even wet as a dog, the captain couldn't disguise the gleam in his eye. No doubt he had some indignity in store for us. I was sure of it.

Even if Odette and I left the ship in one piece, we would be changed. Our fates sealed. For better or worse.

"What should our pirate names be?" I mused, watching Odette still. Though she'd stripped down to her sodden undergarments and was wearing a worn blanket like a cape, she didn't look uncomfortable in the least. I, on the other hand, had hesitated to slip out of my own clammy getup. My dress was usually my comfort, a second skin, and I resented it for failing me when I needed my armor most.

"Didn't you hear? Only by accepting the path of the rogue do we acquire pirate names," she chirped, looking up at me with a halfhearted smile. She was tugging at a locked drawer, testing its resistance to her charm.

"Ah." I found it strange that she would take the captain at his word. Odette never listened to anyone else. "We must call ourselves something."

"You pick, Regula. You're a champ at these sorts of things. You know everyone better than they know themselves." She gave up on the drawer with a sigh, and plopped herself down on the exceedingly sad daybed. She was a picture. A sad-faced, soggy girl on a threadbare chaise on a rat-infested ship going gods only knew where.

"Give me a good one." She threw herself against the lifeless pillows and reordered her blanket. "It's been quite a day."

I leaned against the back of a sterner wooden chair and considered. The crew must already call us something. Would it be better to play into their imagining of us? Was Odette to be princess or milady in a mocking tone and I her lonely maid?

I looked out the many squares of window, ignoring the seafaring spider that had taken up residence in an empty pane. The moon had risen early, a slice barely visible in the not-yet-deepening blue sky. Odette and I had never had our affairs so far out of order. We were used to a boring sort of life in Sanctuary, a safe one.

I was all too familiar with my own past, my failed marriage and subsequent fading away in the walls, but Odette was as yet untouched by that cruel fate. Perhaps she never would be. There was some slight possibility her husband would be suitable for her. The kind who'd allow her to do as she pleased, to chase whomever she'd like to become. It wasn't the usual way of things in the inner walls, nor in the whole of Sanctuary, but if anyone could do it, Odette might. Besides, her beau was a Vestal. The subjects of the Vestine Empire had decidedly different expectations of their wives.

I hadn't fared half so well as I hoped she would. I looked at myself, alone for all intents and purposes, when I wasn't trailing on the heels of fresher blooms, and knew it was because I'd allowed myself to be used as grist for Sanctuary's mill. I'd been married after a furious summer of courting. My father had been a hairsbreadth away from advancement when I'd come of age. He hadn't hesitated to pluck me from the fragile nest I'd been born into and barter me two walls up to cement his political chances and assure our family a home in the inner city.

My husband was somehow worse. Easily bored. Cruel when

provoked. When I proved less charming and less fertile than he'd imagined, he dropped me. I had done my duty, over and over, and still borne no fruit. My fall from grace was quiet, for I'd made no impression on the society of my husband, and my father was too busy with his next scheme to notice. When I hit the chair in my parents' house, papers signed to release me from my marriage, I was relegated to something more horrid than childhood. I barely knew who I was.

Odette had saved me in some ways. Or, at least, the opportunity she presented had. I'd wandered in and out of rooms as a chicken might, head full of nothing, until her family's offer came. I was the perfect companion for their daughter and their gold was the right fit for my father's pocket.

All at once, at the feet of a slip of a girl to whom running headfirst was instinctual, I came back to myself. Odette had thawed out my frozen life with the easy sunshine of her friendship. There was no satisfaction in simply watching, not when a hand was extended to me. The partnership had been intoxicating, and I, surely, had done nothing to deserve it. Just as I could do nothing to save it now.

"Venu, I think." The old story had come unbidden into my mind, carried by the cold memories that played behind my eyes. Venu's tragic tale was whispered mostly as a warning to temper youthful enthusiasm.

Venu was a maiden in some far-off kingdom, beautiful as a dove with the will of a bear. She made a habit of disobeying her parents. The king and queen of…oh I forget, decided that rather than deal with her, they'd lock her away in a great cave. The cavern was only accessible through an opening in the ground, which left her stuck at the very bottom, looking up at the sky.

After some raging over her circumstances, Venu's spirit broke. She gave up and cried. Seven lonely tears fell from her eyes. From each, much to Venu's surprise, sprang an eagle. These mighty birds were upset by her pain, and asked what they might do to ease her suffering. To each she whispered the same thing, and the eagles promised to return when they'd found a way to make her happy again, then flew up and out of the cave.

She waited one day, until the first eagle flew back with a bag of gold. That wasn't what she'd wanted. She and the first waited two days, until the next returned carrying a sack of sweet peaches. This didn't work either, and the eagle settled down to wait. A week later, the third eagle returned with a beautiful dress. It fell to the floor of the cave. Two weeks after that, the fourth eagle dropped a barrel of fine mead. A month passed before the fifth eagle brought a set of exquisite paints. The sixth eagle returned in another month, and dropped a jeweled crown to the floor. Everything lay in a great heap, and none of it made Venu feel anything but misery. All of her hope rested on the seventh eagle. She and the other eagles waited days, weeks, years. It never came.

Again, Venu gave up. Her eagles could not make her happy again. Hope was lost to her.

Venu asked the six eagles for one final service. They lifted her, their talons wrapped around her wrists and ankles, out of the cavern where she urged them to seek out their own destinies. As soon as they'd disappeared, she threw herself back into the hole, wishing only that her parents would find her bones.

"You're Venu, I mean."

Odette was watching me, her curiosity piqued.

"Oh, am I?" she asked archly, but I could tell a noble sacrifice for the sake of her own principles pleased her.

"Remind me why we're playing along with this pirate farce?" I paced toward her. The planks beneath my feet were worn in what felt almost exactly like this path.

"Would you rather be dead, Regula? It's their law or nothing."

I stopped in front of her, my shadow creeping across her prone form. No matter how tired she was, she would bite if threatened.

"The pirates? They seem content to leave us well enough

alone. You're the one who cares about our names." I had her, and she knew it. She wanted to play marauder, she was already half a pirate herself. That was the real difference between us. I hadn't the courage.

"Say I am Venu, what does that make you?"

I didn't have to answer. I was, as I had always been, the eagle on her shoulder.

5

REGULA

Venu, huh?"

The captain chewed on his lip. Relying on my limited knowledge of pirates, I wondered if this one wasn't too young to be in charge of much at all. Far too pretty too, once I looked past the broken nose. It didn't track with the grotesque pirates who graced the tales I'd been told.

He turned to me, destroying any hope I'd had of staying safely in Odette's shadow. How could a pirate have such honeyed eyes, hardened not at all by his profession? I hadn't considered that a ship's deck would be the perfect place to watch the sun sink, turning everything it touched to gold, including the captain of the *Wretched Lady*.

It seemed they'd left that out of the stories.

His interest in me sharpened, and I realized I'd missed another of his questions.

"Her eagle, sir," I said, with all the menace I could muster. No matter how friendly he seemed, or how proper his crew, there was always a chance that they might threaten my charge. Me? I cared little. I held no such sweetness as Odette. I wore the many years between us without complaint. If I was troubled by any of these pirates, I'd relish a chance to live up to my name and peck out their eyes.

"Ah." His gaze trailed over me. More to assess than to leer, I thought. It was a relief from those eyes boring into mine.

The corner of his mouth quirked up and he shook his head ever so slightly, disturbing the sandy strands of his hair and giving the sun an even better opportunity to kiss the tanned planes of his face. I stood in the blue shadows, wondering when I'd last seen a man. I was the one leering. I blinked, his outline cut bright on my dark lids.

I shook away my ill-mannered thoughts. My brush with drowning had awakened some long-sleeping piece of me. Danger was no longer distant. My situation was surely to blame for this fascination. Adventure had a way of quickening the breath and making the heart race.

As if to prove me right, the captain's attention returned to my charge, the movement draping his face in warm darkness, shadows gathering past his crooked nose. I shouldn't even have been looking. He couldn't be much older than Odette—an age I wouldn't wish to be again for a whole chest of gold. I'd spent most of those years transitioning from girl to wife. While I raged that Odette might repeat my experience, it didn't mean I should leave her to the whims of pirates.

Rogues though they were, they'd lent us bits and pieces of their wardrobes, and it was ridiculous what passed as fair dress on this ship. Kitted out in their tight knee pants and threadbare shirts, we must've looked a sight. Or at least, I must have. Odette probably doubled as a sailor's fondest wish on a long voyage, though she still wore her blanket as a cape for warmth. Mine waited for me in our cabin. I supposed I should be grateful we weren't in our wet undergarments. This was just the sort of thing that would send Odette's parents into an early grave.

I stepped in front of Odette, the movement made easy by the utter lack of fabric around me. I was mortified to be so exposed, but it was rather powerful to be able to just... do anything I wanted. If I hadn't been about to open my mouth and make demands, I might've done a jig.

"How'd you two end up my problem? Ladies rarely leave Sanctuary's gates much less…" The captain spoke before I could, despite my posturing. He trailed off, waving his hand toward the side of the boat.

He was flanked by two other pirates. One was the woman with the soft brown skin and long black braid, whose face I'd known in my strange drifting between this world and the next. She'd been the one to wake me from my watery sleep. Whether she'd used medicine, luck, or some magery, I knew not.

The other was a barrel-chested redhead who towered over the other pirates, threatening in the extreme. He shifted on his feet, arms crossed, and I wondered at the glint of gold in his brow. Three rings pierced the freckled skin around his ginger brows. No one else seemed concerned.

"We've already told you more than enough." I made sure my hackles were raised. I wished I had a comforting hilt on which to rest my hand.

The captain's jaw tightened. He hadn't expected any pushback.

"I think it best you go over it again… alone."

I shivered. Over my dead body.

"Sheathe your claws, Eagle. I promise no harm will come to you or your Venu." I must have scowled harder, because his lips twitched into that not-smile.

"He'll have his way whether you like it or not," the lady pirate grumbled, her tone verging on commiseration.

"His way is just what I'd like to avoid," I barked, effectively turning the attention back to my target. The pirate with the braid pinned me with her gaze, then shrugged. I took it to mean she wouldn't be standing in anyone's way.

The captain laughed. It was loose and rolling, childish even.

"Whatever fears you have, I'm afraid I can't assuage them."

I frowned. I hadn't expected unadorned words.

"I'll speak to you first, Eagle, so you might have the measure of me."

I opened my mouth to argue, then shut it. He'd rightly guessed that my worry wasn't for myself, but for my companion.

"And if I do not approve?" I said.

"Oh, you will." He smiled at this, his confidence so practiced as to be alarming. My hands curled into fists at my sides. Without skirts, I quickly realized they were visible to all.

The woman leaned in and whispered something to the captain. He shot her a look, but said nothing, only pursing his lips. She turned on her heel, braid swinging behind her, and disappeared up the stairs to the next deck.

Did all pirates keep this many women aboard? In all the horrible tales of marauding ships and captured prizes, I'd never heard them mentioned. And yet, here they were, dressed to some strange, dazzling code and shoulder to shoulder with their captain and all the rest of the men.

The giant stayed where he was planted. I was glad of it, for I found myself quite without the guts to confront any of them, much less the biggest.

I felt a touch at my wrist, and jerked.

Odette.

She slid her fingers over my fist, easing it until I merely clasped at her hand. We were fine, she reminded with a touch. I turned ever so slightly to catch her eye. Safety was never guaranteed.

I was furious at our chartered ship and its steely eyed captain. He'd been charming too. Officers always were. They'd given no indication that they'd dump us over the side at the first sign of trouble. In fact, I was certain the navy had rules about protecting all passengers and cargo to the very last.

These pirates were a stand-in for the men I couldn't curse. The ones who'd nearly killed me. But it did not mean I would let them mistreat us, or act with impunity. I was fashioning myself an eagle after all.

Around us, the sun had finally settled into the cloud-crowded horizon. The bustle of the ship was stilling too. Duties finished and folded away, by pirates who were fast becoming smears of gray in the low light.

"Out here?" the captain asked. I blinked in response. "For our meeting. Your charge will wait for you in my cabin until you return."

Ah. I supposed it was the best I could ask for. A rapidly darkening deck did not feel so dangerous as an enclosed cabin on a strange ship, not by a long shot.

"Yes, I believe this will do," I said, knowing little about ships beyond the four walls of the cabin we'd been confined to on the last one.

Again, I wondered at the improbability of our being on a pirate ship at all. While men were herded into the navy without a second thought, the women of Sanctuary rarely saw the sea. That we were anywhere near it was a testament to Odette's power of persuasion, or to how badly Sanctuary wished to show itself again on the continental stage.

"I'll see her there, Eagle." It took me a moment to realize the giant had spoken, since his tone was so mild that I couldn't believe the words came from his mouth. He stepped around the captain as easily as a dancer and swept an arm out toward the stern. Whatever reservations I might have had, they were not shared by my companion. Odette unclasped her hand from mine and stepped lightly in the direction he'd indicated, her blanket swirling behind her.

They weren't a pace away before she started peppering him with questions. I did not envy the towering pirate one bit.

Odette could take care of herself, as much as I wanted to coddle her.

There was little to do but wait for the captain as he flagged down another crew member. This one was all choppy black hair and hard edges, with green streaked eyes I almost couldn't look away from. She stood nodding in only her shirtsleeves. If I remembered correctly, Odette had soaked through her coat. It matched the reddish belt at her waist and the patches in her stockings.

Coming to some agreement, the new pirate briefly caught my eye before disappearing across the planks.

"I'm not sure how long this will take," the captain muttered. He was still some way down the deck, rubbing at his neck absent-mindedly under the high collar of his black coat, and I wondered if he'd said it to me or to himself. He'd changed at some point, though we'd never seen him enter his own quarters. As it was, his coat gleamed—oiled, I guessed—making him a beacon in the last of the light.

I was struck by the traitorous thought that perhaps today had been nearly as long for him, and for all the pirates, as it had been for Odette and me. They hadn't expected to do any rescuing, and must have sorely needed whatever they'd wanted from our old ship, or else they'd never have risked it. This one was falling apart.

Still, it wasn't my job to keep a handsome pirate afloat. Certainly not one who referred to himself as "comely" with a wink. In fact, I was of half a mind to keep my mouth shut the entirety of our interview.

6

CONNOR

I offered the Eagle, as she now called herself, a seat on a less than genteel crate hastily covered with scrap canvas. If it bothered her, she didn't show it.

She avoided my gaze, and I took the opportunity to look at her. Beneath her tough exterior, I knew she felt more than she showed—amazement, perhaps, or fear. Her body spoke more truth than her face, her fists clenching every time something got under her skin. She puzzled me. Her situation was troubling in the extreme but the Eagle herself was the mystery I most wanted to solve.

As captain, a woman—our passenger—should have been the last thing on my mind.

The ship tightened up for the night around us. Talk brewed below; the crew debating the lost prize and the women we'd gained in its place. They'd be frustrated with me, but forgiving, I hoped. We were all more than willing to stop a drowning and stores weren't low enough yet to see me marooned. If my bad luck continued though, I wouldn't have a crew to return to Griffin.

My worries didn't rest fully with the *Wretched Lady*. That low-life captain had known a touch too much about us pirates for comfort. Stories told only a pinch of the truth. Our reverence for the sea and hard-held superstitions rarely made an appearance. He'd bet on both and won. In all likelihood, Sanctuary's iron had squeezed the information out of someone. We pirates were used to their shot, but not the weight of city's attention.

Sanctuary had a nasty set of dungeons. Prisoners were plentiful, as were turned pirates—men who were happy to give up their knowledge for gold and refuge behind the walls, no matter who suffered for it.

Venu and the Eagle had been a valuable distraction. A purposeful one, I was coming to believe. The *Wretched Lady* had been thoroughly diverted, and the naval ship draped in its merchant's colors was free to carry on, unmolested.

The prize had slipped away.

I settled directly opposite the Eagle, wishing I'd sent Billy for another coat. The Eagle was stiff backed, doing a good impression of her namesake. Even her toes were politely pressed into the deck, as if she might spring up and fly off.

The way Trenna's old shirt whipped around her arms as a breeze rose gave the distinct impression of wings.

Ah, seas. I shrugged my coat off my shoulders and offered it to her. She looked like she wanted to refuse my gift, until the wind picked up, my ally in this, singing around us. The Eagle put it on, the slight shine of it lending a glow to her face and the column of her neck.

"I take it time is of no essence on a ship like this," the Eagle said, her tone as flat as the western beaches. She'd been watching me, picking her words to best prick at me. I was easy prey for her assumptions. My time was hardly precious, and I cared little for the whims of the world. It was the shadow of her blasted city that had me and my ship running scared all the time.

"Have I been wasting your time?" I got the sense she didn't like me much, even if she did look comfortable in my coat. "Forgive me."

I fixed her with my widest smile. My fakest too. Griffin

wouldn't have bothered. Where he spoke plainly, I used my charms. If they didn't want a flirt and a carouser, the crew should have voted someone else their captain.

I hated playing nice with city folk—even lovely ones with cutting words—and it rankled to have let her ship go free.

"It may be that I owe you an apology," I said, though I didn't believe a word of it. "In some roundabout way, the *Wretched Lady* might be to blame for the misfortunes you suffered at the hands of your previous ship's crew." I peered at her, waiting for her reaction. She gave none.

I found the seriousness of the Eagle's dark brows and even darker eyes distracted from any of her milder features. Her face was pale, perhaps from her brush with death, but something told me she did not see much of the sun. Her hair, earlier a mermaid's spoiled midnight tendrils, had been salvaged with tidy knotting about her head, adding a touch of primness to the figure she cut in the crew's castoffs.

She'd been lying on this same deck in a ripped corset puking up the sea not an hour ago.

"Surely you had no thought of us when you drew alongside for the sake of plunder," she said, her eyes meeting mine without flutter or bluster.

"The *Wretched Lady* is a pirate ship through and through." I tilted my chin up so she would not mistake my meaning. "You've seen the state of this place. Would you fault me for seeking a bit of refurbishment? A taste of riches?" Was that a twist to her lip? Or a trick of the lengthening shadows?

She didn't answer, and I wouldn't dance around it any longer.

"What happened on your ship? Why were you thrown over?"

The woman snatched at the collar of my coat, drawing it up around her neck.

"It's not much of a story. O—Venu and I were sitting in our room, where we'd been confined from the moment of our boarding." She looked at me evenly. "We weren't even invited to the captain's table. It's considered very bad luck to have women aboard a ship, you see."

I snorted, startling her from her story.

"Fools. The sea's a woman herself. Far more risky to allow none aboard than to have some to appease her." I felt certain she was storing away my every word.

She nodded, charging forward with the rest of her tale.

"We were not told of the skull and dagger on our tail until your ship was quite close, and then only in whispers through the door. When the captain finally came in, we were half in a terror from the crash of the boats and the lack of news. We expected an update, not the brutal handling we received from the men he brought with him." She was staring at me now. "Venu's family paid a pretty penny for our berth, and I believe they would be horrified to hear what has become of us. I'm sure there will be a reward for your assistance."

A reward in the shape of a rope. She sucked in a breath. I waited.

"You saw the rest. They grabbed us and dragged us outside. Rebin, he was… he was our guard. I'm not sure what happened to him." She paused again, a furrow forming on her brow.

"Death or conscription most likely."

"I fear so." She did not flinch at the suggestion. Another might have fainted in her place.

I motioned for her to go on.

"We were pulled across the deck. Venu first, then me. All hands and bad breath, those sailors were. They had trunks too. They threw those off first." The Eagle frowned and tugged one of the panels of my coat over her thigh. I kicked myself for not being cleverer in choosing the location of our interview. Her eyes flicked up to search my face.

"It was a ruse, I think. Some attempt to see if you'd abandon your pursuit if they dropped coin in the water." She plucked idly at Trenna's threadbare cuff and stared out toward the horizon. "Nothing of value in those trunks, I'd wager."

"I didn't take you for a gambler." I couldn't help but tease her. She huffed a barely discernible laugh through her nose, but otherwise ignored me.

"O—my charge was screaming, and then we were both over the edge and then the cold and the wet and—"

I held up a hand, staying her words.

"Forewell was the captain's name, I think. It was a blessing, in a way, when they threw us off. I could not stand all those hands on me." She shook her head, her pinned hair staying in perfect place. "Never thought I'd say this to a pirate, but thank you for the rescue. I'd make poor fish food." It took me a minute to realize she'd snuck in one of her quiet jokes and was waiting for me to recognize it.

"Seemed a pity to waste a feast." The words were out of my mouth before I heard them myself. Wash it all, I should throw myself over the side. Old Connor had no place here, no matter how this woman intrigued me.

She let it pass, seemingly, without comment.

"Can you tell me what the ship carried? Were there other passengers?"

"No idea. We weren't allowed out of our cabin and no one bothered to visit us." So she might not have even seen the measures Forewell had taken to disguise the ship. A little closer to Coisume and they might have passed as one of the merchants that regularly ran the seas around the continent.

"Was your own journey of great importance?"

"No. Yes. Important to us, yes, but others? I can't be sure. O—Venu's father booked the passage for us on the *Edgewater* somehow. The first ship heading to Coisume in nearly twenty years, and we managed to get on it. There was a big fight about it, us being women and all, until word arrived from the First that we should be allowed aboard."

I snapped to attention. A naval vessel dressed up convincingly as a goods ship, running late in the season with a special dispensation from the top ring in Sanctuary, heading to Coisume of all places. Was Sanctuary opening back up? The *Edgewater* stank to the clouds with secrets.

I wished I knew what lay below her decks, and I wanted to teach her captain a lesson he wouldn't soon forget.

"Captain Forewell played the gentleman. Personable enough, but much distracted in his few short visits." The Eagle ran her fingers over the oiled leather of my coat. "You must have guessed that I have little experience in the way of sailors. I have a little more in the way of men. That one set off no warnings with his conduct." Her sharp brows drew down. "Had he made himself known sooner, I would have barricaded the cabin."

"I have no doubt you would have stolen a private's pistol and learned to use it by trial and error." That brought a pleased smile to her face, though she tried to repress it. Gone was the prostrate victim from the deck, if she had ever been there. This was a woman who would not let much stop her, nor anything surprise her.

"Forewell, you say…" I racked my brain. Famous navy men were generally the cruelest. Their names, cut from the bodies they left behind, traveled to us pirates in the Reaches. We did our best to keep well clear of their bloody wake.

"You say you know little of sailors, but did the walls whisper of him? Any exploits? Accolades?"

"I couldn't say. We… The concerns of the navy stay around card tables in our wall. I'd never seen him before, if that helps."

"I'm not sure anything will. He's leagues away. Though he'll need all the luck he can get should we meet again." I squared my shoulders.

"We both have a score to settle, Captain Connor." She sat up straighter too, and I could not find it in my heart to doubt her.

7

CONNOR

I t was then that three of the worst scoundrels aboard strutted past us. I would have given a measure of gold I didn't yet possess for Pella and Cesare to walk on by. They pretended to be very much enjoying each other's company but I knew their ears were pricked. Jack, who shadowed them, didn't deign to speak to me most days, so it stood to reason she wasn't the one who'd chosen to come up here.

"Connor!" Pella said with theatrical surprise, rendering my fantasy coins as worthless in my head as in my hand. "Silver has the discussion well in hand downstairs, but we're longing for your input."

She and Cesare, despite their well-turned heels and devious tongues, were the boat's best eyes, spared a turn at the grueling night shift to save their talents for the light. Thus, they could always be found up to something while the rest of the ship was at watch or at rest.

"A captain's duty is never done," I said, the words strange on my lips. Years past, I would have readily joined them. While there was much delight to be found between those two—barring Jack, of course—I noticed the Eagle shrinking away from their intrusion. Any openness I'd won disappeared back down her shoulders and into the tight knit of her hands. The Eagle's eyes didn't latch on to the newcomers, but I had no doubt she was taking great care to learn them, just as she had me, over the short course of our acquaintance.

"Do introduce us to your castaway!" Cesare cut in, his half cape jingling with copper fastenings and the occasional silver coin as he swirled it, bowing to the Eagle. I choked at the insinuation, but no one was paying me any attention. "A nightmare, my lady," he added with a sympathetic frown, his hand spooling out toward the Eagle in greeting, the inked tentacles that adorned his knuckles visible in the graying light.

"Indeed," was all the Eagle said, ignoring the gesture, though she did duck her head in his direction.

"You were harshly used, in my opinion," Pella rushed to add with a pout. At least her sympathy rang truer than her reasons for walking the deck.

"I've promised our guests a smooth passage." I eyeballed the three of them, trying to infuse my voice with some authority. If I could not stop the tiptoeing and whispering entirely, I might at least scare them into keeping it to a minimum. "In fact, we were nearly finished."

I thought all my implying would go right over their heads, but I found myself with the most unusual of partners in my task. Jack, stony at their backs and in possession of both their elbows, whispered rather loudly about her urgent need for the head. Probably the damned excuse the pair of them had given to come up here in the first place.

The rest of my harsh words buried themselves when I noticed an undeniable twitch of the Eagle's cheek. She sought to stifle her laugh with a yawn. I covered for her with a hearty promise to join the crew belowdecks as soon as I'd finished.

It was not long before Pella, Cesare, and Jack wound their way back downstairs, though they were sure to pass by again. The Eagle seemed content to revert to silence until we saw the back of them.

"Our trip was in service of a marriage. A proposal, that is. Important to someone, I suppose, since it landed Venu and me on the ship." The Eagle started up again, saving me from pressing her.

"To cement it? But surely your portrait would have been enough to sway the betrothed?"

The Eagle stilled, regarding me just as her namesake might have. The white-bellied birds of prey sometimes landed on our ship, and their keen golden eyes were just as penetrating.

I could not bring myself to believe she was satisfied with whatever cage Sanctuary had built around her. Courting rituals from the city were baffling, uncomfortable, and ended poorly for most involved. I'd left the walls very young, and was glad of it. I had only to measure myself by the pirate code. The truth was all that was required of any parties looking to indulge with one another. Without it, one would face the wrath of one's lover, or worse, one's crew. A fair price to pay.

Give me a bawdy night under a full moon over the lace-bundled burden of life inseparable and cold until death.

"My portrait? Comely Connor—" The Eagle said my name with the same reproach as the hardest quartermaster. "—do not presume to flatter me. You will accomplish nothing. We sailed to fix Venu's prospects." She couldn't fool me. The suggestion that her own portrait might satisfy a stranger had not gone unnoticed. All the sharpness had disappeared from her gaze, and if she were a pirate I was sure I would have had her grinning.

"No prospects of your own?" I couldn't help myself. In another life, we might have shared a bunk.

Her face fell. Ah, it was in poor taste then.

Even frowning, she was a very lovely woman. Anyone would be lucky to have a minute of her time, much less a chance to tumble her. She'd tempt all manner of lovers, and had enough fire behind her eyes to keep whomever she chose on their toes. Strange that such a woman would have come straight from the innermost walls of Sanctuary. Stranger still that I should pull her from the sea's maw myself. Was it—

No. There was no point in wandering down that path. Lusting after the Eagle was folly. I might be a pirate, but I'd been tasked with her safe, and imminent, return to Sanctuary.

"I concern myself mostly with the prospects of others," she said, having fixed her expression back to neutrality.

"She's your charge then? Venu?" I could not quite relegate this woman to a babysitter in my mind. Nor could I reasonably believe that Venu needed much watching. She'd inspired a great deal of terror in my men when first introduced to the ship. Sanctuary was truly a backwards place.

"I'm her companion, yes."

"She doesn't seem one for minding," I mused.

"Oh, she'd be much worse without me." She half smiled, and we both waited for the other to speak.

"I thought you city folk kept to yourselves." I had to steer us back to more important topics. "Why would Venu be searching among the channels for a match?"

"It wasn't—It's not my job to ask questions." She answered a touch too fast to mask the feeling behind the words. "I find I'm chilled to bone, Captain, even with the kindness of your coat." She eyed me, and I imagined her weighing the danger of my refusal with the chivalry I'd been so careful to display. She was right, the temperature had dropped with the sun, and it was no lazy summer night to be drawn out as darkness swallowed us.

"Another time then, my lady." I wanted answers. She had them, but I wouldn't stoop to torturing them from her. I'd saved her from the water, and I'd save her from the wind too. For now.

I SHOULD NOT HAVE BEEN SURPRISED TO FIND VENU HOLDING court with Rory and Billy when I delivered the Eagle back to the cabin. Shame she hadn't been with us a few months ago when Griffin disappeared, she might have picked up more votes for the captaincy. It was clear to me that both women would have made good pirates, albeit for different reasons. Where the Eagle was cold and subtly calculating, her charge was inescapably bright. Warm, even, when she wasn't screaming at you. As I closed the door on the four of them, I could not shake the feeling that they fit. Not only with each other, but with the *Wretched Lady*.

For a moment, in the black of the hall, I wanted to turn back, to return to their rooms—my rooms, really. To sit with Rory and Billy and forget all of this. Those chambers had never been so cozy when I was supposed to be sleeping in them.

I banished myself to the ship's rail instead.

Even if the crew was taking a shine to the women, they could not stay. Common decency would have them delivered home as soon as possible. We pirates weren't a threat, but we'd been left in a strange position by the *Edgewater*. One from which the *Wretched Lady* might yet stand to gain. We'd spent all summer looking for a way into Sanctuary, and now, just as we'd given up, Venu and the Eagle had landed in our laps. Perhaps the women would be the key to Griffin's rescue, a chance finally dangled by fate herself. My mind raced.

"Ho there."

Silver hailed me, picking his way through the perils of the dark deck. It was a relief to have my thoughts interrupted. He had no lantern, choosing, like I had, to let the sliver of moon guide his way. Once, the deck would have been lit well into the night. No longer. The charms for light that the *Lady* had been outfitted with at her construction had run out before my time, leaving empty holes in their stead, taunting me with their uselessness.

"Busy day, kid." He joined me at the railing, leaning forward toward the endless water. It wasn't a question.

Hah.

"Needed a break from the masses?" I jerked my chin, indicating the way he'd come.

"They threw me out when I didn't have all the answers. Said they were expecting their captain."

I groaned. "You know, I couldn't do it without you."

He looked at me sidelong, what little light there was catching on the bright curls that had long since replaced the black in his hair.

"Today and every day. The *Wretched Lady* doesn't know how lucky she is."

He barked a laugh at my words.

"She must know, she assembled us." I settled back onto my elbows, keeping the aft cabin in my line of sight. "You too, Connor. She's got a purpose for you, just like the rest of us," Silver added. I avoided his thoughtful gaze.

"You sound so sure. I thought you picked me, you old bag o' bones, out of a batch of the worst ship's boys the seas have ever known." Now I was the one with a laugh caught in my throat. "Thank you though. I couldn't have found a better crew if I'd had all of Sanctuary's stolen gold to offer."

Silver nudged me with his shoulder.

"If you had all that gold, we'd take turns slitting your throat." That was about as sentimental as pirates got.

"And if I let you, I wouldn't deserve an ounce of it."

Light spilled from the hallway that led to the captain's cabin, and a figure emerged, his bulk unmistakable.

"Left Billy with 'em, Captain," Rory said, sidling up to me and Silver.

"Good riddance." Silver snorted. "I can't hardly sleep with all that snoring."

"Says the man with the loudest snore I've ever heard." Rory regarded us both for a moment. "Captain, our guests are owed at least a meal and…" He trailed off.

"You can't stomach feeding fine ladies the same rat droppings we've been eating?" Silver said.

I nodded. The ship was on its last stores, and they weren't pretty. Hard biscuits and salted gannet. Nothing for the stew pot but more of the rotgut we guzzled during the day.

"If things'd gone differently we'd be dining on smoked goose and crated apples, but as it stands… they're just as far out of luck as we are." Even if I wanted to treat our guests better than my crew, which I didn't, there were only crumbs aboard.

Rory set his mouth in a hard line. He'd tallied the storerooms with me.

"We could set into Penny's Cove. They won't have much, but what they do have might go for coin," Silver suggested.

"City folk eating goat and dried beans? We can't leave them in the smallest town in the islands. They'd find a berth when their hair turned gray," I chided.

"We have to do something, Captain." Rory crossed his arms. "We won't leave them there, but we can trade the last of the salt. I wouldn't mind something other than seabird."

Silver murmured his agreement.

"The last of the salt is the end of it. We dock and sell it, and then what? Wait for the admiralty to dangle another fat ship under our noses?"

"We catch the last one." Rory said it stone-faced.

The idea tickled me. I wanted to see that cold-eyed captain keelhauled.

"They're half a day ahead."

"Ten to one they're still docking in Coisume. If we turn from Penny's east, through the isles, we'll beat them if they take Sanctuary's main route around the middle lighthouse."

I scratched at the beginnings of my beard. He had a point.

"You'd risk the ship on rocks and sandbars?" I asked.

"You risk the ship by starving us all to death," Silver said, surprising me, and while he wasn't wrong, the words hurt.

"Besides, Trenna's been that way before. If anyone can steer us clean, it would be her."

"You'd mutiny over meat, huh? I take back what I said earlier, old man, I need a new crew." The words were light, but I felt Rory's eyes boring into me. He had an uncanny ability to sense my moods. Silver was older, and had plenty of years of pirating under his belt, but Rory had been my closest companion since I'd boarded this ship. I had no doubt he was recalling the tears I shed into his shoulder when I'd first heard of Griffin's leaving.

"Sleep on it, Connor," Silver suggested, eyes back on the blackness blanketing the horizon.

"No. No, you have a strong point. As does Rory. That ship was a gift. The only one they've let out in ages without men or firepower." I was barely a captain, but I knew the value of listening to wise counsel. "If it's goat that'll keep you from dumping me on one of the lonely islands, I think I can afford the expense."

"They won't have women to throw overboard this time." Rory's lip curled with disdain for the cowardly Sanctuary sailors.

"Maybe we get these girls their own cutlasses and send them over the breech. Might scare the men into submission." I laughed at the image, though it didn't seem far from reality. We wouldn't be able to offload them until we found a proper harbor, and if their first day aboard was anything to go by, they were well on their way to becoming terrifying pirates.

"We'll end up on the wrong side of their cutlasses if we don't bring their dinner soon." Rory chuckled. "Connor, can you help me carry them something up?"

"They might run us through when they see the biscuits." I clapped Silver on the shoulder, and started belowdecks.

"Aye, that's why you'll be the first through the door," Rory said as he followed me.

8

REGULA

Of course Odette had already made friends of the pirates. It was only natural. She had the constitution and the mouth of a renegade. I, on the other hand, had only managed to piss one off: the captain.

The same captain who'd just marched back in with plates of the worst food imaginable. A pity the pirates hadn't been able to raid the *Edgewater* after all. We would all suffer without its stores.

I managed a curt thank-you under the weight of the captain's attention. Up close, in the light, he seemed no older than Odette, though a day's growth of sandy beard and his careful manner masked it somewhat. I found myself rather captivated by the golden hoop in his ear, winking at me from behind a mischievous lock of hair. A shame the glare of the oil lamps hid the true color of those eyes.

Or perhaps it was for the best that they did. I knew better than to let my gaze rest too long on the captain. I'd had enough of men for one lifetime. I was in danger of becoming a pirate myself following such frivolous, flirtatious thoughts. Thankfully, he retreated from the room as quickly as he'd appeared, content to leave us to our awful supper.

One pirate stayed for our protection, or so she said. I wasn't convinced we'd need the help, but Billy seemed at ease on the chaise, even as Odette teased her, their meals forgotten.

From my seat on the sturdy chair, I tried to ignore accusations of hair pulling as Odette combed through the pirate's short locks. I had only a mug of watery beer and my bowl to entertain me. A hunk of what I guessed was fish sat dried, salted, and deathly next to a biscuit that might have been better described as a rock. I didn't eat fish. At least, not willingly.

Tonight my stomach mutinied against my rules. No matter how poor the options, I was starving after my near drowning and the excitement of the day. I nibbled at the edge of the biscuit, unable to get a good bite. The fish was far less appetizing, though softer and blessedly without a hint of the fishiness I'd expected.

I sighed.

"Crack it on the desk, woman!" the pirate called over to me. I looked up, startled. "Unless you plan to soak it in your beer, you have to break it into pieces."

I tried and failed.

"Oh, do show us, Billy," Odette said, stretching out over the chair to see better while the pirate made her way across the room. She had a confident stride, and none of the meanness of expression I have expected from someone hardened at sea.

"Give it here."

She held out a blunt fingered hand covered in blue markings.

"A tattoo for every man I kill," she said, when she saw my face, and then motioned for my biscuit. I let her have it. I hadn't missed the shine of gold in her ear either. It must have been a custom among the crew.

"Billy, it's impossible to shock her. I would know, I've had years trying," Odette remarked from where she lay, catlike. To me, she added, "These ships are awfully boring for stretches, and Billy says tattooing passes the time well." As if she couldn't resist the drama of it, she kept on. "They go all the way up her arm!"

I should have asked how she knew such a thing, but the pirate interrupted, smashing the hard bread into the edge of the desk.

Billy held the thing up, spurred on by Odette's squeal, and I saw a distinct break in the crust. She smiled to herself, and turned to better show off her triumph.

Odette stage whispered to me, "Seems quite a lot of muscle for one measly meal." In the space of a breath she said to the pirate, "Do me! Oh please, I'm ravenous."

Billy could not hide her blush when she passed back the halves of my biscuit. She'd unfortunately already chosen the most dangerous course of action with Odette. If one didn't want to become her willing servant, one had to completely ignore her.

Odette nearly smacked her in the face waving around her share of the hard bread.

As Billy guided Odette to break her own, I tried mine. It wasn't satisfying, but I hoped my stomach would accept it anyway. Laughter filled the room. Odette's particularly harsh attempt at the biscuit breaking sent the baked rock flying across the wide desk to land in my lap.

The shock of a biscuit to the gut was one thing, but the absurdity of our situation—playing with our food like children—was another, and before I knew it I was laughing too. Tears streamed down my cheeks as I clutched at the cursed thing in my lap. Had they been hidden in the corners of my eyes since my brush with death?

Lifting the blasted biscuit, I gasped. Odette had broken it! I held it high over my head like a hunting prize, and the girl puffed up with delight. Both she and the pirate followed my hands with their eyes, like two kittens going after the same string. It was only fair that I launched it back at them, letting them scrabble for the pieces while I returned to my meal.

I'd swallowed two grisly bites by the time they'd settled down to their own supper.

"Billy, is that your real name?" Odette sandwiched the asking between delicate mouthfuls. She'd eat anything.

"You know it's not, my lady." The pirate shook her head, her attention on her own plate. The honorific sounded wrong on her lips, but charming nonetheless. It as much as anything prompted Odette to set her food down and persist in her line of inquiry.

"Yes, I know all about you pirates and your names." I watched as she fixed the pirate with the full force of her blue eyes, dinner now forgotten. "If I learned your name, I could make you do what I want all the time."

The pirate choked on her biscuit.

"No—That's not the way of it."

"Oh no? So I couldn't get you to do my bidding, Veronica?" Odette planted her chin on a fist as Billy turned to her, mid-snort.

"Do I look like a Veronica to you, Venu?" She emphasized Odette's fake name.

"No, rather more like a Bradley."

Billy made a pained noise.

"If you don't enlighten her as to the nature of pirate naming, she'll keep guessing until you both turn purple," I cut in. I'd seen this play out more than once. In fact, this sort of prodding had gotten us on a ship to Coisume in the first place.

"Druzj," Odette said. Then "Fiona."

The pirate shook her head, voice lost to silent laughter.

"Even if you guessed it, it's not about control," she managed. "Any true sailor offers their name to the sea before they first sail." Her tone turned serious and Odette's attention sharpened "One day the sea will use it to call us back to her."

"Like me today," I mused.

"No! You didn't give your name, so she wouldn't have taken you," Odette practically shouted from the chair.

"I don't think the sea needs a name," I shot back. "People die every day in the shallows, even if they never step on a ship."

"Right enough, but it's the worst of luck. The Lady of the Sea isn't happy to take those souls." Billy hastened to explain. "That's why..." She looked at me from behind her choppy bangs.

"Why, what?" Odette was never scared to ask what I couldn't. The pirate blinked at me, then down at her dish.

"Well, it's why we let your ship get away. The Lady of the Sea would have plagued us for the rest of the season, maybe two. If the captain hadn't decided to disengage, and if he hadn't pulled you up, who knows what sort of sailing we'd be in for."

"The captain?" I was appalled at my own frailty as warmth shot through me at the thought. He'd saved me.

"Yeah, he brought you up. The sea must have guided his dive. He's one of the best swimmers aboard, practically raised in the water, but there was no telling where exactly you'd sunk. I'll admit it wasn't looking good." Billy's face broke into a smile. My rescue had been a relief. "The navy's so damned underhanded. We all thought you were beyond saving, and we'd be left with this screeching monster blaming us for your death."

"I'm hardly as bad as your Lady of the Sea." Odette leaned back, the lounge creaking with use.

"No, my lady, but you're a load of trouble upfront. She'd just send a storm and sink us later."

Odette growled with mock outrage. I knew she quite enjoyed being "trouble" and would probably be glowing from the unintended compliment long after our eyes closed and we drifted off to sleep on the unfamiliar ship.

CONNOR

Rory and I snuck down through the makeshift mess under the cover of chatter. Hammocks had been cleared to the edges of the crew's quarters and crates carried in to balance extra planks. Jack had even sacrificed a few barrels for seats. Pirates clung to every surface like barnacles, all waiting for me. Supper was usually served out and squirreled away to every corner of the boat. The crew only did this when they wanted to hear from their captain.

I ignored them, busying myself with my own bowl.

They were much closer to silence when I'd finished.

"You chased Silver out of here with questions and yet you don't have any for me?" I meant them jokingly, but the words came out with a bit of challenge to them. It was different speaking to the *Wretched Lady* as its captain.

"You hardly know more than he did," someone muttered nearby. Jack, I'd wager. Always the first to argue with me in front of the others. It pained me to admit but, in this case, she was right. Today had been a surprise for me. I avoided addressing her specifically, instead letting my eyes bounce around the whole of those gathered. I owed them the truth.

"Whether Sanctuary is growing bold or foolish, I don't know. We might have frightened them." I waited for more pushback. If it came, I didn't hear it. "Their navy has a code. Not the same as ours, I reckon, but dropping passengers into the drink can't be in it. I'm choosing to believe whatever we saw today was an act of desperation. Of carelessness. Whatever the cause, we can't scuttle around trying to predict and outmaneuver their cruelty."

I settled into my seat.

"That those women made it out alive, against all odds, is a testament to the spirit of our crew. We didn't hesitate when it mattered most. For that, I thank every one of you. I know this has not been the easiest of years." To this there was a murmuring of ayes. "Hanging around in enemy waters, waiting and watching, is not what any of us had planned. I meant this prize for us! To fill our bellies and our coffers, and it hurt to let her go." The crew was nodding up at me.

"I, for one, would like to see her again. Show her what the *Wretched Lady* has in store for gutless cowards like her crew."

"And that captain!" Alecto added, setting off another wave of assent.

It was my turn to nod.

"I have spoken to one of the women at length, and will interview the other tomorrow. While I haven't gathered much, they strike me as exactly what they seem. Innocents at the mercy of Sanctuary's navy. No matter our feelings on the matter, I'd appreciate it if we could continue treating them with the dignity deserved by any passenger or fellow pirate."

"You telling us to leave them alone, Connor?" Pella asked from halfway across the room. I could hear the frown in her voice, even if I couldn't see it very well.

"Not at all. Both seem well able to voice their discomfort, and have a hearty curiosity for our life out here. You might find that they come up to you with questions of their own. I don't think the *Wretched Lady* has ever had city dwellers aboard, bluecoats or no."

"Pssh, Captain, half of us were born in the walls," Trenna said. I hadn't seen her set up in the doorframe, but it made sense that Silver would have relieved her.

"We didn't choose to stay there!" Cesare hollered.

"Choose? You think those city dwellers have a choice?" Trenna scowled at him, pointing a finger at the planks above us, and took a step farther into the room. "Either laboring on the outer walls, or in labor on the inner ones, plenty don't get another option." It took me a moment to understand Trenna's meaning. "We got lucky, Cesare. We got out."

There were a hundred layers to that. I'd left young enough that I'd had only traces of my life in the city to hold on to before the navy claimed me. Better to remember nothing than to revisit real scars like some of the other pirates.

I cleared my throat. Trenna and Cesare could trade blows later. This was about Venu and the Eagle. They'd landed on our ship for a reason, and we would keep them safe.

"No matter the temptation, we aren't gonna gawk or poke at our guests in the process of getting to know them."

"You'll be poking at them enough for the lot of us then?"

Jack said, all stony sarcasm. Even though I knew her game, going just far enough to get under my skin, I felt a betraying blush start up my neck.

"I'll find out more about that ship, yes," I said. More than half of the *Wretched Lady*'s crew was in the room. There were plenty of reasons for my ears to go red, if she was looking. "I'll be sure to keep you informed."

Rory appeared at my side. Not stepping in or speaking up, but letting me know he stood where he always did.

"If there are no objections, Wretches, we'll set into Penny's Cove. We can replenish and regroup. If you have any business on the island, attend to it quickly, for we'll not stop long."

"Did you hear that?" Alecto whispered a little too loudly to Isadore, the ship's new carpenter. "I would kill for some goat!"

The conversation devolved from there, though no one argued with our heading. Penny's Cove was a refreshing destination after a summer spent hiding in empty inlets and at the edge of long-abandoned isles.

I sighed. Every time I spoke now, it was a speech. I was no longer looked to for fun, but for information and authority. The mantle of captain had changed me in the crew's eyes, though I hadn't really changed at all. Commanding was a skillset all its own, one that I had never been particularly interested in. Now I suffered for it. The crew, if they listened to me, did it out of respect for Griffin and on the understanding that I was only a stopgap.

Rory leaned into my shoulder and whispered, "Good enough, Connor."

I scowled at him, resenting that he saw the struggle I tried so hard to hide beneath the surface. He cleared my bowl, drained the last of my mug, and set his elbows down in their stead, forcing me to forgive him. It helped to have him at my side. I was a better captain with him to guide me.

We'd shared an upbringing, coming aboard the *Wretched Lady* at the same tender age. We'd sunk easily into friendship as we grew, and thankfully that hadn't changed with my untimely promotion. I wondered if one day he might put himself up for the role I was suffering over.

Trenna, too, had the natural qualities of a leader. If she'd wanted to lay into Cesare in front of the whole ship, there were those who would follow her unasked. Thankfully, she'd pulled a crate up next to Rory and was about to goad him into an argument over their last game of cards.

I envied both of them. They hadn't had to pick up the captaincy, better for the role or not. Pirates were a complicated lot, without the regimented nature of a navy. We all wanted different things, and we all got a vote in important matters. It would be less work to captain a ship full of cats.

Today was the most action we'd seen in months, and it had taken far more out of me than I'd expected. I would have to push myself further if I truly wished to see Griffin free. Whether the crew believed in me or not, I wanted to do right by them.

9

REGULA

W hen we ventured out on deck the next morning, we had Billy as our guide. I found myself squinting into the sun, hoping for a glimpse of the pirates above us, tending to the sails. The ship had found its heading, Billy informed us, which was the reason for such fervent activity in the rigging.

Any further explanation was lost as we were accosted by a knot of familiar pirates. The first, who I remembered gleefully stumbling into my conversation with the captain last night, held a roll of red canvas uncomfortably in her arms and was smiling at us with lots of teeth. The second wasn't hard to place. She had been there as well, quiet in the dark behind her friend.

Without shadows to conceal her, I was struck by the strength of this pirate, the short cut of her hair setting off a square jaw and teasing eyes. The roll of canvas she hoisted over her shoulder was black, and she didn't look at all perturbed to be carrying it. The third was a stranger. Tall, with a pirate's tan, longish dark hair, and a pair of twisted metal spectacles set high on his nose. He looked a lot like—

"Ah, Billy! I had to replace you." The first woman tossed her head in the direction of the other two, deep auburn curls flying. "Couldn't carry everything alone."

"You don't have to carry anything at all," the man said, frowning down at his empty hands.

She hissed at him, resetting her grip, and returned her attention to us.

"We didn't meet properly last night. I'm Pella, short for Pelican. This is Jack, short for… I forget." The redhead cocked her head prettily and pointed at her muscled friend, who flashed us a winning smile but didn't elaborate on her name. "I'd introduce Robin, but he was just leaving. Seemed to think he could replace you, Billy."

Robin looked ready to argue with Pella's dismissal.

Neither Odette nor I had time to return Pella's greeting. Billy beat us to answering with a shrug, "Got our guests to look out for today."

The whole crew already knew who we were, so there was little lost in our staying quiet.

I focused instead on the similarities between Billy and the unfamiliar pirate. Dark hair, white skin that somehow tanned and freckled, a shocking streak of green in their mostly gray eyes, his a little magnified behind the glass. I'd have bet my breakfast Billy and Robin were family.

Pella struggled with her load. Jack sighed and held out a hand.

"We can carry them both, Pella, I told you." The pirate's voice was deep, not precisely how I remembered it from the night before.

Frustration danced over Pella's face before she gave in. "He's needed elsewhere, I'm sure." Her eyes shot daggers at Robin.

"I stand the midnight shift, you know that."

"So go to sleep!" She hurled the words at him.

I glanced between the pirates, then over at Odette. Her eyes were overly bright and her brows were slowly creeping up her forehead. It was as if we'd accidentally walked onstage during a play.

"Anyways, we can't find Connor. You'll have to do, Billy. You're used to this," Pella said after a beat. Then she scrunched up her face and heaved the canvas to her friend. I watched as Jack swung the second roll onto her empty shoulder, twisting it into position one handed. She hadn't been wrong. There was little sign of strain on her face.

"I said—" Billy started to object.

"Our guests can help too!" Pella exclaimed. "Flags are by far the most interesting part of any pirate ship." Her eyes glittered at us, bright against her dark liner. Robin crept out of Pella's line of sight, situating himself between the two rolls and adding a hand to the back of each to ease Jack's burden. Curious.

"Billy, I'd like to see them. I've heard horrible stories." Pella had aimed for and caught Odette's attention perfectly. "Is it true you stitch them after a great battle, using the clothing scraps from your defeated enemies?"

I laughed under my breath. I had never suspected Odette of reading sensational pamphlets about pirates until now. She must have been sneaking them.

"Here! We'll roll them out and you can see for yourself." Pella waved a hand at Jack. Her smile fell into a scowl when she noticed Robin, helping against her wishes. The flags thumped down onto nearby crates, looking big enough to cover them fully once unrolled.

"They haven't even broken their fast yet!" Billy muttered, though no one was listening to her.

"Oh! Thats…" Odette trailed her fingers over the first flag.

"Pretty, huh?" Pella replied, brushing a curl behind her ear, scowl gone.

"It's lovely."

It was. The red canvas was marked across its middle with an X. A black petaled rose on a long green stem crossed a silver sword of the same length. Where they'd gotten the thread for the sword, I couldn't imagine, considering the state of the ship. It would shine when they flew it, just as pretty from far off.

"This one is worse," Jack said, having just finished unfurling the black flag. Now this looked more like what I'd pictured. In bleached white canvas, a skull peered out from a field of black. A rusty red flower was sewn over its mouth, with petals spilling down like drops of blood.

"Is that... real blood?" Odette asked, running her fingers over this one too.

"Do you want it to be?" came Jack's answer, her gaze clear as it swept us.

"Long Legs, you rat," Pella said, coming around the side of the crates. "We aren't meant to scare them. Or, well, not more than they already have been. It's just madder, love. Blood wouldn't hold its color half as well."

She said it so matter-of-factly that Odette hardly realized the girl was testing her. I watched her bite her tongue in response. She wasn't one to blanche at such things. Knowing her, she'd just come up with a hundred more questions.

Robin snorted, which reminded Pella of his existence.

"I told you to make yourself scarce," she said.

He fixed her with a terrible glare, prompting Jack to step in. "Get some sleep, Robin. It's been a rotten few days." She slapped a hand on his shoulder and grinned. "Wouldn't do to be groggy when we sail into Penny's."

This snapped him to attention.

"Penny's? We're going to the cove?"

"Why d'you think we're fussing about with the flags?" Every word underscored Pella's annoyance.

"I can't understand why you do anything, Pella," he replied. "Perhaps I should give up trying."

"Seas, man, get out of here before you embarrass yourself." It was Billy who grabbed his wrists and forcibly marched him from our group. He was a touch taller, but their black hair stood up in charming peaks as if mussed by the same hand.

They squabbled like siblings too, all the way across the deck.

"So the flags are for this Penny?" Odette and Pella were the only two without their heads turned.

Pella perked up.

"Yeah! We use them to communicate." She tapped the fabric, rolling her lip between her teeth. "If somebody's not familiar with our ship and they're looking through a glass at us, our flag will tell them whether we're friend or foe."

"Why the fearsome one? Is it an enemy port?" I chimed in.

"Not at all. I know it doesn't make sense, but this flag is pretty standard across all the ships that sail hereabouts, except your navy, that is. It doesn't mean the same—" Pella'd realized we city dwellers might be dangerous people with whom to share such information. She shot a look at Jack, who just shrugged.

"The red one's for us alone, practically says our name in symbols." Jack more than made up for her friend's sudden silence. Odette beamed at her.

"It's beautiful."

"We pride ourselves on beautiful things," the pirate said with a wink. Pella elbowed her, perhaps to shut her up.

Odette turned to me and said, loud enough for the whole ship to hear, "Beautiful things? I bet we're the finest passengers this tub has seen in a while."

I had to button my mouth closed or else burst out laughing. Both pirates' faces split in matching grins.

Billy rejoined us then, completely lost to the conversation. Instead of letting her in on the joke, Pella forced her to choose a flag or else be banished from our company. Billy frowned like she was born to do it and picked the red one.

"Might as well show it off."

10

CONNOR

Venu rattled on in front of me, spilling Sanctuary's secrets wrapped in societal frippery. I probably needed them, but I was having trouble listening to her. First my eyes, then my mind, wandered across the deck to her companion. I wanted to understand the Eagle. I asked and she answered, and yet I walked away with nothing but her words stuck under my skin like thorns. I should have found it easy, speaking to her, except I was possessed by an urge to sink my fingers under the surface she showed me.

Now, I interviewed her opposite. For every question I asked, the girl had two more, posed with an exuberance that was growing wearisome. Didn't she ever rest? I was being talked in circles. Perhaps there might have been some credence to my initial fear of espionage, except spies would not waste their time listing off the ten most "heart stopping and dangerous" experiences of their life up until this point. There had been an adventure in climbing while wearing lace and a frightened horse loose on a city block and a...

It was impossible not to let my mind drift, the shrewd answers and studied mannerisms of the Eagle seeping in around her companion's nonsense. She was only half a ship away, her head in one of Silver's handy books. He was probably telling her about his own lady back in one of the pirate towns. He made sure to write her a love letter at every port and always had an arsenal of poetry on him. No doubt she was helping him pick out the best lines to send from Penny's Cove. Whatever they spoke about, I envied him. The Eagle was enjoying herself.

I wanted to stop worrying about her. I'd confirmed with Isadore, who was the closest thing to a doctor we had aboard, even though she'd been hired on as a carpenter, that the near drowning would not impact the Eagle further. She hadn't been worried about either of the women, reassuring me that the sea and the cold that came after it were the biggest threats to their health before returning to her shop belowdecks.

I'd hired Isadore on while we waited for Griffin, hoping to patch the gaps in the *Wretched Lady*'s coverage. Her family ran a trusted apothecary in the Tross—one of the bigger pirate haunts —and while she'd chosen to apprentice in the shipyard, she'd still learned enough of medicine to help us out until we could attract a sawbones of our own.

As I watched Silver and the Eagle over the girl's shoulder, I was glad of her words. The Eagle shouldn't suffer further.

"—your own?"

It was only when Venu cleared her throat that I noticed the quiet between us. The girl turned to follow my gaze.

"I'm sorry. I—" I shook myself.

"Worried about my Eagle?" Venu turned back, her eyes glowing. "Don't be. She's got more spine than any of your pirates."

Her charge was merely stating the obvious. I was well aware of the strong defenses of her minder. I'd run up against them yesterday and I was having trouble forgetting the experience.

"Might I be excused?" Venu asked, shifting on her seat. We'd set up on the ship's benches this time, our elbows on the wood, the ocean rolling in the corners of our eyes. Our backs were turned to the fore and aft of the boat, sitting like two strangers stopped for a chat on a stroll. "There's absolutely nothing about that ship or that captain or Sanctuary itself that I haven't told you." The girl continued before I could consider my answer. "Whatever you're looking for, I just don't know."

She was right. She'd talked for an hour or so. It wasn't her fault I hadn't been listening.

I dismissed her.

She leaped up in delight, thanking me profusely. If I should need her or any of her many, many details, I knew exactly where to find them. Neither she nor the Eagle would be leaving my ship until I was ready to let them go.

Astounding, really, how quickly Venu caught the attention of Alecto and Pipes and cajoled them into a tour of the deck. Saved me the trouble of finding something to entertain her. Venu did not strike me as the type to languish in her cabin for long.

I stared after her.

It was clear I had not been the only one with an eye across the deck. The Eagle was quick to peel away from Silver and join her companion in exploration.

Their dynamic was unusual; the younger one always rushing off toward some new adventure while the elder tailed her, staid and wary of the world. Her words yesterday had hinted at a wilder spirit, at a woman with a great deal of heart and a mind starved of excitement. Perhaps Venu and the Eagle were putting on a show for us, or perhaps they were worn into these patterns from long years in Sanctuary.

Nothing about their conduct smelled funny to me, but I'd always been accused of seeing the good in people. It was easy to ascribe innocence as I witnessed the two of them turn wide eyes to the world of the *Wretched Lady*. A taste of freedom from their walls and whatever lives they led behind them.

Had they been naval men, they would have been offered the pirate's bargain. Stay and take a place aboard our ship—or any other in the nearest port—or be stranded somewhere Sanctuary wouldn't have too much trouble finding them.

These women were special, and their arrival unheard of. With our circumstances being what they were, and Griffin held captive in Sanctuary, I wasn't sure we could afford to give them anything but an unremarkable ride home. Were they important enough to barter for Griffin's life? Venu, maybe. I knew too little about the city to be certain. Sanctuary might laugh in our faces just like their captain, putting the women in far greater danger.

Venu and the Eagle had disappeared up onto the bow, and only a few pirates worked at the cranks and pulleys in my line of sight. I ran a hand through my hair and turned to face the ocean, thunking my chin down on my crossed arms. The ship was sturdy and comforting beneath me, same as when I was a lad.

We on the *Wretched Lady* had fallen into a dangerous pattern. We'd expected—I'd expected—Griffin to handle Sanctuary for us. He knew more about the world than the rest of us combined, except Trenna, with all her time traveling to make her maps. It had made it easy to rely on him when dealing with our greatest enemy.

None of us had guessed he would fail.

This year, Sanctuary had come out of winter baying for blood, patrolling heavily just as soon as the ice broke up. After the brutal razing of Old Ryme's Port, pirate towns made a point to move around, and so far, they'd avoided any further aggression. Secret signs and half-hidden signals pointed our ships to safe harbor, often ports that larger craft and worse captains would never be able to reach even if they did decipher our coded messages.

This left their juggernauts frustrated in the extreme, crashing down the shipping lanes. They'd taken craft after unlucky craft, showering the sea floor in blood and bodies. Bad news flew faster than the gulls and waited for us every time we tied up.

When we'd learned that the *Ruby*, one of the biggest and best armed pirate ships in the isles, had been sunk in the far north, I'd watched a little of the light go out of Griffin's eyes. We'd been friends with the *Ruby* for as long as I could remember. Ships were lost all the time, but the *Ruby* was the first defense against Sanctuary's goons. She could be called upon to blast their galleons to smithereens on short notice, and even if she didn't fire her guns, the sight of her would send their navy running. The isles would miss her.

There was nothing the *Wretched Lady* could do but carry on. We stationed ourselves in her stead and set about harrying whatever fleet happened to pass by.

Raiding the navy was good for a while, until it became the only thing that whet Griffin's appetite. He wanted revenge for the *Ruby*. He could sink a hundred ships without scratching the surface of his hurt. It had been folly, looking back now, to trust the pitiful cries of Sanctuary's sailors as they begged for their lives. They confirmed the *Ruby* had gone down, but not before the navy brought her captain off in chains. Griffin showed scarce sympathy after that, and gouged more information out of them.

Every trail he found led right to Sanctuary's dungeons.

The navy usually didn't bother taking prisoners, especially not from the far north just after ice break. More mouths to feed and more people to worry about in the unpredictable weather. Torture could be done off the side of the boat far more easily.

The *Ruby* had been a nail in Sanctuary's boot, sure enough. Her captain, Mags, was ex-navy herself, which was a story I'd never heard in its entirety, except that she stole the *Ruby* from right under their noses. She was responsible for plenty of the city's losses and more than one pamphlet published in Coisume condemning Sanctuary's horrific deeds. Maddening Mags. The Magpie. The navy cursed her in all her many names. Why they hadn't killed her was anyone's guess.

Word of her capture brought the color back to Griffin's cheeks. We spoke late into the night. He was sure Mags had been taken to satisfy some pirate hunter's grudge. She'd made enemies of them all. There was little other possible reason. His rage hardened from a gathering storm to a tempered blade. Finally, after our brutal spring, there was someone he could save. No matter that it reeked of a trap. He wanted to spring it.

Trenna, Silver, and I all tried to stop him. We wanted Mags back, but it wasn't worth losing him or the ship. The city had been closed for so long, breaking in would be an undertaking. The other two he listened to with the respect due to his equals. Me, he treated, as ever, like a brother, one he didn't particularly appreciate butting into his affairs. Finally, he held up his hand and told us he was born to do it.

He wouldn't elaborate, and the next day he was gone. A note asking us to wait for him at the Silver Buckle on summer's longest day sat on his bed in the captain's cabin. He hadn't risked the ship. He'd left us nice and protected at the Tross and taken an old rigger out into the strong currents around Sanctuary, the chain's largest and most dangerous island. Alone.

We set off as soon as we found him gone. The seas must have blessed him. Even in a bigger, faster craft, we couldn't catch up. He'd hidden the rigger in an open-mouthed cave on the cliffs behind the main city. Rory and Silver paddled in to investigate, but he was long gone. Whether he climbed up the face of the cliff or went further into the caves, they couldn't tell.

So, we bided our time until midsummer.

He didn't return.

Griffin was gone. The man who practically raised me, who taught me how to be a pirate and showed me how to really live. The *Wretched Lady* missed him, and we were not ready to mourn him.

He was good enough to get into the walled city, but he wasn't good enough to get himself back out. And I was stuck here stomping around in his boots trying to figure out the best path for his ship and his crew and his future. I wasn't cut out for the job, but I would do it, even if it killed me.

I longed to be Connor again, without a care in the world.

I'd spent the summer uncomfortable in my duties as captain,

growing more harried and worried as weeks slipped past the longest day.

Yesterday, from jumping into the sea after the Eagle to listening to her testimony as she clutched my coat about her, I'd felt like I was finally bridging the gap, becoming both myself and the leader of the *Wretched Lady*. Old Connor would have eaten the woman alive, a pretty thing like that, but the *Wretched Lady*'s captain was supposed to be wringing secrets out of her for the good of the ship. I'd battled both impulses and walked away sure of myself for the first time in a long time. I wondered what she would let me wrest from her before our time together was through.

11

REGULA

It was easy to blame Odette when we found ourselves out in the cold night air, hanging as far off the railing as our fear would let us. It was our second night on the pirate ship, and it felt markedly different from the nights we'd been shut in our cabin aboard the *Edgewater*.

We'd spent the whole day being whisked about the *Wretched Lady*, learning about flags and the names of the sails and avoiding those horrible biscuits that seemed to make an appearance at every meal. There was always a job to be done and a pirate more than happy to share a bit about life on the ship. I'd taken in so many names and bits of jargon that my head was chock full. At least there'd only been one proper way to coil a rope, and I had port and starboard down pat.

After such a day, the salt air on my face was refreshing. In Sanctuary, our ring was carefully removed from any hint of port or commerce. I had only seen the sea from a distance before we'd stepped onto the naval ship, even though our city took up the better part of an island. Even the cold was firmly shut away, with tight window dressings and covers over walkways. My every sense was alive out here.

"So we just whisper our names down to her?" Odette asked,

as polite as she got. She'd tried to press herself into one of the gaps, as it would get her closer to the water, and was still pouting a bit because Billy hadn't warned her it was the closest spot aboard to a toilet. I'd had to bite my hand to cover my laughter when she realized, and she'd brought two of the night watch running with her screams.

"Usually you do it at the docks, or ankle deep in the surf before your first sailing, but this'll do. It's more the spirit of the thing than doing it right." Billy swept her hair out of her face and spit over the side. "You don't have to, you know. No one mistakes you two for sailors even if you're wearing the clothes."

I plucked at the strings of my borrowed shirt.

"It would be rude of us to bring you any more bad luck, even if we aren't meant to be pirates," I said, stepping up onto the rung below the railing. Odette was already hanging half off, her upper body doing a good impression of the figurehead.

We'd paused and stared at the *Wretched Lady*'s carving earlier in the day. There was nothing so fearsome or so beautiful where we hailed from. In Sanctuary, art was decoration alone. A statue of a boar woman with a big sword might well land one in a cell for lewd and unmentionable behavior, no matter how skillfully it was whittled.

"Seeing as how we're on a pirate ship, odds are we're well on our way," Odette said, laughing back at us over her shoulder. I gripped the untended wood and leaned out with her. Billy stood a pace away, her body aimed toward us instead of the dark sea. She'd brought a lamp from the cabin, its waxen light dancing with each roll of the boat beneath us. Billy seemed torn between leaving us to our mischief and muscling in to stop us.

"Do I address her? The Lady of the Sea, I mean," Odette asked.

"That's between her and you, Venu. I couldn't say." Odette bent forward, eyes fixed on the inky ocean below. I looked a moment longer at the pirate, who crossed her arms, watching us. "I'll just…" She looked to make her escape.

"Oh no, Billy, you can't possibly leave us. Without you, the sea might think us charlatans." Odette didn't look, but her words worked their magic, and the pirate was back at her elbow in record time.

"Aren't you scared I might hear your name?" She plunked her elbows where Odette's body extended over the rail.

"I could be lying... Or perhaps I'd like you to gain control of me."

I wondered if Billy even remembered I was here, with her attention so fully focused on Odette. I was an instant from hopping off and heading back to the cabin in disgust. It was one thing to flirt shamelessly, as Odette did with everything that moved, but quite another for her to string along a pirate.

Odette had no trouble ignoring me to better play her little game.

She waited a moment, and then with a pretty, calculated scream, lost her grip on the railing, one hand flashing out against the expanse. Billy, who'd watched her all along, was quick to wrap an arm around her, pulling her back. The insufferable girl turned her head and fixed the pirate with a devilish grin.

"If you wish it." Billy's words were laced with promise.

"There's no danger. She had a good hold on this side the whole time," I said through gritted teeth, backing away from the rail—and the show. I'd had quite enough. Odette could handle herself for a while.

I turned, and ran straight into a warm and confoundingly firm wall.

Someone's chest.

Much to my shame, I realized I'd just run into a pirate. I gulped air back into my lungs as warm hands set me back on my feet.

Not just any pirate. The captain.

My face flamed, safely hidden in the dark.

It would be impossible to forget the dangerous scent of salt and tar and the slight tang of liquor that lingered between his skin and shirt.

As soon as he saw me steady, his hands fell away.

"I heard screaming."

I blinked at him.

"I'm teaching 'em how to be pirates, Captain," Billy answered his unasked question, still huddled at ship's edge with Odette.

"Is that so?" He looked between the three of us. "And you? Are you well?" he asked me. For once, I didn't have an answer.

CONNOR

I NEEDED A DRINK. THE EAGLE WOULD HAVE TO FORGIVE ME FOR encroaching upon her roost—though it was my cabin in the first place—to retrieve one.

Griffin had hidden all the best liquor in there.

I'd walked the Eagle back to her lodgings, all the while trying to shake the memory of her touch. Since becoming captain, I'd tried to separate myself from the crew, which meant turning down invitations and avoiding casual contact. I hadn't realized how long it had been—

A whiskey would temper my racing thoughts.

I pulled a chair over and climbed up to the captain's stash.

There. A slight click from the worn panel's latch revealed thick glass bottles, most coated in a fine layer of dust. One, by far the finest, was mottled with fingerprints. Ships like ours were run on a take and share alike principle, so it was a fair bet most every person on board had a taste or two of the good stuff when the regular guzzle ran out. That was, if they didn't have their own secret cache.

Desperation didn't drive me to the bottle usually, but I needed to settle my nerves. The cold of the glass against my lips and the burn of liquor down my throat would shock me back into myself.

"Ahem."

I nearly fell off the chair.

The Eagle.

I'd forgotten her in my haste to slake my thirst. She'd taken off her coat, and was standing a few paces away, staring.

I saw myself through her eyes, balanced precariously on a chair, swigging straight from the bottle. Rough around the edges with an unnatural shine to my eyes. A rogue, through and through. She was right to fear me, right to stay far, far away.

Instead, she raised an arm, her sleeve billowing as she motioned, unmistakably, for the bottle. I swallowed what remained in my mouth and handed it gingerly over, not quite sure what to make of her. Would she toss it from the window? I hopped off the chair, knowing I could stop her if it came to that.

She brought the damned thing to her lips and took a long pull.

"Not half so bad as I expected," she said through gritted teeth. I stifled my surprise with a laugh.

"And you say you aren't cut out for a pirate's life," I teased.

Her gaze sharpened like the bird whose name she'd borrowed. She took another swallow.

"I find I owe you a great deal, Captain." I was trapped in her gaze without the distraction of the bottle. "My life, it seems," she added, softer.

"Luck had more to do with it than me, truly." I believed it. One didn't simply find and rescue people who were meant for watery graves. Especially not as the colder currents washed in for winter. A fortnight later and there would have been no saving her.

She shoved the bottle back at me, and watched as I took another drink. Cool fire swirled over my tongue.

"Either way, I'm grateful." She perched at the edge of Griffin's desk, folding her hands in her lap. Clearly she was used to hiding them in skirts. Without concealment, she fussed with them for a moment before stilling.

I swallowed another mouthful, figuring that to be the end of our conversation. She didn't seem to mind silence, nor did she turn down another shot at the bottle. When she handed it back, I corked it and stowed it away.

"We… There may be rough seas ahead. We're still a long way from the channel city, and we were in a desperate state before your ship escaped us." Taking the Eagle into my confidence was risky, but I wanted more than anything to know her secrets.

"I hadn't guessed, what with the luxurious fare you've been serving us." Her voice was wry.

"There's a port not too far from here. We'll restock a little before heading on." She was sitting on the maps that would get us there.

"Do you think…" she said, glancing toward the windows, "…we might meet our ship again?"

"There's plenty of ocean between us, but I hope we do." I pushed the chair back into place, her eyes tracking me as I came toward her. They were glowing in the light of the oil lamps; a warm darkness. The drink had smoothed yesterday's furrows from her brow. She was relaxing, if only by fractions.

"Each of us has a score to settle," she murmured.

"The words of a pirate, my lady. Again," I chided. At this, she smiled a little, and I could feel the weight of fatigue on us both.

The door creaked behind us, and in came Venu and Billy. The city girl was smiling the sort of breathless smile that was coming to mark her, and she flopped, boneless, onto the lonely chaise.

"I rather like this ship life." She recovered from her delighted swoon and regarded us as she tucked her hands behind her head.

Billy ogled us too, shaking with silent laughter, as if she weren't just as much in need of mocking for following the new arrival around like a puppy after five minutes.

"Don't expect me to hire you on just yet," I said, resolved to leave them to the rest of their night.

"Oh, I'm afraid I wouldn't be caught dead on a ship with such terrible provisions," the girl shot back, crossing one trousered leg over the other.

I'll admit, it stung. She'd zeroed in on the biggest crack in my armor. I had to press down the growl I wanted to give her.

"Do you have a bedroll?" I chose instead to ignore the girl, and turned to stare at Billy, slouched against the wall. I caught her slight frown at my words.

I glanced at the wide bed set into the far side of the chamber. The covers were well tucked, without evidence that anyone had slept there last night. I'd made a point to avoid it when the cabins were passed to me. It was certainly big enough for a few, though I wondered at Billy's balls if she thought she'd be allowed in it with two proper ladies from Sanctuary.

"I… Uh, I sat up last night."

I cocked a brow, trying to lace my face with some steel. It wasn't my business who bunked with who until I had to apologize to the newcomers she'd scandalized, being unaware of the way pirates tended to flirt and fuck.

"On the chaise, Connor." Billy was unamused by my insinuation.

Some captain I was. I could hardly stop myself from imagining that the Eagle's eyes had followed mine to the bed, coming to the same conclusion. When I did sneak a look at her, I was pleased to see the slight blush that danced over her cheeks and down her neck. Though, whether it was Billy or the mere implication of a shared bed that heated her, I didn't ask. In either case, I would make my exit sooner rather than later, for everyone's comfort.

"I keep a bedroll under the desk, for just such times." I nearly choked on the words. I didn't have time to wonder why. Billy could sit, or stand in the corner for all I cared. The pirate sure as hell didn't ask me why the bed was always untouched in here. Code and courtesy were linked on this ship.

I let myself out, the click of the door drowned by the beat of my heart.

12

CONNOR

Tucked sweetly away to the south of Sanctuary, along a coast of struggling greenery and craggy rocks, stood our intended port. Penny's Cove was slung proudly above the largest slice of beach on its island. A humble dock welcomed us in from the deeper water of the bay—the only town on this isle still standing against the wind, the tides, and its neighbor.

With her fairly hidden shores and iron-willed leadership, the little place bustled with activity, pirate and otherwise. If you knew where to look. No map from Sanctuary marked it, nor did the walled city's navy search for it, choosing instead to chase more exciting prey: the ever-moving skull and daggers who sailed out of the northwest.

The town was also damned convenient if one wanted to replenish stores right under Sanctuary's nose. There were hundreds of islands to the west, and many to the north, but Penny's stood on a chain known as the Gate, which put her closest to the riches and politicking of the continent. Without a knowledgeable navigator or a barrel of luck, ships were forced to take the safest path, down the string of islands where the currents were gentlest, before they could cut over to the east.

The Gate did not easily give up her secrets, and Sanctuary had long ago deemed the islands too harsh for further interest. They'd planted an outpost at the southernmost tip of the chain, complete with a wall or two of its own and a shining lighthouse, and left well enough alone. Though they sank any pirates foolish enough to fall into their clutches, the navy had only recently begun to venture off their boats to strike at the many settlements scattered across the isles.

Penny's Cove flourished yet, and had eyes enough to mark the passage of any and all vessels in the well-travelled shipping lanes along the western edge of her island. The town was rich in information, but it was even richer in goat. The cliffs and crannies of the Gate were an accidental home to the largest population outside of the continent.

It was these goats I watched marched up the gangplank on the backs of my men. Rory's advice had been sound. The last of our salt had secured us supper. Goat for the cookpot, gutted and bled, and more cut into strips and smoked. My mouth was watering already. It had been so long since I'd had anything but tooth-breaking tack.

Penny waved me over with an imperious hand, brown and calloused. Unlike her town, she was an imposing figure; taller than me by a head even as she leaned on an oiled cane. I wasn't sure if the town had been named after her or if it was some title passed down through the ages. I did know that if you wanted to do business in the cove, you had to impress Penny. I hastened to her side, ready to argue over the quality of our salt.

"Mighty strange minnow we saw today, lad, considering the hatchery's been locked up tight for an age." She watched my men as they heaved goats aboard. I'd almost eaten her minnow. A naval ship dressed as a merchant ship in a sea without healthy trade.

I hummed my agreement and weighed telling her about the *Edgewater*. Maybe I could get another goat for my trouble. I tapped my tongue against my teeth as I watched her. She had eyes on every island in the Gate, but their spyglasses could only glean so much.

Her hand tightened on the head of her cane as she stared me down. Her face was lined, her dark hair shot with gray and tucked into a woven cap that looked to be more salt than yarn at this point.

"I call Griffin my friend, Connor. You can speak straight with me." She sniffed, leaving my uncomfortable title off. "None of their ships have stopped here, but we grow wary. Nothing is left untouched when the navy has its way. Sanctuary cannot abide any it cannot control."

I watched the loading rather than face her head-on.

"Penny's Cove has stood a long time," I said. "There are no more people to be brought within their walls, no remaining ground to conquer on that big island of theirs, except the salt flats where they dare not go. They sink our ships and burn our towns when they run across them. It's no coincidence."

Before Sanctuary closed its gates, news traveled to us freely in the Reaches. Now, the arrival of their ships was all the warning we got.

"We hear nothing and see much. Things I can't make sense of. I would know what you know." She motioned for me to follow her. I didn't argue. The *Edgewater* was already ahead of us.

Penny's Cove bustled with small vessels, all docked farther in, and as we trotted into the city, heads turned to follow us. Penny walked alone, her cane leaving a mark in the pounded dirt, and I didn't doubt for a moment that I would be in trouble if I tried anything. Griffin had always been of the opinion that Penny's Cove was known for its goats: the human ones, stubborn and fearless enough to climb up any cliff. It was his flag Penny had recognized, and because of his reputation she'd come to shake my hand. She'd deal with us fairly, if only out of respect for Griffin's name.

The largest building on the wharf was a saloon, marking it as my favorite type of town, and it was no surprise when Penny led me through open doors and into a great common room. Balconies framed the ceiling and a battered bar sat at the edge of my vision.

As it was, we were alone in a sea of chairs and tables. Penny signaled the barkeep, who promptly disappeared. She dropped heavily onto one of the stools, resting her stick in a welt carved into the bar, and stared at me until I joined her.

"We won't be disturbed." She folded her hands before her and leaned into the wood. "You may be the last ship to stop in before the ice comes, and I can't wait a whole winter without news."

It would have been much easier if I had what she wanted. Something solid. Not two half-drowned Sanctuary women with a puzzling story.

"You think your salt paid for those goats?" She pinned me with her eyes, the corners of her mouth turned up. "You got lucky, kid. I need word. Give me peace of mind, or give me a reason to prepare." There it was. I'd been naive to assume we'd simply made a good trade.

There wasn't anything about the city's behavior that I wanted to hide. Sanctuary had its seasons. They pillaged with one hand and locked themselves up with the other. The city wasn't interested in anything but proving it was the biggest, strongest, and in their opinion, the only viable place to live in the Far Flung. Sometimes we referred to Sanctuary as the Mouth, because it devoured. We didn't call its neighboring towns and provinces anything, because they were nothing but burned bones. Any survivors were added to the tenth or eleventh or fourteenth walls.

"Aid that requires payment is still aid, and I thank you for keeping the price low." I balanced myself against the bar, attempting to call back the calm exterior I'd perfected when I was not the main focus of such meetings, when the fate of my crew did not rest upon my shoulders. "If you'd met me a few days ago, I'm not sure I'd have had anything worth knowing, but those blue-coated bastards have sunk to a new low."

Penny listened, urging me on with a hand when I faltered, as I launched into the tale of Venu and the Eagle. Not the fable, but the two who sat aboard my ship.

She stopped me only twice. First to confirm that women had indeed been allowed to leave the city. It surprised her, and while I knew it was unusual, both the ladies aboard seemed so comfortable in their new circumstances that I'd discounted just how rare it was.

"I remember the last—wet nurses or maids, weren't they?—and that was nigh on twenty years ago, just before the city shut itself up," she muttered before allowing me to continue.

When I described the captain and his cold-hearted plan, she stopped me fully, drawing herself to her feet. The scrape of her stool on the hardwood brought the barman hurrying back in. She called out some names to him, and he disappeared again.

I stood too, unsure of protocol but interested in avoiding any disrespect that might keep us from trading in Penny's Cove again, or leaving the sheltered bay.

"Stay with us tonight," she commanded. "You have nothing else to say, and I would speak with your city women." She retrieved her cane from its notch. Staying in Penny's would be good for us, except that we'd lose all hope of finding the *Edgewater*.

"Penny, if you had a chance for revenge, a chance to find the captain who offered those girls to the sea, would you seize it?" I didn't think I'd manage a real argument with her. She could order my ship harried and run into any one of the tricky sandbars that protected this place. Worse, she could send her people over the *Wretched Lady*'s side and bring anyone she wanted here at a moment's notice. It was possible she'd done it already. If she hadn't, it was only a testament to some former feeling for Griffin.

"The ship was sailing for the channels. It stands to reason they would continue, especially if their need was so great as to dump passengers to keep their course." I could feel sweat gathering at the back of my neck, but I kept on. "The *Wretched Lady* doesn't look like much at the moment, but we nearly had that rotten excuse for a captain. If I can catch them before they pass the guns of Coisume, I may be able to wring the answers we seek right from their cowardly mouths."

Gears turned in her head. Good. I wanted a chance to beat the glee from that scum Forewell's eyes. Or perhaps I would watch Venu do it; let the women deliver their own retribution.

Maybe Penny would appreciate it if I got on my knees and begged.

"I want to see that ship sunk," I added, trying to bolster my own spirit along with my case. "If we stay with you, we'll never catch them."

She tilted her head and a smile played at the corners of her mouth.

"Have you heard of the Graveyard, lad?"

13

REGULA

My pulse raced as we were herded from the boat. Even without the bite of our old captain's knife in my back, I hesitated at the gangplank. Captain Connor followed behind, loaded up with letters and requests from the pirates. Silver's barely fit in the sheaf of his shirt, it was so big.

Odette, of course, was unafraid to walk in only breeches and a shirt among strange folk. She made it very easy to follow her, as was our pattern, since no one had eyes for me when she passed by.

My first step onto the ramp was as shaky as the breath in my lungs. I completed it nonetheless, following it with another, all too aware of the sliver of wood between me and the sea. I knew a cove was far shallower than the open ocean, and the water here could not suck me down even if it tried, but my heart ignored my head's counsel. It threatened to beat out of my chest, and I stood, teetering, vaguely aware of Odette's mild encouragement from the solid planking of the dock.

A hand landed on my shoulder, almost hard enough to shake the board beneath me.

"Breathe."

It was the captain, his tone so easy and unbothered that I wondered if people balked at every port.

"Again."

I had managed just one gulp, and forgotten to continue. His firm pressure didn't guide me anywhere, nor did it feel like a trap, just warm weight pulling me out of the panic.

Finally aware of more than terror, I shrugged him off.

"Keep your hands to yourself, Captain."

I didn't need his help or his gentleness. My life was on its way to great change. If I let something as small as a gangplank stop me, I was truly in for misery.

"Of course," he murmured behind me, withdrawing his touch. I allowed the loss of it to drive me forward.

I came down off the plank so fast I couldn't change my mind.

At the bottom, Odette had forgotten all about me. She was peppering a nearby fisher with questions. The poor woman was stuck with one foot on the dock and one in her boat, braced against the onslaught of words.

I snuck a look back up the plank and found the captain close behind me, mirth in his eyes. He nodded at me as he passed, heading straight for Odette. The look of relief on the old salt's face when the captain offered my charge his arm was immense. I bristled a little as she took it, whether at the action or the brilliant smiles the pair seemed to call from thin air on contact, I didn't know.

The dock stretched on forever as I dogged their footsteps. The town rose up in front of us, small and crowded with build-ings. It was strange to see a place without walls separating the various strata. Penny's Cove might be a handful of sand in comparison to my home, but there was a warmth to its size that was absent when I thought of Sanctuary. People hopped from sleek fishing crafts and wandered every which way down the hard pack of the broad main street, greeting neighbors and towns-people alike.

No one waved at us, though I could feel eyes on my back.

Captain Connor matched Odette's sunny conversation word for word, pointing out each of the buildings we passed. Finally, we stopped at the biggest, a lumbering two-story boasting a huge set of weathered wooden doors and the telltale reek of old beer. After yesterday's liquor, I wasn't sure my stomach would cooperate in an alehouse.

Odette let the captain hold the door open and brushed through first. I was next, succeeding, if only by a hair, at ignoring him as I passed. Once my eyes adjusted to the darkness inside, a sea of empty chairs and tables greeted me. Only one, the farthest, was occupied.

A woman rose from the far table, eldest and perhaps tallest among the group, and gestured for us to join them.

She seemed impossible to disobey, so I took the first seat, directly across from her. Odette, too excited to stay still, I imagined, set her fingers walking across the top of the chair to my right before finally settling in. Captain Connor took the final place between us and the strangers.

We were watched by a dark-haired woman who was going gray at the temples, her red lips pursed against the white of her wrinkled skin, a younger, obviously quite sunburnt man, and a bald woman with soft eyes who was tanned but not half so weathered as her companions. All three were dressed plain and kept quiet. They waited, it seemed, on the giantess beside them, who loomed over us.

We learned shortly that the woman was the Penny of Penny's Cove, and the others were her advisers. I'd never seen a governing body so full of old women.

Penny wasted no time wringing our story from us. The captain hadn't bothered to warn us.

Each adviser looked like they'd be happier on the wharf than in an embroidery circle, and for some reason that brought me a sparkling, uneasy joy even as their questions intensified. I sensed Odette next to me, itching to get their measure, though she sat and spoke with the dignity required of a young woman under immense scrutiny.

Nothing surprised the brunette, nor the eldest. The man took breaks from watching us to scribble in a leather notebook that he slapped open and closed on the hard wood table. The kindness I might have imagined in the bald woman's eyes turned to confusion the longer we spoke, and a line was slowly eating into her brow.

Captain Connor leaned forward, listening intently even though he'd heard the entirety of our tale already. It was good of him and respectful to these cove folk, who did not seem to be pirate-kind, but something else altogether. I was not the most familiar with Sanctuary politics, but it was a great shame that I had never once heard of these islanders.

Our story was growing thinner with each telling, even to my own ears. Of course, the truth of it was layered with my secret hopes for Coisume and Odette's final gasp of freedom. It was true to us, for ourselves, but there was a decided hollowness to our ship's murderous behavior at the first sign of trouble. I'd had little time to question the reason for our trip, from Odette's parents' perspective or the navy's, since the agreement had been such a coup for the two of us.

Silence met us when we finished. All our companions, questions answered, looked to Penny, whose lips had thinned in thought.

"The record is taken," she said finally, "with only one thing needful now. Dispense with the pirate names, and tell us what families you hail from in the city." There was no question in her asking, not really. Loath to drop her game, Odette waited, liking, as she did, to have the upper hand over our pirate saviors. I suspected the captain was listening closely, though he hid his interest well.

"The lady is a scion of the house of Sessleny, first ring," I proclaimed, as I was wont to do in the city. Here the reaction was somewhat different. Instead of awe, the women of the port sucked in a collective breath to the scratch of their fellow's pen. One repeated the words under her breath just loud enough for me to catch. Odette and I had argued about how to present ourselves, wondering if we should switch around and present me as her and she as me, before deciding on the meager protection of Venu and the Eagle. Having escaped a wet and untimely death, we'd both decided that her ransom was worth risking. Odette would forgive me for the reveal, as long as the rest of her trip home proved exciting.

"And you?" Penny did not pin an honorific on, as one would expect for politeness. I didn't much like to be a matron, so I paid it little mind.

"I'm no one. Merely her governess."

Penny whistled away my nothing pronouncement. I chanced a look at Captain Connor, the closest thing to an ally we had at the table. He'd turned slightly, opening his body to the two of us, and there was a twinkle in his eye. If someone was going to push back at the old woman, it wouldn't be him, it seemed to say, not for all the gold in the world.

It wasn't that I meant to hide myself away behind her, but Odette had made the last few years a safe haven where I wasn't required to breathe my status or think about my family. Neither name came quickly or without a fight to my tongue.

"I'm of House Belau, third ring, though I did marry into House Toine, exchanging for first, for a time." There was a relief to saying it, oversimplification that it was. Odette knew my story, all the sad trappings of it, and helped me keep it from the lips of every gossip. We'd hidden it quite neatly until now, under all of her charm and my ability to blend into the background.

I swung my gaze back to the leader of Penny's Cove, noting the twist of Odette's fingers and the shadows in the captain's eyes, his sparkle lost to seriousness.

"It is unusual for anyone to leave the first ring for something as simple as an errand, hmm?" the old lady said, ostensibly to everyone. "More so for a slip of a girl and her caretaker."

"There was a ship full of men to protect us," I said. "Though they did not prove the best at the task." This earned me a snort from the bald woman that quickly faded into the charged quiet.

"The women will stay with us for now, Captain." The eldest addressed Captain Connor with a bit of fire in her mien. "No, don't argue. We must both consult amongst our own. It is customary for your ship to keep to its code, I believe. Your crew deserve a say in this."

His mouth opened and shut, tension shooting into his hands.

"They need a bath, boy. Such gentle folk as the first ring can't be used to your salty berth," the brunette added.

"I've kept them very well, thank you!" He leaned back at her insult, any fighting spirit bridled and tamed by his relaxed posturing.

"A bath wouldn't go amiss!" Odette piped up. She laid a hand on the captain's wrist, and added, "Our accommodations have been first rate, especially after our misfortune, but a real soak would be a comfort."

Penny nodded.

"Harvest is near over, and we have plenty to share for the night. If you'd be gracious enough to stay, we can offer a meal for you and your ship."

"How generous." The captain's brows rose. "And you'll return them to our decks afore we leave tomorrow?"

"There is plenty to discuss, and more to plan around." The elder pressed her chair back, coming to a stand solidly, a polished cane I'd missed on my entrance in her hand. The others at the table followed her.

The captain took his time, crossing his arms. "They're safer on my ship than locked in here, with a full winter to set their families worrying. I must insist they return to the *Wretched Lady*."

"There are ways around the frost tides and the ice, if one has had time to learn," the old woman tossed back. "We can return them to their great city just as well as you, and with less danger to their persons." Her face relayed just how fragile and poorly suited for a pirate ship we were.

"Wise as you are—" the captain said, "I cannot in good faith leave them, even for a bath, if you'd barter them back to the city. The *Wretched Lady* saved them, and we'll not be collecting bad luck using them as pawns and market tokens, no matter how pretty a piece they may be worth."

I was sure something more was written into the words, for the old woman frowned. She leaned over to the bald woman, who nodded in response to whatever she whispered.

"Of all the ships in the Far Flung, you've the only one to whom I'd release such fine folk, if you promise to see them to their rightful place," she decided at last. "And that's only if you swear on Griffin's name, since yours isn't worth much yet."

The captain's face darkened and he stood, looking up at her across the table, square shouldered and hard jawed.

"I've already sworn it to the deep, and I've no problem swearing on my captain, except that he's not yet a soul to swear on. Not close." His words burned, and it was impossible not to hold my breath as he pressed a finger into the oiled wood. "You can't make me damn him, but you can't keep the women here either. Trust that I'll see this through, or we might all find ourselves in the same cage that holds Griffin."

The strong words didn't sour the old woman, in fact, she cracked a smile.

"So be it, then. The cove'll trust you on this, and should you fail, we'll hear about it soon enough to tan your hide and sink your ship." She threatened him so cheerfully that I wondered if I should shiver. Our lives hung in the balance here, at the table and on the sea.

"I know he'll see us safely home." Odette couldn't contain herself. Whether she'd missed the layers of conversation or chosen to ignore them I wasn't sure. "A bath! Sensational!" she exclaimed, turning to me, her excitement lifting me just about out of my seat.

The elder waved a hand, dismissing us. The brunette at her side came over to escort us out.

Captain Connor ducked between us and whispered, "I consider that well won." With a glance back at the cove's representative, he raised his voice a hair. "If they mistreat you, the town's small enough that you can shout and we'll hear you in the harbor."

Odette gasped gamely, and I shrugged.

"Surely nothing they can do will be as bad as a dip in old salty," I said, all my humor pent up from the last hour of interrogation. Pirates always found new and interesting nicknames for everything, including the sea. I was beginning to adopt the practice.

I surprised the captain, I'd say, and it showed on his face for just a second, before his grin stretched back out and he waved us off to our bath.

Penny's adviser was quick to lead us to the nearest building, a squat thing done up in the same yellow and black rock as the cliffs, and into one of a set of rooms. They were sparse, but offered us a view of the main road and gave truth to the captain's words.

The *Wretched Lady* waited proudly just outside our window.

14

CONNOR

My crew's patience held only as long as it took for my boots to strike the *Wretched Lady*'s deck. They were splayed out across the width of her. Duties done, goat packed away, and flour already halfway to hard biscuits. Once they saw me, they clamored to share their opinions on our heading.

"Men like that can't be left unchecked on the seas!" Rory cut through the noise, somehow, his voice surprisingly level.

"If they're men at all! Hardly better than beasts," Cesare said.

"That's what they call us pirates, I'll bet." Pipes whipped herself around to spar with the tattooed pirate.

"Better to remember how small our lady the sea is, when it comes to it. We'll meet that tub sooner or later, and be glad we delivered our precious cargo long since," Silver said once they blew themselves out. He was cross legged on the largest pallet with a little book open on his lap.

The conversation carried on around me. I'd weighed our options, and was quietly waiting for my crew to get stuck in the same cursed spot as me.

We could turn now, drop the ladies back off in their own city, and risk our pirate necks in the process. Or we could race the *Edgewater*, catching them in the open near the continent, or not, while delivering the women to Coisume in relative safety. Without an escort or any documentation, the women might be worse off in the channels, but it would be knots better for us to rush forward with the second plan.

There was only one pressing issue complicating both. Around Penny's wooden table, I'd been handed an uncommon gift, and with it, a grave decision. I was sick with myself, two-face that I was, invoking the ancient rights of safety and courtesy for the ship-wrecked to cow the old woman and cap her ambitions toward Sanctuary when I... Well, I didn't see much choice besides using Venu and the Eagle to further my own agenda.

I was a damned bad captain anyway—a fact emphasized by the fight brewing around me—so I could only pray that the Lady of the Sea would spare everyone but me when I skirted her customs and drew the only card I had to play.

The women were valuable to Sanctuary. The city had finally made a misstep, handing them off to us. Penny believed it, so I believed it too. We could use them.

I waited.

It was inevitable that they would reach the same conclusion.

"What say you, Captain?" Trenna asked, always careful to include me, and to reach a hand out to any shipmate that might look too green to speak.

"Sod him, Trenna. What would you do if you had the helm?" Jack of the Long Legs called from the corner. I didn't flinch at her words. I knew I wasn't what some of these louts considered a captain. Trenna would not be in this predicament, had she been left in charge, and every man among us knew it. If handed the captaincy, Trenna would be good, but she'd also be permanent. No one wanted to cast such a vote until we had Griffin's bones here to return to the sea. I had been a compromise, a bandage on a bleeding wound, and I hoped none of them would pay for it.

"I do have the helm, Long Legs, and it's because Connor's given it to me." Trenna, ever the diplomat, deliberately cut her down, eliciting a sullen silence from the corner full of her supporters. Jack was a popular and competent sailor who held some sway with her peers and had made it quite clear she'd rather have Trenna running the boat. There were many such clusters across the crew, some whose allegiance was to Silver, some to themselves alone. If I weren't in charge, I'd have been as loud as the rest. I couldn't argue with any faction, not when I agreed heartily with the meat of their problem.

We needed Griffin back.

"I've been chewing this over since the Sanctuarians were hauled aboard." I addressed the whole of those gathered. Anyone who'd rather sleep than vote was in their hammock belowdecks.

"You have been too long without a true captain, I know," I said to Jack's corner, and to the rest. "I picked up the mantle in hopes that we would see Griffin back with us within a week, and it has been months. Worse still, we have chased our own tail trying to find some way to break him out of the walls and we've suffered for it. I, Comely Connor—" This got its customary laugh and I hardened myself to the rest of my speech. "—am responsible for this, above anyone. Luck pokes and prods us, and I believe we have a real chance of getting him out this time." I took a deep breath, grateful for the silence that greeted me. They were willing to hear my piece.

"Griffin's capture has proven more permanent than we expected. We have no way of knowing where or how, exactly, he is, but I have chosen to trust in the man who raised me and to hope we'll find him in fine condition. In Penny's Cove, it was made clear to me in no uncertain terms that we have the best weapon against the city among us quite by accident. The two women delivered to us by the navy are both from one of the great houses within the first wall."

I paused for dramatic effect, not at all recalling the way the

Eagle had slipped her marriage so lightly into the telling at Penny's table. It wasn't for me to mind, much, except that she had seemed so unlike one of the wedded and bedded city women. *My mistake.* Worse than Billy, I was, caught up in a lady's whims. A pirate waiting on the word of a delicate like her, as if our worlds were really meant to collide in any sort of pleasurable way.

"Are you suggesting we ignore the rules of courtesy?" Rory's voice rose a fraction higher than usual. I'd expected him to disapprove. We'd always been each other's conscience, and now as captain, I had come to realize I would trade mine for a way out from under the burden.

"I am suggesting we use what leverage we have over Sanctuary while we have it. I am suggesting we win our true captain free." I turned to him, forcing myself to witness the wound in his eyes. "No one is more important than Griffin. The women will be returned well and whole to their families, and we will benefit only from the threat that they might not."

"They are our guests! To use them as bargaining chips is to make ourselves fools of fate. All of us were welcome upon the *Wretched Lady* when we most needed it, without reason and without artifice. You would spit in the face of that, and us." Rory didn't pull his punches, nor did he soften his words.

His eyes bored into me. He was right and he knew it. Some things were sacred. Some things were not to be stepped on or coiled up and tossed out. Ships lived and died by the code, sailing by luck just as we did the seas.

"If it unlocks the shackles at Griffin's wrists, I must stand before Lady Luck and beg her forgiveness, for I can see no other way." I wrenched my gaze from Rory's, turning first to Trenna and then to Silver. My eyes were pleading. One word from either would knock me off my precarious post and onto an island somewhere.

"I hear the rumors. I see you whispering. Any man among us who doesn't want our captain back is welcome to raise a hand."

No one moved.

"I thought not." I pressed my feet firmly into the floor. "Does any one of you see another way to spring him? Is there a jailer we can bribe? A cannon we might wheel up to the city's walls? A mole to pay to dig under their stones with no proper map? No? I may be spitting in the face of luck and our code, but I will not ignore the gift we have been given."

Across from me, Trenna's face was tight. We had already run through a dozen schemes. We'd tried a few of them, wasting dangerous weeks anchored too close to Sanctuary's waters. None of it had worked. The walls of the city were sealed shut to us. I hoped my navigator would do anything to have Griffin back, because I needed her support in this.

"I do not ask this lightly, and I promise to shoulder the burden of the choice on my own. If we vote—and we can, I'll not stop you—then whatever ill luck I've brought down will surely spread to you who vote with me. If we don't, well... then we'll see."

The deck was awash in whispers. It was up to my crew now.

"Unconventional, Connor," Silver said. "I don't like the idea, but I understand why we may need it." That was as close to an agreement as I would get from the man.

"Without a vote, we still need to settle the question of our direction," Trenna reminded us, her thoughts ever with the ship's wheel. I was ready for her.

"We need time to plan our moves against Sanctuary. Were I to choose, we would race for the channel city, cutting off the ship that escaped us. Should they slip away, and they won't, we can re-provision on the bounty of the continent, all the time plotting how to best leverage our guests." Nothing sounded pretty about that, but we were pirates. There were ships to be taken, full of Coisume's goods, if need be. The women, on the other hand, would be far harder to bargain with.

"Taking the ship must count as coin in the Lady's pockets, to offset some of the damage we intend to do to the sea's courtesy.

That captain deserves as good as he's about to get for putting those women in danger in the first place, and the whole navy could use a good swabbing, if you know what I mean," I said.

Agreement rose to a fever pitch around me. None of us pirates could resist a bit of vengeance, especially for a good cause.

A cause we'd be treating similarly poorly in the coming days… If it weren't for Griffin, I wouldn't be up here to suggest it. I would be down on the pallet deciding to leave the fellow who did on the next island.

"So do we vote? Or do we leave it for later?" I called into the whirlpool of speculation.

Calls of "Later" slowly picked up around the room. Trenna had been the one to start it, as I'd hoped she would, her clear nay paving the way for others. Skipping out on courtesy was bad, and the only thing worse was knowing that Griffin's freedom hung on the doing of it.

I tried not to think of the women. Griffin would have offered Venu and the Eagle safe haven for as long as they needed it. Maybe Venu could have avoided her upcoming marriage and the Eagle her ongoing one, written off back home as having drowned at sea. Half the women on the ship were from the walls of Sanctuary themselves, stowed away on merchant vessels before the city shut down or press ganged by the navy when pretending to be boys, defecting as soon as they were offered the bargain because they'd heard the pirate life was worth living.

But Griffin wasn't here.

It was only me.

15

REGULA

P enny's Cove had brightened up during our bath. Chatter accompanied us down the short stretch of dirt that served as the main road. Penny's adviser, Alyna, was again at our sides. Under Odette's onslaught, we'd learned that her family had left Sanctuary to settle here around the time the second wall was built. It was hard to imagine, with fifteen walls and some outposts since constructed, and only five of them in my lifetime.

More, she wouldn't tell us due to our "unfortunate place of birth," as she called it. I couldn't blame her, since it was clear the cove and our city weren't on the best of terms. Between the pirates and the islanders, Sanctuary had no friends in its neighbors. The neighbors, however, got along heartily.

Clean, fresh, and finally in some semblance of dress, generously gifted by the cove's women, Odette and I were delivered back to the alehouse. This time it was full of people mingling, eating, and drinking. I would have been hard pressed to tell the pirates from the people of Penny's Cove, if the pirates weren't so ragged about the edges.

The picture was endearing to a fault. For all their wrinkled clothing and dirty fingernails, the pirates looked downright relaxed, stuffing their faces and trading jokes. If the state of their boat was anything to go by, the sailors themselves could use a bit of rest and refurbishment. Penny knew it too, judging by the spread she'd laid out. One side of the bar was stacked with well puffed bread, the last of the summer's orchard, and a steaming pot of stew, big enough that Odette could curl up in it. Bowls peppered the room, filling the place with the satisfying aroma of meat and spices.

I caught my stomach growling and realized Odette had abandoned me to fill her own. The food was tempting enough without the harrowing memory of ship's biscuits and salted fish. So tempting, in fact, that my nose soon led me clear across the room, following in her footsteps.

Pirates clustered around, some I recognized. The imposing one with the thrice pierced brow and fiery beard was deep in conversation with a barkeep, drinking dark liquor out of decidedly smaller glasses than everyone else was using. A few stools down, Robin, who I'd worked out to be Billy's brother, stared across the room, spectacles shiny in the many lamplights. I followed his gaze to find Pella and the pirate with the octopus tattoos half in the shadows at a far table, hands disappearing into each other's clothing. My cheeks heated and I quickly looked away, scanning the room. It was so different now, full to the brim. I felt rather foolish when I did not immediately spy the one person I'd come to find myself watching for.

A crystal clear laugh drew my eye to the woman with the long black braid who'd stood over me after I'd nearly drowned. She was presiding over the largest table, which to my great surprise included Penny, looking for all the world as if she belonged to the same crew. The pirate had coaxed a handsome islander out of his seat and was inviting him, quite theatrically, to dance. The delighted table was hooting and hollering, a wave of their mirth washing across the room.

The point of an elbow broke me out of my observations. Odette's, of course.

"You've got to try this! I swear it's better than the stuff at home." Ever the lady, she shoved a hunk of bread into her bowl for a soaking, and then into her mouth. I sniffed at her, admitting to myself that the meal looked delicious.

"You're a picture! Sit down before you're wearing your stew back onto the boat." I was halfhearted in my chastisement. We'd agreed long ago that I could mother her only to the degree that I was willing to mother myself. As such, she ignored me.

That is, until Billy enthusiastically waved her over into an empty seat. If the pirate considered herself Odette's captor, she was sorely mistaken. She was an admirer, at best.

I sighed. Another thing I wouldn't be successful at mothering Odette over. There was no changing her mind about anything. If she chose to stick with someone she was like brick and mortar, and there was little my lecturing would do but make her more attuned to the task.

There was a secret part of me that wondered if she should stay here, taking up the pirate mantle she loved so much in stories. If my marriage was anything to go by, it would be a wiser course than subjecting herself to whatever her parents had planned.

Leaving her to make her own mistakes, I grabbed myself a bowl, grateful for the gritty texture of it beneath my fingers. Odette and I were different at our cores. Her youth and temperament made every problem seem a mountain to be climbed or honey to be charmed from the hive. Even her wedding didn't scare her a whit. There was no man, even one from the continent, who couldn't be twisted around her littlest finger—a lesson Billy was no doubt learning at this very second. I envied Odette her certainty and her hope. I'd lost mine years back.

Tossed from the *Edgewater* and sucked under the waves by my gown, I'd felt a measure of fear, but more than a hint of relief. My unearned and unending suffering was the perfect match for the might of the sea herself. She could have quenched herself in me.

The cove's stew contained a week's worth of meat and a wealth of vegetables. Pillaged, I was sure, from the garden's odds and ends. Anything that hadn't fit into canning jars or brine for the winter had been donated to this pot, or perhaps the cove folk had plenty, even in the darkness of the coming season. I knew little of their lives here.

In Sanctuary, the only time we spent listening to newcomers was when we were ushering them into our walls. If guests from the isles or the continent had ever come to our fine halls, it was too long ago for me to remember. Odette's unusual betrothal had been agreed upon through a series of stately letters, ferried by the navy. I supposed this might change when the two of them were actually wed. The city would hardly break its solitude and set up such an alliance without a reason.

I plucked a soft bun from the pile and deposited it right in the middle of my stew. After all, what need had I for scrupulous manners among pirates.

My supper secured, messy as it was, I faced the hall. I didn't have Odette's knack for finding my place among strangers, nor much stomach for the rowdy energy of the nearest tables, even if the pirates would have me as their guest. There was space at the edges of the room if I wanted to risk exposure to whatever pirates got up to in the shadows.

During our meeting with Penny, with the room illuminated only by weak light, I hadn't noticed the balconies. Situated over the floor, they were connected by wide-planked walks. High enough to look down, but not so far off that I left the room altogether. *Perfect.* I was the Eagle, after all, more comfortable soaring over things than in the thick of them. The stairs were close enough to the door that I could skirt the room without drawing too much attention.

I steadied the bowl, warm against my fingertips, and made my exit. Each stair put me a little higher above the merriment. Warm air welcomed me to the landing, fenced off neatly to prevent a fall. Balconies jutted out to the right and left, perfect places to survey drinking or gameplay. It was a clever setup, and I wondered if the owner sat up here to watch over the floor. Or… Well, one could never discount the need for privacy in an alehouse. Not everyone was as brazen as the pirates below.

Whatever the reason, I appreciated the distance the balconies afforded me, and chose the one on my left without much thought. Anything with a chair and a table would do nicely. Though, with my new piratical lifestyle, I should not count myself above sitting on the floor if it came to it.

I resisted the urge to peer over the side to search the room one more time. I was fine—better than fine, actually—supping alone.

16

REGULA

"Why am I not surprised to see an Eagle up here?"

All the air rushed from my lungs. I could have sworn no one was on the balconies. I'd scanned for heads and shoulders above the railings.

It took me a minute to find the captain himself, though I recognized his voice immediately. He was sitting on the floor with his back to a corner post. No wonder I'd missed him. An empty bowl, a full tankard, and a battered book full of scribbled columns sat around him in a half-moon.

"Are you hiding?" I asked, taken aback. There were chairs here, and a table too, made out of what looked like barrel scraps. The floor was the last place anyone would think to check for him.

"If I were? Would you think less of me?" He was watching me, his head tilted back against the wood, eyes tired. "Not the dashing captain you imagine, no, but a coward tucked away from his responsibilities."

"Not at all. Weary, perhaps. Witness to more than his fair share of tiresome, unpredictable events." That won me a snort. Though his mug was full, I suspected him of being in his cups.

"Unpredictable... That is one way of putting it." He scrubbed a hand across his brow. It was a pleasant hand, square and strong, likely at home wrapped around a rope or clutching the hilt of a blade. Though… No, he shared plenty of duties with his crew, no higher or mightier than the other sailors. He hadn't directed anyone else into the water to save me when need arose.

"Yes, quite." I wondered if he might be lured out of whatever maudlin mood had him splayed out on the floor. I'd left the bother of the hall, but wouldn't mind some steady company. I was hesitant to admit to myself how much I admired the man after only a few days on his ship. It had been jarring to catch myself looking for him below. There was a comfort to his presence, even if we might occasionally spar.

"Would you like me to leave? I was, myself, looking for a quieter spot amongst the chaos." I gestured over the edge, down at the full tables.

"Don't let me stop you."

"Well then, you must join me, for it would be passing strange to have me up here and you down there." I deposited my supper in front of the far seat. "I promise not to be a bother."

"Fair enough, Eagle. You're too polite to tell me to stop wallowing on the floor." Now it was my turn to snort as he got up. Dusting himself off, he dropped the book and tankard on the table, as well as his empty dish, before sliding into the open seat.

Not wanting to bother him, I dug into my stew using the soft, and now soggy, bread. It was divine. I closed my eyes to savor the unfamiliar taste. Layered with peppery spices, the chunks of meat were gamier than I was used to in the first wall, but a vast improvement over the bland food Odette and I had shared on the *Edgewater* or the *Wretched Lady*. I knew Captain Connor, too, had been making do with poorer fare. I swallowed and looked over at him.

"Delicious!" I said in response to his questioning gaze. "Never had anything like it."

He blinked at me in the strong light of the hall's lamps, and I watched the entirety of the action. The slight golden touch of his eyelashes to his cheek drew my eyes next to the unnatural but endearing curve of his nose. His brows went up.

"No goat on the wall?" he asked.

"Fowl mostly, and fish. Pork if it's a holiday."

"They must have left them all here." He chuckled. "You see, there weren't any," he explained, seeing my curious face, mouth full of stew. "Round about a hundred years ago, one of the city's galleons got stuck between two of the reefs outside these isles, and had to offload their furry cargo in an attempt to get their bottom up. They were too scared to venture back in, so they just left them. Now there's so much goat the cove'll practically pay us to take them."

I smelled a lie in that, having met the head of Penny's Cove. She would have to be a shrewd businesswoman to have kept her folks healthy and happy and outside the city's walls for so long. There was always room in Sanctuary, and until recently, my understanding had been that islanders were a vital part of the city's growth.

"They've been very gracious," I said. "I, for one, could not have carried on much longer without a bath." I held my wrist up for a mock sniff, which won me a sidelong smile.

"You city folk aren't fashioned from the sternest stuff. Us sailors are plenty happy with a bucket of old salty and whatever soap we've got to trade between friends." He looked down at his hands, turning them over in a dutiful inspection. This too, reeked of a lie, for he was clearly enjoying the relative luxury of the isles.

"One bar won't last long between you pirates. Though I suppose you don't use much of it."

"Eagle, you wound me. Take a look for yourself." His hand drifted over and, in the name of observation, I took him delicately by the wrist. A specimen for the moment, not a pirate, skin hot and alive under my hand.

"We pirates are vain creatures. We bathe far more than you lot in Sanctuary," he continued, unruffled by my touch. His nails were free of the dirt I'd expected when I checked them. "This week, for instance, my hour of soaking was rudely interrupted by a damsel or two in distress." He raised a golden brow at me.

I choked and relinquished his hand.

"I cannot be blamed for that. And it seems you have suffered little in the sacrificing, because you've got the cleanest hands of any pirate I've seen." I paused, busying my fingers with the bowl in front of me so they wouldn't itch at the memory of his wrist. "On the wall, all we hear about are marauding men with no room for anything but hate and gold in their hearts. Certainly no soap to be found in their pockets."

"Plenty of room for gold in my heart. I might use it to buy soap, though. Rory has a fondness for the rose scented kind that they sell over in Coisume. Costs a pretty penny, that." I'd know exactly which pirate he was talking about if I met one that smelled like flowers. I would not allow myself to consider what kind of soap Connor preferred, or if I might catch a hint of it in the air around him.

"Venu loves pirate tales, no matter how gruesome. She says the charm isn't so much the violence as it is the freedom. I confess I never thought much about you until now." I'd finished my bread and was debating whether to drink straight from the bowl.

"Your walls wouldn't know much about us." His eyes clouded for a moment before they cleared. "Nothing worth knowing, that is. And if they did, it wouldn't do to tell you the truth of us. We pirates are known for some extraordinary feats." His mood must have fully recovered, for he waggled his eyebrows at me, making it impossible to mistake his meaning. I decided I could certainly slurp my stew in such company.

"Comely Connor, do tell me what you mean," I said in my flattest voice, before taking a long, loud, thoroughly unladylike gulp of stew.

"No, no, I couldn't ruin your fine ears. Well, perhaps it's best you know that soap isn't the only thing we like to share on a ship." I almost spit my mouthful back in the bowl. He was a scoundrel, captain or not. A blush traveled unbidden up my neck.

"Pah! No need to paint a pretty picture for me, Captain. I've seen your ship. Perhaps you should pull your head out of your shared trousers and get to polishing, refurbishing, and, most urgently, stocking the place." Let the red in my cheeks be evidence of anger and not whatever had put it there in the first place. Flirtation? Unbidden lust? I'd had enough punishment in my life when it came to passion, and I would be paying further now, I was sure, surrounded by pirates with practiced tongues and no lock on their forbidden emotions.

"Rake me with your talons, Eagle." Connor grinned and clutched his stomach, pressing a hand over my implied wound. "I would feed my crew better if I could. In all truth, it's why I was hiding up here."

"They'd rather eat you than that indulgent stew?" I shot back, and while his face didn't make it quite to serious, his smile dimmed.

"Maybe. I'm not much of a captain. I came by it recently— for the wrong reasons—and it's a job many would be better suited for." He released his grip on his stomach, his shirt falling back into its place as his fingers found his tankard and raised it for a long drink.

As I said, I knew little of pirates, nothing beyond the horrid stories that would run up the staircases of the walls. He was young; at least, younger than I'd imagined a captain. All his charisma, and he had a great deal of it, could not make up for inexperience, especially in a place as harsh and unforgiving as the sea.

"They must have chosen you for a reason. Is a vote how it's done? Or did you tie them up and force their hands to gain the captaincy?" I couldn't help adding a saucy bit. His face had gone all flat and faraway, and though we were near strangers still, it was much harder to abide than I liked to admit.

"Tie them up? No, I'd never!" he sputtered, setting his mug

down. "Not unless they asked, that is, very nicely." I'd done it, drawn the twinkle back into his eyes.

"If they didn't stick their daggers in your back over it, those you consider better suited must have meant for you to have the position. The one with the braid looks quite fearsome, and her people wouldn't follow you if she didn't wish it." There was a reason sailors crowded around her table downstairs, dancing or no.

"Trenna. You see everything, Eagle. A ship is only as good as its navigator, and we have one of the best in all the Far Flung." He planted an elbow on the table and leaned his chin on his palm, studying me. "I'd follow her in a heartbeat."

"I'm coming to see you'd follow anything in a skirt if given the chance."

"Trenna in a skirt? Oh no, there's a sight you'd not soon forget. Completely and utterly scarring." His brown eyes widened comically, the strong lamps turning them shades lighter than shadow had allowed on his ship.

"A beauty like that? I doubt it. You pirates must wear skirts sometimes." I motioned to my own. I considered them my best barrier against the world and was grateful to have gotten one from the women of the cove.

"We'll do anything we damned well please, Eagle. Ask Trenna to put on a skirt and you'll be laughed out of the hall. Ask me and you might find yourself with a different answer." He was so obvious in his attempts to ruffle me, as if I were some shy girl just out from behind her mother's apron.

"I believe my skirts are drying nicely in your cabin, and I'm sure we could fit them for you tonight." I watched him process the different parts of my dare, his face running from amused to wolfish and back into some form of polite, affected enthusiasm.

"I would never deprive you of your wardrobe, lady." *Hm. Would he not?*

"What a sobering promise, Captain." I frowned pointedly, moving to pick up my empty bowl.

"I wasn't... I didn't mean..." His hand shot out to cover mine, keeping the dish firmly on the table. "I misspoke. Forgive me." He gave my hand a squeeze, and then let go. "Pirates make their skirts out of sail. That's all I meant, that I had no need for your pretty things."

I raised an eyebrow, as now we were both thinking perhaps too closely on my "pretty things," and recommenced clearing my bowl. He watched me with a slight furrow between his brows.

Only when I stood did he fully grasp my intention to leave, and he leaped up with me.

"Stay, Eagle. You've easily banished my earlier worries." He reached for me, or the bowl, I wasn't sure. "Do you drink, lady? I can bring you up a cup and we can continue wallowing."

I laughed, louder than I intended, and nodded. I wouldn't mind a drink.

17

REGULA

I brought two tankards of ale back up the stairs, half expecting the Eagle to have flown off somewhere else.

Even though we'd both come up here to escape the party downstairs, I was finding her company much better than my own. I was tempted to explain my growing heap of problems and let her put together their answers for me. She'd already picked up on the crew's preference for Trenna as their captain.

To my relief, the Eagle sat right where I'd left her, wings spread over the railing and her concentration fixed on some spot below. Her charge, perhaps. Or maybe she admired the view. I admired it too.

"Here," I said, to keep her from startling or catching me with my eyes on her. I slid her beer onto the table, steadied my own, then returned to my place in the hard-backed chair.

She came away from the edge to take a sip of her drink. Or a gulp. She wasn't one to do things by halves. There was no hesitation to her. She'd been raised on stories about pirates, lies and half-truths meant to scare children, but I'd been raised on stories of city folk, especially their women. Fragile creatures in need of protection, in need of a sanctuary. All buckles and bows and not a drop of spirit in them. I'd had no reason to question these tales till now, but the Eagle was rewriting them completely.

She gazed at me over the rim of her glass, smacking her lips in satisfaction. "Is there anything Penny's Cove can't make?"

I eyed her. The beer was the long-brewed stuff served after a hard harvest's work. Penny's leftovers were still better than the watery swill my ship called beer in tough times, and, judging by the Eagle's reactions, at least as good as what was served on the wall.

"The cove smiles on us, I reckon." It was a risk to expose any island town to city folk. One Penny had been willing to take, even with the threat of the navy hanging over all of our heads. I wouldn't have judged Penny if she'd locked us out, so I kept my words as guarded as I could when I spoke about the cove.

I should have been grilling the Eagle about the walls. I should have been unsettled by how much I wanted to take her into my confidence, except she didn't seem to have much loyalty to anyone but the girl downstairs, no matter which ring she came from or to whom she was married.

I stared into my mug, considering.

Again, the story I'd been raised on was in the forefront of my thoughts—of Sanctuary folk who stood behind their banners, who cheered on the razing of towns and separated families, who reveled in the obliteration of their enemies. Entire communities, islands even, eaten in the name of their safety and growth. I didn't know where the truth lay, or at least not with the woman in front of me. She was a force, as thoughtful as she was hard to read.

My dilemma came down to my own reaction to the Eagle. I was attracted to her, her looks and her wits so clearly entwined that one couldn't see one without seeing the other. Altogether too quickly, I was ready to sweep aside all caution in her presence. I'd need to get myself under control. I could not plan to trade her and her charge in for Griffin and woo her in the meantime. I would not. No matter how different she proved herself from my stories.

"You know, we haven't truly been introduced, Captain,"

I snapped my eyes up to meet hers.

"Pirate names are fine, Eagle," I said, though I desperately wanted to know her name.

"Are you offering me a place as a pirate?" she asked, her attention narrowing.

I balked. I would if I could. Griffin would have, but I needed him back.

"I thought not. So we can dispense with the games. In the city, we wear our names rather proudly. Mine isn't worth much there, so maybe it will mean more here." She paused, her teeth pressing lightly into her lower lip. "I'm Regula."

She held out a hand. I was sure I was meant to shake it. I kissed it instead, unable to resist. Her skin soft under my lips, and cooler than I expected.

"Regula. My pleasure." It was. Oh, it was.

"Perhaps it's mine, Captain."

"None of that. Call me Connor."

Regula. The name fit her. Regal and uncommon. A little strange. Easy on the tongue.

"Connor, then." She nodded, knitting her hands back together, far from me. She turned to glance down from the balcony.

"Tell me, Regula—" Now I knew it, I was afraid I wouldn't be able to stop saying her name. "—what would your husband think of you stuck here among us pirates?"

My question had her head whirling back, puzzlement written across her face.

"My husband?" She hesitated, heat rising in her cheeks. "Why, he has no right to think anything at all about me." Her skin was so fair, the red could not be mistaken.

"You said… Downstairs in the meeting with Penny—"

"You listen far too carefully." Regula glared at me, the effect softened by her rosy cheeks. I waited.

"If you must know, I was a girl of good enough breeding with a husband of better who cast me off after two years of barrenness. Thoroughly ruined and without prospects, I might add." She tossed this at me like cannon shot. I wanted desperately to catch at her hands and soothe whatever raging part I'd pricked with my question.

"My own family could not stand to have me back. It was only the position with O—Venu that saved me from tumbling down to the seventh wall's dockside. Perhaps we would have met in a room there if things had gone differently." Regula's hands curled into fists on the table, and she was practically spitting. "There. That is why. He has long since washed his hands of me. Are you satisfied?"

I wasn't. She was furious in one breath and implying I might have hired her for an hour or two of passion in another life with the other. I was mightily unsatisfied by the whole of that, except that I would have enjoyed her immensely in the second scenario.

"You at a dockside house for the taking? Why, I might have married you and forced you to live as my pirate queen." I tried to shape my mouth into an easy grin when the last thing I felt was easy. She was still frowning, though her vigor had gone. "You'd have had salted gannet each night, which is a bird, by the way, not a fish." I wanted to see her eyes shine, and the lines fade from her forehead,

"We would install a special golden port off the deck where you could do your business—"

"You rotten thing!" She smacked me on the arm. It stung rather deliciously in the aftermath of my imaginings. "I tell you the whole of my sad tale and all you latch on to is that I might have been a pirate's whore?"

"You dreamed it up." I shrugged. "And it did seem the most exciting of all your options. You should have considered it."

This stopped her in the middle of her next thought. I waited, watching her try to lock down her indignation. Oh, I'd gotten under her skin, alright.

"I've made it to the pirate ship without much trouble." She'd regained control. I got a smaller smile than her eyes suggested I might.

"Trouble or no, seems to me the other way would have been more fun."

"Oh?" She reached out, ready to swat me again.

Instead, she caught my shirt and pulled me forward, closing the distance between us, knocking the smug curl of my mouth into something breathless and unsure.

While I prepared for the fresh sting of her hand, Regula snatched a kiss.

My next words were lost to the determined press of her lips. The demand of her fingers. The cut of my shirt into my neck. My heated blood spilling its way all the faster to my cock.

There was beer on her breath as she pulled away, and a hint of soap in the air around her. Simple and clear, unlike the woman before me.

I wanted to get to the bottom of her.

All I needed was…

I reached for her, found her shoulders through the soft fabric of her dress, felt the warmth of her skin beneath.

Regula, so different from anyone I'd ever kissed before. I must have looked a sight; possessed, incapable of anything but pursuit. It was too much. We were too far apart. And I was set to return her to a cage I could not hope to free her from. I loosed my hands, against the screaming of my every instinct, and let them fall.

"You'd deign to kiss a pirate?" I asked, hoping my words would mask the wildness of my eyes and the storm of my heartbeat.

She stared me down.

"I wanted to see how I might benefit as your pirate queen."

Her head tilted slightly, birdlike. The Eagle again. "I don't think I'd have accepted the post."

18

CONNOR

"**W**ouldn't accept the post?" I paced the hallway outside the galley. "The gall of her!"

I'd been banished from the crew's berth by irate, unfeeling seamen and I'd been kicked off the quarterdeck by heartless, mocking seawomen. My cabin, unused to it as I was, was again in the service of the very creature who'd driven me to the edge of my patience, and a hammock hardly suited my agitated state.

We'd been interrupted, Regula and I.

I hadn't been able to argue her barb. I'd had no chance to try my charms or give her another kiss, a better one. One that rocked her back and made her consider what a pirate might truly give his queen.

It was a good thing, even if I fought it.

I couldn't have her, not as captain, not as the man who planned on sending her right back to Sanctuary. I wanted her, true, but for the novelty of her tongue and the strange frankness of her company. There would be other dalliances. I'd never had any trouble finding someone to fuck. But would they fascinate me as she did?

We'd been caught moments after intimacy, heated but

circumspect, by Silver, come to corral me back to captaincy. This hadn't spared me a few pointed questions as the pirate dragged me off the balcony and back to the ship.

The last I'd seen of Regula was her triumphant smirk, disguised to all other eyes as a polite smile.

I hadn't impressed her.

If Silver had waited an hour longer, things would be... No, there was no point in desiring a woman I intended to use poorly. Her kiss had changed her so dramatically in my eyes, ripping away the veils of myth swaddling her, but there could be no changing the reality of bargaining with Sanctuary. Her lips could not best what was to come, or save her from the role I would force her to play.

Ah, I wished now, as my feet hammered the dust from the floor, that I had been honest with Silver as we left the cove's hall behind. We might have argued over my behavior, or hers, but my desires would be forced to ride much further behind my duty to my crew.

Instead, I'd avoided a row, and was left to stew with the memory of Regula's lips. Best to forget them and become the captain in all of this. If she chose to press her attentions again, and I doubted she would, I must rebuff them. My admiration for Regula could only be that; admiration.

"Ye're driving me to distraction, ye know that?"

Serafina stood in the doorway of the galley, her shadow falling into the hall. She clutched a dirty spoon in one red splotched hand and her braid looked halfway to unraveling. I flinched, so sure I'd been quiet enough to avoid her notice, as she was hard of hearing.

Even with a slight dusting of flour over her whole person, Alecto's mother was a striking figure. She'd agreed to cook for the *Wretched Lady* after the last one quit, and it was like having my own mother aboard, if I'd ever really had one.

"I'm sorry, Fina," I said, debating whether to bring her in on my problems.

A familiar mop of hair popped out behind her. Alecto. Ever the dutiful son. Begging for scraps to sop up the beer in his belly.

"How are the biscuits coming along?" I asked instead, hoping to bury my obvious unrest.

After the *Wretched Lady* had snatched me off a naval ship, and Griffin had taken me under his wing, we'd stayed so many times in the Tross, our favorite of the ever-shifting pirate towns. We were safe under Fina's roof, treated like family when we had no other home but the ship.

Pleading with her to help us through yet another hard time had been one of my first acts as interim captain, though I think she'd signed on more to keep an eye on Alecto than because of any argument I offered. Her cooking was leagues better than we were used to, provided she had the right ingredients.

"It's tack, Captain," she replied. "Hard as I can make it, for as long as I can cook it."

"Horrible little things," Alecto muttered behind her, too low for his mother to pick up.

"I leave it in your capable hands." It was easy to ignore him when the cook was still staring me down.

"My hands would be a lot better at it if I didn't see ye out of the corner of my eye every time I pause to take a breath. I already have one barnacle here. What's the matter with ye?"

I sighed, appreciating her concern. Alecto stopped craning his neck and jumped down from his perch, squeezing into the doorway beside his mother. He was much taller, with his father's darker skin and curly hair, but they had the same face. If they weren't practically my family, it would be akin to being accosted by two wolves in the night, all narrowed hazel eyes and sharp-boned intensity.

"Nothing, Fina. It's nothing." She'd faced her own share of troubles, I knew.

Fina had grown up the beauty of a small but prosperous fishing town on Sanctuary's isle. When the town was swallowed by the walls, Fina was the prize they brought with them when they traded in their language and tradition. Rather than let herself be bargained walls over in marriage, she'd run off down to the cliffs, spending months in hiding, fending for herself in nooks and crannies before coming across a group of smugglers who let her earn her keep as a cook before she left them for one of the pirate havens in the Reaches.

She told stories fit to give Rory, Alecto, and myself night-mares when we were kids. Of caves that ran so deep into the earth one could barely breathe, and of white-veiled ghosts that walked the tightest edges between the sea and the land. Even her husband, a weathered pirate originally from the continent, was too superstitious for her talk, leaving us to soak up her tales like sea sponges. Griffin, older than the rest of us, pretended she didn't scare him at all.

"She'll find out one way or another, Connor." Alecto grinned.

His mother was a gift to the ship but a curse for him. He'd been forced to rein in his considerable charms the moment she stepped aboard. He was a hermit now by pirate standards, much to the chagrin of many on board. Probably part of the reason he was down here in the first place. Avoiding temptation.

Fina set her hands on her hips, heedless of her spoon.

I looked past her to the doughy disks she'd lined up, waiting for room in the oven.

"Griffin never liked it either, ye know." She shook her head, still watching me.

I didn't know. Neither did Alecto, by the looks of him.

"There's no such thing as a perfect captain, Connor." I blinked at her. "It's why we live by the code."

"There are plenty better than me, Fina. You know it as well as I."

She nodded.

I wanted very much in that moment to be back around the hearth of her home, half listening to her stories and half listening to Griffin and Bellus bickering about when the frost tides would roll in. I wanted it all back. To be small again, and protected. With someone else to make the decisions.

"I miss him," I whispered. I didn't think she heard me, but she read what I said on my lips. Alecto busied himself staring at the floor. Her flour dusted arms came around me, and I sank into her embrace. Fina wasn't Griffin, but she was close. She cared about me. I couldn't let her down.

"We'll get him back," she murmured before setting me away from her. "No more worrying. I've enough to manage with this one." She punctuated this by swatting her son with the spoon.

I nodded.

"Ye've got work to do and I've got biscuits to burn." Fina teased a laugh out of me. Biscuits were hard, dry, unforgiving things, but she wasn't one to ruin anything she touched.

"You wouldn't!" I pretended upset. It was my hard earned flour, after all.

"Nor would ye."

She didn't fall for my fooling, instead fixing me with one of her looks—the kind that mothered and pilloried me at the same time. I might very well burn it all down, and I was desperate to replace myself with the real captain before I did.

Then she shooed me out, banishing me just as the rest of the crew had.

Alecto followed me, his arm finding its way around my shoulders in silent comfort. I fought the urge to brush him off.

The *Wretched Lady* was mine—in name, at least—for the foreseeable future. I would have to muster the strength to steer her true.

19

REGULA

I was proving myself quite the pirate, I thought, on waking in the captain's cabins next to Odette. I'd been downright impish yesterday, bratty and overzealous. I didn't regret it one whit. I also didn't quite understand why I'd done it.

On the *Edgewater*, it was like I'd been given permission to picture myself in the channel city. My life in the walls had been clearly marked, like a badge on my blouse. Nothing was afforded me besides a position. No risk, no enjoyment beyond what Odette was able to conjure for us, and decidedly no flirtation. I'd existed in the eyes of the ring in the same way a pair of drapes or a writing desk did. Useful or not useful, pleasing or not pleasing, and nothing much beyond that.

The promise of a new life, compounded by the fact that I had begun to make it real, made me hold myself a little differently.

Then I'd nearly died, sucking down a good lungful of the sea, at the hands of men who were meant to be my protectors in the walls. Odette, too, had been exposed to grave and unnecessary danger.

Whatever had changed in me had then been forced to harden and regrow. I was not just different but new. Everything

I'd shoved down and hidden in Sanctuary was impossible to contain any longer.

I glanced at the sleeping girl beside me and wondered if she'd sensed my transformation.

I'd tell her about the kiss today. What would she think of me? For Odette, things were simple. Either I loved or I didn't. Either I would leave or I wouldn't. She was the only one allowed to be complicated, even if she mostly went with gusto wherever the wind blew her.

Nothing was so certain for me. Everything was tenuous. Old Regula had been cautious and calculating. This new one... she was surprising even me. And in the crisp light coming through the captain's windows, I decided I was growing to like her.

The starfish and seaweed and ocean silt could gather on my sense of decorum and what my life should be. I had long wanted to escape the path laid out by my ambitious family and traitorous womb, and now... now I really could.

Regula the pirate had a ring to it. This ship. Another. A house on a quiet isle. A trade in Coisume. The future waited before me, unchosen.

Out here on the open sea, some looked at me as an oddity, but none looked over me. Comely Connor himself had seen fit to play for my attentions, touching me more than anyone in ten whole years, looking at me like I was a real person, fit to be admired.

I could not begin to describe the depth of that feeling—a warm hearth after a long and cold journey. Instead of a second chance at the same, I'd found instead the glimmer of a life I might actually enjoy.

Deep in my thoughts, I did not immediately notice when Odette woke, leaving her no choice but to paw at me like a misbehaving kitten. Her voice sleep-rough as she demanded a recounting of whatever I'd kept from her last night. I had very selfishly refused to elaborate on my strange, bullish mood when Billy escorted us back to the boat. She would forgive me for holding a secret to my bosom for a few dark hours, especially since I'd known she'd enjoy it much more as medicine for her headache this morning. I wasn't the only one who'd been drinking Penny's beer. Besides, I hadn't been watching her very closely, and I thought it only fair we trade stories for once.

Since I wasn't half so bleary eyed, I helped Odette up and over to the basin. It wasn't a bath like we'd had in Penny's Cove, but it would do for a quick scrub of the necessaries. The water was refreshing, cold from the night. She was decidedly perkier after a good splashing, and I was ready to spill my guts.

In pure Odette fashion, she fell back to the bed in a pretend faint after I gave her an abridged version of our accidental dinner, Connor's flirtation, and my kiss.

"Oh, dear gods, return my companion." She pushed up to her knees and bent her head in supplication. "She is solemn and scrupled, and surely has been replaced by a foul spirit after taking a drink of the deep."

As the new, unprincipled Regula, it only took me a moment to kick her in her well-presented, praying backside.

She recovered quickly, flopping down to swing her feet and regard me with judgmental blue eyes. "Regula, I cannot believe you. All these years and not one stolen glance, not one peep. I thought you stone-hearted. Only a pirate could catch your interest."

"I know. It was rather impulsive." I sat down beside her. There was no need to lay out clothing for the day, since we were roughing it. We'd wear yesterday's dresses. "I don't know how you survive all the attention you get, even back home. I melted under the heat of one man's gaze."

Odette snorted at my crude description.

"It was *Comely* Connor." She emphasized the rakish name. "I'm sure many women have crumpled in the wake of the captain's amber eyes and delectable lips"

I fought the impulse to frown, thinking of scores of other women, none of them as old or as buttoned up as I.

"I could not have chosen better for my first kiss since…" We did not, as a rule, mention my former husband's name.

"I'll say. Quite shocking, Regula. I'm pleased with you, and for you." There was a hint of pity in her voice that I wondered if I'd ever escape. I knew my situation was almost unthinkable to a girl of her age and beauty. It simply wasn't to be considered, and I had always tried to keep it from rubbing off on her in that way.

"There were times—" She played with the coverlet. "—when I wondered if you were one for the finer sex." Odette looked up at me, her hair a little wild from its dip in the water. "Or if you weren't interested in any of it. Or if what had been done to you was a great harm which had put you off the pursuit of love at all."

"It was a great harm, though not in the way you mean. A disappointment. A betrayal, certainly." I was serious for a second, hearing the second part of her words before the first. "The finer sex, my hat! You never hesitated to lose your petticoats around me!" I laughed at her implication. She scrunched her face up and shrugged, giving me just the opening I needed.

"Oh, so you have a taste for the finer sex yourself? And you decided you'd never tell your dearest and most beloved companion?" I gaped at her.

"Who I considered to have been done rather poorly in love, and would do anything to protect from further injury!" Odette retorted. She didn't get half so red as I did, but she was blushing now, furiously. "Besides, you are sister to my heart. I would never risk you, even if it meant keeping some things to myself."

"Some things." I huffed. "You minx! Telling me now so I can sort back through every casual acquaintance I forgot to scare away because they were in skirts and beat myself up about dereliction of duty."

"Regula, I'm afraid you were very bad at any duty meant to keep me from the attentions of anyone, man, woman, or otherwise." She shook her head in mock seriousness. "In fact, it is the reason I begged my parents to hire you."

I tutted at her, exactly in character as chaperone and governess.

"We served each other well, did we not?" I relented, pulling at one of her errant curls.

"The very best," she replied. Neither of us was ready to say a final goodbye, especially with the day of our leave-taking suddenly lost to fate.

"Now you know I've kissed a pirate, and I'd like to know where you've been laying your considerable favors." I eyed her. "Perhaps with Billy, who follows you like a lost hound?"

She shook her head, back to examining the sheets.

"Surely not the big one with the metal in his eyebrows."

That startled a laugh out of her.

"Regula, I have been very good, considering." She smacked a hand on the linen. "I'm sitting at a scrumptious banquet, but I cannot eat because the pit of my stomach is filled with fear." She buried her head in the bed.

I could only agree with her. We were adrift on a strange sea, in no small sense of the words.

"They are quite handsome, these pirates." I tried to rouse her from her worry.

"Comely, even," she said, her glee muffled.

I waited for her to sit back up. We were the best of friends, the sort that form when there is no one else. As far as I was concerned, we would be until our end, no matter how many tantrums she pretended.

"Do you think I'd make a good pirate?" I asked when she finally resurfaced.

She smiled at me, clearly thinking of other things.

"I mean it. What if I stayed here? After." It was the first time I'd brought it up. I knew she'd guessed my plan for the channel city, but the idea had been so frighteningly delicate in its inception that I hadn't let it past my lips.

"I shared my name with him, Odette. I haven't signed on, but

I have given up our game." It was easier to admit this than tell her I had begun to daydream about a pirate's life.

Her smile fell away and her eyes sharpened on mine.

"You would make an excellent pirate, Regula. You are exceedingly competent, a trait it seems this ship needs in spades." She pointed lazily at the cracks in the *Wretched Lady*'s once proud timbers. "I think all that exhausting lawn bowling you enjoy will transfer very easily to cannon balls," she added, poking her tongue out at me before looking away.

I gave her a second to take the question and think about it, for her response felt hollow and practiced, no matter how nice it was.

Finally, she met my eyes.

"I will be very sore to lose you, dear friend." *She wouldn't be half so sore as I.* "At least these pirates have proved kind. They have their code, you know. It really is very fair. Better than how you've been treated in Sanctuary by far." She cocked her head. "I would worry about you less as a pirate than in Coisume, where you might never make it out of the gutter."

I knew her words to be the truth. I felt the same way. This ship had the closeness of a family, a home. The continent loomed large and wholly unknown in my mind, a battle of its own.

"I'm thinking on it, Odette," I promised her, even as I whispered the same to myself.

20

CONNOR

I was up in the crow's nest, spelling our best eyes, Pella and Cesare, for the day ahead. I'd been a regular up here before my promotion to the captaincy, and it was nice to have only the wind and the sea for company again.

I could only guess at the *Edgewater*'s path to the continent, but there was little chance they'd veer from the safest plotting this late in the season. I had my eyes trained, but I didn't expect we'd spot them on the horizon for a day or so.

Most of today would be lost to weaving among the rocks that scattered the shallow ocean on the eastern side of Penny's Cove. The Graveyard, Penny called it, and for good reason. Too small to be considered islands themselves, the outcroppings were enough to take a chunk of the hull with them. As such, the navy avoided this side of the Gate entirely. Sneaking through it, we'd have a chance at catching the *Edgewater*. The *Wretched Lady* was slim, quick, and full of pirates well used to escaping down the least trodden path.

Cesare was waiting below, tattooed hands full of biscuit, his feet up until we got the first glimpse of rock in the water. We used brightly colored flags and whistle signaling in times of careful sailing, and he had the best touch with them. I was saving Pella to spot our enemy, assuming we cleared the rocks.

I did not bet the *Wretched Lady* lightly. With the great mono-liths jutting up from the ocean floor at eerily regular intervals, there were only a few headings that did not lead to a coffin of stone for the ship itself. There were enough dead ends to trap anything bigger than a fishing boat.

If the actions of the navy had not been so offensive to the sea herself, we wouldn't have been risking our own safety. Even with the hearty backing of the crew, I wondered if I'd overplayed my hand. We would fix for the north-north east with the wheel in Trenna's calm and experienced hand, though the continent was directly east and the channel city a little south down the coast. Choosing the fastest way would surely kill us in the rocky maze. Trenna had sailed it before, trusting these old routes.

No certainty could stop the worry that twisted in my gut.

I'd come up here to ensure us the best chance. By spotting the Graveyard in the distance, I allowed Cesare and Pella to rest up for our complicated trip.

Trenna... I wasn't sure. She would get us through the rocks, likely the only one who could, though it might mean taking her off the helm when we needed speed. The woman hardly slept, and would not protest if I simply left her there for the duration. I couldn't chance it. If things went sour, we might need her to run us safely through more dangerous waters.

Maybe I'd throw Silver on the wheel since I had no skill with it myself.

The crow's nest was one of the best places to work such prob-lems out. Eyes on the horizon as my mind fired furiously away.

In the Graveyard and with regards to Sanctuary, fate and my crew could be nothing but trusted.

There were other courses: The ship turning back toward the Tross or wintering in Coisume without moving to free our captain. Griffin swinging for it, body hung on the walls. Waking in a warm bed with someone who looked decidedly like Regula.

Venu ushering in a whole new age at the tavern in one of the pirate holes. I knew which future I must avoid at all costs, no matter how tempted I might momentarily be to seize the others.

Giving Venu and Regula back to Sanctuary would not be the betrayal I imagined. The women were used to their city. Beyond the minor upsets of life, the walls were what they knew. The girl did not fear her marriage and... Regula did not face anything like it. I was not turning them toward grief and suffering. I was giving them back what they expected and no doubt would have demanded if given a choice.

But Sanctuary was no future. Not really. We pirates knew it well. People were chewed up, fighting for sticks and stones to humble one another. That was why we gave all liberated city folk the bargain. Some were loyal to Sanctuary and its navy and quickly returned at their own request. Others were the sort who might take time with the choice, who had been ill used in their current circumstances, and eventually jumped at the chance. Women, when we found them, almost always joined on.

I'd been a ship's boy pressed under the boot of the navy.

I'd taken the bargain. Changed my life for the better. Never again to suffer would be a lie, but never again to suffer needlessly, a truth.

I deserved whatever ill luck I attracted for taking that choice away from Regula and Venu. I would take it on, even if I regretted it for the rest of my days.

They'd go on to the lives they'd been meant for if they'd never met the *Wretched Lady*. I alone would be left wondering what might have been had they stayed.

I vowed to give them a say, in every way I could, up until I needed to offer them for Griffin. It was the least I could promise. Perhaps there was a way...

My eyes caught movement below, not on the calm sea, but the deck, where a flock of pirates, their coats making patches of color against the tarred wood, gathered around the two women, their cove dresses standing out bright.

I laughed to myself. Venu and Regula were again the center of attention, with all my pirates buzzing about them. I wished I could see the *Wretched Lady* through our visitors' eyes—a little dinged up and needing a good oiling, but worthy of her crew. Worthy of everyone. Even me.

I couldn't hear them up here, not unless they yelled a'purpose, but I watched them swirl across the deck, side by side, and swarm up to Trenna at the helm.

With her quick dismissal, the group gathered around the main mast. It was only when I felt the phantom sweep of Regula's gaze from below that I turned my eyes to the sea again, and was the first to cry, "Graveyard."

REGULA

THE PIRATES FELL DEATHLY QUIET AROUND US.

A yell came again from above, settling over the silence of the deck. And then another, an echo, from the bow.

The crowd around us dispersed without a word. One went scurrying up the ropes in front of us, giving me a moment to admire the sea creatures tattooed on his hands. Others disappeared into the sails. Still more unearthed a set of brightly colored flags which were passed in a line between the stern and the main deck, pirates holding flags high enough on the staircase for the navigators to see. Odette and I were left with Billy. A little farther off stood the big one with the pierced brows, his arms crossed over his chest.

What they were setting up, I couldn't fathom. I stared up at the highest part of the mast. The pirate who'd disappeared up the rigging had called it the crow's nest on our tour, and had delicately fended off Odette's requests to climb up to see it. Eyes and ears only, he'd said, very sternly for a rogue.

As I watched, he scampered over the edge of the tiny platform.

"Something's happening!" Odette whispered feverishly in my ear. *A little late to notice.*

I rolled my eyes at her.

"Oh, look, there." She pointed at the wheel, where Trenna wielded a burnished spyglass, light reflecting off the lens.

I lost Odette to the side of the ship so she might see the object of everyone's attention. Billy followed her, allowing me a measure of relief that she would be quickly rescued if she got so excited she launched herself off.

Nearly scaring me out of my skin, the big pirate appeared at my side, his neck craned back, the sun glinting off his piercings. Someone was climbing down toward us.

"What is it? What's happening?" I took advantage of his nearness to whisper, jarring the man a notch from his concentration.

He looked at me, quite obviously considering his answer.

"I can start guessing and work myself into a faint," I joked. He didn't laugh, merely lowered his gold pricked brows at me. Against his shaved head, the bright flame of his brows and beard punctuated his face, eclipsing even the jewelry above his eyes. I'd never seen anyone quite like him. He looked the perfect example of a pirate.

"Sea's dangerous around here," he finally said. "Lots of rocks." His voice had been surprisingly soft when Odette had held court in the captain's chambers, but it was even lower out here. The pirates were being very careful. I didn't hear so much as a heavy step from the rest of the crew.

He looked back up at the mast.

A shout came from above. One of the flags went up from the pirate on the staircase, a flash of yellow. Trenna bellowed an "Aye" toward the crow's nest from where she stood at the helm.

I gazed up just in time to see a long pair of legs and a firm backside, well-shown in worn brown breeches. A sailor nearly finished with his descent. It was no wonder the city was so deeply against piracy. A girl might encounter unspeakably fine things on a pirate ship.

It was only when the admirable ass swung around and dropped to the deck with a mop of sandy hair and a decidedly familiar smirk, that I realized I'd been gawking at Connor.

"You better not be winking at me, Captain," came the big pirate's rumble beside me. "We have work to do." The man was rather menacing, even without raising his voice.

Connor planted himself in front of us, looking the other pirate up and down.

"What, pray tell, do you mean?" he asked, though his calmness suggested he already knew.

"I've been told to get you out from underfoot. Will you go, or do I need to carry you to quarters?"

"I'm your captain, Rory, as I believe you acknowledged a moment ago." There was no worry or hurt in Connor's eyes. No betrayal.

"Aye, and a captain's meant to be at his maps or speaking up to his navigator in times of need." Rory cleared his throat and uncrossed his arms, adding, "Not scuttling over the deck as a runner or flag boy."

Connor frowned, giving the impression of a child who'd been told to stay away from the sweets cart.

"Don't do it, Connor." Rory's voice was somehow even lower, reaching only the two of them, and me surely by accident. "Let them see you as the captain, not as the ship's boy."

These words seemed to find their mark, though Connor did not respond immediately.

"There's no need to carry me, brother," he finally said, clapping the pirate on his muscled shoulder. "Join me in my cabin." He turned and proffered an arm.

"I must go over the maps," he added, much louder, shaking the elbow he held out. To me. Oh, he had been speaking to me.

I snuck a look at the big pirate, Rory. He shrugged. It seemed getting Connor off the deck would be worth it no matter who he took with him.

"Will you keep an eye on her?" I asked, still close enough to Rory that my whisper carried. Odette and Billy had not left the side, and I jerked my chin their way.

He nodded.

"He'd better," Connor whispered, wedging his crooked arm between us so I could hardly miss it.

I took hold of it and let him lead me across to my own cabin, which I supposed was really his.

21

REGULA

"What was that all about?" I whirled on him the moment the door closed, still whispering.

"An old friend looking after me so I don't make a fool of myself," he said, eyeing me, his lips pressed together.

Connor was framed perfectly by the sturdy ship's door. I had only to step forward, once, twice, and push him up against it. To bring my hands to his neck, fingers curling in his hair, and kiss him senseless. The tension of my first attempt still lay between us, easing the imagining, last night's taste of him on my lips.

Clothing rustled.

Oblivious to my daydreams, the man was taking off his coat. In just shirtsleeves, he was a present unwrapped: forearms molded by climbing ropes, strong shoulders beneath thin linen, brown-gold stubble creeping down his neck to flirt with the hair that curled up from the apex of his shirt.

He crossed to the far wall of the cabin, sending the close air of the cabin eddying past me. I felt compelled to follow. Sitting on the bed or the ratty chaise was a touch too intimate now I'd been reminded the room was really his domain.

I avoided the only chair too, perching instead on a corner of the wide desk. Connor proceeded to open one of the diamond-paned windows, letting in a little of the crisp ocean breeze. It was as the Eagle I watched him, unsure whether I would peck at him further.

By the time he finished and fell heavily into the desk chair, I was half lost to looking at him.

"Truth is, Regula, I'm captain in name only," he said, placing his elbows on the desk, not far from my seat. "You noticed. There are better options aboard, better captains. The trouble is that we already have one. The best captain I've ever known. Someone I'd never willingly replace."

I raised my eyebrows. Connor was regarding me earnestly. He hadn't shared nearly as much with a mug in his hand at our erstwhile dinner. He steepled his fingers, looking like an authority figure, no matter how hard he denied it.

"I was taken aboard the ship very young, after some years as a cabin boy in your navy." I had never considered how pirates were made. "Before he was voted captain, Griffin took me in and raised me as a brother." His voice broke on the name. I remembered the leader of the cove mentioning his patronage, marked with pride.

"He was captured by Sanctuary some months ago, attempting to rescue a fellow pirate. It caught us all off guard." His words heated, then cooled as I watched him recall to whom exactly he was speaking. "Another man would be dead, but we have reason to believe Sanctuary isn't finished with him yet. We anchored off your coast for a few months, attempting again and again to spring him, but nothing has worked. All we've managed is information."

I very easily filled in what those attempts might have entailed. While I'd never seen the dungeons with my own eyes, they loomed large in my imagination. His crew was competent from what I'd seen, and very obviously loved this Griffin. Those months must have been a torture all their own.

"I'm here, holding his place, until we get him back." Connor leaned into his hands, not quite meeting my eyes. I shifted on the hardwood. "We missed our usual season. There's little food and no gold. Everyone's worried they might be stuck with me. I'm not much of a captain." He dropped one hand and rubbed the other across his brow, something warring behind his eyes.

"You're wrong, Connor. You dove into the deep after me rather than risk another sailor." I paused. "These are growing pains, made worse by unfavorable conditions and the loss of your friend. Don't blame yourself."

"That's exactly it." He tripped over the words, his frown deepening. "I... I didn't want to save you. I resented the loss of your ship and when I was down there searching for you, I gave up." He hung his head.

I started to reply, but he held up a hand, cutting me off.

"I can't begin to excuse it. Only by the grace of the sea herself did I manage to get you up to the ship. If my hand had not become tangled in your dress, I am afraid I would have left you to the waves. I... wanted to save myself."

He snuck a look at me, guilt lining his features. The picture of shame.

I couldn't help myself. A laugh bubbled up my throat and burst out.

"What—"

"Connor!" I tried to catch my breath. "That is hardly a confession! Our bodies are not meant to spend so long under water. I would have sacrificed Venu for a gulp of air when I first went down. It was so oppressively cold, and I could not get anywhere with my dress pulling me deeper. I even—" I stopped. It was too embarrassing.

The slight brightening of his manner urged me on.

"I swore I saw a... a man down there. Or a fish. A man with the tail of a fish, sliding past my legs, touching them as he went by."

Connor quirked a brow at me, and I rushed on.

"It was so dark and I was gripped with a fear greater than

any I'd felt before. Connor, our minds play tricks on us at every opportunity. Our bodies, too. The panic you felt pulling me up was no different from me seeing things in the water. There's nothing to be ashamed of, and nothing to apologize for. You saved me. That's it."

"That's it," he said, a faraway look in his eyes. Gods, he was handsome, even as his shoulders drooped.

"You see? You haven't let anyone down." I fought the desire to reach for him as he shook his head.

"You have no idea the sort of man I am."

"I'm coming to know you. I see someone who takes great care…" I trailed off, mentally cataloging the best I'd seen of him. His face shifted, as if he'd come to some internal conclusion, then he winked.

"I'm not sure of my next step." He sat forward in the chair, his leather-clad knee a hairsbreadth from my skirts, and gazed up at me. "I'm liable to break the pirate's code and…"

His head tilted, his eyes locked on mine. I raced to recall everything I knew of their code. Did he mean…? My heart sped up.

He was so close.

We were alone.

Any second the ship might scrape on one of the dangerous rocks, and send us back into the deep.

The brazen part of me, the part that had driven me to kiss him, rose closer to the surface. Gone was my old self. I would no longer go unseen and unheard and less than lusted after. I couldn't count on fading away if I wanted to begin anew in Coisume. Nor if I stayed aboard this ship.

I had nothing to lose.

"You win, Connor." I sounded less wanton than I'd intended, and more commanding. "What if you relinquish it all right now? I'll take charge. It's only us. Just this cabin. I can steer for you."

Connor released a long breath, still looking at me with inscrutable eyes, nuance lost to the brightness behind him.

"I'd be relieved. Shall I call you Captain?"

I chuckled at the thought, fingers twitching. I wanted to touch him.

"No, Regula will do, if you'll be Connor." I only wanted to lift his burden, not take it too far from him. It was easy to slide my fingers over to brush his on the desk.

"Aye, I can do that. What would you have of me, Regula?" He leaned back again, opening himself to me.

He was all smirking contradictions. A rogue of the first order. Waiting for me to take control. I was unsure. Slow to choose. There was an ocean of possibility, one I'd only swum in a few horrible times during my marriage. I was no innocent, but also hardly aware of what one might expect from a man who would ask such a question, much less a pirate.

"I'm afraid I was brought up quite sheltered. A few days on your ship and..." I drew the words out, wanting to drink the shine from his eyes. "I barely know what to ask for, not when I'm missing so much."

I made to stand up and found myself quickly deposited in his lap. My legs pressed to his, my side to his chest, his arms around me with enough force to draw me down without feeling like a trap.

"You'd learn from a pirate, then?" He spoke softly, just at the level of my ear. His breath fluttered against my skin, drawing my awareness as it went. There was some threat to the words, but it was belied by the sweetness with which he held me, a sweetness I had seldom, if ever, felt.

I could do with more of that.

"Show me what a pirate might share with his queen." I hungered for more.

"Regula."

I could feel his stare now, like a touch of its own.

"A pirate might take his queen over to the bed and practice for their wedding night. Or he might shower her in gifts, expecting nothing but a sharp kick if she didn't like them. Tell me what you need."

I snorted, which I was sure was quite becoming. "I have no urge to kick you. Yet. Be assured, I'm no spring flower, delicate enough to be trampled on."

I turned then, in his arms, and stole my second kiss. It was different this time, because he did not let me just take it, coaxing me after him with deft lips. Our tongues met and parted and met again. I flattened my hand across his chest, more and more aware of the heat of him. I might melt out of his lap and onto the floor should his arms leave me.

Could I fall into him? I pulled away, pressing up off his chest before he drowned us both. My breathing was heavy, my lips lighter without his.

"Not a pirate queen, then." I curled toward him, whispering into the spot between his neck and ear, where I had not known to be fixated a moment ago. "What would a good Sanctuary girl seek in the arms of a pirate?"

He twisted, regarding me with darkening eyes. Thinking. I tucked a finger into the collar of his shirt, skimming the flesh beneath. Would I ever be looked at like this again?

"There is something… they don't teach in your walls." The words were an invitation.

"So, teach me," I whispered, setting myself away from him with straight arms, my body balanced on his knees.

I wanted him to come with me. When he didn't, I let myself look at him. The rise of his chest, the light kissing the hollow of his throat. The line of it, falling over his shoulders and down his arms. He was well practiced, I imagined. Holding me with care. I hadn't known men could come in such a lovely package. The dim corridors of the city certainly had not been to their best advantage.

"Learn this. Pirates respect our own code, and it's a strict one. We don't take what isn't offered, not in matters of lust."

It was charming that he could speak so solemnly when I had only a moment ago felt the want of him between our bodies.

"Fine, then. I'm offering." When he didn't immediately shut up and kiss me, I rushed on. "Would it be better if we invited someone else in? A witness of sorts? I know you pirates all dally in each other's beds." I spit this a little too cattily, having ready a list of hints he'd dropped.

Connor's eyes widened and his brows crept up to meet his hair.

"No. No, I—You want that?" he asked, incredulous.

I shrugged, sinking my fingers farther into the meat of his thigh. I wasn't a pirate yet. There was no telling whether the channel city would be a return to my dull, entirely sexless existence. There hadn't been a spark with anyone else, but the thought didn't terrify me, not if it spurred Connor into my arms. I could almost see my fragility reflected in his eyes.

"No, I don't want that. Sometimes that's the way of things but not now, not with you," he said. I hadn't shocked him badly enough to shake the seriousness of his tone. "It's more that we pirates are loud about what we want and what we don't. I can expect to hear about it immediately if I step a foot out of line with one of us. You? You want to play the naive city woman, but I can't be so sure you aren't her. I'd be risking the luck of the *Lady* and all the goodwill of my crew on it."

"They'd run you off the ship?" My eyes were the wide ones now.

"Worse." He shook his head. "Much worse, and I'd deserve it too." He brought an arm up, his palm wrapping around my wrist, heavy against my sensitized skin. "So as much as I want this, Regula—" He brought the other up to my chin, a finger skimming my jaw. "—and rest assured, I want it like a drowning man wants a good gulp of air."

We kept watching each other, the air between us fizzing with possibility.

"I won't let you regret this," he said, voice quiet and suddenly hard.

His hand dropped, and I mourned the loss of it.

"Already ready to blame yourself." I was getting frustrated. I wanted him closer. "I could very well get carried away and do something you don't enjoy." I frowned at the thought. It had been so long since I'd been with anyone, the chances were high I'd do something wrong.

"Of course," he agreed, and yet moved not a muscle.

I was very close to marching back out to the deck. His hands sat just beyond the edge of my awareness. His kiss had riled me, but it wasn't worth this, reminding me of his worry and his pity. I was strong enough to chance his arms. He wouldn't break me.

"I can't force your trust…" I let the words hang between us. I wanted his hands back on me, even if what he was saying was well meaning, and sensible in the extreme.

He studied me.

"You'll be the death of me," he finally said, relaxing into indolence with me on his knee.

I nodded, desperate. What he wanted and what I wanted were far from enemies, if I correctly read the heat in his eyes, the tension in his frame.

I reached up to cradle his neck. He caught my fingers.

"Regula."

It was his turn to steal a kiss, surging up, my hand still caught in his grip. There, and then gone.

He pulled back to regard me once more. More punishment.

I stood up, meaning, truly, to leave.

"Let's see how a Sanctuary girl likes this."

22

CONNOR

There was nothing quite like Regula splayed across my desk, with the windows mirrored in her eyes and my name on her lips.

She would not beg, no. Not yet.

I'd tossed her there the moment she'd talked me out of my reservations. I'd lied to her. Well, it was an omission, but that was almost the same thing. I hadn't counted on wanting to touch her so badly I couldn't remember my flimsy ethics. I was no better than a rogue, and yet... and yet I could not take my hands off her.

Seas, it hadn't taken much. Her dark curls were not quite undone, threatening to spill across the wood. Her skin was a stark contrast, brightened by the sunlight pouring in behind us and glazed by the blush I'd drawn to her cheeks. Tantalizing.

I vowed to mark her further, with lips, and perhaps teeth, if she did not protest.

I stared at her, my fingers bracketing her waist, her hips. Near impossible to choose a piece of her to devour first.

Her knees parted slightly under her dress, calling to me. My hands were already there, between her legs, rucking up the fabric, wanting—no, needing to crush her skin to mine.

She gasped. I leaned down to steal the sound from her mouth, kissing her into the wood. Her fingers whispered up to my neck, as if it were possible to pull us closer. I tasted her, felt her bones where we pressed together.

Regula had claimed her own corner of my mind, her teasing rejection a nail I could not quite pull out. My resolve was fully drained, leaving only want. I was finished sating myself alone, her image urging me on. She had surprised me. She was, in this moment, surprising me. Taking just as much as I could give her.

If it was lust, if it was desperation, on either side, I didn't know. I was lost and the only chance of finding myself was in the curve of her calf, the unassuming softness behind her knee.

Having abandoned my principles, it was now of the utmost importance that I show her what a Sanctuary girl might be missing behind all those walls. I was fairly certain, as I stole back my lips and danced them across her jaw and down to where her hair curled against her neck, that her experiences had been selfish ones, born of duty, not desire.

Had she ever played at pleasure, the greatest prize of all?

My nose was made to fit into the hollow of her throat, my lips to scatter kisses in time with her heated breaths. Gone was the trace of soap from the cove, leaving her smelling only of herself and the tallow bar I kept near my cabin's basin. There was nothing particularly intoxicating about her, and yet every inch of me was as one on fire.

Where her breast swelled from the stern fabric of her bodice, I bit down. Not so hard as to hurt, but to leave her a memento while I made short work of her skirts. She cried out—for me— breathless, when I did not immediately return to her embrace. Blood jerked to my already aching cock, my body delighted by her urgency.

I did not let her suffer further, my fingers finding the warmth of her thighs, freshly bared to the light. I sat back in the chair, letting my gaze rove up the slope of her belly, over the valley between her legs, down the hills of her knees and again to those darkening eyes.

Regula watched me back, the Eagle once more, the corner of her mouth quirked up. In impatience? I vowed to tease her a little—it seemed only fair—letting my hands toy with her thighs, just far enough from... Her curses broke my concentration.

I ended my caress, instead wrapping my hands around those strong legs and jerking her to the edge of the desk.

I'd had plenty of lovers. Pirates liked to fuck, especially without attachment. We were known for it. But I'd cut myself off from everything the instant I stepped up to the captaincy. Probably the reason I couldn't shake my attraction to Regula. She was arresting. A perfect mix of interest and inexperience. Soft and sharp at once. I doubted I'd find her so willing to learn on any other topic. I was coming to believe it impossible to surprise the Eagle.

I licked my lips and snagged the waist of her undergarments, pulling them to her knees, then farther. I wanted them off, but she pressed herself up on an elbow, protesting.

I stilled my hands, my head cocked.

"Shall I stop, Eagle?" I asked, stroking a finger up one of her legs. I would stop, if she asked it, no matter how good she felt.

"I... No, I... Carry on," she muttered, settling back without breaking her stare.

I grinned and let my eyes drift from her face. She was a feast. I bent and kissed the line I'd drawn on her sensitive thigh, then thought better of it and bit down. Red pricked her skin in the shape of my teeth. Of me.

An indulgence.

I smoothed my hands up and over her ass with enough pressure to set her squirming, petting her. I closed in, slow enough that she could stop me if she wanted. End this before I'd tasted her, before I'd had my fill.

Her sweet, insistent whimpers and the subtle shift of her hips suggested she'd follow me as far as I was willing to take her.

Regula stared at me, lids half-mast with want, hair disheveled, so thoroughly debauched looking that I wondered how she would react if I—

I traced my fingers through her dark curls, my mouth glancing over the inside of her hip. My view—seas, I could not get enough of her. So slick for me. I was hard in my trousers, set to spill from my other senses alone.

Her tart, heady scent was all around me. Ah, I would savor this.

She scrabbled against her skirts, gathering them higher across her belly, unwilling to fly without watching me work. I liked that curiosity. Regula's gaze might be enough to bring me off, starved as I was.

I dared her to look away. Then I licked her, lingering. It was a question in itself. She shuddered lightly against me, but did not stop me, did not break our held gaze.

Ah, I will make sure her eyes roll back.

If only I wasn't about to betray her back to her city. If only I had some other choice and could keep her in my cabin until she tired of me. The things I would do to her were beyond counting.

I was swiftly becoming addicted to her expressiveness, her unwillingness to shut down in the face of the unknown. I had tricks to bring to her bed that would spark the pirate in her. How I wanted to...

I would have to settle for her gasping around my fingers. I'd taste her and let her go, leaving her satisfied enough for both of us.

She squeaked, unable to stop herself, as I gave up thinking and lost myself in her, tongue delving deep. Unbelievable. Forbidden fruit upon my tongue.

Trading my kiss for a finger, I reveled in her shiver of surprise. I added another and let my free hand drift up to tease at her clitoris.

Her breath caught; a compliment. I played her patiently, fingers and lips in turn, dancing around the pleasure she hardly trusted me to give her. It wasn't long before she dropped her dress, taking hold of my hair and trying to force me where she needed me.

I took the hint, unable to hide my smile, cock jumping at her impatient guidance. I slid a third finger in and curled them up toward her belly button, sending her bucking into my hands and moaning against the wood. My tongue was close to seducing its target, tight on the prize itself. I could lose myself in the sensation, in the sharp breaths I heard above me, in the grip of her hand, but I wanted to make her writhe and remember it, so I bit back my urges and watched carefully, outside of myself, as she inched closer to oblivion.

Almost.

There.

I redoubled my efforts, plying her just so. No more playing, I would wring her out. Half desperate, surrounded by the taste and touch of her, I threw myself wholly into her pleasure. Regula had left off watching, her head falling back and her hips rising to meet me, thighs tightening. My arm curled under her ass, holding her to me. Regula. So beyond beautiful, captive and panting.

She was very nearly—

23

CONNOR

The door opened.

The seas-cursed door opened.

I was not in the best position to notice the interruption, caught as I was on the cusp of Regula's orgasm. When she clamped her thighs around my face, I did not immediately recognize it as a sign of anything but ecstasy.

It wasn't until she started pulling her skirts down clumsily over my head that I registered her stiff words were directed at someone else.

I pressed one last kiss to her cunt, earning a hasty cuff to the side of my muffled head. I couldn't stand captains who governed through blood, but perhaps today I would join their ranks, beheading whatever poor sod had entered my chambers without a knock.

I retreated from Regula's skirts just as she swung a leg over my head, scooting herself back to the edge of the desk beside me, facing away from the door, all her effort focused on reclaiming uprightness and dignity. I, however, had none to lose, and grinned up at the culprit, my face covered in her juices.

Whenever Rory was mad at me, I could do nothing right in his eyes until his anger passed. It always had. Now he stood, just inside the door, scowling for all the world like I'd set his beard on fire, and I wondered if I'd incensed him past the point of forgiveness.

"Little busy at the moment, old friend," I said, letting my hand snake under Regula's skirts and back to her lovely thigh. She shot me a pointed look and twisted enough to see the intruder, giving me slightly better access to her comforting warmth.

Rory double checked that the door was closed behind him, then stalked farther into the room.

"When I told you to find something to do, I meant something useful, not—"

"Regula," she supplied. The heat had retreated from her cheeks, leaving her just as proper as her undone hair would allow. He nodded at her, his complaint still with me.

"Did you fall and get a splinter up the ass?" I baited him. His eyes lit with rage. "Last I checked, my cabin was my own." This was less than fair, for I knew his issue was not with me wasting my day between a woman's legs, but that I was feasting on a city dweller I intended to betray. An innocent, in his eyes.

"Your cabin, yes, but not the blessed passengers, Connor!" Rory was near boiling.

I hadn't seen him this upset since I'd bet and lost his silver shaving kit in our twentieth year. He was far too furious to consider that our guest might have begged me to toss her up on the desk and have my way with her.

"He informed me of your code." Regula was quick to come to my defense. If he wouldn't listen to me, perhaps he'd believe the lady in question. "The choice was mine. Besides, it was clear you had little use for him above." She didn't pull her punches.

"Oh, aye, lady. I bet he bent over backward for you. This one here's all for the code." Rory took aim at me, lacing his words with vinegar. Regula didn't deserve her place in the middle of our squabble, not without context.

She looked at me, then back at him, and I caught familiar calculation behind her eyes.

"He told me about your captain too. The one who's stuck in Sanctuary's dungeons."

This only hardened his rage, but he had to quell it. The Eagle was clear about what she wanted, and it wasn't for him to question her.

"Even without the code, you've been kinder than any pirates in our tales."

I squeezed her leg, then. She didn't have to protect me.

Rory stared at her, and then turned his eyes, still ablaze, to me.

I shrugged.

"I figured there was no harm in telling her about Griffin." It was the truth, after all, if only part of it. The Eagle was keen, and quiet about it. She might be the key to his freedom even if— no, it was impossible to hope for anything more than what she'd already given me.

Rory, to his credit, didn't argue. Not in front of our guest.

"Well, then. Why are you here?" I regretted, immensely, not locking the door on our way in, even if I had only intended to review some maps with the Eagle as a distraction from my nerves. It was irresponsible, but I was tired of doing the right thing all the time. She'd neatly fished for my secrets and baited me into kissing her again and... Had she found satisfaction, before Rory ruined it?

I wanted to wind my hand a mite higher and...

I wouldn't embarrass her in present company.

"Trenna said she left her maps of the Nearways Sea in here last night." Now he was the one blushing, as well he should. It was a slim reason to bust the door open. "They aren't in her cabin," he added.

I made up my mind to switch out his perfume for piss.

"And you couldn't *knock*?" I was incredulous. His eyes darted between Regula and me, discomfort clear on his usually stoic face.

"I *did* knock. Long enough that I wondered if you'd gone into one of those midafternoon naps of yours." He matched my tone perfectly. I clenched my jaw.

I'd taken the captaincy and in doing so given up all my bedmates, and now my crew was bold enough to walk right into my chambers chasing rumors.

"Do you think he's learned his lesson?" I addressed this to Regula, who regarded the two of us with a mix of curiosity and concern.

"Him? Not at all, Captain. I believe he appointed himself your minder the moment you stepped up to office." She narrowed her eyes at him. "I would know; I have a charge myself."

Right enough. Rory had been struggling to keep me on the right path. Taking obstacles out of my way and catching me just as I was about to ruin myself. I wasn't giving him enough credit, no matter my current vexation.

"The maps?" Rory ventured again. "We're nearly clear of the Graveyard."

"Thanks to our fearless navigator." I slapped my hands on the desk and scanned the room. We'd been poring over them before everyone returned from Penny's feast.

Nothing on the desk now. I thought I remembered her rolling them up. Navigators were only worth as much as their maps, and Trenna knew it. She'd been robbed once, all her maps disappearing with an errant lover when she first started out. She'd spent years retracing her steps to acquire new ones, hating the thief more deeply each day. It wasn't uncommon for her to leave them in the safety of the captain's cabin, but they were never misplaced.

"What do they look like?" Regula asked, glancing around the room.

"Like maps," I answered her, then turned to Rory. "They're

not here." We held each other's eyes a moment. "Unless you moved them?"

"Not me. Never touch them if I can help it, not after I spilled all over the Far Flung one. She never lets me forget it." Rory was worried. He never rambled.

"They're not in her cabin," I repeated to myself. "They're not here." I frowned.

Only our crew and the main council of Penny's Cove had known of our intention to head toward the continent to catch the *Edgewater*. There were only so many places a lost map could be on the ship. If the maps were truly gone, then we'd need to figure out who stole them.

A rat was aboard, and not the kind we could cook and eat.

Rory's eyes were grave on mine, his expression a little bit sorry. He'd come to the same conclusion.

"Regula—" My mind raced. "—Rory and I must discuss something privately." The last thing I wanted was for her to leave, but I had to spare her what Rory was about to say.

"I've been away from my charge quite long enough as it is." She shot me a soft smile; forgiveness for our ruined moment, maybe. "I expect to find her covered in parrot feathers or attempting to swing from the ropes."

Rory ignored her attempt at levity, and she didn't bother to continue, leaving us with a swish of skirts.

24

CONNOR

He waited until the door creaked shut, at least.

"She's clever, the Eagle." He emphasized the false name, the separation between us. "A stranger. From Sanctuary."

"No. No chance. I think I'd have noticed if she'd shoved those maps up her skirts." I wouldn't hear of it. There was a world of nonsense between his insinuation and Regula herself.

He eyed me, his lips pressed together.

"And last night?" I blinked up at him. How did he—ah, yes, she and her charge had had the run of my cabin. The whole night they might have been...

"That's what I thought." Rory came up to the desk, crossing his arms over his chest. Looming, one might say. I let myself settle further into the hard-backed chair.

"Connor, you're being a fool. She's smart, you say. Smart enough to tangle you up so fast you'd never notice. You can't even see she might be working for the city."

"Is that jealousy I hear, Rory?" It was a cheap shot. Rory and I hadn't fucked in ages, and when we had it was for the comfort or fun of it, without a hint of connection beyond our camaraderie.

"Seas! You can't admit for a moment that you're in over your head! She's damned right I'm minding you. I have to, or else you'd be all muddled up." He tapped against an exposed nerve, finally voicing his true thoughts on my captaincy.

I would do anything other than admit he had a point. I couldn't very well tug on his beard when we were both this pissed. I was agitated, annoyed, and an ocean away from sated, but none of it was his fault.

"You're reaching. We don't know that the maps are gone. Trenna sent someone to check her cabin, didn't she?" I kicked a foot up to the desk in a grand show of ease.

"Me. She sent me to look." He glowered at me.

"Nothing?" My worries swelled.

"Nothing. The window was open, but you know how she is about fresh air."

"Still, it does not mean—"

"Connor, the crew knows she sailed for five years without any maps when she lost them the first time. She'd be on the end of someone's knife if they really wanted to steal her knowledge."

"They're half as valuable as she is," I agreed.

"If the maps are gone, whoever took them isn't worried about the Graveyard."

" No... but doesn't she have that one tattooed?" My mood lightened at the thought. Rory choked.

"As if I've seen it. She's not one to show much skin. Not since..." He trailed off. Trenna had been different when we'd first met her. Happy, maybe. Not anymore.

I shrugged.

"Could be anyone," I said. Trenna wasn't one to misplace her dearest work. I didn't bother hoping the maps were still around. The way things were going, I was thankful we still had the navigator herself.

"When did we last see a city dweller, much less have one aboard? Why would something go missing now? There's no new crew and the seabirds don't concern themselves with maps," Rory continued, refusing to let it drop.

"In case you forgot, we were both born in the walls," I spat at him. "It doesn't prove anything. It barely speaks to Regula's character, or the girl's.

"Rory, there's plenty of reason for our crew to be fed up with the status quo. You're an example." I waved a hand at him. "You've been steaming at me since the meeting, and you've a right to be. I've gotten us into a mess. Anyone can see it."

He leaned down to the desk, not bothering to disagree.

"It would be a risk to depend on us, or any pirate ship, rescuing those women. Spies or not, it's not the usual game the city plays." Rory was well lit by the windows, all shoulders and bright beard, face full of doubt.

"Most like they were expendable. Insurance," he said.

"The women to be dropped if anyone harried them?" I considered it. That felt more like the Sanctuary I knew, schooled in all manner of backstabbery. "There's more than enough reason here on the *Wretched Lady*. Those maps could be in anyone's hands now."

Rory pursed his lips.

"And that's not counting Penny's Cove. If the city's on their back, what better way to get them off than an alliance to cement their safety. You can't tell me you trust Penny? Or think she's ancient enough to have forgotten how to play Sanctuary's game?"

None of the islands were free from the threat of Sanctuary's navy on their doorstep. Old Ryme's Port had been besieged for two seasons before the city's cannons broke through and their people were killed or swallowed. Any place that wasn't Sanctuary was in danger of being sucked into its walls.

Fear like that forced leaders to do all manner of things. If Penny had worked something out with Sanctuary for those maps, I could not judge her too harshly, preparing as I was to bargain Regula and Venu back for our captain.

"The maps might have walked out with a hundred people, Rory. Provided they walked out at all."

"Oh, aye, with everyone but the woman you've got in here on her back." It was unlike Rory to be this riled over a bedfellow.

"If you're right, and she is a spy, I'm much better off with my head between her thighs."

No matter how mad I might be growing, I still needed his counsel.

"I'm tempted to confide in her. I haven't yet, and I won't... not until we're ready." I settled for that much, though it did not melt his stern demeanor. "I know, I know. Judge me all you want."

He tilted his head, brows raised. His striking blue eyes caught the light. Another time I would have teased him about his sparkling sapphires.

"Connor, you can't be serious. It's been a few days and you're already halfway to tumbling her. Your head is calling the shots, and not the one with the mouth!" He scowled at me. "I can hardly follow you! Punishing yourself for Griffin's capture. Pushing everyone away in the name of your captaincy so long that you can't keep yourself from mauling a city dweller! Really?" He blew himself out quickly. "If you needed touch so bad, I've a hand." He withdrew from the desk and paced over to the windows.

I snorted at him.

"Your hand has enough to contend with! It's not—" He shot me a punishing glare. "Regula's got a fascinating curiosity, and... and I wanted to show her a thing or two about pirate life." I was shaping the words for Rory's benefit. There was a pull between us alright, but I hadn't bothered to get to the bottom of it.

"Don't you ever feel sorry for them?" I continued, wondering how long until he'd leave me alone. I was far from hard, but the memory of Regula across my desk was fresh in my mind's eye. "That kind of life? Is there any sort of loving in it, carnal or not? We get to sit out here on our ships with our agreements and do whatever we want as long as our partners want it too. Sanctuary demands their women do little more than carry babies."

Rory scrubbed at his neck, his eyes narrowing.

"You're fucking the Eagle because you feel sorry for her?"

I didn't have a chance to respond, cut off by the bang of the door.

"Again?" I growled at Rory, staring past him at—*ah, perfect*—Jack. Her eyes flashed at me for a second before she bothered to look apologetic at her interruption.

I shot to my feet. Enough was enough.

"What in the tide's name are you doing in here?"

Rory shifted around, careful to stay between me and the pirate. For my sake, probably. He didn't want to watch me throttle a crew member.

"Trenna's looking for her maps, Captain." She had the good sense to use my title, treading as she was on my territory.

"You're looking for her maps? He's looking for her maps. I'm fucking looking for her maps. How many sailors can we get in here, do you think? The midnight shift? Perhaps we should look through their pockets while we're at it!" I slammed my hands down on the desk.

I wasn't sure I'd ever seen Jack jump before.

"I... I'll just be going then." She backed out the way she'd come.

"Yes, yes, go and tell Trenna we'll be enlisting the ship's rats to search the hold. She can go down there and herd them. Or if she'd rather, she can send you."

Jack didn't say another word, and the door clicked behind her.

"Was that necessary?" Rory asked, returning his attention to me.

"Seas, yes. This is my cabin. Trenna has her own trunks to send Jack diving in."

"She's worried, is all."

"And I'm not?" I snapped at him. "If Griffin were here, things would be different," I added sulkily.

He snorted, uncrossing his arms and coming around the edge of the desk to muscle into Regula's abandoned spot.

"That's the truth. You might get to keep your lady, for one," he said, setting a hand on my shoulder, face smug.

"She's not my lady," I hissed. "It's just—"

"The first drink of water after a long dry spell?" He could not suppress his laughter.

I shook off his hand and clouted him on the side.

"You want to try being captain? See how long you last!" I barked at him. "In charge of everyone you might want to take to your bunk? A ship full of hungry bellies? A veritable sea of better sailors pitying you the job?" He was still smiling. "A best friend who has started to act like your mother?" I poked him in the ribs. Wherever his anger had gone, and for whatever reason he'd loosened up, I was grateful.

"Why'd you think I pushed so hard for your name to go forward to the vote?" He raised a brow.

"Ah, get out, you shark!" I levered him up from the desk and toward the door, following right behind.

"Sure you don't need a hand?" he joked, pulling the worthless thing open, and carrying himself outside of it.

I slammed it behind him and leaned against the wood.

The world waited outside. There was Trenna to talk to, the crew to be arranged for the night, and Regula and her charge to sort out.

Perhaps I was driving myself too hard. The Wretches, as well. It had been a slog of a summer for each of us in turn. We all needed a break, something to crack the shell of our recent failures.

The *Wretched Lady* needed release.

Me too.

No amount of bureaucracy eclipsed the need I'd been holding on to since Rory's interruption. The picture of Regula was seared in my mind—pink cheeked, knuckles white on her skirts, knees framing my view.

The only way to ensure I wouldn't be bothered again was to unbutton my pants right here, with my back firmly blocking even the most determined intruder.

So be it. My flagging erection had forgotten nothing, and rose to my hand without much wrangling.

Those last few moments when she'd gripped me with her thighs and gone rigid against my mouth, ah, my whole life could be spent reliving them. I had hardly needed breath. Had she bucked against the wood, her spine curling, on the cusp of crying out, before she was interrupted? I'd worked her nearly there. I knew it from the sweet swelling of her cunt and the impatience of her hips. Those whispery, barely contained moans of hers had been just as satisfying as a sack full of sweets after a long journey.

She could not know how she enticed me. All warm curves, every unraveled inch of her. I could simply bite—

And there.

I came with great, body-racking jerks.

I would find Regula out there and apologize. I'd pay her every courtesy, and hold myself to the captaincy. I would not at all think of the mess I'd left in our wake.

If I could no longer indulge, I would make sure my crew was not to suffer the same sentence. It was high time for a little celebration.

Although perhaps I should wash my face first.

25

REGULA

I 'd been ravished and banished.

That fact sank in as soon as I exited the cabin and found myself in the bright light of day. The flags were still in use and while a few crew members stood about, watching, the rest were up in the ropes, fixing the sails to Trenna's command.

No one would bother with me, or if they did, there was nothing about my dress or—

I put a hand to my head and sighed. My curls were seriously askew.

Quick fingers made for short work as I tucked the strands back into their places. No pins missing, at least, though I mourned the pleasure I'd been denied. The captain had known exactly what a city girl like me might enjoy. I hadn't realized a man could kiss with such passion or in such places.

Presentable, and just in time too, as the affable pirate—Jack, I thought her name was—marched past me toward the captain's cabin. She tossed me a smile that I tried my best to return. My knees were still a little shaky as I made my way out of the hallway and over to the side of the boat.

The crew was scattered there in twos and threes, pressed up

to the railing. Odette and Billy were not far from where I'd left them, a ways down the boat.

I resolved to join them in a moment. I collected myself first, settling into an empty space at the rail. My heart was beating somewhat too near my throat for comfort, and my skin tingled all over where the wind brushed it.

Inside the captain's cabin, I hadn't realized the magnitude of the stones Trenna was carefully avoiding. They stuck out, gargantuan, on either side of the *Wretched Lady*. Rock, layered like candles dripped from the heavens, trailed into the distance behind us.

A graveyard it was, alright. One for oceanic gods, buried long before we humans had sparked to consciousness. Bastions of another era.

One passed us as another ship might. I notched my elbows into the wood and watched it. White and gray birds dotted its face, making a racket I'd missed in the haze of pleasure. Their hollering against the mighty stones was an invitation from a new world. One where I might run up the stairs and throw myself over the bow with a sword in my hand, sinking it deep into the heart of a sea monster. Fish bones and bright shells under the birds' feet reeked in the sun, serving only to underscore the strangeness of my situation.

It did not help, I thought, eyes on the stone monolith, that I could see myself here, dagger in hand, feet in pirate's boots. I was guzzling freedom for the first time, swilling down the possibility of a life where I chose everything. These pirates shaped people to their strengths and not their faults, seemingly with ease.

I could see myself staying with them.

A stone pillar slipped past, soon lost to the horizon. There was a yell from far above and a flash of yellow appeared in my peripheral vision.

I turned, boosting myself to see farther over the edge of the boat. A few others leaned over for a better look. The deck would still have been deathly silent if not for the birds and the calls from the crow's nest. The ship groaned beneath me, a twisting, menacing noise that set the hairs on my arms pricking. The pirates in my line of sight turned as one to look back toward the wheel as Trenna roared from her post.

I copied them. Her furious hands were clenched on the great wheel, struggling to keep it over as far as it would go. Trenna's face—what I could see of it—was hardly strained, even as she finished shouting to the sailors above. Her fingers though, were near to snapping the wooden handles. Holding and holding, they yanked another great noise from the ship.

Twisting back around, I locked my hands over the worn railing. She'd changed our course, and now I worried I might go right over.

"You alright there?"

I hadn't noticed Jack at my elbow.

She stood without an ounce of fear, the usual twinkle caught in the corner of her eyes, her short hanks of blond hair matching her sunny skin. An earring gleamed fat and gold in her ear.

Jack looked at home on the deck, comfortable even as we tilted toward the waves.

Upon closer inspection, she was neatly stitched into somber colors and half a head taller than me. Her fitted trousers and loose indigo jacket whispered of strength in the body beneath them. She looked dangerous, except that she was covered in a thin layer of dust, especially noticeable in the joins of her clothing and just above her cuffs. She smelled strongly of wood chips, which was pleasant in the face of the birds' stink.

"I think I can manage." I shot her a tight smile. I kept my voice low, since no one else seemed to be making a peep. She nodded, shifting her stance and sliding toward me anyway, not a foot out of place.

As she inched closer, I was made aware of the reason for our sudden course correction. Another stone monolith, squatter, but no less covered in nesting birds, stuck out of the water just off the side. If the last had been in viewing distance, this one was nearly touchable.

I sucked in a breath, arrested by the sight.

Terrified.

A hand caught my tense wrist.

"May I?"

I nodded, much closer to a watery grave than a moment ago. Jack stretched long arms under mine, bracketing me, and putting her firmly at my back. She held herself away, not really touching beyond a whisper of forearm, not unless the boat forced us together.

"Jackdaw," she said.

"What?"

"Jack, short for Jackdaw. I like Long Legs better if you're adverse to Jack, but…" She trailed off.

I turned as best I could to look at the pirate, taking a second to realize she was completing our introduction from the other day.

"There's little point in playing the Eagle any longer. I'm Regula. Pleased to meet you in truth, Jack."

I could not bask in her grin long before the threatening pillar in front of us drew my attention back.

I was lucky Jack was so solid. We were so close to the stone, sliding just barely by, even with Trenna's best maneuvering.

Had any of the other pillars come so close?

I must have loosed my thoughts aloud, because the pirate behind me unlocked a hand and gestured across the deck. I spun to look, well supported in the case that I slid.

My eyes went saucer wide. Another great grave rose over the far side, much taller, almost fully obscured by birds.

We were threading a needle between the two, with what I had to guess was only the length of a person to spare between the rocks and the *Wretched Lady*.

"Mercy…" The word slipped from my mouth.

"This last bit is the worst," Jack gamely replied. "Do you

see?" She nodded back toward the first sentinel of rock, her bright hair bobbing with her. Near as she was, I could not help but notice the deep brown of her eyes and the freckles that played over her slightly hooked nose.

I craned my neck, this time unsure what I was meant to be seeing.

Another deep protest roared up from the ship, and the deck shifted, strong enough to rock me forward into the barrier.

The pirate leaned in a little, pointing again with her head rather than her hands, and I was grateful for the steadiness of her arms around my middle.

"Don't worry," she said, and in the next breath, "Under the water. Right along the pillar. See that?" I followed the line of the stone down to the waterline, and—oh yes, it did not disappear down, but spread out toward another pillar some distance away, never dipping far enough that I couldn't see a hint of it.

"It's all rocks?" I ventured.

"They call it the Graveyard not because it looks like one, but because ships don't leave it." Her voice was hard. "Almost none survive the traveling of it. We're lucky enough to have one of the few aboard." I didn't have to look back to know she was speaking of Trenna. I was beginning to wonder if everyone aboard didn't love her a little. She seemed the sort to have lived a thousand lives, even though she couldn't be older than I.

"She's a fearsome navigator. There's no easier way out of here?" I twisted around to see the other column. We'd turned a hair farther from it, but it was hardly less terrible. Trenna must have had nerves of steel. She was the only one yelling now. With the flags still and the crow's nest silent, the whole ship seemed to be relying on her skill alone.

"There's a rocky bottom all through here," Jack replied. "The clear day makes for an easier path, but I wouldn't trust anyone else at the helm." I snuck a look at her. Her gaze was focused on the woman who held the wheel. "We'd be tinder if we tried this in a storm."

"The captain chose her well," I said, baiting her, catching just what I guessed I would: a contemptuous quirk of her lip, before she noticed me staring. Connor was right to suppose that a portion of his crew would rather follow Trenna.

"I understand you aren't much for the seas, being a city dweller and all, but I promise you a good navigator is worth ten captains on a voyage like this," she said with only a hint of the vitriol I was expecting. Surprisingly diplomatic, these pirates.

"I'll take your word for it, sailor."

She laughed at my reply, a pleasant rumble, close as she was to my ear. "I'm for the sea, alright. Been on a boat as long as I can remember. Will be until they get tired of my dramatics and kick me off." She gave me a cat's smug smile.

"Ah, a fair punishment for rescuing a city dweller from going over the side." I smiled back, politely mocking her.

"Cannot, for the life of me, let a lady face the danger of the high seas alone." She reformed her face into an example of perfect respectability, and added, "Especially if she has already drunk enough of the deep to make anyone sick."

Now I was the one to laugh. Everyone on the ship must have watched me cough up half the sea.

"Much obliged then. My life is forever changed." It was truth, I think, slipping from my lips, though it sounded like flattery.

"As are ours," Jack murmured. She was in danger of painting herself a horrific flirt. Perhaps further gone than Comely Connor himself. I rolled my eyes, but could not hold back the roses blooming on my cheeks from the unsubtle compliment.

26

REGULA

Connor and his towering shadow, Rory, strode past. Despite my grin, they spared Jack and me only a cursory glance on their way up to Trenna's side. I could have sworn a cloud passed over Connor's face.

My good humor stumbled, a frown dragging my smile down. Jack noticed, unsurprised to find the captain at the heart of my trouble when she followed my gaze. For an instant, I got the sense that she knew exactly what I'd spent the last hour doing.

Impossible.

She wouldn't ruffle me. I wouldn't be the one to give away the game, especially if Connor didn't want to play anymore.

We women of Sanctuary could not be so different from these sailors. We all required a little care and attention after—it didn't matter. There *was* another pirate in front me. I wasn't the one being rude, though Jack was now watching me closely.

"You could call me Long Legs, you know. All my friends do."

All of the calculation was gone from her face, the wide, white expanse of her teeth showing.

"Long Legs, then. I don't have many friends."

"Doubtful, Regula. You and the young one have half the ship running around after you." Again, I wondered if she made a habit of hiding in the captain's closet. Secrets hardly stood a chance on a berth like this.

My paranoia was comical in its essence. Only a few moments ago, I'd been basking in a pirate's propensity for pleasure. If there was a prude on the *Wretched Lady*, I was sure Jack wasn't it.

"It is exhilarating. Makes Sanctuary seem quite boring in comparison." I tossed my head. Jack was distracting me so nimbly from Connor's snub that I'd nearly forgotten why I needed her as my anchor. Without the lurch and cry of the ship, I'd taken my eyes off the Graveyard.

The great stone off the side did not allow itself to be ignored for long, rising up out of the water closer than I remembered it.

I stumbled back, a reflex that was at least better than falling forward, except it sent me crashing past the careful distance of Jack's arms. I was suddenly very aware of the sturdy and altogether too real woman at my back.

"Steady on, we're nearly through." One of her hands settled on my hip, effectively guiding me out of our accidental embrace before withdrawing. "Few people ever get to see this, you shouldn't miss it," she said, encouraging me to look.

The pillar of rock was within touching distance, all wind and rain hammered edges splattered in white droppings. I held my breath, trying hard not to think about the width of the boat. The grave on the far side had surely been just as close. Did the pirates ever climb on them?

We were squeaking by, metaphorically, since there was no screech of tinder and rock, no bone-shaking collision from either direction. My shoulders crept toward my ears, readying for disaster.

"She's worth her weight in gold, our navigator." Jack leaned in a little, breaking the spell of our stiff-armed politeness.

"I can see that. It seems everyone is pulling their weight." I tilted my head back to get a better view of the sailors scurrying up in the ropes. "Is that what you do?" I pointed.

"Not very often. I'm the ship's cooper."

I puzzled over the title before she added, "They lock me down in the hold and force me to make barrels." She winked. I wouldn't have believed her anyway. She was as tanned as any of the others.

"They pay me in the nice bits of wood," she spun her yarn further.

"I know your code! Everyone gets a share of the plunder." I pretended indignation. "Some people must get more, but none are left empty-handed!"

"You've caught me." She laughed, practically into my shoulder. "I beg them for the good bits so I can make baubles that'll sell for twice my share." This explained the sprinkling of dust.

"You do? Have I seen any?" I took a mental inventory of the ship. No wooden dolls, no— "The statue at the front of the ship?"

"Nay, Regula! Do I look as old as the *Wretched Lady*?" She was aghast, watching for my response. "Besides, that's better work than I could hope to produce in the corners of the day when nothing needs steaming, cutting, or fitting."

I snorted.

"I'd lay good gold that the crew covets your work." I'd be the last to know what these pirates held precious, but I was sure of this.

"Good gold, huh? And here I thought you came to us with nothing. Where've you been hiding it?" She teased her tongue over the point of a tooth and let her eyes wander down my person.

"A girl can dream, Long Legs. I've lost my purse, but not my spirit." I did not suppress my smile. Today, I was definitely proving myself a gambler. Besides, everything was easy with Jack.

I'd thought the same of Connor.

"Aye, you've plenty of that." For the second time in as many hours, I felt like the nicest cut of meat on the feasting table. Perhaps I should retire my "woe is me" moping. Clearly, I was born to steal hearts on pirate ships.

It was the thought of hearts that sent me—against my better judgment—searching up near the helm, where I would surely find...

Connor was staring down at me. I'd never seen anything like his expression. His features weren't stormy anymore, but plaintive. Only for an instant, then he turned to confer with Rory.

How long had he been watching?

Perhaps he regretted the hour we'd shared. There'd been no time for his own release.

We'd been interrupted. Did it rankle that he'd yet to bring me off as well? It seemed something of a sport to these pirates. Not selflessness, no, but they took a special delight in the chase.

He'd been happy enough to service me, just as I'd been happy to receive, for the first time in my life. My firsts were piling up, with the good soon to outnumber the bad. My past was drifting further out behind me. Or had been.

I wound my fingers into the fabric of my skirts.

His hand had been seeking up my thigh, my... my juices fresh on his lips, and he'd still sent me off. I could not possibly be responsible for these dour looks.

"You're staring, love," Jack said, her voice a river pouring into the space between us.

Was she the reason?

Good Gods. Was Comely Connor jealous of the second biggest flirt aboard? We hadn't spoken any vows. There was no more than a dose of pleasure to bind us. A pirate lark. Besides, he'd been quick to point out that pirates loved to share. He wouldn't be stewing over Jack if he intended that, not with her dashing manner.

My face was surely dipped crimson at the thought.

I would call him a fool, and possibly a hypocrite, if he'd deign to speak to me.

But Jack... now, Jack had been nothing but respectful. Calming, honestly. I wasn't used to this sort of thing. Connor hadn't bothered to escort me from his cabin, or even to say a word once he left it. If he had, perhaps he wouldn't be mooning down at me. He'd be the one clasped to my back, showing me wonders over the side. I wanted another stolen moment with him.

None of it was even worth entertaining. There *were* sturdy arms around me, but even in the worst of the ship's momentum, they weren't for anything other than ship's courtesy.

Had there been a flash of attraction? Perhaps, though I was unfamiliar with how such things presented from a woman. She could very well be giving me the sort of treatment she'd give anyone.

I hadn't heard all the pirate code yet, but passengers obviously benefited from the *Wretched Lady*'s rules. Or else, Jack and Connor had been brought up to take pity on every spinster that set foot within a league of them.

Connor could think whatever he wanted up there.

If he was frustrated with my attentions or lack thereof, he could rot. I'd used him only to the degree that he'd begged for it. My former husband was one of those, ever wrathful if things didn't go to his plan, in the bedroom or outside of it. But Connor... No, I could not believe that was in his nature.

"Know the captain well?" Jack asked over my shoulder. I considered this as I stared out at the sea where the rock now passed behind us.

"Not so well as you know half the ship," I hedged, cutting her a glance.

I'd yet to see a pirate flinch, but Jack came very close. Her body tensed for the length of a breath, then with a blink, her easy demeanor poured back over her.

"So pretty well, then." She smirked.

I shouldn't have dignified her with a response.

"What do you take me for?" I raised a brow at her.

"A pirate," she said after a moment of thought.

I did not have time to formulate a clever reply.

A cry went up from the surrounding pirates. A cheer of delight. The flags I'd seen earlier were worked up and down, wheels of yellow and orange against the knotted wood. I spun in the cage of Jack's arms to find there were no more menacing stones. They'd all been left in the middle distance.

I took in the crew, clapping here and there with a fervor that pointed to the seriousness of the situation. The right navigator was life or death. I wondered how they'd gotten Trenna on this raggedy boat. Her knowledge was surely worth enough to employ her for life.

I felt, rather than saw, Jack drop back from the railing. I'd adjusted subtly to her arms at my sides, and the loss meant I could breathe again.

I smiled at her, finding it impossible to convey how helpful she'd been. Other sailors began scrambling down from the ropes and disappearing off the deck. Whether they went to their next task or a nap, I didn't know.

The tension of the Graveyard was not gone from my muscles yet. I peeked back behind the cabin, using the railing as my guide, and saw a horizon dotted with stones, thick as a cloud of hornets in places.

The two pillars we'd slunk between looked ill-placed and impossible to attempt, the true roots of the rocks completely hidden by the sparkling water. A white bubbled wake was the only proof of our passage.

"Bloody miracle, she is." Jack's growl had doubled in volume to match the renewed hum of the ship. She'd moved away, but not far. Her gaze was directed up at the helm.

Trenna had been relieved by Silver and was shaking out her hands, surely sore from her expert sailing.

I did not expect much from Connor, not now, but he marched to the edge of the upper deck and shouted from its height. He did not address me, as some part of me had hoped, but rather the crew still gathered.

"Wretches, we have tempted fate today and come out with luck on our side. In an effort to keep her, I say we take tonight and celebrate. It's been ages since we let loose, and it may be longer still before we have our captain back and a summer breeze to call us home." He paused, surveying the mess of us, careful to avoid meeting my gaze.

"The moon is far from full." He began again with a touch of sternness I didn't quite understand in the context of his words. "But tonight, belowdecks, we will revel if you will it." His crew howled up at him in delight, hardly allowing him to finish.

"For the *Wretched Lady*!" he shouted as his pirates fell into pleasant chaos.

27

REGULA

Odette could tell I was hiding something. Ignoring the cheering pirates, she caught up with Jack and me in the darkness of the lower deck. As much as I wanted to tell her all, as we neared the cooperage, I wasn't sure I should.

What I'd shared with Connor had been fun of the first order, but nothing had come of it. It would be cruel of me to get her hopes up in regard to my love life.

Odette did not press me in front of Long Legs. She, however, shot me a series of quizzical looks over my newfound friendship. I shrugged her off, having learned everything I knew about befriending pirate-kind from her in the first place.

Belowdecks was a great change from above, with everything tarred watertight, and the only sunlight sneaking in through cracks and the occasional salt-crusted hatch. Tallow candles winked at us from old brass fixtures, their protective casings blocking only a little of their animal stink as we wound our way toward the ship's belly.

Odette and I marched briskly along behind Jack. The passage was a fickle one, opening into a gallery with bunks and hammocks neatly running the width of the ship, then closing in on us again with all manner of doors to be opened. Jack turned sharply at the fourth such door and swung it wide for our benefit.

Much to the chagrin of the pirate who'd been standing right behind it with a bucket of tools in her hand.

Any awe we might have felt at the well-appointed, many stationed room was lost to a colorful string of curses and the clatter of said tools as they tumbled from her grasp and rolled about our feet. Luckily, our toes avoided any serious injury, and we three quickly recovered them.

When the pirate finally stood, tools in a semblance of order, she looked like she might say something to us all, but thought better of it. With a moment to look at her, I decided she had to be one of the prettiest pirates aboard. She rivaled Odette for physical charm, with big brown eyes, freckled, softly bronze skin, and not a speck of sawdust on her fetching skirt and blouse.

She ignored Odette's butterfly apologies and squared up to Jack, short and curvy against the cooper's height and bulk, unafraid to stare the bigger woman down.

"My apologies, Isadore," Jack finally said, not backing up one inch.

"Yes," was all Isadore said before marching ahead with her bucket. We scattered to get out of the way, and I found myself watching her springy black curls disappear down the hall, wondering what we'd just witnessed.

"Ship's carpenter," Jack supplied when I looked askance at her. "She's just worried about the *Lady* getting blown to bits under the navy's bombardment. It's her first time on a ship with any action." She settled further into the room.

"A hard job, no doubt," Odette chimed in, halfway through the door behind us.

"But we won't meet the *Edgewater* tonight, surely?" I asked at the same time.

"Not unless they come to our party." Jack smiled, addressing us both. "Our last carpenter was a character, seas keep him. All bluster and bite about the littlest things." Jack tapped her fingers lovingly across one of the work benches. "Isadore isn't half bad, I promise."

I peeked around Jack. The room, which combined a shop and a cooperage, was large and brightly lit. Sitting somewhere near the bow, grates had been set up to drain sunlight down, banishing the feeling of a lower deck. It was tidy and far better kept than any other corner of the *Wretched Lady*. Tools lined the walls, with tightly hasped boxes and seamless barrels stacked in the crevices. Rougher looking work took center stage, ready to be fiddled with.

Like Jack, the surfaces were mostly clean but for the wood dust that had settled into the cracks. The crisp smell of sawdust was inescapable. What wasn't wood was iron, which Jack explained was actually far more essential.

She showed us, rather proudly, the ceiling vents that could be opened with a rope and pulley to let out steam and smoke from the controlled fires, which let her round a barrel or reshape it. Apparently, cargo was stacked above so no one would fall through into the cooperage.

"That's clever!" Odette said upon witnessing the demonstration. She'd always been interested in gadgetry of all kinds, though usually only the sort that applied to city ladies. I was forever searching out clocks and music boxes for her to tinker with.

I had to agree. If the ship looked beat up and shoddy, it did not mean there wasn't the proper tool or person to fix it, only that the materials were lacking, or perhaps the time hard to carve out. The cooperage was making me wonder what other secrets the ship might hold.

Odette and Jack were shoulder to shoulder at a bench on the far side of the room by the time I left my thoughts and returned to the present moment.

"You can't just use any old scrap for these. We've been short just about everything or else I'd have made a few more." I couldn't quite see what Jack was talking about. I edged around her to get a good look at a row of figurines, some pushed back into the shadows of the wall.

"You weren't lying. They're magnificent," I exclaimed, a little too close to Odette's ear.

My charge turned to Jack with a look that asked "Can I touch?"

When she got a nod, she leaned down with curious fingers. The figures were all more or less of a size. The front pieces were mostly animals, with lithe little bodies and dancing feet, as if the wood had grown specifically for the purpose of making them come alive. Even without paint, the creatures were lovingly oiled and in a variety of rich hues.

"There are more—" Jack said, then paused, eyeing us fiercely. "I'm not sure they'd be to your taste."

I did not immediately see the glow in Odette's eyes, since she was still pressed forward, examining Jack's work, but I knew it would be there when she turned, as she could not resist a challenge.

"You must show us, dear Jack," she said, shooting back up to our level. "Don't hold out on us. I know you all see us as silly city dwellers, but it's not the truth." Her tone dipped into the mewling of a cat for milk, and she did look very sad indeed to be excluded. I was content to press my hands into my hips and watch a master at work.

"Who told you that?" Jack's voice was laced with outrage. "None of us think you silly. Unfortunate in the extreme, perhaps, but not silly." She tapped a finger to her chin, suddenly the serious cooper rather than the roguish pirate.

"Besides, we're halfway to pirates ourselves, aren't we, Regula?" Odette cast me a pleading look.

"Aye." I gave my best toothy grin. "The high seas or nothing for us." The impression was so bad, both Odette and Jack succumbed to giggles.

"Alright, alright," Jack said, once she'd finished laughing. "If anyone asks, you will lie about what I've shown you today."

She guided us across the room to a set of cabinets, bigger than the woman herself and locked with intimidating iron bars.

"If I'm not to be accused of corrupting you, I'll need you to swear—" She paused, looking between us. "—to having been thoroughly corrupted before I got to you." Oh, now the professional was gone and the pirate was back.

Odette gaped, then recovered, slapping at Jack's coat with a playful hand.

"And that's as good as answered." Jack whistled, gazing between the two of us.

"You rascal! Wipe that smile off your face," Odette commanded. She looked like she had a mind to set the pirate straight, her eyes boring holes into the woman's head.

Jack merely slipped a hand into her pocket, bunching up her blue coat and sending a sprinkle of wood dust off its breast. Out came jangly keys, which she deftly applied to the lock.

28

REGULA

"If I was smart, I'd ask you to pose, so when Billy comes down here all hangdog because you left our pretty ship, I'll have something to sell her." Jack tugged open the cabinet doors.

"What do you mean?" I asked. She ignored the question, the answer right before us.

The shelves were chock full of all manner of erotic statuary. There were figurines engaged in raucous acts, in states of undress, and—

"You carved a cock?" Odette had skipped the suggestive pieces and was peering straight into the back, where a row of beautifully polished penises stuck up in varying degrees of excitement.

"Gods. There are a lot of them." My jaw hit the floor.

"Cocks are good money around here," Jack replied, matter-of-fact. "You never know who might need one." Pride filled her voice. She raised an eyebrow in Odette's direction.

The workmanship on these pieces was just as stunning as the animals, with a wide array of tones and shapes to the wood. The figures were perfectly presented mid-coitus, and the wooden cocks well-hewn. I'd heard people sometimes made do with a stand-in, but I'd never seen one with my own eyes.

The pieces ranged from smallish, which I could vouch for as some men's reality—my former husband's, certainly—to rather large and too wide to fit in my hands. There were still others that did not necessarily match what one might consider a cock, but sitting next to all the others that did, one might easily guess their purpose.

"Do you—" I snapped my mouth shut. I hadn't truly considered what I was asking when I started the question.

"Do I make 'em? Yes. Though Isadore helps with the more detailed ones." Jack answered rapid fire. "Do I use 'em? What a question! Any artist had better use their own handiwork or else what's the point? I'm the best in the business."

I choked and sputtered that I hadn't meant to ask the second.

Odette, meanwhile, snaked a hand in and helped herself to a curved carving of thick ship rope, pressing out of a flared base. Rather than asking, she merely looked from the piece to Jack and back, her eyes gleaming.

"It's very detailed," she said finally, giving me time to catch my breath.

"Some folks like to feel it all, every knot and thread." Jack chuckled. "It's not for everyone, but I try to make sure there's some variety. Keeps people coming back, you understand."

"Oh, I can see why they'd come back, since these are nearly impossible to find on the common man." Odette had traded the rope carving for a branch of a cock, almost as thick as her leg. I could see the muscles in her forearms working to hold the piece up.

Jack just shrugged, but she must have noticed Odette's struggle, because she gently took the cock away. It looked much safer in her hands.

"It's not my job to judge. I collect my coin from satisfied customers, and that's it. Besides, if you search hard enough, you can find any size bruiser you like, on a man or a woman." She flashed a grin before setting the penis back into its place. "Likely they got it from me, though."

"Who buys this stuff?" I asked, my eyes lingering on a lovingly carved bust of a laughing woman, her big shoulders and breasts thrown out in invitation.

"There's someone adventurous in practically every town, a whole lot more if it's got a port. Most of the pirates commission something for their lovers, or send a figurine to a spouse at home. Some'll even use them as courting gifts, or for their own pleasure." Those words forced my eyes back to some of the larger and more impressive pieces in the collection.

Had Connor ever purchased from Jack? Had he... posed?

Thankfully, the creak of the door behind us kept me from boiling over at the thought.

When I turned, I expected Isadore and another stream of curses, but it was a thin young woman with assessing eyes and hair pulled up in a mountain of tiny braids. She fit the room almost perfectly, her rich brown skin shining in the swathes of light from above. Her ears were filled with golden hoops, all sparkling.

"Jack..." She said the name tentatively. "You're going to get yourself in trouble." She'd clearly seen past us into the cabinet, and now she searched our faces for our disapproval.

"Pipes..." Jack copied her wearied and protective tone. "These women had been fully... filled in... on all things pirate without me needing to lift a finger. They asked to see the embarrassing stuff! I could only oblige." She shrugged her big shoulders. A dog in sailor's kit.

"Practicing the word 'no' would be in your best interest, Jack," the stranger suggested, her tone lighter, as she slung a sack onto the desk nearest the door.

"Why should *I* have to learn it when the captain—" Jack nodded suggestively at me, starting my blush up aggressively. "— and Billy—" She cocked her head at Odette. "—haven't bothered to? Go knock on their doors first. I'm but a humble merchant."

The other pirate gave a noncommittal hum, that very clearly stated she would not be checking with anyone about anything.

"This is my bad-weather assistant, Pipes." Jack addressed Odette and I with a wink. "I only see her when the weather turns sour and she can't be up in the ropes with her friends."

"Oh, is that true?" Pipes sent her a withering look, then began to unpack the canvas bag. "I must have bargained for these odds and ends in Penny's Cove at the request of one of my friends up in the rigging." She dumped out a few pieces of wood. "Isadore wouldn't mind having these for a fix here or there, either." She inclined her head toward the far side of the room.

Jack chewed on her lip, digesting the threat.

"That was very thoughtful of you," the cooper finally said, drawn over to the chunks of wood. "Isadore has plenty of her own scrap to work with." Jack picked one up. "Pipes, this is nice! I thought there weren't any trees in the cove?"

"The island doesn't have much, but you aren't the only whittler on the seas. Convinced a few to share their spoils..." Pipes was proving to be a talented actress, all rolling words and dramatic faces. "...for my other friends, up top."

Jack frowned, her hands clearly itching for the wood. Odette and I stole a glance at each other, silently laughing.

"Oy, alright, I take it back. Pipes is by far the most talented and best hand on this here ship." Jack aimed this at us, catching us at our giggling. "Pipes, meet Regula and..." She paused. Pipes stepped a little closer, all her artifice forgotten with the compliment.

"I'm not a pirate...Yet. So I suppose I have no need to conceal my name. Call me Odette," she said.

My stomach gave a flip. Would Odette stay aboard? Would I?

"—Odette. Ladies of the city, who might one day be the proud owners of a Long Legs special." She looked especially hard at my charge, who didn't do her the favor of ignoring the insinuation, bestowing instead a devilish smile.

"You can't go wrong with one," Pipes said gamely. "If they don't make you faint, they'll, well, they might make you feel faint, if you know what I mean." I didn't immediately get her meaning, not until Odette was taken over by a wave of laughter, and finally it dawned on me. Ah. I was, in some ways, still such a Sanctuarian.

"We'll have the pleasure of your company a while yet, ladies, so no need to buy now." Jack edged past us to lock away her considerable assets.

"Yeah, don't let her swindle you." Pipes paused, her face going soft. "After that ordeal with your old ship, I'm glad to see you both in better spirits," she added. Of course, she'd been present for my near drowning. The whole of the *Wretched Lady* had been in attendance. Oh, gods, Jack had probably seen my breasts torn free of my corset, too. I'd flashed the whole lot.

"Well as can be, given the circumstances," Odette said.

She didn't elaborate, because we were interrupted yet again. Not by the brusque carpenter this time either. The four of us turned as one to find Billy barging in, her face pained when she realized, too late, that she might have knocked.

"Captain wants you at the helm, Jack, Pipes." She jerked her chin at the two of them, body hanging halfway through the door.

"I know. I'm fetching for Isadore at the moment. You know how she is when the ship is in mortal danger," Pipes replied, cleanly slicing over to the far side of the room to scoop tools and scrap into her canvas sack.

Billy rolled her eyes.

"We're not even in spitting distance of danger."

"You should thank me, Billy," Jack purred, clearly no fan of the captain's orders.

"I doubt I want to know why." Billy's lip curled. She'd discarded her steady demeanor and adopted something a little more bullish for dealing with Jack. Interesting. "Ladies? We'd better make ourselves scarce."

"Surely we can help?" I asked. Pipes wound around Billy and into the hallway, her bag banging against the doorframe.

"No, no. I'm not even sure if— they have all the hands they need." Billy hurled this last part right at Jack, who had made absolutely no move toward the door. Billy glared at her. More and more I picked up that Jack was one of Connor's detractors, resisting his will with her every breath.

"When the captain orders, I oblige." Jack's manner was light, almost playful. She saluted us like valued sailors.

"Jack, thank you," I managed, giving her a squeeze on the arm as she passed.

"Your work is tremendous," Odette said.

"Illuminating, to say the least." I wondered if it would... Yes, Billy's jaw had tightened up noticeably, and while she didn't bother saying anything, her eyes took on a volatile aspect. Jack just grinned at us over her shoulder.

"My pleasure." She ducked through the door. "And my best to the both of you. Stay out of trouble."

I was fairly certain I heard "You're the trouble" mumbled under Billy's breath as we followed her out.

29

CONNOR

With our heading set well out of Sanctuary waters and our stores replenished, my crew could afford to cut loose.

All the other decisions I'd made in Griffin's absence had been desperate ones. I'd asked the *Wretched Lady* to waste months in the rocky coves and barren islands nearest the walled city, running risky midnight missions whenever there was a ghost of a chance we might get to our missing captain. I hadn't considered the cost to morale, only our bellies, when I'd sent them after the strange merchantman.

The *Wretched Lady* needed more than Griffin back, more than hard biscuits and dried goat. She deserved a return to normalcy. In lieu of that, I would give her a little fun.

A pinch of the old Connor slid in to act.

I hadn't consulted my mates, but they agreed heartily. Some revelry was in order.

Silver muttered something about missed opportunities as he slid into Trenna's abandoned seat.

"Missed the whole summer, you mean!" Rory exclaimed, elbowing me in the side. "And all for the benefit of our guests."

"If they'd like to come, yes." I pretended I had not spent

some time wondering just how Regula would look in the candle-light, her skirts caught up to dance, with fiddling lively enough to lift her from her feet.

"Beer and song and celebration. That's all. The rest we'll save for the next full moon." I tried my hardest to ignore Rory as I listened to myself.

Raiding was a good life, but it was a hard one. Most pirates chose the full moon to let the intensity go, fighting and fucking and feasting across the deck in the warmer months, and below it during the cooler ones. Who was I to ask them to rein it in?

Rory let me wallow for only a moment in my hypocrisy.

"How about whiskey? I won a cask from the cove's barkeep." This put a smile on most everyone's face.

Trenna wasn't pleased.

"We're returning those girls, aren't we? Maybe we should give them a night to remember."

"Seas, Trenna, you can't mean that." She couldn't see me sweating. "Things are different in Sanctuary. The walls might well be built on consequences instead of bedrock."

"Connor's right. They aren't pirates, and aren't to be pirates." Rory glared at me, even if Trenna was the one in need of convincing.

"They're people, you brutes, who *can* decide for themselves."

"Decide they want to join a pirate orgy?" We all startled.

Jack of the Long Legs was perched behind us, smug bottom resting on the curve of the railing.

Trenna huffed out a laugh.

"If they want to fuck, they'll fuck. Whether at your revel or in that big empty bed," she grumbled.

"Don't worry, Trenna, Connor'll see them satisfied..." Jack uncrossed her arms and leaned back over the deck. "One way or another." She winked at me.

Furious heat streaked up my neck. I was going to—

"Enough!" Trenna said, throwing her hands up. She stepped back from our argument and disappeared down the stairs.

Rory jogged after her, leaving Silver to the wheel and Jack and me at each other's throats.

"Packages safely trussed up and locked away, eh, Captain?"

I didn't owe her a response, nor was I foolish enough to be caught in a trap of words.

"You've got a sharp one there. Pretty too. Pity you'll be serving her up to the city." Jack watched me a touch too closely.

"It's none of your business, cooper," I spat, baited against my better judgment. "You disagree? You should have spoken up at the meeting. Never bothered to stay silent before."

"Hadn't had the pleasure of the lady's acquaintance," she said, talking casually out of the side of her mouth.

My body tensed again. I bit back my reaction.

It was unreasonable to be upset about anyone's acquaintance with anyone else. For all I knew, Jack had struck up this little friendship to goad me. Regula and I were bound by no promises. There was nothing for Jack to muck up. My fists refused to listen to reason, bunching at my sides where they should have been resting.

"Take your petty squabbles off my deck," Silver boomed at us over a shoulder. "If you're going to argue, save it for tonight when you're soused and we can all watch."

I debated declaring it my deck, but decided against it. Silver waved us both toward the stairs despite my scowl.

"She's a pirate through and through, Connor," Jack hissed, her words carrying up the steps to where I followed. "The other one too, the fancy one. Give them half a chance." She shot me a look more poisonous than her usual. "You don't even want them at the revel, do you?"

I should have fought her on that. I wanted Regula at the revel, in my arms. Or anywhere, any way she'd have me. Hardly Jack's business, though.

"I wouldn't have to lock them up in my cabin if rogues like you weren't sniffing around."

We squared off on the open deck, circling each other. For months now, she'd questioned my every decision, my every move.

"That's rich, Connor. I'm the one sniffing, but you're, what, pillaging? If she'd rather spend her night on my lap than yours, she should be given that choice. Shit, she might pick my lap for the rest of her life if you weren't tide bent on sending her back."

I snatched at Jack's elbow, digging my fingers into the fabric of her coat, dragging her with me. She fought me every step of the way to the bow. A little more privacy for our brawl.

"There is no other choice, Jack," I grunted. She ground her boot heel over my toes. "Tell me another way to get Griffin back. We have no sailors. We have no money. We can't get into Sanctuary. Can't even open the door."

"No other choice?" Jack regarded me with bared teeth. "None of us had a choice in anything until we became pirates."

I tried to remember where she'd come from, but we'd never been close, and I hadn't bothered to learn.

"There's no guarantee the city will even want them back. Maybe we'll sacrifice them and ourselves in the process. Griffin would dunk you in the deep for this, at least a few times." Her words were a curse. Her eyes flicked toward the heavy wooden door of my chambers.

"There is naught else I can do! Would you rather gamble, or lose everything without even playing Sanctuary's game?"

"We've all played it, Connor. It is only luck that stands between us and the gallows. There is no beating them. All we pirates do is run and hide." She pressed in so close I could see the points of her canines. "That city can and will eat a person up. It very nearly got you, I reckon, and half the ship as well. Will you resign Regula to that? Is that what your interest buys her? Your tongue? Your touch?" She jabbed a square finger into my chest and shame crept over me.

Did Jack have a spy in my mind, to so thoroughly sense my own misgivings, my own fears and doubts? I'd packed and stored them away, but she'd brought them out in simple, unavoidable terms.

"Consider it, Connor. Consider them," she said finally, her cold eyes searching my face. With the wind gusting and the sun beating down, holding her gaze was like being accosted by a creature of old—something my ancestors had trembled at, the sort with a secret knowledge of the human heart.

She turned on her heel and marched off. I doubted I would be able to summon her again.

Seas, Regula was a vision.

She spun from Rory's arms to Trenna's and back again, exhilarated and breathless from laughing. Her hair was half-down, beckoning me against her back. I was beginning to understand her insistence upon her Sanctuary skirts, watching them flutter and kick in time with Billy's fiddle.

I stopped in my tracks just to watch her. If all it took to shake off her mysteries was a turn about the dance floor, I would have to wait in line. Both Regula and Odette were well attended, with pirates on their feet all around them, stomping and whirling their partners to the music.

I was late. Late enough that there was only a whisper of liquor left in the bottom of Rory's barrel. Cups were strewn across the rest of its crate, and someone had already tapped the beer behind it. I contemplated leaving for the haven of Griffin's cabin, where I'd have plenty of whiskey and none of this... distraction.

Unfortunately, I was captain now, and was expected to show up to my own parties. Ignoring the cups, I lifted the oak cask to my lips and let the last of it burn down my throat.

Lost in the darkness of my drink, I felt rather than saw the arms that circled my shoulders. It was an effort not to choke when I turned my head to find Trenna an inch from my nose. Her breath gave me a good idea who'd been drinking all the whiskey.

"Makes sense why everyone's been so touchy, Captain," she murmured, plucking the upturned cask from my grip with both her hands and sending the final drops flying toward the dancers. "Those girls are a treat."

I turned, choosing to stare her down rather than lose myself in the object of her booze-soaked musing.

"Pity, that." Trenna peered at the cask's empty bottom with a frown before dropping it. Whether she was talking about women or whiskey I didn't have time to figure out. She grabbed my wrist and tugged me over to a nearby bench, shoving Pella and Isadore over to make space for us.

I sank down, grateful there'd been no choice in the matter. As enticing as it was, dancing wasn't an option for me today, not with anyone. It was doing my crew some good, though. No hint of our regretful summer, nor fear for our future mixed in with the merriment. We were pirates. We were meant to live like this. Sanctuary's walls or the comfort of an island town would never have been enough to satisfy us.

Whiskey surged into my bloodstream. I felt fucking good for once. I set an elbow into the wall and didn't fight the grin that spread over my face.

I could handle being captain if my crew kept dancing, especially if it meant they left me alone. I was hardly betraying my station if I watched, my eyes lingering on one figure in particular.

Rory twirled Regula almost close enough to touch, her heels endangering Trenna's freshly shined boots and her fingers an inch from tangling in the lace of Pella's extravagant pants. Faster and faster, as Billy raced toward the crescendo with her bow.

And then stopped, her heel slamming into the floor to end the song.

Every pirate in the room dipped their partner, whooping and

whistling for more. Rory dipped his right over my open lap, so close I felt the caress of her loose hair.

I was halfway to outrage, and Regula to realization, when Rory stopped teasing us and dropped her against my chest. My arms circled her body, my knees tucking under hers, instinctively. Her weight and warmth were a welcome surprise. It was a battle to keep from nuzzling her hair as she gasped in indignation.

Rory roared with laughter until Pella and Isadore linked his elbows and dragged him back onto the dance floor with them. Trenna snorted at his back and scooted down the empty bench. Her hand snaked around my shoulders and caught my chin from the side, turning my face her way.

"Don't be a fool, Connor." I could guess what she was talking about this time.

With that, she winked and stood, heading back to the beer.

And then Regula and I were alone in a room full of pirates. Our bodies pressed together. The perfect column of her neck within kissing distance. Her chest rising and falling against mine.

I felt her hand in my hair and, for the life of me, I thought she would kiss me. Here. In front of everyone. We shouldn't, not in the middle of a revel.

If she did, I would fucking kiss her back. Tonight. Tomorrow. Damn the consequences. Damn my own plans.

But she was wriggling out of my clutches with more than a dose of fire in her eyes. For an instant, my arms would not cooperate. Holding her felt right, even if it was far beyond bounds.

I let her go.

Regula only went as far as the bench beside me. Her spark was reserved for Rory, who was dancing too fast to really burn beneath her gaze.

When she looked at me, her face was full of regret.

"I'm sorry, Connor. I swear, I didn't put him up to that." She didn't quite manage a smile. My brow furrowed. I opened my mouth to reassure her. Whatever she thought—

Long Legs stomped up to us, appearing from some shadowy corner or another.

"You just can't help yourself, can you?" she snapped at me. She'd been at the drink too, by the looks of it, her tanned face flushed and her jacket lost.

To Regula, she managed a polite bow, holding out a hand.

"Dance with me, lady?"

Bloody seas. Would that I had wiped that smirk off her face earlier. Old Connor wouldn't have hesitated.

I was up on my feet before she could blink, stepping in front of her offending hand.

Regula, a hint of annoyance in her voice, ignored me and accepted, and Jack reached out, pulling her past me without a second thought.

I stared after Regula, unable to blink when the pirate swept her up and off across the planks.

I wanted to snatch her back. I wanted—

I shouldn't. Jack of the Long Legs wasn't the one who planned to sell her back to Sanctuary. Jack hadn't lost herself between Regula's legs with a seas-cursed lie on the tip of her tongue. I sank heavily back onto the bench, my fingernails cutting into the meat of my hands as I watched the two of them fly around the room.

Even as my blood boiled, the truth rang inside of my head. Regula deserved more than me. If she picked Jack…

I should just swallow my pride and bow out. I should never have bowed in.

I kept searching for her, even as she twirled. It would be far easier to do the right thing if her eyes didn't lock with mine on every pass.

Regula—

My gaze was interrupted.

Jack had just backed the two of them into another trio of dancers.

Everything slowed, as the pirate took a look at the scene she'd interrupted.

Isadore was sandwiched between Pella and Cesare, dancing close enough that it wouldn't be unusual for a full moon's night. Pella and Cesare were one thing. Whose heart hadn't they made a play for? Robin sat half-broken on the far side of the room, mooning over them.

Isadore was another. She was new, beautiful, and obviously interested in their game. She and Jack, though... There was history there. She'd asked about Long Legs when she signed on. Grown up in the same town or something. I hadn't thought a thing about it. The "or something" was looking more and more realistic. If I was heated that Jack had stolen Regula from my side, Jack was as mad as a dog over a bone at Pella and Cesare.

"Stay away from her, you leeches!" Jack bellowed, loud enough to freeze the dancers and startle Billy into lowering her bow.

"Seas, Dore, they don't care about you. Look at Robin..." She switched to pleading with Isadore, in a voice that would have been soft if it hadn't been for the freshly silent room. "Nobody matters to them."

"None of your business, Jack," Pella said, inserting herself between them.

"*You* keep your hands off her."

I popped up from the bench. Regula was standing a little behind Jack, a discarded toy. I shouldn't revel in Jack's outburst, but it—

It was the sort of thing that called for a captain.

If they came to blows, it might be more than their friendship could handle. Or more than the *Wretched Lady* could. We needed our cooper, our carpenter, and our best eyes all in working order.

I started moving, weaving in between the frozen dancers. The whole room watched.

"Does it look like I mind, Jack?" Isadore coiled herself back into Cesare's embrace, her voice clear in the quiet.

Jack sniffed. I was almost close enough to step between them.
"You don't want—"

"I don't want what? You might be better off asking what I do want, Jack." Isadore stretched over to turn Pella's head, speaking an inch from her lips. "But you'd never do that. You've never bothered. Fuck off."

"Your hands are more than welcome," Isadore said to the other two, her arms looping around each of their shoulders. "Let's find someplace a little quieter."

Pella's face split in a grin, and she stuck her tongue out at Jack as she was pulled along toward the companionway. Cesare didn't bother looking back, his head tilted against Isadore's.

Jack's fists clenched.

I caught her by the shoulder.

"Leave it, Jack."

I expected a punch. I welcomed it. Let me be her enemy right now. Griffin would have handled things differently, but I wasn't him. Connor was all I could be.

Her blow didn't land.

It never even launched.

When she turned to me, Jack's face was worse than a punch. She looked like she'd taken a shot through the chest, all her blood drained out, the anger she'd held a moment ago lost to despair.

We weren't friends. Never had been. But I hesitated to take my hand from her shoulder in case it was the only thing holding her up.

I scanned the room, desperate to avoid the deadened look in Jack's eyes. The music hadn't started back up and everyone was still. Everyone except Regula. She stepped forward and took Jack's elbow, her eyes full of questions as she started whispering nonsense in the pirate's ear.

My jealousy retreated, and pity took its place.

"Alright, alright, I think we're in need of some music," I called out.

The tension in the room whooshed out with the first note from Billy's bowstrings.

30

REGULA

It was unnerving how easy it was to hustle Jack to a seat in the corner as the revel reignited around us. Connor was close behind.

After a moment, she started to perk back up, though her mood was far fouler than before.

I'd seen Connor grab her, goading her as a distraction. It should have worked. Now Jack seemed willing to take him up on the offer, shaking me off and shooting up into his face.

"Should've let me—"

"Jack, you're acting like a fool. The carpenter was clear." I cut in, before Jack worked up enough spittle to shower Connor. Or worse. I feared no one would win if they went at it, especially here where the other pirates might join in.

She seemed to remember me then, her fury falling away. Even at her most pissed, Jack was ever the gentlewoman. She'd rather fight with her captain than a lady, no matter how ill I fit the title.

It took a moment for her knees to follow the corners of her mouth, buckling. She thumped back into her seat.

"Leave me. Both of you."

Connor opened his mouth, closed it, and opened it again. "Someone should—" A hand landed on his wrist.

"Someone will." Rory was at his side.

I stayed stock-still, not sure what I might add.

"Seas, just leave." Jack dumped her head into her hands. Rory dropped onto a nearby crate, shooing us away with his hands.

Connor was the first to turn and walk off.

I followed him, my eyes alighting, as they were trained to do, on Odette in the mess of dancers. With Billy occupied, she'd been constant companions with Alecto, who seemed to be much in the company of his own mother.

The captain ducked out of the room toward the deck, and I decided Alecto's mother was probably a better chaperone than I would ever be.

The cold sea air was lovely against my heated skin as I stepped out into the passageway.

I peered around, Connor having disappeared, until I spotted him leaning behind the door.

"What are you doing?"

"Told me to leave. I left." His voice was clipped. I couldn't quite see his face without the golden light from the revel. It was late and growing later.

"Aren't you their captain?"

"I don't care, Regula. Not about anything." He came away from the dark, though the shadows remained in his eyes.

"Connor, that can't be true."

He shook his head, taking another step toward me. Had it been someone else, I might have felt afraid. Not Connor, though.

Connor whose hand circled my wrist and drew me to him.

"Come with me."

He leaned to the side, sliding open a port I hadn't even noticed. Hidden stairs extended down to the lower decks under the soft but strange pulsing of what I guessed was one of the ship's only working charms. Then he stepped through, looking up at me with those deep honey eyes. His face was at once resigned and hopeful, bathed in the uneven light of the first magic I'd seen in years.

I couldn't return to the revel without him, and maybe I didn't want to return at all.

I let myself follow him once more.

"I'll be damned if I leave you to the cooper," he muttered, almost too low for my ears, before continuing down to the next floor. I was sure I should not have heard him.

"Jack's not so bad." It hadn't been a jab, but he stopped dead in the doorway and whirled around.

His hand flew to the planking at my side. I did not run into his arm, but I might have, had I been looking anywhere but at his back. His eyes pinned me in place.

"You like her?" His lip curled in a way that seemed quite unlike the captain I knew, and more like a hardened pirate. I shivered.

"Whatever there is between you and the cooper isn't my concern." I would not be cowed by his big arms, nor crowded into a corner of the stairs. "She was beyond kind until…" I left the rest unsaid. Jack had unraveled in front of the both of us.

Searching my face, he waited a long time to respond. If the answer to his issue with Jack was in that quiet, he kept it to himself.

Finally, he laughed; a soft, smoldering thing.

"Kind? Has Sanctuary's definition changed so much from my youth? Jack'd have you out of your dress and in all manner of trouble in an instant."

I flushed. "Not so different from you, then."

His jaw dropped. It took a moment for him to recover, clacking his teeth back together, the muscles in his jaw tightening.

"If I remember correctly, your skirts stayed on, love." I watched as the heat in his eyes smoothed over into practiced flirtation. Bright but not intense, interested but not overly.

I was the one to pause, for he set my heart racing far faster than all this evening's dancing, and I would not, under any circumstance, let him win this battle of words.

It was a simple matter to duck under his arm, letting our bodies press close for an instant, and to murmur from the hallway ahead of him, "I'm amazed you remember anything of me at all, with your cross looks and penchant for ordering me around." I minced a little for his benefit, less sure of my heading than I pretended and a trifle afraid of the murky depths of the ship. "It's enough to hurt a girl's feelings."

I did not pout, as Odette might have, but my challenge found flesh. It was satisfying how fast he caught up.

"That is not..." he started. "I didn't mean to..."

I decided to end his misery. "Unless you'd like to let Jack sour our friendship, I would suggest you wrestle with her another time."

I chanced a look back at him. I was not walking very fast now, as I had no real destination, and he was very close behind me, so much so that the bells of propriety instilled in me in the city were ringing loudly in the back of my mind. Let them. I might never see Sanctuary again.

I spun lightly and stopped, letting him run right into me.

His arms swept up to my shoulders and back, keeping me on my feet. Caught well and truly before I could come to any harm. Any, that is, not of my own making.

"You are entirely right. Forgive me, Regula, I've been a swine," he said, our bodies crushed close.

"One would almost believe you to be ruled by impulse rather than logic," I teased, skimming my finger over his lapel. "Are you a captain or a rogue?"

"Can I not be both?" He bit at my finger, his breath skating over my hand. The snap of his teeth was loud in my ear.

"Please," I whispered, rather forgetting the stairs behind us and the party beyond them.

I tousled his hair where it tapped the curve of his jaw, and pulled his head down into a kiss. It was a breathless, argumentative meeting, with none of our earlier accord. The sort that can only be finished in the dark. We were spectacularly exposed in the half light of the hallway.

Connor must have had the same thought, pulling away for the space of a breath to fumble with the handle of a nearby door.

I barely had a chance to take in the space, a closet of sorts, before I was swept into it and the glow of the hallway was lost.

NOW HERE WAS MY DARKNESS. CONNOR WAS THERE TO MEET ME in it, his hands never quite leaving me, even as we maneuvered around the cramped space.

"I could have sworn you were upset about this," he said, tugging playfully at the neckline of my dress.

I didn't bother to answer, my fingers fighting with the fastenings. The captain pressed me to him, stopping my fumbling, his hands taking the place of mine. He undid the few laces over my back, my face cradled against his warm shoulder. How could a closet be so full of him?

He peeled my sleeves down and let the rest of my dress slide with them, forgetting the task in my neck for a moment, where his lips whispered against my sensitive skin.

"Seems a shame you can't see this," I whispered in his ear, my fingers weaving into his hair.

"Oh? Shall we return to the hallway, then?" He spoke into my bared bosom, stooping to follow my clothing.

"No!" I squeaked, holding him tightly to me, so he might not reach for the handle.

"No? Alright, my Eagle, have no fear." He chuckled against my shoulder, sliding his hands back to my waist, sending my skirts finally to the floor, and my chemise shortly after them. "Now, what would you like, Regula? How might I satisfy you?"

I was well on my way, breathing in the consuming blackness of the space and his warm, salted scent on the close air. I wanted plenty, like the fairness of our nakedness to be addressed, but I could not sort my thoughts out for the life of me.

"Are you sure you're capable of satisfying me?" I asked, drawing him up for a kiss. I caught his outrage on my tongue, and let him joust with it until we met the wall and set all the hanging implements to twisting and rattling.

"With you by my side, Regula, I have a feeling I will accomplish much," he said into my mouth. "Much more than before." His hands found the curve of my buttocks and lifted, spinning me so my back was as good as a lock on the door. "Is this—" He accentuated the sweet friction between us with a roll of his hips. "—what you need, my Eagle?"

Ah, yes. I squeezed my legs tight about him, his arms and the door providing support enough for me to enjoy myself.

"Or do I disappoint?" He released his hold ever so slightly, his hands promising to disappear just as easily as they'd slid over me.

"No! Don't you dare move!" I half screamed, my desperation echoing around the small space. "I want you, Connor." I let the tips of my fingers trail across the shirt I longed to rip off his back.

It was near pain to wait, all bound up, naked, in his arms.

"Is that right?" He did not, however, need me to repeat my words. "A little help, love?"

In our haste, we had not bothered to free his cock from his pants, and now it pressed between us, all trussed up. I slid a hand down, loosening things only as much as I needed to pull him hard from his breeches.

"Regula, wait, we should… I should get a sheath." I blinked at him in the dark. I didn't intend to, but I found myself laughing —a fresh, real kind of laugh, like I hadn't in a long time. I slipped from his arms, my feet hitting the planking. It took me a moment to catch my breath, his calloused hands attentive on my waist.

"I'm barren, Connor." I was quite unused to saying such a thing out loud, though it had haunted my inner thoughts for years on end. "It won't matter."

He made a noise, of acknowledgment I think, for there was nothing in it of pity or disgust, before his hand came up to my cheek. He stroked me there like a pet, reassuring, solid.

"All the better." His growl did not mesh with the care of his touch, but he soon matched the two, his hands rediscovering my thighs and scooping me up in a single demanding motion. I gasped, draping my arms around his neck as he kissed me brutally.

My admission had been fragile and uncomfortable, but this touch was anything but. Perhaps I could trust his words. Perhaps it was better this way, with nothing between us, no threat of a child to bind us, no fear of consequence.

Yes, I thought, conceding the point to myself and banishing the last of my fears. I could not blame myself anymore, or hide in my own regret and unhappiness. I decided to become something new against his lips, worthy of the attention. My hips lost their shyness and I let them meet his, grinding. His cock slid against my wet cunt, over and over, less of a tease and more of a promise.

It was the work of a moment to reach between us and guide him where I truly wanted him. Connor blew out a breath against my neck, my touch a shock, though a welcome one. For all his pressing me against a door and ravishing me, he was gentle and unbearably slow as he entered me.

Too polite by half.

In the dimness of the closet, I was brimming with confidence, and could not bear his care. I was used to the short pain of entry, and unused to the pleasure I'd felt at the mercy of his mouth and his hands. I scored my fingers under his shirt and over his back, hurrying him along.

"Is that all?" I goaded him, unable to hold back my discontent. I nipped at his ear, rolling the lobe between the tips of my teeth, until he slid all the way in, my back flush with the wood and my pussy full of him.

"It is *not*." He pulled back and thrust as he spoke. "As you well know."

I could not, by any means, have stopped the moan he called from me as he continued. I was as one possessed, meeting him and riding away, chasing my own pleasure. The confinement of the closet, the strange headiness of his attention, and my shrinking fear of discovery drove me to a shaky madness, unrivaled in all my years.

I knew he felt it, as I did his hot breath on my ear. His hand snaked up to play with my nipple, reordering my consciousness. I thought I might very well split from my skin, falling to pieces under the practiced, relentless sweep of his cock.

I did not have much experience in losing myself, but he surely had brought many to mindlessness, for he found my mouth again, shifting our angle ever so slightly, throwing us even further into delicious contact. I tried to kiss him back, I did, but that I could now feel every stroke, every inch he took from me. I was an exposed nerve, and he'd set me aflame.

The feeling splintered, streaking from our joining to the tips of my fingers, down the bend of my knees, and up to bolster the unruly roses in my cheeks. I gasped into him, mouth to mouth, riding the peak he'd wrung from me. He smiled against me, circling an arm around my ribs and clenching me tighter, bucking into me faster and harder, until he'd drawn the same heat for himself from the coils of my last climax.

When he slowed, empty and softening inside me, we clutched each other in the velvety blackness, beads of sweat tracing the hollows we'd just kissed.

Connor lowered me to my feet. His cock slid away, though his hands stayed steady on me. I was grateful, for I wasn't sure my shaky legs would hold. I felt him search for me in the darkness, felt the brush of his cheek and nose before he caught my lips.

It was a long time before we ended our unhurried crush of limbs. A true exploring. Nothing like the lust we'd burned out, but beautiful in itself. I cursed again at his clothes and the lack of light, allowing my fingertips to discover as much they could, even impeded.

I enjoyed lingering with a lover, I realized, never having had the opportunity before.

Much was unspoken, or said with the touch of an eyelash or the soft glide of a hand. I did not so much ask for his help, as he intuited I should be drawn back into my dress. The sensation of it sliding back on was perhaps more stimulating than it coming off in the first place. I was raw against the fabric, so different from the hard heat of his chest or the knowing flex of his hands.

We gave ourselves the best reordering we could manage in the closet, knocking about the tools and cabinets as little as possible. I was certain I would look so thoroughly ravished that even a perfect handmaiden could not have set me to rights. My lips buzzed, and I did not doubt my skin was rosy from his touch.

"Exquisite," he whispered, rough and conspiratorial, into the final clasp of my bodice.

I ran a hand through his hair and contemplated whether we might lose more time to another kiss.

31

REGULA

I t was a long time before we returned to the revel. So long, in fact, that when we stumbled in, there was little point in keeping our smiles to ourselves.

Most of the pirates had disappeared, along with the music. A few lingered on the edges, but the center of the room, which had doubled as a dance floor, was empty.

I was relieved to see Odette keeping Rory company on the crates where we'd left him. Jack had abandoned her chair and now sat with her wrists braced on her knees against the wall a few paces away. Her eyes were locked on a horizon thousands of miles away.

No matter how much straightening of clothes or pinning of hair we'd done in the closet, we were close to being found out, because we couldn't stop whispering to each other. Already, Rory and Odette's eyes narrowed from across the room, and we'd drawn even Jack's attention.

Thinking it best if we separated, I went to Odette and let Connor continue on to check in with Long Legs. There seemed little danger of her blackening his eye anymore.

Odette's pretty face was split in a grin, her eyes alight at the sight of my happiness.

"Now, wasn't that fun?"

"Yes, for my first pirate revel," I said. I was hesitant to reveal more, though Rory was hardly innocent of the situation. He'd walked in on Connor with his head between my legs. "I found it quite satisfactory."

It was impossible to contain my giggle. Gods, I was sickening. Was this the Regula I'd been shoving down for years?

Odette was outright laughing at me. Rory was politely watching after Connor and Jack, even though I had surely heard a baritone snicker following my words.

"Regula, I did not expect to enjoy it so much when you finally lost your head around a lover, much less a pirate," she said in a stage whisper. Finally, I had the perfect candidate on whom to practice my glare.

"Oh, you brat. I have only a few scant days left in the company of people who don't see me as your shadow or some sort of stain on my family's good name. Should I not enjoy it?"

Odette frowned prettily, a furrow appearing between her brows. I think she considered us sisters in all ways. It was nice, sweet even, though I was her much pitied and nearly unmentionable nursemaid to all others in Sanctuary.

"I suppose so. I didn't mean… I'm glad, Regula. I would rather see you like this than forgotten in the corner of a great salon." Odette's frown lightened. "It suits you. You've brightened up, especially for someone who nearly drowned."

"Feels like a lifetime ago," I muttered, gentling my own expression.

"Do you think your captain will catch them? The *Edgewater*?" she asked, serious now. Her eyes darted toward Connor.

"My captain?" I scoffed. "I suppose so." If I weren't in such a good mood, I'd swat at her. "He seems sure of the *Wretched Lady*. The ship craves a good many things. Our revenge is one of them."

I followed her gaze across the room.

Jack was standing now, the dead look on her face gone. In its place was the disdain Connor seemed to bring out in her. She wouldn't let go of whatever was between them any more than Connor would. Pirates.

"I was thinking of retiring, but if..." Odette trailed off, her implication clear. I wasn't sure I could sleep at this point, riled as I was, whether I curled up next to her or Connor. Rest was far from me tonight.

I could not help myself, looking again at Connor, only to find Jack storming over. The captain stared after her, shades of worry in his eyes.

The pirate yanked at my shoulder, spinning me around. Rory's boots clattered on the floor, but even he wasn't fast enough to keep her from opening her mouth.

"Don't think for an instant that he cares for you. He's going to return you to Sanctuary. Sell you back for our captain." Rory dragged Jack off. My skin was red where she'd gripped me. Her words echoed in my ears. "You'll never be pirates, either of you. Not if he's left in charge."

Connor was a step behind Jack, but it wasn't his face that betrayed the truth of her words.

It was Rory's.

He looked anywhere but at us, even as he snatched the cooper back.

For once, I was too shocked to think or speak.

I hadn't—

"No. No, you can't." It was Odette who responded first, almost too quiet to hear. "I'll go back alone, if I must. Don't... don't take her back. They don't care about her. I'm the one they'd trade for."

My stomach sank to my feet. Jack shook Rory off, two giants struggling, while I felt as small as a mouse.

"He won't risk it, will you, Connor? Returning a lady is one thing, but returning her with a witness? A chaperone? Even better." She addressed the captain, then me. "Ask him. He won't ruin his best chance to get Griffin back."

With that, Jack stormed out, leaving us with her revelation.

I didn't have to ask Connor. Only to look at his face.

Ah, what a mistake I'd made. *This* was what had haunted him. *This* hung between us. Not Jack. Not my drowning. I hadn't bothered to look past the obvious, fool that I was.

I'd imagined myself a pirate. I'd let him style me as his queen.

All for nothing.

In an effort to keep my face from the floor, I tightened my lips and left.

I stomped all the way from the room, and all the way up the stairs, and all the way across the freezing deck.

I even tried to slam the heavy door to the captain's chambers. Against its battered wood, I swore I would not venture past its protection until I quit the *Wretched Lady* for good.

32

REGULA

Odette had returned shortly after I had, her fury matching mine, and we'd worn ourselves out with talking and crying. Then more talking and more crying.

Morning came sooner than I was ready for, bringing Billy with it. She tiptoed around outside for a while, meaning she, and probably everyone else on board, had heard what transpired last night. I felt a hint of relief when we let her in and she wouldn't meet either of our eyes.

She *should* regret conspiring to get rid of us. Just as I would regret sleeping with her captain. The *Wretched Lady*'s kitchens could serve remorse instead of those rotten biscuits, for all I cared.

She came bearing the message that we—that the ship had caught up to the *Edgewater* in the night, much sooner than expected. Odette and I were to be confined to the cabin until engagement was ended, no matter how the fighting went.

I was so exhausted from the night before that this did not concern me at all. I had already taken a pummeling; what was the promise of cannon fire on top of everything else?

Last night I'd thrown away my pretty ideas of pirate life. I'd tossed away Coisume, as well, for I could not outrun Connor's crew in a city I'd never set foot in, not if the *Wretched Lady* wanted to catch me. Sanctuary was all that was left to me.

I no longer tasted freedom upon my tongue, and found no satisfaction in anything.

Well, no satisfaction besides shooing Billy out and shutting the door on her.

It was so much worse to press my back against the door this time. The world I wanted to keep out was far more real by the light of day.

What truly hurt, more than anything else, was that Connor was right. He wanted his friend back, his captain, and we were the best way to do it. Perhaps his only way, if he was to be believed about how the *Wretched Lady* had spent her summer.

I could explain it to myself, but I couldn't ease the ache in my chest.

He hadn't lied, exactly. And we'd never promised each other anything.

It still hurt.

If he'd told me... No, it wouldn't change anything. Odette and I would always come second to his ship. It was folly to think otherwise, to have hoped for more.

We were stuck.

Odette flopped, as dejected as I was, onto the creaky chaise. I counted my blessings that she'd avoided the desk, considering, well... I opted for the chair, shoving it over against the wall in an attempt to look out the high windows.

Billy hadn't told us much. There was no sound of cannon. No stomping of boots.

What was happening out there?

The wide seat was enough of a boost to have me head and shoulders above the sill, where nothing awaited me but waves and wake.

Odette watched me as I placed my elbows on the thin ledge, pressing my nose to the glass. My life was to be all closed doors and unfinished, unfulfilled business. Hers? I hoped hers would be better. I sighed, my breath fogging the window ever so slightly.

"You are suddenly quite free with the furniture," Odette remarked. I did not bother to turn to her, letting her pointed comment fall between us. "I've never seen you stand on anything before."

"My last chance at piracy," I bit at her, hoping my words did not sound as harsh to her as they did to me. I was rarely desperate for my own company, and often avoided it, but right now, I longed to sink into my own bitter lot and wallow in my own unrest.

"Don't tell me you considered it? Becoming a pirate, I mean. Regula, I did not think—" Her pity was as strong as perfume in the air, and I was in no mood for it.

"Was I the only one?" I crooked an eyebrow at her. "Your days of playing chase with Billy are just as short as mine."

It was a long time before either of us spoke again.

I tried to focus on the horizon, but all I saw was my own reflection, distorted in the old glass.

"I've never been in a battle before." She'd gotten quieter.

"I should hope not, Odette, though you do have the look of a killer." I shouldn't have been teasing in a mood like this. "Perhaps they made a mistake locking us in here. You should be the first over the side so you can scare the navy half to death."

"Regula, don't joke. I cry when they shoot the stag on the First's holy day. Spilling a man's blood must be much worse." That was one way to reason it.

"Well, we're out on unfamiliar waters, with pirates who barely tolerate us. Did you expect to bundle yourself up in compliments and finery to keep yourself safe? It might have worked for you in the city..." I turned to her then, settling a hand on the sill to balance myself. "I suppose you might still manage it. Besides, the navy cannot truly mean you ill. Your father would have their heads. And we know the pirates won't kill us. They need us."

"My father isn't here. The navy already—" Her voice broke at the thought. Odette was not a crier, unless it suited her and I was tempted to leap down to her.

I stopped myself.

I could no longer be the one to wipe away her tears. Even if we both stayed in Sanctuary, rather than carrying out our grand plans, she would soon be married, and I would be nothing more to her than a memory.

"Odette, who are they to decide whether you are a pirate or not! If the need arises, you will protect yourself." My tone verged on scolding. "You're skilled with your hairpins, and a well-placed bite or scratch can be as effective as any blade. Perhaps, if we had more time, you could master a pistol... or we could commission you a golden hilted dagger to conceal in one of your puffed sleeves." I was trying to rouse her from her mood, to distract her from the fact that I could not control the path of a cannonball or predict what a man like Captain Forewell might do with us should the *Wretched Lady*'s luck turn foul.

Betrayed and heartbroken as I was, the pirates had treated us far better than the ship we'd sailed out on. I prayed to the gods that no harm would befall the crew. I squeezed my eyes shut and found Connor's face pressed there.

He had to survive.

I needed to hear him beg for my forgiveness, just as he'd begged for my favor.

CONNOR

I HATED MYSELF, AND I STILL HAD TO CAPTAIN THE SEAS-CURSED ship.

Griffin wouldn't have made even one of my mistakes, much

less the full set. If he hadn't left… Regula and I never would have met. She wouldn't be barricaded in my cabin, pissed as hell. I never would have seen her soften. Never tasted her salted skin.

I was struggling to maintain my focus.

I had to run the *Wretched Lady*. My crew was half-drunk, and the *Edgewater* was within our sights. I would not sail on by.

Leaving the revel early had done Cesare some good. His eyes had been fresh when he'd spotted the ship on the far horizon. The night crew was carrying us now, as everyone else stole a few more moments to sober up.

If I could not keep Regula with me, if I could not be the man she needed, I might at least mete out a little vengeance in her name. Forewell would regret dumping the women. That I swore.

Now that the prize was back in my spyglass, I wondered if there was another way, one where Odette and Regula might stay with us, or wherever they wanted.

Would the city trade a captain for a captain? We'd had no problem routing Forewell the first time. Sanctuary had gone to great lengths to dress up his ship, so his mission must be of some importance. Perhaps he would be a better bargaining chip.

Better for me, anyway, if I could convince Regula to forgive me.

I found I wanted her to stay. I could use her counsel. I wanted it even now that I'd ruined things between us.

I shook off my thoughts and headed up to the helm. Rory stood at Trenna's shoulder, and Silver leaned against the railing, banished by the better navigator.

I took a moment to thank the seas for them; the best crew I ever could have asked for.

The deck was calm and settled, the day crew slowly marching up from their bunks to their stations. Ready as they'd ever be.

The navy would regret the day they'd trifled with Regula and Odette's lives. All sailors, pirate or otherwise, knew the cost of the sea's service. It was the greatest cowardice to sacrifice the innocent to protect oneself or one's secrets.

I would relish the crunch of wood when our cannons hit.

"Captain." Trenna sounded far too excited to press the *Wretched Lady*'s nose into the enemy. "How would you like us to approach?"

It was a formality really, a kindness she did me. I'd been a runner in most of our battles, a gunner on occasion. What I'd learned of strategy, she and Griffin had taught me.

"The third maneuver," I said, after a long look toward our quarry. "What do you think?" She'd invented the maneuvers, after all, sharing long nights with Griffin trying to guess at all the ways one might enter a battle.

The third was effective. Subtle, when the navy would be on the lookout for sharp. It was a zeroing in that could easily be missed by the other ship. A deflection, almost.

If we'd seen them, the *Edgewater* most certainly had eyes on us. Whether they were taken in by our false flags or not, I had to give us the best chance at them.

Forewell would be punished. It was almost a shame it was me doing it, for there were other captains who might bleed him like a stuck pig.

She nodded, considering.

"They will see us," she finally said.

"They already have, if they've got any wits at all," I replied. "If they remember us—and that's a big if—they deserve to quake in their boots."

She looked over at me with a cocked brow, her long black braid swinging.

"Very well. We will meet them in the third."

I was dismissed, grateful to have finished my part in the play.

"Silver, Trenna has the helm." He snorted at my words, for she'd surely told him so only moments before. "Lend a hand where you can, and prepare to board her when the time comes."

"Seas guide you, Connor."

"Guide her, you mean. I'm just the figurehead." I jerked my chin at Trenna.

"Us, then." He grinned at me and made himself scarce, taking the steps two at a time down toward our guns.

Rory situated himself at my elbow. Solid and dependable, he was, especially if you had a girl under your mouth and no need for his company. We'd seen ourselves through tougher situations than this one. He had on his three usual pistols, and I was sure two more were close to hand.

"You'll cover her?" I asked, since no one else was around.

"Always," he said. We couldn't stand to lose Trenna, not for this naval boat, not at all. He'd make sure any undue interest in her was returned tenfold.

I tried to smile at him, gripping his wrist. He returned my rictus.

"To arms, Connor." His hand mirrored mine, just as powerful a clasp, but hopeful too. I let its strength propel me down the stairs and to the center of the deck.

It was imperative that I survived this. I wasn't sure I could apologize to Regula even if I made it through, not really, not when I needed to free Griffin. I sure as hell couldn't offer her a place on this ship, even though I was starting to think she deserved one. I just hoped she'd let me see her, speak to her.

Ah, I'd mucked it all up.

My place now was in the thick of things, and when the time came, I would play my part. I'd be the *Wretched Lady*'s captain, no matter what it took from me.

I had to take on a little of Griffin to do it. There were pieces of me that would help: the swagger, the sharp sword strapped to my waist, the hazy confidence of yesterday's fuck that hadn't yet faded. More I'd learned from my captain, as surely as I held his burnished brass looking glass. I stood under the overhang of the deck, preparing to take up double the space, to become elbows and knees.

A little closer and I'd step out, jaw squared in challenge, to the wind, to the water, and to the navy itself. It was imperative that the *Edgewater* see me here, the threat of me, whenever they deigned to look.

I'd show them the whites of my eyes. My teeth. Let them worry over my blade, set to rend their flesh. I would ignite their fear, and finish it when we boarded. Like my crew, I was ready.

But first, we had to catch up to them, as a regular ship.

The *Edgewater*'s colors shivered against her perfect white sails, the pretense of simple merchant-hood long since abandoned. All pomp and ceremony, but not an ounce of class. I itched to take her. I wanted to plant my boots on her deck and on the throat of her captain. I would shake him a bit, shatter him. There was very little forgiveness in my nature for those who'd exhausted it. What practice I'd missed in making men weep, I would make up for with Forewell.

Our maneuver would sweep us in line with Sanctuary's ship, running slowly as we were across the wind, until we turned with our front cannon primed for their tail. It would take us longer, but would allow us to pretend to be nothing more than a passing ship, with our continent colors, until it was too late.

I eyeballed them, waiting for their attention.

Sure enough, the gleam of a glass sparkled at their helm. I raised a hand, knowing nothing much could be amiss. My sword was tucked away under my belt, my face vague. All our preparations were below, any hint of our attack veiled firmly. If they were smart, and I knew they were not, they might catch on to us for the lack of men in the rigging or out on deck. A seasoned captain would trust his gut on this, but not that lilyliver in his blue-blotted coat.

Or perhaps, I wondered aloud, as I watched a stream of blue appear at the side of the far ship, I should follow my own. My stomach gave a little jump as their hands came up, and shouts echoed across the sea.

They could not know us with these colors. Not with that careless captain. They were guessing. We had not menaced them yet, had hardly even turned in their direction.

I scanned my own deck.

Everything looked normal, a simple ship upon the sea. I checked myself over. Sailors had earrings and captains kept a rapier or two on them. These Sanctuary men were untrained and jumping at shadows.

They were yelling at us too, making a great fuss across the expanse of sea.

I chewed on this, not sure what to make of these bluecoats, yet again. I turned and went back up the stairs for another opinion.

Trenna took my looking glass, though she had her own. There was a comfort to using Griffin's things, a familiarity that I could not fault her for. One could practically feel his fingers where they'd worn into the tool.

When she finally brought it down, I caught the worry in her eyes. Mine were not half so transparent, until a great boom echoed across the water.

Our heads snapped toward the *Edgewater*, and we warred over the glass for a moment. I won it, but not before I saw the puff of black smoke billowing up from the center of our quarry.

"Bloody far to engage," I murmured, my eye to its accustomed hole. The spyglass did not clear anything up. Bluecoats still clamored at the edge of the ship, undisciplined and far from fighting formation. Their faces were full of glee. The cloud behind them rose slowly, unattached, a blip on the horizon. Had they fired? They were out of range, and it did not explain the men who grinned at us from their railing.

"I don't like this," Trenna said through gritted teeth. I agreed wordlessly, my eyes glued to the strange sight.

33

CONNOR

We drew nearer to the *Edgewater*, for we did not change course in our confusion. Not so close as to put ourselves at risk of their cannons, but enough that we could see the city's sailors make a mockery of us without the aid of the spyglass. It was the sort of thing Griffin would have known exactly what to do about. Me, I could only hedge.

The *Wretched Lady* had two options. Attack, though the element of surprise had been lost, or sail past, giving up the chance at Regula's revenge and a fattened purse.

I sucked on the problem. The two urges warred in me.

My strategy was only as good as what I could guess, and the actions of the *Edgewater* were not fitting neatly in with my plans. Trenna did not go against me, holding the ship steady where we should have turned. I was halfway to thanking her when another great cry went up from the men on the far ship.

At first I did not see anything to inspire their shouting.

Then the nervous whirl of my stomach coalesced into a lump, leaden, that threatened to drop from me and straight through the deck.

Tiny specks dotted the horizon at measured intervals. Five, no, at least seven, approaching vessels.

I swung my spyglass back to the *Edgewater*. Ah, the captain had come up top, and he too was laughing, his gaze fixed on us like a brand.

How had they...? It didn't matter. My advantage was gone. The *Wretched Lady*'s revenge would not hold up against eight ships. I had only been betting on the one.

"They're moving fast," Trenna said beside me, a hand on the till and an eye on our adversaries.

I looked closer. The crafts were becoming clearer with each passing moment. They were sleek and small. Lovely, if I saw rightly. Almost reminiscent of the continent's beautiful battleships.

"They're tiny enough to sneak up on us." I frowned down at the top of Trenna's head. I often referred to Sanctuary's fleet as a swarm of flies, but these boats seemed to truly exemplify the concept. A cluster of little vessels, the likes of which I'd never seen, moving faster than should be possible on these waters.

"Captain..." Trenna started. "Connor—"

"Shall we go back the way we came?" They wouldn't follow us into the Graveyard, I was sure.

"Their size, Connor. They could very well risk the maze."

Our ship would be stuck to the razor's edge path only she knew, whereas their boats might be able to skim over the top, cutting us off or harrying us from the sides while we were defenseless.

"No, then." I chewed my lip. "And without the wind we'd never make it back to the Gate..." Our run to the islands would get us nowhere and would put towns like Penny's Cove in danger. The open sea was good, for how seaworthy could something so small be, but it was too far off, and they'd be on us before we could starve them out, nor did we know what followed behind. Obviously Sanctuary had called for reinforcements, albeit strange ones. Damn their pigeons for flying true.

We still had some distance from the *Edgewater*, and more still from the newcomers. Pointed this way, the wind was with us, ready to blow us all the way to shore. We could not hope for the continent, unless we wanted to bash ourselves into an uneven coastline, for a safer path would lead us straight through the smattering of ships that now lined up against us.

There was, in my estimation, only one possible move, and it would require more luck than I wanted to barter with. We needed every second we could get.

It was time to shed some weight.

I looked up, finding the *Wretched Lady* aligned already with our only chance. Trenna had gotten there before me, deftly shifting us toward the channel city and its blessedly neutral waters. If we cut our anchor, and the wind stayed with us, we might make it.

Coisume was a sprawling port with lively trade and allegiance only to itself. It stood lonely against the empire on the continent, welcoming any sailors who washed in. With a wall of mountains at its back and the rumor of a sea monster to protect it in its infancy, the city state had grown powerful enough to remain neutral through long years of aggression between Sanctuary and Vestine. Even in peacetime, it was equipped with guns heavy enough to dissuade either party from striking the other within reach of its waters.

All I had to do was get us there, and Coisume's guns would put an end to any trouble on my boat's tail. On land, well, we could head off whoever followed us, or else lose them in the streets. In the channel city, there would be options. Out here, I had none.

It would cost us.

I couldn't afford food, much less a new anchor.

The price was cheaper than our lives.

"Let us fly," I commanded Trenna, my hand on her shoulder. It steadied me much more than it lent her strength, I was certain. It would be close. Those ships were small and maneuverable. I couldn't tell what other surprises they had under their decks; might be magic or rowers. I only knew we had the wind at our backs, a good head start, and our nose already pointed in the right direction.

"Trust the *Wretched Lady*," she replied, all calm steel. And in that moment, I did. "Give the command, Captain."

I nodded. "We cut and run."

34

REGULA

Odette and I waited a long time for cannon fire, for the clash of boats on the water, and the possibility of violence. Cooped up, curious, and more than a little worried, I regretted my willingness to sequester myself in the cabin. We had nothing to go on, no clue as to the happenings outside, no word at all, and, in my case, no pirate I'd like to speak to either.

We'd tired of peering from the rear windows, finding only ocean and open horizon. If I counted myself bored and tired of waiting, Odette was doubly so. She'd gamely agreed to join me in my protest, but she was unable, on even the best days, to keep to one place for long. She deserved a medal of sorts for lasting as long as she did against the call of the unguarded door.

As it was, she skulked just inside of it, not bothering to hide her debate from me. The odd argument slipped from her lips, either for imposing herself on the crew for the sake of information or holding back so as to stay faithful to me.

I felt the same pull on my own principles, and told myself I would look one more time from the squared windows at the back of the ship. Perhaps things had changed.

It was now somewhere toward the middle of the afternoon and the slowly wintering sky was glowing around the edges. The sun had its sights set below the sea, but still some ways to sink.

I maneuvered the chair over the hardwood, climbing it for the best view out, expecting more of the same nothing.

I was dead wrong.

Where the *Wretched Lady* had been the hunter, she was now the hunted. For all our moping, we had missed a whole new set of ships.

I hissed at Odette, hurrying her hand off the doorknob and her feet over to the window. We barely fit on the chair, but found a happy balance using the chair's arms and each other's shoulders.

I could not mistake the smear on the horizon. The *Edgewater* should have been dodging cannon fire by now. The *Wretched Lady* had, it seemed, left it behind in a hurry.

I did not have to wonder at this.

We were pursued, not by the naval vessel, but by smaller boats with billowing flags, red and gold with the thinnest line of green to separate them. Flags I recognized, if only I could—

Odette sputtered beside me. I thought her caught up in the action before she cleared her throat and spit out her words. She almost smashed her fist through the glass in her rush to point at the boats.

"Ocuis! Regula, they must be *his* boats!" she shouted, her breath fogging the window. I gaped at her for a moment, and then it all clicked together in my head.

Her betrothed.

He'd been chosen from one of the greatest families of the continent. I hadn't been privy to pedigrees, but could remember strains of breakfast conversation. The family was known for its expansive trade and enviable fleet of ships. It had been key in the argument Odette had made for a fashionable trousseau that had won us our trip to Coisume.

"Ocuis," I whispered in agreement. Odette was practically jumping up and down. One of the ships was gaining, with another not far behind. Others fanned out in the background. That could not be good for the pirates.

The *Wretched Lady* was running away.

I did not know to where, or whether we would make it, but I battled with my wounded pride. We might be of help.

Odette knew all about her betrothed and his family, and should hold some sway with them if the boats caught up.

"Come on." I circled her wrist with my hand, drawing her attention. "We have to take this to Con—the captain."

Her eyes were sharp when they met mine, and we fought silently for a moment.

"Of course, of course," she muttered. With a last look at our pursuers, she followed me down from our lookout.

We did not encounter resistance at the door. The crew, to their credit, had left battle stations to aid the speed the ship was now relying on. There were more men in the rigging than I'd seen on the deck.

Connor was where I imagined him. Well, where I imagined him when I was in my right mind, at least, for all other times he was regarding me, flushed and glistening, from between my own legs. But that was before… He was at the helm. Nowhere else. His arms crossed and mouth tight, eyes somewhere over the navigator's shoulder.

His face was grim, just as grim as it had been when I'd left him last night.

The worry in his eyes quickly turned into frustration as he registered our presence.

"I thought—" He fixed me with his stare, stepping toward us in what looked mightily like alarm. "We are running for our lives, ladies, and I would prefer—"

"Odette's betrothed chases you." I cut him off, my words hitting him almost as a cannonball might, his movement arrested. "Or his family."

"Connor, take it somewhere else," came a reedy command from beside us. I had been too busy to notice Trenna's poker-straight spine, and I could not have predicted the clench of her teeth, for her hands were strong on the steering.

The captain's response was to herd us down the stairs and out of his navigator's domain. No information was worth unsettling his savior at the *Wretched Lady's* moment of greatest need.

Sheltered under the bulk of the helm, he studied us.

"Explain."

We answered together, our voices a muddle with the rush of the sea around us. I shut up and let Odette take over.

"I'm promised to a son of the Ocuis. That's why we were allowed to travel for my trousseau. The same Ocuis who own a fleet of ships that fly red, green, and gold." She slapped a hand on her hip.

"We saw them from the window," I added. "The city was already to be allied with them by marriage, why not for ships too? Why not use their dumping of us to their advantage, to rile up the continent?"

"They can't know you survived." His eyes traced over me, flinty in the afternoon light. I returned his stare with iron of my own.

"We don't matter. It's you they want, or else they knew you could not resist a second chance at their ship and they could not hope to outrun or outgun you. The navy has clearly been studying pirates." It was plausible. "I expect they intended to have their backup carefully arranged by the time you arrived in the lane. You surprised them with your speed." I frowned over it. "But there is no doubt they were waiting for you."

"Aye," he said, dropping his gaze as he digested our words. "What else do you know of them? The city is insular by nature, they do not ally easily."

"No, not in years. Perhaps time and isolation have done their job and worn down whatever animosity made Sanctuary withdraw in the first place." Since learning of Odette's engagement,

I'd pondered this myself. I had been given a basic primer on cross-seas politics, due to the nature of my former husband's work. I was meant to be a feather in his cap, a wife who could navigate the dangers of an important dinner table, had I not been such a disappointment in the birthing room.

"The family's in charge of Vestine's trade, having held the emperor's shipping contracts for a hundred or more years," Odette piped up. "My betrothed was to be a Vestal emissary of sorts, splitting time between the empire and Sanctuary."

Connor eyeballed her, a brow raised. "And you were to be Sanctuary's bargaining chip?"

She gave a dainty shrug. "A good wife is worth more than an armada, they say."

"No, they do not." Connor snorted. "They offered you up as sacrifice for this, lass." He waved a hand. "An Ocuis fleet to further Sanctuary's agenda, I'll bet. This is the first of many possible uses for your husband's generosity." His eyes went faraway and a muscle ticked in his jaw.

His words chilled me to the bone. The ships on our tail could easily maneuver the dangerous waters that protected places like Penny's Cove.

My throat tightened at the thought.

It was no wonder Sanctuary wished to forge an alliance with the Ocuis, especially if they held the ear of the emperor. Had Sanctuary given up all of its long-held grudges?

I supposed I should be grateful I'd be returning to the city, nigh impenetrable in its construction. If they planned to sweep the seas clean of the pirates who harried their shores, it would be much safer to be within the walls than on one of the smaller islands or on the sea herself.

Alecto ran up to us, dark curls flying against his shoulders, interrupting Connor's questions. There was no sign of his mother.

"Channel city ahead. Rory can almost see the battery," he

said without losing a breath. He nodded at Odette and me with the air of a perfect gentleman.

"Alecto, you remember our guests?" Connor did not look easy under the weight of his realizations.

"I could hardly forget them." Alecto gave us a slight bow before turning back. "Anything for me, Captain?" No wonder his mother hardly let him out of her sight. He was dashingly handsome. His hooded, earthen green eyes were ethereal against his light brown skin and spare, fashionable getup. His manners, too, measured up. If he weren't a pirate, I'd take him for one of the continent's dandies.

"Not until we're in range of Coisume's guns." Connor said, strain leaking across his face.

"Rory said—"

"Rory's guessing. That will get us killed."

A boom came from behind us. The sound echoing over the planking.

"Cannon at the stern" came a shout over our heads, quickly followed by "Missed us."

"Coisume may not be close enough," Connor muttered to the three of us. "Forget that, Alecto. Round up anyone with a pistol. We'll fire on these Ocuis before they put a hole in us." He chewed his lip for a second then added, "Nothing larger. We do not want to risk drawing the attention of Coisume's guns ourselves."

Another nod and Alecto left us.

"I thank you for your help, Odette, Regula," the captain said, taking considerably more time with my name. "But I would thank you more if you stayed where I knew you were safe." He was such an unforgivable liar.

"Safe? Your cabin might be taking on water," I bit out. I was desperate to rile him. He deserved a slap, a real one.

He barked a miserable laugh. Despite my anger, I was overcome with the urge to put an arm around him. He seemed brittle in the face of his responsibilities.

"Fine. Fine." He relented, motioning the nearest pirate over. "You there! See to it that these two are made comfortable in the cooperage." He raised a brow at me, and spread his hands magnanimously, snuffing out my urge to comfort him and reigniting my fury.

I bared my teeth in a smile. Let him take it as a challenge.

35

CONNOR

I t should not have felt so good to tuck Regula away safely in the lower decks, I thought, blowing powder down at the boat harrying us. Even if she hated me, I would protect her for as long as I could.

The ghost of hope hung around me still. I imagined Regula staying, her arms wrapped about me, holding me fast against the nightmares I'd wrought, steadying my gun.

As it was, I was less one worry. That would have to do.

The Ocuis, if Odette was right in her guessing, were astonishing ship builders. The craft following us was exquisite. What the small craft lacked in power it made up for in speed and agility, things the *Wretched Lady* had always taken for granted against the bulkier ships at Sanctuary's beck and call. It was almost a pity to shoot at it.

Almost.

I took a chunk out of the starboard decking, my satisfaction caught between grimace and grin.

We were only a few moments from Coisume's boundary, where the great guns were always primed to fire on impolite visitors. The other ship's single cannon, placed like a unicorn's horn on their bow, would quiet from here on out. Not even the Ocuis would run the risk of being blown out of the water. They knew Coisume's rules as well as we did.

Rory passed me the last of his pistols. If I weren't so busy, I might consider why he was letting me shoot his treasures without so much as an owed favor. I took aim one last time.

The shot went off without a hitch, right into the planking above the gun. Not close enough to light the whole thing on fire, but hopefully my shot, and the few Alecto had gotten off in the same amount of time, would force the gunners to keep their final cannonballs to themselves.

They would not dare shoot at us now.

The range of Coisume's guns was predicated on rumors, mostly, but there were those who'd seen ships taken down. The channel was especially deep here, with the channel city perched on a shelf that did not extend as far as their harbor.

There was plenty of room to sink ships.

Crews manned the big guns day and night, and would not hesitate to respond to the sparks and sounds of a ship on the offensive. I let the breath leave my body, long and slow, my eye still locked on the boat below.

Triumph. Of a sort.

The Ocuis were very close, too close for my comfort, and showed no signs of slowing. Another craft followed a length or two behind them. They would tail us into the city, no matter that Coisume stood as a declared neutral ground. Neither Sanctuary nor Vestine could fell their enemies there without paying a price.

As if confirming my suspicions, a figure emerged from the hatch on the nearer ship. When he stood, I had no doubt about Odette's theory. The man who swayed below us screamed continental money, from the shiny leather of his shoes to the starch in his collar and the stiff pomade of his hair, both managing to stand strong against the wind whipping over his back. The sun caught on his golden skin and reflected off his dark hair, making him look more like a statue than a person from this height.

Rather than let us enjoy his illusion, he unsheathed a long, straight, and utterly useless—in most situations—blade from his hip, and held it high in warning. I could not hear what he shouted, but the twist of his handsome face was evident.

"Do you wager he blames us for the death of his betrothed?" I said to Rory, who'd joined me to peer over the edge.

"He blames us for a few things, I reckon," my second replied. "He's letting us have it. Something of a showman, huh?" Rory's eyes lingered on the man, who was in fact still going at it, no matter that the sea was eating up his words. I could not let myself worry about the rage that sparked from his eyes, even at a distance.

"What are the chances of him calming before we reach the docks?" I mused, watching the silver flash of the man's blade, as it moved with his gesticulating hands.

"Not good," Rory said. "Better, maybe, when he knows you've saved his woman."

"Could be… It's a match made on portraits and polite words, if that, so it may not be Odette he's riled up about." I cut him a look.

"You know that type, Connor." Rory rolled his eyes, but kept them trained on the Ocuis below. "He doesn't get out of bed unless there's a pretty face to wake him. He had good reason to race us across the Nearways."

"A pretty face or daddy's favor," I agreed, which made him snort. "He's not firing, though. I guess we'll see if he's had a change of heart by the time we make port."

We stood in silence, aside from snatches of the continental's cursing.

"He may not be shooting, but he'll want Odette the moment he hears she's aboard and breathing. No man in his right mind would entrust a woman to a bunch of pirates, much less his betrothed," Rory said, leaning over so his shoulder tapped at mine. I understood his implication, a little mortified that I hadn't thought of it.

"I'm sure you'll convince him to let us keep her," I joked, the lump in my stomach back with a vengeance.

"Aye, and he'll marry me instead, just as I've always dreamed." Rory replied, quick as a whip with a lilt to his voice, trying to sell me on his starry-eyed maidenhood.

We looked at each other, then down at the man, who was beginning to tire of his yelling, and we both broke out laughing.

"I think I know what to do," I said as soon as I could breathe again. "If she'll let me."

Rory eyed me, saying nothing in such a way that I wondered if he wanted to argue. On which count, I could not guess. His gaze turned back to the now-still figure on the ship below, and I left them to stare at each other while our boats battled through the rush of water.

36

REGULA

W hat a foolhardy scheme, hung as it was upon a nest of hope. It would surely get me killed. Nonetheless, I pulled on the salted mess of Odette's traveling skirt. It was not quite white now, its blue ribbons traced over with ocean. It would never swish or sway like it once had. Well, not without a proper laundering.

I couldn't think of a better plan, not with at least two of the Ocuis ships escorting us into the channel city, sure to dock close enough to challenge the pirates and keep an eye on anyone leaving the ship.

Someone had to play Odette, and do it convincingly, as much as I wanted to open my mouth and say otherwise.

There were younger women, prettier too, among the pirates. It would have been funny, perhaps, to have Billy do it, as I'd suggested, but she could hardly be prepped on social niceties in the short time it would take to sail into the city. Besides, there was no possible softening of the callus on her hands.

Odette's portraits hadn't been doctored, but it was common practice in Sanctuary, even for folk who walked the same balconies and ran in the same society. I was counting on the continent to abide by similar courtesies. What was hair a shade or two darker or a face with a few more years on it? This Ocuis was a second son, or so the dinner table said, and would not necessarily be scared off by a woman who had lied about her age. His line would continue with or without him.

Odette had gone to perfect her own pirate's costume, and I was left to the captain's chambers yet again. I had broken my vows to the place, but I could tell the *Wretched Lady* didn't fault me for it.

Connor stood beside me, his betrayal festering between us.

Odette's ruined muslins did not bother me half so much as he did, even if they had been his idea. Even if I could never be Odette now, I had been very like her a long time ago. Would be still if my ovaries had cooperated. Ever since, I'd lived as a ghost of that woman, but she existed deep inside of me.

I felt Connor's presence at my front, and his fingers on my cheek before I realized tears threatened, one escaping into the stroke of his thumb.

"Regula…" He lost his words, but kept up the sweet pressure on my cheekbone.

I wanted to rip the pity with which he said my name right out. He should not feel so safe. I could not collapse into the weight of his touch. Not when he…

No, I would not lose my nerve. I would not ruin the charade, not by crumbling into him.

"Why didn't you tell me?" I batted his hand away.

Connor looked at me—no, through me—without saying a word, his mouth set in a hard line.

"I would have understood." I was dangerously close to falling apart. "If it was the only way."

He sucked in a breath, blowing it out at the planks beneath our feet. "By the time it mattered, it was too late."

I hardly heard him.

"What mattered?"

"This. Us. We never should have—"

"Fucked? Kissed? Come to know one another?" I launched

my words as if they were shot meant to hit the deck, shaking the two of us apart.

He finally lifted his gaze from the floor.

"Yes. Any of it. All of it," he said. My fingers twitched, and I buried them in Odette's skirts. My skirts, now. "I'm a captain, Regula. I'm meant to be above it all, but I was lonely." He continued after a moment. "Lost."

Suddenly, after a lifetime of taking what was given me without complaint, I could not bear it anymore. I knew I was not the choice of loneliness.

I was more.

He had wanted me, not to fill his own emptiness, but for my own strengths. He still wanted me, as shocking as that was to admit to myself. It simmered in his amber eyes. His coward's eyes. Even here. In our last moments together.

There was no place for me on the *Wretched Lady*. There was no place for me in Sanctuary. I would be walking off into Coisume with only Odette's clothing to protect me in my pretending.

I would make sure Connor remembered me before I went to my fate.

For the first time in a long time, I took something I wanted without first weighing my own worth.

I kissed him, searing him, so that he could not hide. It was not my arms that tightened around him, pulling him against me, but the telltale curl of his own fingers in the many fastenings of my dress that brought us flush.

He could give me up as many times as he liked. To Sanctuary, to the Ocuis, to Coisume, to the sea herself. He would never rid himself of my memory.

CONNOR

I WAS LIKE A MAN POSSESSED. I COULD NOT GET ENOUGH OF HER.

I was to blame for this fresh loss of her, the one who'd dressed her up in her charge's clothes, like a lamb to the slaughter.

For all that I had protested, I was happy devouring her. She had goaded me into it, taking from me everything I was too afraid to give her. I had never been so hard in my life. Why should I keep myself from a final tryst, when I'd never tasted such respite except in her arms?

This time, we battled. Every apology, every word unsaid, stolen from each other's mouths. I didn't dare undress her and demand another solution, one that might let me keep her a day or two longer. I could only take what she offered me. This moment. I would have to work for it. Wring tenderness from her fury. Settle the score between us.

I warred with desire, without knowing exactly what I needed from her.

I did not want to relinquish her mouth.

I had to find a way to pull her from this trap, out of these unfamiliar clothes. I'd set it for her, and now it was really sprung. Somehow, if we survived this, I would convince her to stay on the *Wretched Lady*. With me, if I was lucky. But it was naive to want that way while looking down the barrel of a very different future, one that could not be solved by divesting her of her skirts.

She saved me from my spiraling thoughts, leaning out of our kiss and gazing up at me with liquid brown eyes. She was all heaving chest and spit-rubbed ruby lips, and I could not deny her when she whirled around to bend over the desk where I'd first tasted her and said, "Our time is swift running out. Want something to remember me by?"

I must have lost my mind for a second in the turn of her head and the curve of her ass. She offered it, propped up on an elbow, one hand rucking up the pompous layers of her dress to reveal skin I would never worship again.

How could I deny her? How could I cheat myself? I was hardly capable of speech when I took over, flipping the troublesome fabric over the arch of her back and finding her wet against the fine linen.

"Come on, Connor," she growled at me. "Tick, tock."

She emphasized the words with a roll of her hips, expertly drawing my attention. I was helpless to keep my hands from her, one settling on her hip, where it felt altogether too comfortable. The other I busied, drawing apart her drawers and exposing her pretty pussy. I could look at it for hours, for days. If I took no other memory from this journey, I knew I would treasure this.

I drew a finger down her folds, near drooling at the feel of her. Again, I wanted...

"Don't minister to me, fuck me," she said. Her scowl would have been unbearable but for the roses in her cheeks and the buck of her hips against my questing hand.

As the lady demands. I unbuttoned the flap of my pants, where my cock waited, more than ready to oblige. I did not let go of her hip, my hand burrowed between my least favorite dress and the inferno of her skin.

I did not need to be begged to lose myself.

If she wanted to feel me, to walk away from this, from us, with the ache of our pleasure between her legs, I was more than willing.

Before she dared ask me again, I slipped over her, drawing a gasp that tempted me to spill right on her buttocks, hopelessly declaring myself hers. I rallied, sucking in a great, fortifying breath and willed my mind silent. My wishes must stay buried deeper, my control must prove stronger.

I was the last man who deserved her. She could use me however she wanted, but I would not ruin her life again.

Everything else was lost as I entered her, harder and faster than I had before, deep and tantalizing. Almost never did I crave this sort of violent joining, beyond dreams or as the occasional second in a stream of partners, but it was right.

She grinning at me, feral, wondrous.

Her anger, my guilt. We shook our frustrations off the bone.

She'd known exactly what I needed, I noted, my thoughts half-formed as I drew out and thrust back in. Regula somehow always knew.

This. A brutal taking, rocking her onto her arms and listening to the muted, unintelligible sounds coming out of her usually sharp mouth. This would be balm, should she find her way back into my mind on a cold day, alone in my bunk. This was visceral. The slap of my hips against her ass, the clench of her around me as she fought against falling apart. I did too, fearing I'd fail her and lose myself too soon.

I was so close, and she couldn't be far away. I gave up, and swept my arm under her, pulling her ass up and back from the wood so I could get to her clit and send her over the edge before I spent myself inside her.

She met me, moan for moan, our flesh melding, both of us incoherent. And then, we rode over the heart-stuttering crest of our pleasure together for the final time.

When the last of it washed out of me, I felt tears at the corners of my eyes. I had wiped hers not so long ago, but it seemed a sacrilege to wipe mine. She'd earned them, wrung them from me along with a climax so spectacular I could still feel it in my knees.

I slumped over her, muttering her name, begging her… for things I couldn't have and shouldn't consider within my reach. Her heart was all thunder under mine, her neck lovely and pink, like I'd held her there in my frenzy. I was a mess, and I could not, however much I wanted, be her mess.

"Shhh." She seemed to know it too, quieting me until our breath synchronized and I had the strength to stand and offer her a hand up.

There was only one thing I wanted to say, that perhaps I had said in the throes, but her eyes begged me to forget it. I had to let her go.

We parted quietly, then and there, the truth of us left on the desk. I worked my comb through her hair, and she pinned it up, humming a song I'd never heard.

A fast, hard fuck was easier than saying "I'm sorry," and it was a good enough substitute for saying goodbye.

37

REGULA

O dette's betrothed hadn't stormed the *Wretched Lady* the moment we docked, but he had tied up a berth over, waiting for the authorities to pronounce us welcome before he and his cronies streamed out of their boats and up to our gangway. He was a dandy alright, all pomp and flash.

I was disguised as Odette and surrounded by female pirates for the illusion of modesty. There was a chance that her bridegroom would be so ecstatic to see Odette alive that a week among pirates wouldn't matter. Hopefully he hadn't put too much stock in her portrait.

I probably should have taken more time to prepare my new role, but my distraction had been worth it. Connor would be hard-pressed to forget me, and the wound between us was a little mended; enough that I would not regret my time with him.

The real Odette was high up in the rigging, staring down at us from under a cap. They'd never expect a lady—from Sanctuary *or* the continent—to be grubbing around in the ropes. Besides, it would soon be dark.

The captain and Rory met the Ocuis at the dock, having gone down to register the ship anyway. While I still waited just out of view on the *Wretched Lady*'s deck, I could hear everything the man said, including his upset over Odette's untimely demise. Feigned or otherwise, he was laying into the captain in perfectly accented merchant's tongue. Connor let him moan for a moment before putting him out of his misery.

"I'm afraid there's been a misunderstanding," he said, his tone gentle. "Your betrothed is alive and well." He waved a genial hand and I stepped up, every inch—I hoped—a lady.

At the sight of me, the Ocuis, whose given name I still could not remember, swallowed whatever charge he'd been about to level as shock rippled across his handsome face. Little surprise showed in the men behind him. They were either well trained, and he well liked, or her betrothed was the only one who'd expected to find Odette dead.

"We—" Connor said with a flourish. "—found your lady near drowned and nursed her back to health." It wasn't the whole story, but it played to the expectations of the man before us.

Odette's betrothed ironed his expression back into something resembling his portrait before he spoke. He ignored the captain and addressed me alone. "Lady Sessleny, I feared the worst. Are you well?"

I stopped holding my breath. At a distance, at least, my face was proving enough like Odette's to fool the man. I was grateful she was hidden well above us and not available for comparison. While we were far from sisters, I knew I could copy her manner perfectly. Only my face might give me away.

I assured Odette's betrothed of my well-being and began showering the "merchants" of the *Wretched Lady* with compliments over my treatment.

The newcomer kept his whole focus on me, which might prove to his credit in his eventual marriage. I'd learned the hard way that many men never bothered to listen to their wives.

I knitted my hands together at the waist of my dress and continued with my charade. "I was betrayed by men who should have been my protectors. My family entrusted me to them on this journey, in preparation for our coming marriage, and they…" I trailed off. "I survived their unkind treatment, but I have lost a dear friend and companion to the waves."

Tears came easily. It was no great leap to imagine my bodice open on the deck and my skin cold and clammy from the sea. These past days, I had more than once tasted salt in my throat. I'd fought the memory of breathing underwater and felt again the strange sweep of scales against my legs. I was haunted by the shadows I'd seen beneath the waves.

My false betrothed did not bother with words. He strolled right up to the gang plank. Would he rush the pirates?

Instead he stuck out a hand to the captain. "I offer you my thanks."

Connor's back was to me, but I still noticed how slow he was to shake the man's hand. For one short, sharp instant, I wished to tell the truth. Consequences be damned.

Claim me, Connor. Sweep me off my feet and back onto the Wretched Lady.

I was not one to rush in headlong—or to rush at all—but Connor made me wish I was different. Bolder. Bold enough to begin my life anew, as a pirate.

I longed to feel the captain's arms around me. I wanted his attention, his approval.

But there was no room for my wants, not when I was meant to be Odette. I could more easily step into her shoes than refashion myself as a pirate. No matter the desires of my secret heart. It was a good thing I was accustomed to walking a path that had never felt like my own.

Connor and the Ocuis were still going at it, trying to top each other with polite, empty lies. The two men argued over who might retain my company, and I waited, perfectly posed, as if I didn't care a whit where I ended up as long as it had a warm bath and a fresh dress.

"I won't leave her in the hands of the same men who abandoned her in the first place. It's not the way of my ship,"

Connor said in the face of my false betrothed's obvious impatience.

"That's rich from a pi—" I watched the man bite back his words and reframe his argument for my gentle ears. "I assure you, had I known those Sanctuary scoundrels would treat her so, I would have taken her on a tour of the continent myself." He was clearly angry on Odette's behalf. I was leaning toward believing he'd been the patsy in all this, lied to by the navy and sent to pick up the pieces of their poor decision-making.

That didn't mean I trusted the man, though. Connor clearly didn't either. "I'm disinclined to take your word for it. I've taken great care with her keeping, at significant risk to myself and my ship. I would be a fool to place a lady like that in further danger."

I almost snorted.

Connor was walking a fine line, hinting at a bribe and poking the man's pride all at once. It was not the most subtle conversation, but he did sound exactly like the pirate we all knew him to be.

"As her betrothed, I will not allow her to come to harm. In fact, I promise to deliver her back to her family myself. Sanctuary's navy has lost my confidence," the Ocuis said. "I am, of course, prepared to reward you handsomely for your fine keeping of her."

"A reward, huh?" Connor tilted his head. "Take your money and double it if you want us to seriously consider your offer. Oh, and add your finest anchor."

"An anchor? My purse will surely be enough to satisfy."

"Wouldn't you do anything to ensure your lady's safety?" The pirate winked and flicked his blade from its sheath. The Ocuis sighed.

"An anchor it is."

With a wave of his polished hand, the continental sent a man scurrying back toward his ship. I bit my tongue. It was clear Odette would have her hands full with her betrothed just as soon as she actually met him.

Both men gazed up at me. One was a portrait, the other my captain.

Want was written so clearly across Connor's face that he was lucky the twist of his body kept our pursuers from a clear view. It sent a secret, possessive thrill through me. There was a nakedness to his brows, the bristled corners of his mouth, and those sun-gilded eyes that I would cherish.

A fist clenched around my heart so hard I almost forgot myself. If he hadn't planned to leave me all along, I would have let the same hunger and regret show in my face, ruining our delicate plan.

I wished I'd had time to forgive him.

I allowed myself a last look. It was too long, perhaps, but I was far enough up the walk that it would be hard to pin my gaze to any one man. I found myself hoping with an intensity I'd never felt before to find Connor again. In this life, or perhaps the next, we could twine our hands together and explore the channels of this strange new city.

We might move on from the mess we'd made of each other.

For all my wishing, I had a role to play, one that did not guarantee me another meeting with the pirate, even if I played my part perfectly. The *Wretched Lady* would leave with the tide, and I would remain behind.

Pella offered me a hand, ushering me down to the dock, where Connor and Rory stood with the Ocuis. The big redhead was enough muscle to make anyone nervous, even surrounded by Odette's betrothed and his men.

The Vestal stepped up the moment my feet touched Coisume's planks. "My lady—"

Rory inserted himself into the man's path, setting off a great deal of snarling and posturing between the two. It was clear few people ever told the Ocuis "no." And yet there he was, chest to chest with the scariest pirate aboard the *Wretched Lady*.

To his credit, he tipped his face up to Rory's with only a smidgen of fear.

"Excuse me."

My wide eyes needed no exaggeration, for I did not wish to see either of them spill blood over me. I expected to find Connor wrapped up in his friend's battle, but when I chanced a look, his gaze was still on me, drinking his fill.

"Captain, thank you for saving my life." I stepped in, playing the lady in hopes of breaking the two apart. "And for your kindness thereafter," I added, hoping Connor would not mistake my meaning.

"Miss Sessleny, it has been our pleasure." The captain smiled, but it was perfunctory, and not half so bright as I was accustomed to.

A lady would not offer a merchant, or a pirate, her hand, so I did not give him mine, sacrificing one final touch. "I am grateful I've found familiar company again." I sniffed, looking pointedly at Odette's betrothed. The lie did not sit comfortably on my tongue.

Connor, apparently, was playing the rogue as much as I was the rose. He ignored propriety, snatching my hand from its hiding place in the salted fold of my skirt, and swept to one knee, kissing the back of it. This elicited a huzzah from his crew, and a general ruffling in the manner of the continentals. Hands went to swords all around. My cheeks were scarlet as I snatched my fingers from his grasp in mock outrage.

My skin tingled where he'd pressed his lips. Underneath it all, I hoped the feeling would linger.

One false move might destroy our fragile plan. I didn't dare give anything away, for I was the one who would be punished should we fail. If the Ocuis even for one instant considered me— well, Odette—compromised by my time aboard the *Wretched Lady*...

I held my breath as Connor stood.

My worries were misplaced. Odette's betrothed was spitting mad and focused solely on the captain. The man pushed past Rory and extended his hand to me in protest.

I accepted with haste, allowing a little disgust to bleed into the heat rushing beneath my surface.

"Just wanted a taste." Connor grinned at Odette's betrothed. I did consider faking a faint in response to the words, but I had no wish to reacquaint myself with the freezing sea. I gasped instead, in perfect time with the return of my false betrothed's runner, struggling under the weight of a sizable pouch.

I could practically feel Connor's smirk.

"I *am* a man of my word," the Ocuis said with barely veiled contempt. He squeezed my hand in uncomfortable reassurance. "An anchor will be delivered within the hour. Your ship is in dire need of it."

"Much obliged," Connor said as Rory relieved the continental of his expensive burden. "A pleasure doing business with you." I felt Connor's gaze rove over us, cold as tomorrow's butter, before he cocked his head and proceeded up to the *Wretched Lady*.

Rory followed, backward somehow, his eyes on us. The purse clinked in his arms.

The Ocuis spat on the spot they'd vacated before remembering me beside him. He made a pained face at his own vulgarity before waving his men away. Instead of an apology, he offered his arm. "Shall we?"

"I'd like that," I replied, pressing a curl back into place, playing the part of the girl to whom he was promised.

38

CONNOR

"She's bought us a full larder, more powder, and a chance out of our hole." Silver was trying to comfort me.

"You don't understand... I sold her," I said, the words reverberating off my knees. "She's in danger. That Ocuis bastard is sharp enough to figure us out, and he'll do it long before we return Odette and the scandal makes its way across the sea."

At least Silver was listening. I could hear Trenna's fingers drumming on Griffin's desk.

They'd found me hiding here, half curled up, after sending Rory off to spend our poorly won reward. No reason the *Wretched Lady* should pay for my mistakes. I'd folded under the weight of my station, unable to focus on anything after trading Regula away. Not Trenna's maps or Griffin's rescue.

I was stuck in the Eagle's embrace, caught by the bright disgust in her eyes as she left me.

I would have betrayed her no matter how the dice fell. Sanctuary or the channel city. Her family or Odette's betrothed. I'd given her away.

My mates had seldom seen me like this, but I needed a

moment, one where I wasn't the captain. Where I could just grieve.

A moment of weakness, especially in front of two better sailors. I was a liability. Bad things happened to the people I cared about, and not only was I helpless to stop it, but in Regula's case, I had been the one to order it. There had to have been another way.

And yet, neither Silver nor Trenna pressed a dagger to my back. In fact, they were presently engaged in talking me down from my misery.

"She agreed to it, lad."

Silver laid a hand on my shoulder. The touch shouldn't have helped, but it did, and I summoned the strength to face him.

"Aye, and she managed what you could not. She's given us time to mount our case for Griffin's release," Trenna said, her frown a shade more prominent than Silver's. "Give her a little credit. She's a good deal smarter than that imperial show pony." She had a point. Regula's intellect was impossible to ignore.

"There's risk to any plan." Silver shifted on his feet. "What about Griffin? He thought of everything, and look where it got him."

"He's a pirate. He's hard enough to survive rough conditions—"

"Your cooking notwithstanding," Trenna cut in.

"No, by the seas. She's hardly been out of her walls, and now I've doomed her."

Silver shushed us. "Again, you underestimate her. Sanctuary may not seem as bad as a ship without rations or winter on an unfamiliar island, but it is not without its trials. Her horrors may not look the same as yours, but she has surely lived them." He would know. His youth in Sanctuary's navy was obscured by many years and his own oft-buttoned lip.

"I don't… It's not her I discount. I shouldn't have put her out there on hope alone." Would that I could drop to my knees and become one with the *Wretched Lady*.

"I have no idea if this will work!" I was near screaming. Trenna rolled her eyes.

"You're not a fucking child, Connor. We chose you for a reason." There wasn't an ounce of jealousy in her tone, just tiredness.

We were wrung out. We'd braved the Graveyard, nearly battled the navy, and then been chased halfway across the Nearways sea. In fact, she'd done most of the hard work. Silver, too, had pulled more than his fair share of my weight, and we hadn't even begun negotiations with Sanctuary. Rory...

I owed each of them something more than this tantrum, and I owed Regula most of all.

"We are closer to Griffin's rescue than ever." Silver picked up where Trenna had left off.

We'd already begun to plan. Silver would speak for the *Wretched Lady*. Trenna would hide us. Rory and I would do whatever else needed doing.

Griffin's crew was coming for him. With Regula's sacrifice and Odette's help, I did not doubt our ability to get him back. If only he held on.

I had to screw my head on straight. Moping around wouldn't help me measure up to the titans that walked the *Wretched Lady*'s decks. Or, at least, I had to learn to stay out from under their feet.

A knock on the door set my spine straight. Trenna waited for my nod before marching over to open it.

I couldn't hide any longer. Nor should I.

Rory blocked the light on the far side, marking the three of us with keen eyes. He had, apparently, spent the Ocuis purse in record time.

He shut the door before he laid into me. "Never known you to lose your head over a woman, Captain." Almighty tides, how often I wanted to pummel him.

"Never this much weight on my shoulders." It wasn't an

exaggeration. I was sinking. Waves kept coming, each one cracking a little harder over my bow.

"Nah, you never had a reason to suffer before." He exchanged a glance with the other two. They could mock me all they wanted, but it wouldn't change anything. I had to clean up my mess.

"Regula has more than enough guts to keep herself out of danger." Silver returned to his earlier refrain.

"And double the brains needed to outthink even your best laid plan," Trenna added.

"It's not her I'm worried about," I said, a knee-jerk response that had Rory snorting. "At least, not only her. There's a lot at stake here." My thoughts were a jumble.

"She shouldn't have been left alone," I finally sputtered.

"What were you supposed to say? 'Sir, here's your bride, but only if you don't look too close, and here's her pirate escort. Don't worry, just standard procedure. We send a man with every proper lady we meet,'" Rory teased.

"If that's what it took, yes. I'd feel better." I brushed the hair out of my eyes. "She doesn't deserve to bear the brunt of our scheming. If that Vestine bastard lays hands on her, or worse, it's my fault. I'm the reason she's there."

"We. We're the reason. There was little else to do." Trenna smacked a hand down on the desk. "Should you have released Odette to him instead? Should we have hedged and fled with only a bit of goat to fill our bellies? There was no good choice, and no time to work through every possibility."

If only Regula were here in the room with us.

"I wish I could protect her. Or anyone. The only captaining I've done is telling the *Wretched Lady* to wait and hope and worry." I sounded pitiful even to my ears.

"Seas, if that's your problem, you should stop wasting every-one's time. You could do something, you know," Rory said, always the wisest when I didn't want to listen. "Might have to anyways. I saw that louse of a captain down in one of the marketplace pubs emptying Coisume of all her liquor. Spilling his guts, too." Rory had roused me alright.

Forewell had to pay.

39

REGULA

The Ocuis was a complete lush. Handsome enough, courteous enough, and apparently drunk enough to merit his reputation as a dandy.

There was no room for peacocking in Sanctuary. Men interested in fashion and excess were stomped down just as surely as I had been during my marriage. Vestals like Odette's betrothed were another matter entirely. The sprawling Vestine Empire had a near boundless court to match, along with competition. Fads came and went, and riches were meant to be spent.

Valentin—I'd finally remembered his name—came from a powerful family, and it was obvious he'd been given the keys to their kingdom, though for what purpose, I had yet to ascertain. While the Ocuis resided mostly in the empire's capital, Valentin explained that the family kept a place in every important port. Their rooms in the channel city were large and luxurious, if in need of a good airing.

The suites were on the second floor of a modest villa, though I was certain the family was also in possession of the first floor. Coisume was named after its wide channels; ocean avenues that took the place of streets in many instances and necessitated a plethora of bridges and dead ends. The place was almost more famous for its charmed boats, and it stood to reason that some would be downstairs, ready for the family. Perhaps I could steal one.

Valentin had not proved himself a threat yet, but Connor's plan had only extended to the *Wretched Lady*'s escape. I could only linger here as long as the Ocuis believed me to be his betrothed. I was responsible for getting myself out.

We stood in the foyer while servants zoomed about, making the rooms ready. With a word, he'd dismissed his men, but not before one of them had produced a decanter of amber spirits and a glass. Valentin was on his third pour by the time he finally spoke.

"I hope you'll forgive me for the irregular manner of our meeting." Valentin kept a polite distance. "I had hoped... Well, it doesn't matter. I've sent for a chaperone. I didn't think to bring one as I'd been prepared to find you dead." He shook his head and took a sip of his preferred poison.

"Considerate of you." I tucked my hands into the folds of my skirts. I hoped whoever was coming would bring a change of clothes as well. Odette's dress was caked in salt, and I was beginning to itch where it touched my skin.

"Call me Valentin," he said.

"I'm sure my family will inquire. Without my—" I let a sob threaten at the loss of my imagined caretaker. "I was left well enough alone on the ship, thank the gods, though they will have to take my word for it." I straightened up, as if I realized who I was speaking to. "And you, I..."

I was testing him. If he was the sort to raise a fuss and call in a doctor to prod at my maidenhood, perhaps I might find some way to warn Odette before she faced the same examination. That was, if she hadn't been careful, a question to which I had never been willing to subject her.

"I will vouch for your time aboard, just as I will make sure you are returned to Sanctuary unharmed. You are safe with me, lady, I swear it." He followed up the offer by emptying his cup.

Ah, either the empire was a notch less consumed with a woman's virtue, or whatever deal the Ocuis had made with the Sesslenys was of greater importance than what lay between Odette's legs.

He caught me staring at the glass in his hand. Too late, I pretended to study his face. Odette could do worse. His hooded eyes were like dark pools, and he had a lot of glossy black hair that complemented his golden skin.

I wasn't sure I'd ever seen an imperial before. There were great wars between the empire and Sanctuary even before the city had shut its doors. Coisume, too, had ended relations with the emperor a hundred times in recent memory, protected only by a mountain range and their formidable guns from the empire's might.

My interest served me. It would not be hard to pretend to be lovestruck either, not when he looked down at the glass, then back at me, and narrowed his eyes.

"You want some?" he asked, as if I were some creature to tame with treats.

I cocked my head, testing him again. "Plying me with drink? Is that wise?"

He looked down his nose at me.

"We'll be sharing much more than a glass soon enough." He laughed, a twisted, sorry sound. This pained him. "I'd want one if I were you."

That is apparent enough.

"I shouldn't," I demurred, the perfect ideal of his city betrothed.

"I won't tell if you don't. But you'll have to be quick."

"Very well." I wasn't one to turn down a stiff drink.

Valentin muttered something to himself and poured me one. His manner was conspiratorial, if a little off balance.

He passed me the glass, a modest finger of liquor warming the bottom, without any fanfare. I did not know the man, but if I had to guess, it was melancholy that burned quietly at his edges, his impending marriage a weight around his neck.

I sniffed it in a manner I hoped pretty, and looked at him askance.

"Bottoms up, as we say in the north." He tacked on a smile. I raised the glass to my lips for a dainty sip, while he took a draught straight from the decanter.

I did not have to fake my sputter as the liquid made its way down my throat. I wondered if Valentin knew how similar he was to the pirates he hated. They both drank whiskey, though his was far more fragrant and expensive.

"You don't have to look so scandalized." He flipped back his black cuff to swipe the lace across his mouth. The other drinks were catching up to him.

"Am I poor company, Valentin?" I took another sip, bigger than the first, for I was beginning to think all my acting would be lost when he woke up in the morning.

"No, no. I find myself less than prepared to meet you. You were dead, and now you're here, and I'm not ready to be in charge of you." Oh, absolutely the drink was seeping into him.

"Stop worrying. We're far enough from our wedding day." I couldn't help breaking into a smile, to reassure him, perhaps. "I'll return to my family, and you to yours, and there will be time to ready yourself. I promise, I am not at all as fearsome as you've imagined me." I gulped down the rest of the whiskey to under-line my point. It didn't matter what he feared or how he'd imag-ined Odette. I wasn't her, and he would find that out soon enough.

"Did I mention how glad I am that you were the one to find me?" I wondered if he would react to my blatant interest.

Valentin's eyes darted to me, and then away again. He had the air of a man haunted. He was surely drinking like it.

"Yes, well, duty called, Odette. May I call you that?" The clouds passed from his features and suddenly he was charm itself.

"I'd rather you didn't." He'd need that name soon enough. Besides, I couldn't get too comfortable with him.

He watched me. Had I struck him a blow or was it all the same to him? I believed he would do no harm to me, at least as long as I was disguised as Odette, but I was not sure what he might do to himself if left to his own devices.

It should not have bothered me how much he drank. However, Valentin was quite clearly filling a void. What tormented him, I couldn't tell.

His hair had come slightly unstuck from the lacquer that kept it swept back from his face, threatening his forehead and cracking his perfect facade. It was the only tell across the manicured whole of him. Not a speck of dust was to be found on his smart black coat and trousers, even though he'd worn them through a lengthy chase at sea. No button sat out of place. Only a rebellious lock of hair to signal his unraveling.

I was loath to give the empty snifter back, for fear he would take it as an invitation to finish the bottle.

Sensing my hesitation, he held out a hand for it.

"Your chaperone will be here momentarily."

I relinquished the glass, careful not to let my thoughts show. Our hands did not touch as it passed between us.

I nodded and decided to risk something. Anything I could learn about this man might spare Odette from my fate.

"I think it is luck herself that has brought us here before our betrothal."

"Yes, lady?"

"I don't know the particulars, but I know you didn't choose this. Didn't choose me. If there's anything you need to say before we settle things, I'm more than willing to listen." I left the overture open-ended. There was no telling whether he would confide in me.

I wasn't Odette. While I knew her well, I could not speak for her on the topic of this marriage with any confidence. Anything I said had the potential to bite her the moment my subterfuge was revealed. I could neither fake passion nor reveal the marriage was an imposition and implore Valentin to free her from their deal. He seemed the type to take a request like that seriously, no matter his own opinion.

His attention was not wholly focused on me as he processed my words, but somewhere far off. The more preoccupied he was, the easier my escape would be, at least.

I only had to last in his company until the *Wretched Lady* left port. I was buying them time to use Odette as a bargaining chip. With the purse Valentin had given them, they could not need more than a day or two to set sail. As Odette's friend and some-time guardian, I felt I had to use this time to learn as much as I could about her betrothed.

"I appreciate the offer," he said finally, fixing me with his black eyes, "but I have no gripe with you. An engagement would have come around sometime, as my family is much in demand. We're traders at heart, you see, and inclined to offer everything, even ourselves." He scrubbed a hand across his jaw.

I waited for him to continue, again the perfect picture of a lady. Besides one of Sanctuary's daughters, I was interested in what the Ocuis had traded him for.

"All fault is mine. I ignored the marriage game and am finding myself woefully unprepared."

"What could you be lacking?" I asked.

"Mental toughness, perhaps? Ambition?" He was eyeing another drink. "In all honesty, I am not convinced I'll enjoy living in your city." This startled me. He was right to be scared. I doubted he'd fit in.

"It will take some adjusting." I tried to keep my words vague.

"You seem ready," he replied.

I bit back a laugh. "I haven't been able to secure my trousseau without getting myself in horrible trouble. You give me too much credit." I smiled at him. "Besides, I was born to be handed off once I was of marriageable age. It is only by chance that I am to be on your arm rather than a man in my wall. You will be far less boring."

He did not quite smile back. "That's true. You will probably be begging for boring by the time everything is said and done."

"I can't stand boring." I met his gaze and held it. "And I promise you will never see me beg." In this, I knew I might speak for Odette.

As if on cue, the housekeeper stepped in to inform Valentin of the readiness of the rest of the villa. We were no longer each other's prisoners in the spacious front room. Odette's betrothed thanked the man and ushered me farther into his apartments.

The place was pretty. Instead of sconces, crystalline light was captured in clusters at the top of the walls, suggesting the Ocuis had at least one mage in their employ. Coisume was rife with magic. It welcomed official mages and their charms, whether first or secondhand, and it sparkled in every corner of the city.

I'd never seen its like.

Magic or no, the Ocuis's architect had eschewed windows for doors, which had been swept open upon our arrival to let in the night air. Behind them jutted balconies of red-stained stucco and the sound of the channel lapping sweetly against the house, reminding me of the *Wretched Lady* out on the waves.

It was a very different ocean that met the land here. Calmer than the one who'd nearly swallowed me, quieter, but no less insistent. One could not ignore her. The villa knew this, every opportunity to worship the water built into its very walls.

Valentin indicated an arch on the far side of the sitting room. Through it, a row of delicate doors lined a long hallway.

"I occupy the farthest set of rooms. You're welcome to any of the others. They all look out over the channel."

I thanked him. Surely one of the rooms would offer some chance for escape. I wasn't one for sneaking around, but there was something of the pirate within me now, and I was going to give my future the best try I could manage.

"I didn't see any of your luggage, but I can have a man run back to the ship for it."

"Good luck. It didn't survive the first leg of my journey."

Valentin's eyes went wide, then narrowed, his brow furrowing.

"I didn't know… I'm sorry."

"Sorry for what? You didn't throw me off the side of your boat," I said, distracting myself with the invisible dust on my shoulder.

"They'll answer for that, I swear—"

A knock sounded in the antechamber, then a commotion. Valentin only managed a half turn before the commotion made its way through the inner doors.

An old woman stood before us, covered neck to toe in the darkest crepe. She was mostly eyes and nose, and, apparently, bluster, for Valentin's man appeared behind her looking apologetic.

"Mother, how kind of you to join us." Valentin was unperturbed.

She glared at us.

"Did the devil dress you?" she grated at me, holding up a shaking finger. I was reminded of a crow, a furious one.

"Ma'am, I have only the one dress. I was nearly drowned—" I tried to defend myself.

"It will not do, do you hear that?" She addressed Valentin this time. "I thought you imperials doted on your playthings."

My jaw dropped.

"She is my betrothed, Old Mother." Valentin brought his hands up politely to shield himself from her accusations.

"No point in getting sweet with me, boy. Seen one of you and I've seen 'em all," she snarled. "Now, I'll have my pay and my room and the dinner I was promised."

We were both frozen. If I moved, I would be at risk of loosing a bellyful of laughter.

"You—" She motioned to the servant. "—get her something

appropriate to wear. Heavens know I try my best, but there are holes—" She gave a little gasp. "—in the shoulders!"

Valentin's servant fled the room.

"Tomorrow we will make sure the lady has everything she needs. She has only just been returned to us and must rest." The old woman had drawn Valentin from his whiskey haze, his voice now equal parts stern and rational.

Neither one of them managed another word, for there was another knock on the parlor door. All three of us jumped at the interruption.

"That was quick," the old woman said, as if it was a great disappointment.

"A caller, sir, for you and the lady. Said he's a Captain Forewell in Sanctuary's service," One of Valentin's men announced, stepping just inside the door and shutting it behind him.

It took all my power to keep from wilting at the name. The bastard captain who'd thrown me over the side. My hands wanted to curl into fists at the same time as my blood was ready to run from my body. One of the only men in this place who knew what Odette looked like. My game would end the moment he entered.

I could feign sickness, or retire before he appeared, or—

"Another visitor? At this hour? How many dogs do you have sniffing around you, girl?" The old woman saved me, her disgust palpable in the air. She turned to Valentin. "No more men. I won't stand for it."

His dark eyes cut from her to me, the threads of my story weaving into place.

"Very true, Mother." He nodded at her, his face a pleasant mask. "There's been quite enough excitement for one day."

He dismissed his man with an order to turn the captain away.

I inflated again, grateful for the vile old woman and my false betrothed. There would be no earth-shattering intrusion yet. My ruse would survive another few hours at least.

40

CONNOR

My heart weighed heavy as I stepped foot on Coisume's docks a second time. Heavier than the pack over my shoulder. I was doing the right thing, I knew it. And it was about time.

I'd brought the *Wretched Lady* only suffering in my short tenure as captain. We'd rescued no one, won nothing, and lost plenty.

So I'd relinquished the role entirely, letting it fall to Trenna.

I would make one thing right. I would spring Regula from the trap I'd set for her. The *Wretched Lady* could handle Griffin's negotiations without me.

I hadn't expected it to be a relief when the ship cast off, but they would accomplish what I could not.

If all went well, we would meet at the Tross in a month's time, although I hoped to get there earlier. The longer Regula stayed with the Ocuis, the more danger she would be in. We could buy passage on a ship bound for one of the islands and find a likely fisherman to take us the rest of the way with the handful of golden coins I'd borrowed from my ill-gotten purse.

The whole crew had argued with me. Rory was the hardest to disappoint.

Odette had found me after, looking indistinguishable from a real pirate in Billy's clothes, and given me a hug, along with a rousing speech on the importance of her companion. I did not tell her that my heart echoed her every word.

Even Jack, the largest thorn in my side, had clapped me on the back after my resignation, murmuring something about getting our girl that had my fingers itching for my dagger. The rest of the crew stood on honor and saw me off from the taffrail, waving and saluting. I must not have been so bad a captain.

But I could fail no one else.

Night was beginning to fall by the time the *Wretched Lady* disappeared over the horizon. The council's bell tower echoed in the distance, a stark reminder that I'd lost the only ship I'd ever called home. My destiny lay in Coisume, whether she'd have me or not.

I had a choice between spending my gold on lodgings or frequenting a reputable establishment where a pirate might wash dishes and lift casks in exchange for a night or two in a serviceable room. I chose the latter. While Regula had not seemed squeamish or particularly prudish on the ship, she might take umbrage at a room in a brothel, which meant I should save my coin for lodgings when we were reunited.

I would stop into Bobbin's, the reputable establishment where I intended to lodge, just as soon as I found the place. I'd always made it there on Griffin's heels, and while it wasn't too far, Coisume was a maze of a place. It was easy to follow the wrong path and end up in the ocean or on the steps of some grand plaza. Since Bobbin's wasn't the sort of business one asked about, I wasted the remainder of the daylight nosing around in the wrong direction. My stomach was in the midst of a very vocal protest when I finally found one of Coisume's urchins, a smirking girl who had me turned around and on the right path in a flash, my purse lighter a few too many coins.

Ah well. Griffin always managed to get gold into the grubby

hands of the urchins he met. I'd let this one enrich herself in his honor.

The brothel was an unostentatious corner building, painted a soft green, just beyond the confines of the port. A massive wooden sign boasted a larger-than-life needle and thread and advertised the best sewists money could buy.

They were sewing something alright, just not clothes.

I could attest to the fact that the whole place was fine enough, if you didn't mind the occasional pocket picking. The channel city was home to many such places, with a governing council that encouraged the flow of trade in any direction that lined their pockets. We pirates were welcomed under the same policy.

I was betting on the understanding of Bobbin's madam, and namesake, Bobby. She was a hot coal of a person, small and stout and so warm she might burn your hands. It was a wonder she didn't run the city herself with her terrifying husband, an ex-mercenary from Vestine who now guarded her establishment, and much worse wife, great-great-great granddaughter of the channel city's founder and rumored assassin. I'd met them all a few times, but never without Griffin's calming influence.

He'd been invited to their respective weddings, having done Bobby some great—and secret—service at the beginning of his captaincy.

I could only hope that goodwill extended to me as I pushed through the well-oiled doors.

AND RAN STRAIGHT INTO AN ALTOGETHER TOO FAMILIAR CHEST.

Rory. Every hulking inch of him.

It took me a moment to cycle from surprise to confusion, then to frustration. He had no right to be here. I needed him on the *Wretched Lady*, needed him to bring our captain home. I didn't need a minder.

He budged not at all as my vision glazed red.

I wanted to push past him. Or punch him.

"Took you long enough," was all he said, waiting for me to get myself under control.

"You fucking—" I started, trading hot anger for cold, unfeeling fury.

I could now feel the weight of every eye in the huge foyer on me. Bobbin's was exactly the sort of place one came to expecting to go unnoticed, and if I started swinging on a big guy like Rory just inside the door, I would be out on my ass. Never mind that he was my best friend.

"Did you think we would leave you? Truly?" He didn't bother to lower his voice much. The noise of the room had only dimmed after our interruption, not petered out entirely.

"Griffin is more important," I said, shaking my head at him. I wished I could do more. In here, it would be more couth to kiss him than take out my frustrations with my fists.

He laughed, a big barrel of a sound that made almost the same splash as our collision.

"Calm yourself, Connor. I'm here for you, just as I'll be there for Griffin when the time comes."

I cut a glance across the room, skipping over the well-attended couches and the lonely barstools. If my crew had something to say about this, they'd sent Rory to do it alone. The captain in me, which I could not quite shake, was relieved. The *Wretched Lady* could not stand every sailor a night on the town.

"I've set us up a room." He draped an arm over my shoulders, guiding me into the thick of things. "We've only got tonight and tomorrow if we're lucky, as the lady of the house is expecting to sell out for the fool's feast and the rest of winter's celebrations," he said into my ear. "Besides, Trenna will never let you live it down if you delay us too long... for a lover."

My hackles were already up, and his teasing had me near

snarling. I held it in though, for our steps into the room had revealed a figure far more imposing than Rory himself. Bobby's husband, the butcher of the echoed plains, stood against the far wall. His eyes did not alight anywhere in particular, and yet I knew him to be watching all, and perhaps us especially, though we would be known to him by now. His clean white tunic was a stark reminder of his past. White was the color easiest to clean when it was covered in blood. Needless to say, Bobbin's did not often have trouble within its walls.

I smiled at him from under Rory's arm. He nodded back, confirming that my friend had secured the house's blessing.

"Very well." I capitulated. Another pair of eyes and hands would not be a hindrance. In fact, I might, if I let myself, be glad of his company. "Don't forget, we are here for one purpose only." That earned me a hunter's grin from my friend.

"Oh aye, I promise not to celebrate until you're reunited with your lady love." He winked at me, then tightened his arm around my shoulders, as if I should be impressed with his resolve. The man was insatiable, and I didn't doubt him for an instant. If—no—when we got Regula back, I'd be the last to stop him.

Our room was cramped and sparse, located up the banister stairs and to the left, down a long hall of similar doors. An assignation room with a bed wedged in a corner. Were we high-paying guests, or requiring more than the usual entertainment, we would have been shown to one of the rooms to the right, which served a collection of the richest and most powerful people on the continent and surrounding seas. Bobbin's was the second best brothel in the channel city, after Figbough, the much fancier, upper channel club.

They were less fond of pirates.

Rory's things were neatly set on a long pallet on the far side of the room, leaving a strip of floor between the two exits. A light blue ribbon had already been affixed to the front door, marking the room as occupied. There was no such concern for the back door since it led to the building's long balcony and external stairs, and was only used by the workers.

I tossed my sack down on the bed and rounded on Rory.

He beat me to the punch.

"Shove it, Connor. We wouldn't leave you."

"I ordered—"

"You're a half-cocked, poor imitation of a captain, my friend." I tried not to flinch. "*We*—" Rory emphasized the word. "—are a team. *You're* lucky. Silver and Trenna could've had you at the bottom of the ocean if they'd the guts or the inclination for it."

"And you? Would you have marooned me?" I threw the threat back at him.

"I am here, Connor. I have your back. Always will. I would rather see myself in the sands than toss you to the fish." He sank to the ground, crossing his long legs on his pallet.

I shook my head and let myself drift to the edge of the bed, facing him. It was disarming to be so much taller for once.

"Griffin can spare a day," he said, "we all can. You should be there to see him safe. In fact, we might need you, for all that you protest." His point was debatable, but it did not seem worth the effort.

"Where is she moored?"

"The far side of the port," Rory said, as if they hadn't purposely concealed their own plans from me. "Before you give me that sour stare, consider that the Ocuis also saw us leaving Coisume's waters. They will not think to look for us until we've long since gotten your prize back, and unless we're very unlucky, they will waste time searching for her in other ships' manifests."

"She's a fucking woman, not a prize to be won," I spat at him.

"Perhaps…" He eyed me, like one might a dog with foam at its mouth. Would I bite him or would I run away? Neither. I could use his help. "It's clear she means something to you, and I am here to offer my help, Connor. I will do whatever you need of me in her pursuit." His voice was soft, his manner calm, and it did help that he was on the floor at my feet.

"She means nothing! It's the principle of the thing." But it wasn't. The words were a lie. I heard them, dragging their nails across my eardrums.

"Sure, sure. No matter. She'll make a mighty fine pirate." Rory threw up his large hands, the right one scarred white on one side from a blade he'd grabbed to keep it from my throat in our youth. He knew me well enough to guess I had lost a measure of my sense, a measure of what made me Connor in the meeting of Regula and the subsequent relinquishing of her.

I could not stay riled at him after that. Rory wanted the best for me. He'd probably give his life for it. I should talk to him about that. As his everything-but-blood brother, I wanted the same for him, and for the whole of the *Wretched Lady*.

I supposed I should be grateful my crew had not abandoned me, even though I'd ordered it. They were the closest thing I had to a family, and they would not let me forget it.

"Aye, she will," I said after a little too long. "Almost as good as your mutinous self!" I tapped his knee with a boot, uncrossing my arms and letting the last of my anger drain away.

"Ah, but I'm following orders, Connor. Trenna's captain now, didn't you hear?"

I leaned back on the bed and rolled my eyes to the softly patterned ceiling.

"Would you forgive me if I said I knew where the Ocuis keep their residence?"

My eyes flew wide, my opinion of Rory mending faster by the moment.

41

REGULA

Valentin made good on his promise the next morning, squiring me around Coisume. Well, squiring might have been a bad word for it. I dragged him over the cobbled streets, stopping only when blocked by the channels, hungry for the sights of the unfamiliar city. The old woman tottered along on the arm of the handsomest of the Ocuis men, far behind us.

A sleek black boat followed us too, its movements tethered to a delicate charm hanging from the buttonhole of Valentin's breast pocket. It bobbed in the corner of my eye, a reminder of my subterfuge. A real lady would not be racing for the docks. She'd be in that boat, headed to richer shops and cleaner streets.

But I was not Odette, and I forced us up stairs and over bridges, all the time scouring the city. I didn't need to set foot in a skiff to create a map of the channels in my mind.

I led us down a gentle slope, with flashes of sea between the blocks to guide me. Low-slung mansions gave way to spindly buildings with too many windows, their insides spilling onto their outsides. Hooks and pulleys adorned their fronts. Perfect for my purposes. I wouldn't survive my subterfuge if I escaped into the upper crust. Down here, I could disappear.

Briny air kissed my nose, and it was easy to smile. My wonder at the city wasn't fake. After only a night away, I found I had missed the sea.

Valentin trotted beside me, his coat flying behind him.

"This really isn't—"

"Oh, perfect! A sewist!" I'd only just noticed the green building on the corner and its huge sign: a needle and thread. There was a woman smoking a cigarette a little ways around the corner. A sewist herself, perhaps, though her dramatic makeup and expertly rucked up dress suggested something else entirely.

Connor had been clear. Pirates and prostitutes were comfortable bedfellows. While I'd never imagined either life for myself, I needed all the help I could get to survive in Coisume. I had to find a way to speak to her.

"I don't think… My family's seamstress will be more than happy to see us, and we can ride comfortably up the channels rather than walk to her shop." Valentin stumbled over his words, suddenly quite desperate to turn me around.

"I'm sure this dressmaker is as good as any." I hailed the woman, earning myself a slow stream of smoke.

"It's not—" Valentin started, muttering the rest under his breath as the woman stomped out her cigarette and stepped away from the wall.

"He bothering you, miss?" she asked, sizing us up from behind artful fawn curls. Valentin's hand dropped from my elbow and I skittered to a stop in front of her.

"Not at all! It's you we've been looking for." The woman's eyes narrowed, darting over the both of us.

I prattled on. "You see, I lost my wardrobe in the ocean, and the pirates who assisted me didn't have anything suitable." One of her eyebrows shot up. "They were quite nice, for pirates. The *Wretched Lady*. A strange name for a ship. Though I suppose ships are always women." My words were tangled, and it wasn't as if I could tell her what I wanted outright with Valentin standing right there. He was swiftly becoming my barnacle. I hoped she'd catch my meaning.

"I'll need to replace everything. My fiancé is happy to pay any price." I motioned for Valentin to get his purse out.

"She's not... This is not a..." Valentin threw up his hands and gave up trying to explain to me that this was actually a brothel, not a tailor's shop. For all that I was ignorant of the business of sex, I wasn't a fool. Sailors didn't flock to dressmaker's shops. It didn't hurt to let him think me one, though.

This sewist surely knew a safe room for let or where to go looking for employment. Valentin was nice enough right now, but his good humor would only last as long as my ruse did. I willed the woman to play along.

Her initial alarm was now settling into bemusement. With a raised brow, she said, "I *am* quite proficient with wardrobe."

Valentin snorted.

"I'm sure you don't care for the latest patterns," I sniped at him.

"Oh, this one's interested in fashion, if you take my meaning," the sewist said with a wink. It was impossible to miss the impeccable turn of Valentin's collar and cuffs.

He sputtered. Remembering himself too late to keep a blush from creeping into his cheeks.

"By all means, stay and listen if you'd like," I said, meaning the opposite.

Valentin rolled his eyes and clutched at me, his mouth in a poorly disguised knot. For a supposed dandy, I had expected him to be a bit more comfortable with a lady for hire.

He jammed a hand into the breast of his coat and brought out a handful of gold, shoving it at the woman.

"For your time! We seek a different seamstress."

I clenched my fists, ready to protest.

"My services are quality, sir." The sewist clasped a hand over mine, leaning over so that the delicately freckled curve of her bust was very much the subject of our attention. "You wouldn't be disappointed… Or, she wouldn't." She grinned up at me, her eyes teasing. I believed her.

Valentin vibrated beside me.

"We have no need of them. Now or ever," he said, wheeling me away.

"Come back anytime, loves," she called after us.

I let myself go with him, casting a smile over my shoulder at the woman.

She'd tucked something into the curl of my fist, something I was certain wasn't her price list. I left it there, safe in my hand.

"Her costume was quite pretty, and she seemed confident," I murmured over the click of our heels on the cobbles.

"Lady, I know you are unfamiliar with the fashions of Coisume, among other things, but she would have been ill-suited to our needs."

I batted my eyelashes and performed a pout that would make Odette squeal. "You wouldn't like to see me in her garb?"

Valentin scrunched his nose up.

"She does most of her work without her garb, so no. As I said, her sort of sewing would not work for you at all."

I frowned, stomping along beside him.

"I don't understand you, Valentin."

He pulled me to a stop once we were out of sight of the green building.

"Understand this. You nearly hired a harlot." He waited for his words to sink in, and I had to fight a giggle, facing him in all seriousness. "If your chaperone had seen… It is a blessing she is half a city away, " he muttered, mostly to himself.

I smacked my empty hand to my face, feigning innocence.

It wasn't until I was settled aboard Valentin's boat that I had time to hide the woman's gift securely in my boot.

CONNOR

THE SITUATION IN COISUME WAS FAR WORSE THAN I'D IMAGINED.

Captain Forewell was running loose *and* a whole delegation from Sanctuary was in town. Not only had Coisume's council dedicated the whole week of fall festivities in their honor, but they were parading the Sanctuarians around on the city's largest barge. Smaller crafts shot ahead, announcing the reopening of Sanctuary to the citizens of the channel city. Coisume was again to ally with the walls. My enemies were right in front of me, heading toward the lower city. Drinks in their hands, ready to sample the delights of the channels.

I threw myself into an empty seat at a nearby grill to avoid their attention. I could not clearly see the faces of the men aboard, but if Forewell were one of them, he might remember me.

I stared after the boat long after it passed, long enough that the proprietress of the shop slapped a plate down in front of me. I was obligated to pass over a few coins for her smallest portion.

Roasters like this were unique to the channel city, their long grills built specifically for the giant channel eel they served. If there was not already an eel in front of a row of hungry customers, the woman would pull up one of her traps and spear one for our dinner, letting it cook in front of us until we deemed it ready to eat.

She slashed into the meat to mark my piece, the fire jumping and crackling where it met a stream of fat. I sliced along her lines, serving myself.

This place was full, with more customers waiting along the edge of the walkway. *Luck must have spared me a seat*, I thought as I took my first bite. Eel wasn't my favorite, but its rich flesh was nicely dressed up with a marinade of herbs and citrus, their leaves blackened at the edges from the fire.

The shop was situated in a narrow passage between two channels. The barge had passed down the one at my back.

Another, where the shop hung its traps, flowed right behind the grill. I chewed and let myself watch the boats as they rushed past. Some struggled, using poles instead of magic to navigate against the current.

It was good entertainment and fair enough food, except I was in Coisume for one reason. Before I'd seen the council's barge, I'd wanted to find Regula. Now I *needed* to find her. Those men might know her or her charge. If they were anything like Forewell, they wouldn't hesitate to hurt her.

I stuffed the last of my accidental dinner into my mouth, allowing my gaze to rest on the channel a second longer.

My mind was so set on Regula that I thought I saw her on one of the sleek black boats. I craned my neck, even though the channel city was full of dark-haired women.

A flash of cheek, the wave of her hand, dark curls over a light dress. I was dreaming.

She turned toward her companion and I bolted up, knocking the stool from under me.

It was her.

Regula.

There. On the channel. Just out of reach.

The Ocuis sat right beside her, close enough to touch. Close enough to slit her throat if he realized she wasn't his promised bride. When he learned there was a pirate in her place...

I couldn't risk a smile or wave. I wouldn't endanger her, though I wanted to leap the railing and swim to her boat. Her eyes slid over me, as if she were searching too, but there was no recognition on her face. No clue that she'd seen me, that she knew I was coming for her.

Then she sped away, propelled by magic only an Ocuis could afford.

I left the grill behind, tripping over the uneven cobbles in an attempt to follow her path up the channel. I had no boat of my own, and I quickly fell behind.

At the nearest bridge, I stopped and watched her boat until I could not tell it from the others.

I relaxed in the knowledge that she was being shuttled up the channels, while her countrymen were traveling down toward the sea. *Just hold on a little longer, Regula.* I willed the thought toward the minuscule boat, hardly more than a smear of black between the cream buildings of the wealthier quarter.

The winter festivities had been relegated to the back of my mind as I searched for Regula, but it was the first night and the pheasants' ball would be held in Sanctuary's honor.

She might have to make an appearance. I was sure the Ocuis on her arm would never decline an invitation.

Perhaps I should get there first, and bring a few friends with me.

42

REGULA

A gray-coated messenger was pacing the antechamber when we returned to the villa. Valentin was quick to excuse me, shouting a little over the tolling of hourly bells in the distance and brushing off any of my attempts to thank him. I would never wear the clothing he'd ordered for me, but the act spoke to a kinder man than his prickly demeanor suggested. Our chaperone gave me a once-over and, thankfully, dismissed me.

It was only when I retired to my room that I slipped off my boots and retrieved the sewist's gift.

A light blue ribbon tied in a bow. *Poor thing.*

It would have been quite lush if it had not been trapped under my foot for the better part of a day.

I had to find some way back to the sewist's shop, where the ribbon's original owner might help me. I had not memorized the way on our first visit, and it would be much harder in the dark. I wondered if Coisume was the sort of place where one could ask directions to a business of that sort. The channelers seemed affable enough, so far, but one couldn't be too careful. Such questions could get you thrown in jail in Sanctuary.

I squeezed the ribbon for reassurance.

Connor was ever on my mind. I don't know how he'd gotten so far under my skin, but he was so stuck there that I was beginning to imagine him with me. I could have sworn I'd seen him in the city, mixed in with the throng. If I hadn't been in Valentin's boat, I probably would have run up and thrown my arms around a stranger.

I was halfway to forgiving him, even though I would never see him again.

I hadn't realized I had so much to give up, even if I'd been preparing for it. Odette would survive without me. Connor… Well, I would have been smarter to set no expectations of him in the first place. My future, though a little sidetracked, was finally here, and I was on my own.

The door opened, startling me. Valentin poked his head through.

"Ah, good, I'd hoped to catch you before you retired."

I palmed the ribbon and tucked my bare feet under my skirts. I hadn't managed to undress further.

"Tonight's something of a festival here in Coisume, and we've been invited. I'm afraid we can't turn them down." He looked apologetic, at least.

"Oh?"

"The news of your arrival has spread. There is a delegation from Sanctuary that is insisting upon your presence. On top of that, the Coisume council wants to meet you."

The blood froze in my veins.

Valentin brushed a lock of black hair off his forehead and leaned his shoulder into the doorframe.

"Me? I couldn't possibly…" I cast about for words. It was still early yet, and there was one altered dress in the wardrobe I could wear. Perhaps I should fake sickness. I had not planned to play Odette in front of my own countrymen, many of whom were familiar with her father. Not to mention that Captain Forewell would recognize me right away if he was to see me.

"I tried to call them off, my lady." Valentin shook his head. "The pheasants' ball is the last thing you need after your ordeal."

"The pheasants' ball?"

"It's a bit of a farce, really." He rolled his eyes. "Your bad luck to have landed here on the first night of Coisume's winter celebrations. All the gentry dress up as birds and light grand fires and dance around them, roasting themselves, I guess. It's in service of the lower classes." He wrinkled his nose. "They get to laugh their heads off at the spectacle. A little public humiliation for the richest among them. Blow off some steam. Apparently, it keeps everyone happy." He mimed a blade across the throat.

"Dress up as birds? Would I wear a beak?" Some of the fear had drained from me. It sounded like a pageant of sorts, which might afford me a measure of safety.

"Nothing like that. I believe the custom is to cloak oneself in feathers, though I've never seen it myself. We usually summer here."

Feathers? Cloaks? None of that was as helpful as a mask.

Valentin searched my face. I wasn't sure what was written upon it.

"If you're worried about missing the rest, we could come back... together. The fool's feast is great fun, I've heard. Servants and their employers all switch places, and the city eats enough to feed an army."

I nodded.

Gods bless him, the Vestal was trying. Whatever had soured him toward his marriage did not seem to apply to his treatment of me.

It didn't matter.

I would leave him, and I had to do it before we made it to the festival.

I could not face the whole of Sanctuary here in the channel city. Not as myself, and certainly not as Odette. Not if I wanted to walk out of the pheasants' ball alive.

CONNOR

I DID NOT FIND RORY ON MY WAY TO BOBBIN'S, BUT I DID FIND Boris, Bobby's fearsome husband, rousting a misbehaving customer in the alley. The enforcer had tied his long hair back, which meant the lout didn't stand a chance.

Boris had been a warlord. He'd led a legendary band of men in the north. Vestine had spent years trying to pull his thorn from their side. When he was finally routed, Boris had fled to Coisume, where coming after him meant beginning a new war.

His prowess showed behind Bobbin's, as he threw the man around, commanding him completely with his scarred fists.

"One of these," Boris bellowed, "for each time you touched her—" Every hit drove the man into the cobbles, coins rattling in his pockets. "—against her wishes!"

Bobbin's had strict rules. They hung over the bar and were reiterated at every point of contact, impossible to miss. Usually one transgression would be enough to banish a customer. This man, apparently, had committed many.

I made to step past, not minding a splatter of blood on my clothes, and met the customer's eyes.

Blue as the coat he wore.

Captain Forewell.

He recognized me too, pain transforming into shame and anger behind his eyes. Renewing his fight, he twisted from Boris's grip and scrambled off down the alley.

"I know this one," I said, eliciting a long, inscrutable look from Boris. "He'd benefit from a good dunking." I motioned toward the channel, my intention clear.

"Good idea. Give me a hand."

Forewell had not made it far, though he had managed to clamber to his feet. Boris easily caught his neck and brought him around, the efficient corralling a reminder to avoid the enforcer's bad side.

"I told you we'd meet again, you mannerless flea." His eyes bulged as I stepped up beside them.

The water was not far.

"Don't—I can pay!" Forewell squeaked under the pressure of Boris's hand.

"Money isn't the issue. Respect is," Boris huffed at him.

"He doesn't have an ounce of respect in him," I said. "Threw two women to their deaths rather than face me and my crew on the Nearways."

Boris's lip curled, and he shook the man. "That right?"

"No! No, I didn't! I would never—!"

"I've seen your like before, *Captain*." Boris jerked him back to speak right into his ear, exposing the whole of his blue finery. "And I'm inclined to believe *him*." He jerked his head toward me and tightened his grip. "After seeing how you treated my girls."

I stopped Boris a few steps from the channel's railing.

"No sense in getting his coat wet, or the rest of his fancy things." An idea was forming as I watched the Sanctuarian squirm. Boris didn't flinch when I worked the jacket off Forewell's shoulders. "Someone might need them."

The captain fought me alright, as best he could, caught in the grip of one of the most dangerous men on the continent. He lost. I draped his coat safely over my arm and winked at the pathetic excuse for a sailor.

"You said he drowned two women?"

"Nearly." I didn't offer anything else.

"Maybe he doesn't need the rest of his kit either." Boris cocked his head at me as Forewell strained against his hand.

I took his meaning, and set about unbuckling our captive's shirt and pants. It wasn't easy. Sanctuary's clothing was always so complicated.

"Too cold to be swimming, if you ask me, but he's set on it!" Boris said over his shoulder to a curious passerby.

No, not a passerby. Tanza, the icy woman with whom he shared a wife. I paused, unsure whether to continue with a lady present, though she was just as scary as Boris himself. Her pedigree was so perfect that she should have been on the Coisume council, but rumor had it she'd given up the position to become the city's blade instead. I believed it.

She stared at us from beneath black curls, the last of the sun setting off the emerald of her dress and the medium brown of her skin.

"Caught him messing with Clarys," Boris said, as if it was common for him to be dragging a man around like a naughty kitten.

"I'm amazed she isn't here meting out the punishment herself. Any reason we're doing it in front of half the city?" she asked, more curiosity than anger in her tone.

"New information," Boris said. They both looked at me.

"He threw two ladies into the sea. Thought we should repay the favor."

"Ah, this is what I've been hearing about all day. The Sanctuary girl. You must be the one who's after her then? Bobby mentioned a pirate." She pressed a curl behind her ear and ran her gaze over me, calculating.

"Girls. The other one drowned." I kept to Regula's careful lie. Forewell was listening, even if he was a little tied up.

Tanza frowned. In less than the time that it took me to blink, she'd pulled a dagger from her sleeve. It gleamed, wicked against the perfect folds of her dress.

"Don't make me test how sharp this is." She swished it around in Forewell's field of vision. "Carry on, then," she said to me, setting the blade expertly into the notch of the unlucky captain's throat.

Boris relaxed his grip but did not back off, allowing me to unbuckle and pull off the man's shirt. Forewell was trapped with a lethal woman at his front and a mountain of a man at his back, and he didn't look like he had the good sense to enjoy it.

Best to put him out of his misery, then. I shucked Forewell's boots and pants, then I stopped, careful to add everything but the boots to my new collection.

"Won't learn his lesson," Tanza said, her hand steady, eyes never leaving Forewell's face.

Smallclothes too, then. Those I yanked down and tossed directly into the channel. The water made short work of the white linen.

"Please... please," Forewell begged as best he could against the cold steel.

"Didn't know you knew that word," Boris grated just as Tanza said, "It's a little too late for that."

They nodded at each other, partners in terror.

Tanza lowered her dagger, leaving the captain's neck unmarked. Boris wrapped one arm around Forewell's bare chest and grabbed his leg with the other, hoisting him from the ground.

Forewell wailed all the way into the drink.

The current took care of him.

Boris wiped his hands on his shirt and stared into the water.

"Thanks for your help." It wasn't until he turned that I realized he'd been talking to me. Tanza had disappeared from our side.

"My pleasure, really. My friends barely survived his kindness." I shook out my new blue coat a little harder than intended, before I bundled it around the rest of my stolen wardrobe.

"Friends, eh? This the girl you're running around after?"

I blushed. "I'm not... I made a mistake, and I let her go, and now she's in danger."

"Aren't they always?" He clapped an arm over my shoulders, making me jump. I'd known Boris a while, and known *of* him longer than that, but he'd always been standoffish. It was a little scary finding myself this close to him, even if he was smiling as he tugged his long, dark hair out of its knot.

"You tell Bobby about it?" He escorted me into Bobbin's, practically crushing me under his arm.

"A little. I needed her help. I still need it."

We settled ourselves at the bar, and he waved over two tankards while I tucked Forewell's clothing between me and the back of my seat. The barman delivered heady, rich beer; better than I was used to, and probably better than Bobbin's customers got.

I took a steadying gulp and began to share the events of the last few days with one of the continent's most wanted men.

BORIS AND I WERE SUMMONED TO BOBBY'S QUARTERS NOT LONG after. Tanza was there, waiting for us. Rory, too, had been rustled up from somewhere.

Bobby, it seemed, was deeply moved by my predicament. She'd been waiting for me to explain myself ever since Rory had declared me lovestruck when he first arrived in an attempt to secure us a free room. He deserved a good cuffing for that, even if his gambit had worked. We had a room *and* the assistance of three of the most powerful people in Coisume.

Bobby considered me to be abysmal at love. She'd married twice, herself, and was probably the biggest romantic this side of the sea. Bobby, Tanza, and Boris made a strange triangle, and while few were party to how exactly they worked, the strongest point was clearly the madam. She was a diamond pendant, just as comfortable on a leather choker as on a satin ribbon.

As frightening as they'd seemed beside the channel, Boris and Tanza were worse in an enclosed space. They sucked the air right out of the room. I could hardly tell which to be more worried about.

They both stared at Bobby as if she hung the stars in the sky.

"My love!" Bobby addressed her partners, proffering a dainty, freckled pink hand to each. "My darling! Help me smuggle pirates into the pheasant's ball tonight?"

I held in a snort. Boris was anything but someone's darling. At least in Bobbin's open lobby one might forget about his bulk, ignoring the scars that cut through his face and swam down his arms. Here, Boris towered over us all, even Rory, and it didn't even make him the most formidable in the room. Bobby's 'love' was by all accounts much worse, leaving a trail of bodies behind her.

Bobby had coaxed two vipers to her breast, and they all seemed quite happy about it.

My own tortured chest tightened.

"You promised me no work today, love," Tanza said, her tone just shy of pleading as she took her wife's hand.

"This isn't work, it's play," Bobby replied, tugging her in a little closer.

Tanza shifted her gaze to puzzle over Rory and me.

"Not that sort, you beast," Bobby reassured her. "I'm meddling in the lives of others, not dipping my pen into their ink."

I blushed faintly pink and Rory laughed in response. We could toss a coin to see which spouse would be taking our heads if we attempted the latter.

I snuck a glance at Boris. A smile danced at the corner of his lips.

"You promised me tonight." Tanza returned her attention to her wife.

"And you will have it." Bobby paused, her fingers coming up to catch the other woman's chin.

Then she fixed me with bright hazel eyes. "Your Sanctuary girl, you say she's in great danger."

"Yes. She is. She's pretending to be a Sessleny of the first wall. It would have been fine if it was only an Ocuis she had to fool, but now with the festival in Sanctuary's honor and a whole delegation of men who might recognize her for a fake…"

"Does the council know of her?" Bobby asked her wife.

"The whole city does. They'll be inviting her specially." Tanza did not sound happy about it.

Bobby gestured fluidly toward the upper city. "So much is done for Sanctuary's benefit as of late."

Her words sent a shiver down my spine.

Pirates were not welcome in a world where Sanctuary reigned supreme. Nothing was, not unless it fit within the city's rigid morals and ever expanding walls. Coisume would soon regret their renewed alliance.

43

REGULA

The pheasants' ball might very well be the death of me.

No escape presented itself as we readied for the party. Even without the chaperone, who'd declared there was nothing she could do for us if we were set on attending the night's festivities, Valentin hovered nearby. His men went out running, procuring us feathered cloaks to make us proper pheasants.

No amount of pageantry kept my fear from holding me captive on the boat ride over to the council's square. The channel was hardly the sea, but I dreaded going over the side again. Drowning would be a beautiful death, I supposed, compared to whatever Sanctuary would do to me should they catch me.

The air was tinged with smoke from the festival's fires as we made our way toward the upper city, adding to my apprehension. There was no better place to light fires than in a city surrounded by water, but it was still unsettling. Music drifted down the channels as well, growing louder the closer we got to our destination.

Our craft began to slow within sight of the pheasants' ball. We were not alone in our feathers. The channelers spun, whimsical, their cloaks and dresses flying with them in all colors against the light of three huge fires. Those who did not dance were eating, drinking, and watching from the high stone ramparts that guarded the square. This must have been the oldest part of the city. The place from which the rest had sprouted, built by kings but now in the hands of Coisume's council.

The boat released its remaining charmed air in great, concentrated gasps, driving us toward stone steps that doubled as a dock for these small channel craft. I could not focus beyond the sound, barely registering Valentin's voice beside me. I thought I might throw up, everything suddenly too real.

I should have jumped and let the water take me if it wanted.

On the decorated landing, silhouetted by fire and the bluster of the festival, four men waited.

I scanned them, the world closing in on me as I weighed my options. My heart thudded in my throat.

One was a near perfect copy of Valentin. A little taller, a little broader in the shoulders, a little heavier in the brow. Another Vestal, certainly. An Ocuis, I'd bet. The next, a golden-haired shadow, hemmed in on both sides by the others, with clothing so buckled up I could barely make him out. A Sanctuarian, without a doubt. But was he a threat to me? I wasn't sure. A third stood nearly as tall as the Ocuis, and had his attention half turned to the blond man. The careful buckles and folds of his clothing reminded me a little of my former husband. His face—

No, it could not be. He would never leave the sanctity of the inner wall. Never!

He had.

Earnest Toin.

I bit my tongue until rust hit the back of my throat, trying to keep my face blank and a frustrated scream from my lips.

His face was the same. Handsome without much of anything else, unless he let his cruelty shine from him. Laugh lines bracketed his mouth and feathered out from his eyes to the edges of his newly salt-and-pepper hair. He had often laughed at my suffering.

The fourth man wore silver, Coisume's colors, but he was

mostly lost to me. I was unable to tear my eyes from my former husband. I tried to will the boat apart with my mind. Tried to send myself into the deep.

It was no use. The lip of the craft butted against the stones.

Words buzzed around me like flies. I noted things as if from beneath the sea. That was Valentin's brother. This was the pheasants' ball. Everything knocked around, my insides hollow, nothing to grab and hold on to.

My existence boiled down to one thing, and one thing alone. Earnest had not yet noticed me.

Regula, he might not remember. The first thing he did in our marriage was stop looking at me. Besides, I was shined up like a gold piece for the pheasants' ball and wearing someone else's name. Odette was another matter entirely. Her family was famous in the walls, practically worshipped. The next best thing to the First himself. A position Earnest coveted. There was no doubt he'd seen her face in passing.

From the corner of his eye, in a blur, I might measure up to his memory of Odette, but a longer look would damn me.

There was only one thing for it. I would have to reacquaint myself with my fear.

I could not let myself think about the speed of the current, or the cold of the water or the pain of being down so deep I could no longer see the light.

Let the water treat me kindly. Let her hide me.

I purposefully missed the fourth man's silken arm and tripped on my way out of the boat. Half in and half out, I teetered, trying my best to make it look like an accident.

I went down, my chin smacking the landing, my teeth clicking so loud I thought the sky had started thundering.

Fingers clawed at me, finding only my delicate feathers. Ripping them. They were too late.

I didn't immediately find the water, caught between city and channel. When I finally fell in, the cold was a shock.

If I lived, I would hurt.

If I lived…

I was doomed to die, I realized, as someone caught my shoulder, hauling me back up. An arm circled my middle.

I'd cheated my drowning—or Connor had—but this I could not escape. If Earnest had not been paying any attention before, he would surely be looking now.

I was dragged from the water.

I flailed once more, hoping my movements conveyed confusion and pain. The arms around me had to be Valentin's. He was the only one who cared. I levered the boat with my foot, desperate to flip it, to unbalance him and throw us both back into the water, where I might have a chance.

The light craft, fueled by polite magic, was not charmed against upset, and I felt it give.

It was not, however, Valentin who held me up. While the boat rolled, my feet landed firmly on one of the steps.

My hope was lost. Drowned.

I peered out from behind my wet hair.

The blond stranger gazed back. His face, free of shadows now that I was so close, was covered in pinkish scars, like creeping vines. His eyes were feverish, unfocused.

He did not immediately let me go.

Better than Earnest, at least. But not an escape. An enemy.

My time was running out.

I prayed my hair and the remnants of my cloak would hide my face.

"He can't swim!" I bellowed, pointing to where the boat had flipped and was bobbing, held in place by its charm.

This, of course, was a matter of pride across the plaza. Coisume was the city of channels. A city of swimmers. Other guests took to the water, eager to become heroes.

"Strange," the man who held me whispered, an odd look on his face.

I wriggled, thoroughly unsettled. Had he seen me catch my heel under the craft? I could only guess how it had looked from above, even in the dancing light of the pheasants' fires. Shadow surely served me just as well as it dressed him.

He relaxed his grip on me, finally.

"Unhand her!" The command sent the scarred man stumbling to his knees, his fingers clawing at his throat.

New hands settled protectively at my shoulders. I knew these. These knew me.

My stomach sank.

Earnest.

I pinned my gaze to the ground.

Don't look. He might not. He might remove his hands and walk away without a glance.

"Scum doesn't touch a Sessleny. You know that," he hissed at the stranger, who hung his head.

Water sloshed near my feet. The men I'd knocked overboard were pulling themselves up on the landing.

A distraction, if only I could use it.

But I had no further plan. Only to shrink so small as to disappear. It was easy to remember how with Earnest's hands on my shoulders.

"Your family is overjoyed by news of your rescue, girl."

My luck ran out. Earnest stepped between me and the kneeling stranger.

"I assured them that we would bring you swiftly—"

He got a good look at my face and his words caught in his throat.

"She's going nowhere with you," Valentin said, having made it out of the water, soaked but standing.

"I—" Earnest looked between us, drawn back and back again to my face.

"I swore she would come to no harm in my care, and I meant it," Valentin snarled, shaking himself and starting forward. "Your men cannot be trusted. She was left to drown on the *Edgewater*."

Earnest's eyes flashed and he frowned.

"The *Edgewater*? We came in on the same ship, and I heard nothing about a drowning."

Valentin scowled.

My mind raced. Earnest on the *Edgewater*? Another party from Sanctuary? Was that the reason for our trouble? It was obvious now, with all this pomp and ceremony, that Sanctuary and Coisume had formed an alliance. Did it need to be protected against pirates? Or was it the men themselves who were too precious to risk?

It now made sense why we had never been invited to dine at the captain's table.

"My betrothed might be safe in Sanctuary, but not on one of your death traps," Valentin said, adamant. "I will be the one taking her there."

"I don't think so," Earnest finally said. "She's not yours."

"Not yet. Never, if your men had had their way." Valentin spat, actually spat, at his feet.

The surrounding group sucked in a breath.

Then Valentin's brother grabbed him by the collar.

"You embarrass us. This is Sanctuary's night," the other Ocuis said, deadly calm except for his grip. "Their ships are our ships, you know that. It doesn't matter who returns her."

All my numbness fled. My questions were slowly finding their answers.

"It doesn't matter," Earnest said, voice flat. "You're mooning over the wrong girl."

I'd known it was coming, but the words had the same effect as a fist to my gut.

Valentin shook his brother off and bared his teeth. His fingers flew to the hilt of his slender side sword.

Earnest threw his hand up and pivoted toward the silver-clad man.

"I thought you said the Sessleny was retrieved."

The man looked at me, hard, arms clasped, worrying the silk of his sleeves with his thumbs.

"It was the council's understanding…"

Earnest glanced at me one more time, the last he intended to, it seemed.

"You've been tricked. This is a charlatan, a pirate. You lost the valuable one to the ship that brought her in, if she survived at all."

I could not help my flinch. He was the same man I'd known, able to slice down to the bone without the help of a knife.

"You dare malign her?" Valentin was not ready to give up his fight.

"Compare your portraits, boy," Earnest said. "And you, call your guard." He nodded at the man in silver.

Valentin shut his mouth, studying me with dark, inscrutable eyes. I wondered if I made more sense to him now.

A row of men appeared above the landing without much prompting.

No one asked me to defend myself. My fate was already sealed.

44

CONNOR

Regula. Finally.

There she was. In a boat with that insufferable imperial, Sanctuary's delegation there to meet her.

Then she was gone. Into the water.

I scrambled down from my perch on the high walls with the rest of the revelers.

It wasn't my Eagle's most graceful escape, but it would do, *if* it managed to work.

Seas, no. Someone'd got a hold of her, pulling her up as her boat rolled, throwing the men who'd come with her into the channel. *Good.*

If I had not already abandoned my plan, I would have at the sound of her screaming. I joined a stream of would-be rescuers, craning my neck to see around them. I'd set aside my impulsive streak when I took the captaincy, but Regula had brought it roaring back. I could not keep myself from her side, though the crowd was threatening to stop me.

I pushed past dancers and froze. I'd missed something in the throng.

Regula's wrists were tied and the rope delivered into hands I'd hoped to never see again.

Rillen.

Auguste Rillen.

The man who'd burned a thousand ships.

Sanctuary's bloodiest weapon. Pirate turned pirate hunter.

A sailor I'd once considered a friend, who I would now kill with a smile.

I hadn't seen him mixed in with the party from Sanctuary. Only the seas knew why they'd let their hero leave. He was rarely away from the city. He was too valuable.

Suddenly, I knew why Regula's ship had been hell-bent on continuing their journey no matter the cost. If the *Edgewater* was the first ship to arrive from Sanctuary in twenty years, it made a sick sense. There were other, more important passengers.

I could not ignore the implications. Sanctuary was not only opening up, it was back to its old patterns. Blood would be spilled in its name. Regula's would be first.

My heart skipped in time with the drums. The pirate hunter was going to kill her.

My terror held me still longer than I liked.

Rillen in person was different from Rillen on a pamphlet or Rillen in a ballad. His blond hair was unmistakable, loose and wild, just as his scars would be if I could get close enough to see them. It was said he marked himself for each of his kills. Money wasn't enough for him. He had to wear his trophies. Bile burned in my throat.

He looked at Regula, a sidelong, assessing gaze, and my fingers itched for my dagger.

I adjusted the lapels of Forewell's blue coat, uncomfortable against my skin. I'd left the other clothes behind, unable to move under all those buckles.

The whole group started off the landing. Two Ocuis, the men from Sanctuary, Rillen, and Regula, her hands tied. One of Coisume's council walked with them, impossible to miss in his silver finery. A pack of the Channel Guard surrounded them.

Regula scanned the crowd. She would only find me if she was willing to look for her rescue in a blue coat. *Not likely.*

I picked my way across the square alongside them.

Biding my time.

The plan I'd abandoned hadn't needed much from me. A signal when Regula arrived. One she'd given herself, better than I could have, sending a wave through the party. A commotion on the channel itself.

While I stalked one council member, the rest would be introduced to Odette... the real one.

Bobby and Tanza had outfitted a troupe of pirates in the Coisume style to accompany her, but kept themselves well out of the way, because the *Wretched Lady* would be stealing her back at the end of her appearance. We could not risk losing her and they could not appear to be aiding us in any way.

A runner in much muted Coisume silver intercepted the council member, stopping the group. I could not hear his words, but the man's hands flew, growing more and more agitated as he learned of the actual Sessleny far across the festival in the company of the rest of the council.

Regula stood stock-still, but I knew she listened, because a little of her facade fell from her when she heard of Odette's arrival. It was everything she'd sacrificed herself to avoid.

Don't worry, my Eagle, I urged her from afar. *Let us pirates take care of it for you.*

The party from Sanctuary took the news even worse. An older man towered over the council member, jabbing a finger toward Regula over and over.

Eventually, they stopped arguing and took my bait.

Perfect.

REGULA

I WAS GOING TO WRING ODETTE'S NECK.

Then they could kill me. It would be worth it.

She was supposed to be on the *Wretched Lady*. Safe and far from here.

Maybe I would wring Connor's neck first. He was captain, after all. That would be satisfying. He'd broken every promise he'd made me.

She looked right up there though, sitting with the Coisume council. A decadent robe of purple feathers pressed up to her rosy cheeks.

The councilman with us must have left his place to take care of the guests from Sanctuary. He did not look particularly happy to see her in his seat.

We trudged up the low stairs to the platform where they were presiding over the festivities. I almost missed the pirates at her back. Robin and Jack. They'd traded their usual clothing for stark black, looking a bit like the guards the Ocuis employed.

My eyes darted to the crowd. Were there others?

Rory? Trenna? The captain?

They must be here somewhere. Odette was as valuable to them as to Sanctuary.

Earnest began to boil as soon as the council member opened his mouth to explain the situation.

My unmasking had been his triumph. A point of his pride.

As for Valentin... he was silent, trudging beside me. He'd been bludgeoned hard with my deceit. I could not blame him for giving up my defense. His brother was now watching him like a hawk.

The blond one could barely walk in a straight line, though I hadn't seen him drink a drop. Nothing phased him, except Earnest's harsh treatment. The strangeness of his stare and the few words he had managed stayed with me.

He held the other end of the rope that tied me, but I was

beginning to believe he might be just as much a prisoner as I. The men from Sanctuary treated him as they would a tamed beast. The Ocuis, too, seemed wary.

None of this mattered by the time we reached the rest of the council. The Odette show was already in full swing, and everyone was to take part.

"I demand to know the meaning of this!"

Oh, Earnest, shut up. I bit my lip. I had not quite figured out whether he recognized me or if he'd only realized I wasn't Odette. I would be a fool to remind him of any semblance of our married life, no matter how satisfying it would be to give him a piece of my mind.

"This is unusual, perhaps—" The council member who'd escorted us began.

Odette sat forward in his chair, the attention of the other council members traveling with her. She had not merely been waiting for us, she had been charming them in our absence.

"My betrothed and I had grave concerns for my safety at your grand celebration. You'll have to excuse us. We never intended to cause a fuss." Her purple feathers fluttered as she flashed a bright smile.

Valentin went rigid beside me.

He'd never seen her before, besides her portraits.

For the first time since the fight had gone out of him, he looked at me. I dared not turn my head too far, but I managed the slyest of winks.

He had not been so bad, besides the drinking. I might have enjoyed his company, if I had not been plotting my escape the entirety of our time together. He was a continental with a sense of humor, and as a dandy, I knew he would be easy prey for Odette. She was almost irresistible.

"And our fears were well founded, my lady. Look how they treated your double." He was quick to speak up.

Odette did not have to fake her pout when she noticed the ropes at my wrists and the soggy state of me.

"You did this? Why, my countrymen? I—"

Earnest cut her off. "We immediately recognized that the Ocuis was not escorting you, lady! It wasn't to be borne." He would argue with anything.

"Did you not ask her? Or him? We agreed to reveal everything once the festival was deemed safe." Odette's eyebrows drew down and she twisted toward her council of allies, her curls cascading prettily from her shoulders.

He hadn't bothered to ask, but he could not say that now.

It was the standing councilman who saved him.

"Lady, Coisume would never put you in any danger. In fact, we have extra guards assigned to our Sanctuary delegation tonight. Let that lay your fears to rest."

She laughed. "Tell it to that poor woman. Perhaps your many guards will be able to cut her loose?"

Everyone scrambled to free me at once. Everyone except Earnest. His lips were pressed into a hard line.

"I'd like her to stay with me, for questioning," my former husband said. A collective groan went up, and he added, "We do not suffer pirates kindly in Sanctuary." When he looked at me, his eyes were like chips of ice.

He knew me, alright.

I wanted to laugh. I wanted to run.

Odette looked to the council, her smile not an inch out of place. No one else would notice the slight shake to her hands. She knew Earnest as well as I, having learned of him from my stories and my tears. He'd rattled her.

But it was Sanctuary's night, and the council was not willing to cross them, even if many of them did roll their eyes. I'd learned Coisume did not care about pirates, as a rule. The city could not run without a little underhanded business. But this went both ways, and they wouldn't acknowledge their underbelly either.

Sanctuary must have been very important to them indeed,

for they finally nodded as one and banished the rest of the conversation.

"A pleasure to see you alive and well, lady." Earnest beamed at Odette and then nodded at Valentin. "I'll report to your parents that your betrothed will be escorting you safely home." To everyone else, he gave a slight bow before excusing himself.

Odette rose ever so slightly from her seat, but she was just as bound by her farce as we were, and had to play her role.

She could not stop Earnest from taking a firm grip on my arm and marching me up the flat expanse of steps that led to the council's chambers. The blond man came too, though there was no hand guiding him, and a blue coat trailed some paces away. I was grateful for their presence. The last thing I wanted was to be alone with Earnest. The look in his eyes promised retribution for his humiliation.

I was surprised to find Valentin with us as well. He'd left the council and his true betrothed behind. Perhaps I should give him more credit. Earnest did not like this one bit, pausing to send him off.

His grip on me did not falter while he cursed the imperial out. In his eyes, Valentin was just as responsible for his embarrassment.

I rubbed my wrists together, testing Earnest's hold on me. The ropes were gone, but he would not be so easy to lose.

The blond man watched me, extending a hand to hover near mine.

"Are you hurt?" he breathed. It barely carried over Earnest's anger.

I did not have time to answer.

A blur of blue and gold was upon him, sending him again to his knees.

While the man had seemed almost helpless before, except for hauling me from the channel, he became someone else entirely with a dagger at his throat.

Earnest and Valentin left off their arguing and watched as

the stranger rolled, ignoring the kiss of steel. He fought like a man without a thing to lose, as if a cut would simply deliver him closer to the gods.

"Forewell, you should be on your ship!"

Forewell. *Forewell.* Earnest's words took a moment to click into place.

I'd only just steadied myself when the bluecoat pressed himself up from the stranger's chest and my world shattered yet again.

"Forewell's somewhere, but not on his ship, old man."

A familiar face stared up at me.

It was Connor in Forewell's finery. Connor, rolling on the ground with the blond stranger, going for blood.

My surprise was a cliff, but I did not have the luxury of falling from it. Earnest reached for his hilt. I'd spent years on the other side of his anger. He might be older, but he was no less lethal.

Why had Connor thrown himself on the other man?

Earnest was the threat here. I was sure of it. He'd kill me. He'd kill Connor. He would kill anyone who painted him a fool.

Connor would not suffer at his hands. My former husband could not be allowed to draw his sword. I wouldn't let him.

It was a good thing he'd forgotten me. Before I could think too hard about it, I shoved him with all my might.

Earnest fell back, losing his footing on the uneven ground. He rolled down the council's steps, shallow though they were. My breath caught in my throat.

Earnest did not rise.

When I lifted my gaze, it was to meet Valentin's eyes, wide in the flickering light from the fires. I could not read his face beyond that.

My calm left me. What had I done?

I turned back to Connor and the stranger, just in time to watch the blond man hammer Connor's wrist with his fist, knocking the dagger from his grasp. Between one heartbeat and the next, the man had Connor at his mercy, hands solid at his throat.

If the stranger had carried his own blade, or had not ignored the captain's dagger, lying silently off to the side, Connor would surely be dead.

Maybe he would be anyway.

"Regula, get out of here. Now," Connor croaked, voice straining under the pressure of the man's hands.

"No! Please, don't hurt him." I tried to reach the stranger. He had been kind to me, even after he'd heard I was a pirate. It was no use. There was no response.

I was near tears.

"Please! Valentin, do something," I begged. He crossed his arms, his brow furrowed.

Connor flailed his arms and legs desperately, anything to free himself. The stranger did not give him a target to hit.

"Run," Connor gasped.

This time, I listened.

45

CONNOR

I let myself go slack in Rillen's grip, my relief battling my fear.

Regula was gone.

A pirate would find her. She would be free, finally, with the chaos of the festival to protect her.

It was a shame I would not be able to see her on the *Wretched Lady*. If we'd had more time, I could have taught her fishing and swimming. I might have raced her up the ropes or shown her the Tross. I'd have learned her too, if she'd given me half a chance.

My death beckoned instead. My only real regret was that I would not be taking the pirate hunter with me.

I steeled myself.

I could think of worse things than a revel for a funeral, the noisy crowd and drifting smoke from the fires my only companions as I passed on to the next life.

Never thought I'd die on land, though.

I waited.

Coisume's bells rang out. One… two… three.

Rillen's killing blow never came.

His hands loosened and I fell, knees and palms smacking the step. The sting was lost under my surprise.

Ten... eleven... twelve.

All hell broke loose in the square.

I ignored everything else, staring up at the pirate hunter. He towered over me, a shadow among shadows. The Ocuis was behind him, watching us like we were hired entertainment. The older man had disappeared.

Let him look, then.

Rillen was still, silent, his laughter gone.

An overripe gourd hit the ground beside us, covering the both of us in guts. Rillen didn't flinch, merely wiped it off. I was stunned, simply letting the seeds drip slowly down.

I'd forgotten about this. The lower city folk who'd perched in the walls around the square were now the main event, hurling food and wine and whatever else they could find down at the pheasants. The whole of Coisume thumbed its nose at winter, sacrificing what extra they had in the service of their tradition.

It didn't make a lick of sense to me. Empty stores on the *Wretched Lady* meant hard sailing and worse attitudes, but the channel city claimed the practice brought them kind winters, perhaps in part because the pheasant's ball allowed the city's most vulnerable to provision themselves from the excess without having to beg.

Below us, the dancers regained their footing, spinning anew as projectiles rained down from the walls above. Pheasants at their feast. The gentry didn't eat—at least, not from the flag-stones—but they reveled in the ritual, letting their feathery garb bend and whip like the plumage of the birds they pretended to be.

A part of me still waited for Rillen's final blow. I was hardly better than a pheasant myself, presenting myself for the table. I had forgotten to cower or run as the scene around us grew muddier with celebration.

He didn't bother doing me in. The fires raged behind us, wine drenched and smoking. If he was giving me the gift of my life, just standing there with his eyes on the party, then I would be a fool to refuse. The Ocuis, too, held himself off a ways. *Strange.* I would want to fight me, if I were him.

"Thank you," I said under my breath to the far-off sea, or whoever had stayed my enemies' hands.

I wasn't fucking dead, and Regula was out there. I still had a shot. I just had to find her.

The square would be a mess, and I didn't have a clue which direction she'd gone off in, but... the blood was rushing back into my veins. She couldn't be far.

I scrambled down the steps, leaving the pirate hunter and the Vestal to each other's company. Neither came after me.

That left only the pheasants to fight with. I was doused in spirits and subjected to a hail of carrot tops and eggshells before I made it halfway to the first fire.

It was a wonder Coisume didn't lose a chunk of the city every year. If this were a ship, men would be leaping from the decks. But the wide stone courtyard had been built expressly for fire— no wooden buildings to burn on this isolated block, where the bulk of the festivities were held—so its people might have their winter worship. If feathers caught, they were simply ripped off and fed to the hungry flames.

Laughter echoed around me and a new torrent of scraps rained down. I had only to guess which way Regula had gone.

REGULA WASN'T LOOKING FOR ME.

Last she'd seen I'd been at death's door, rasping at her to run.

I'd doubled back. I'd stumbled up and down the length of the three nearest channels, running across Rory on my way, but there was no sign of her. It was like she'd disappeared into thin air.

To say I regretted my decisions in the last few hours would be an understatement. Not only had I failed to get Regula safely out of a dangerous situation, I'd managed to lose her in the process.

Coisume was a big place. Sure, the channelers didn't mind us pirates, but they weren't about to remember if a stranger passed through their pubs. There was Odette to worry about now, too. We'd brought her out into the open, and now it was up to my pirates to steal her back in a manner that would preserve her reputation and keep Coisume's guns from firing on us in the morning.

Due to the week of winter festivities, the port was booming. It would be bad business to close the whole operation down to sniff out one girl from Sanctuary, and Coisume was not known for doing bad business. The council was clearly frustrated with Sanctuary's demands already, even so early in this new alliance.

When Odette snuck away tonight, aided by her black-clad guards, and a ransom note was found in her place, the city would go on high alert.

It was the *Wretched Lady*'s gauntlet thrown down. Odette for Griffin. Time and place set out. Finally.

The three of them would disappear onto the ship, tied up under another name, at a different dock, flying unfamiliar colors. The port master would check his books and find the *Wretched Lady* had left days ago. He might order a search of every ship in the harbor, which would turn our craft up in a week or more— time enough to cast off for calmer seas. That was, *if* he ordered a search at all. Tanza was busy already, working behind the scenes to obscure what we'd done tonight. I trusted the plan.

The only missing piece was Regula. If I couldn't find her, then I would stay. The *Wretched Lady* would sail just fine without us.

Rory and I skulked outside the Ocuis villa, having found no trace of Regula.

"She'd be trying her luck coming back here," he said. Odette's betrothed hadn't returned yet, nor any of his henchmen. I didn't like the man, but he'd surprised me, helping her in front of the council. Regula must have trusted him to some degree.

But not enough to come back to his family's home.

I hoped against hope she hadn't gone straight for the docks. Anyone looking for Odette would surely start there, and the guard would be tripled the moment our note was discovered. Regula didn't have Robin and Jack by her side to get her safely aboard the *Wretched Lady*.

I should not have let her go.

I'd been desperate to keep her from Rillen, convinced I wasn't long for this world. If only I'd known.

Getting out from under Coisume's guns would be the easy part, if the port were watched tomorrow. My stomach was in knots and my brow sweaty. Any strategy I'd started with was lost to the winding streets and overwhelm of the crowds. I kicked a loose cobble and resolved to get myself under control.

It was Rory who finally turned us, forcing me bodily back to Bobbin's. The bells tolled three now. People were streaming down from the middle city, to whatever haunt they'd rather lose themselves in.

I was on edge, and could have searched all night. That, I thought, was Rory's worry. My state might land me on the point of a drunken channeler's blade. Or perhaps someone would land on mine, since I'd stolen a new dagger as we passed one of the taverns. He was right, though I would wait ten years to tell him. A city worked a little differently than a ship. One could be sure of things on the sea, in a way, that you couldn't be on land, and vice versa. I might very well push myself too far.

I grumbled all the way down to the docks, letting Rory shuffle me in with some other men, drenched in the night's fun, to cover us to Bobby's door. My mind was miles away as he marched me up the stairs. Miles I'd already walked, searching for Regula. Our room brought little comfort.

If we had a week, I could enlist Bobby's workers to my cause. Pound for pound, they would make better spies and operators than an army of sailors, especially during a festival week, when the multitude of men and women calling for their services would be as varied as the continent itself.

But my time was running short. If I couldn't... If I didn't manage to find her, they might also be counted on to look out for her. The channel city was a good deal better than Sanctuary, but it was still a new city for Regula to find her place in. A new life.

Sleep took me quickly, no matter how I fought it, bringing with it one thought.

I would survive without her... but I wouldn't like it.

46

REGULA

The blue ribbon was my beacon.

I squeezed it nearly to death, hanging on to a shred of my former self. Plans I'd already laid.

I'd lost almost everything. My feathered cloak had given up and ripped under a dancer's boot, falling behind me in tatters. All my other comforts had been lost, too. Nothing of my time with Valentin remained, nor anything from the *Wretched Lady*.

I'd searched the square for more pirates. There were none to be found, none that I knew. None to rush up and free Connor from the stranger's grip.

I could not risk returning to Odette and the council to borrow Robin and Jack. Her lies were far more delicate than mine at this point, and any misstep might betray her. I did not think for one moment that the pirates had given up their aspirations of trading her for their captain.

They'd need one if Connor was truly gone.

Connor... I could not think of Connor, lest I lose myself to tears. I'd helped him in my own way, but it had not been enough.

The stranger had been too strong for him.

My night was already a blur. I was only coming down from

my panic now, in the relative quiet of the streets. Nothing was left to me but the blue ribbon.

I'd killed a man.

Earnest.

The man who had been my husband.

It was only a push... I hadn't meant—

No. I would do it again, consequences be damned. I would do anything to save Connor, give anything...

Fate had laughed at me for figuring that out as he breathed his last.

There was always a chance I was wrong. Perhaps they both yet lived. And if Earnest was not dead, then he would be hunting me.

A secret part of me was glad that I'd done it. A pirate part. He'd caused me so much pain. Seeing him here, in my new world, was excruciating.

Tying my wrists was the first of a hundred things he had planned for me in his quarters. I would not agonize over saving myself, or trying to spare Connor.

I was tired of running and hiding, of dressing myself up as someone else. The sewist's ribbon was my only way forward.

The city was against me as I retraced my steps. Without the black boat to guide me neatly over the water, I was reliant on meandering streets, old bridges, and staircases stuffed with revelers.

With the risk of pursuit, I did not stop to ask for directions. I wasn't the only pheasant to have lost my cloak, and it wasn't long before I ran across an abandoned shawl of soft brown feathers to help me hide in plain sight.

I walked for what felt like hours, crossing my own path again and again. My memory failed me at every turn and my misery drifted closer to the surface with each step. I'd almost given up when a group of festivalgoers rushed past me, soaked in drink, whooping in excitement about bobbins and sewists and how far their gold would go on a winter's night.

When I conjured the needle and thread sign, the name Bobbin's slotted neatly into the memory, as good a lead as any.

I gave up my own mental map and took to their heels, following a block or two behind. For all their energy, the group was drunk and disorderly. Impossible to lose even on the most confusing streets. They smashed through gates and doors, opening up passageways I would not have thought to examine.

We were soon at our destination. A corner building painted a disarming green.

Bobbin's was exactly where the young woman had secretly passed me her token.

My guides disappeared behind the swinging doors.

I waited.

Was I a wanted woman? Valentin had seen me push Earnest down the shallow stairs. The council had watched me dragged away as a pirate, and would not argue with Earnest if he lived and wanted me back.

A bustling brothel's front room had a few too many eyes for my comfort. I'd be better off finding another way in.

I crossed the cobbles for a look around the back. *Ah, yes, an alley.* Stairs led up to a balcony, which ran across the whole of the building.

I smoothed the pale blue ribbon between my fingers and set my foot on the first stair.

"Where do you think you're going?"

I jumped.

A long-haired giant stepped from the shadows beside the stairwell. A guard of some sort… or worse. How I had missed him when he was wearing all white was beyond me.

"I, uh…" He'd scared the words from me.

His manner was relaxed. People must take one look at him and make themselves scarce.

I didn't have that luxury.

I held up the ribbon like a shield.

"A girl… One of the sewists gave me this."

He zeroed in on the trinket.

"Clarys," he finally said.

"I don't know. She didn't give her name."

"She's the only one who ties those like that." He crossed his arms, serving only to make him look a little more beastly in the scarce moonlight. "What's your name?"

My name? I dared not give him my real one, and I could no longer rely on Odette's, but something told me he could smell a lie.

"The Eagle." My voice wobbled. He cocked his head, unamused.

In fact, he seemed to be leaning toward chasing me off.

"I need to see her, this Clarys. Please."

"She's busy," he said.

"She'll see me. I know she will. I can wait." I was desperate.

"Not out here you can't."

"I don't have anywhere else to go." I was on the first step of the staircase, and still he towered over me.

"That's not my problem. Give me your real name or get out of here."

He stomped a little closer.

I couldn't. It wasn't safe. I could give him something else, though.

"I'm looking for my friends. Pirates. On the *Wretched Lady*. Clarys said she would help me."

The man's brows shot up.

"You didn't even know her name."

"I don't. I didn't. But she was going to help me."

"Was she?" He frowned, then said, "I think you'd better come with me after all."

The last place I wanted to go was upstairs with him, but I had to find Clarys. I knew she would help me. Her ribbon proved it. The man had not yet taken it from me.

I would have to risk it.

O_F ALL PLACES, THE BIG MAN LED ME TO THE BUILDING'S HIDDEN baths. Then he left me there.

If he expected me to clean myself up for him, he was in for a surprise.

A bath would have been nice. I was still sodden in places from my dip in the channel. The night air had not made things much better, and I was sticky with sweat from my search. I sat on the lip of an empty tub, one in a long line. A few were full of steaming water and the place smelled lovely.

Perhaps he knew this would be torture.

It was almost enough to send me somewhere else, a place where Connor was well, and Earnest had never left Sanctuary. Where I was not Regula, and might be allowed a little luxury.

"One of these is for you, you know." I was startled from my revelry by an attendant.

She was a sweet looking woman in simple but elegant clothing. Cherubic, even. With her tamed curls of oak and plush figure, she seemed better suited to the front room of Bobbin's than its bathing room.

I couldn't make myself argue with her.

She relieved me of my stolen feathers, and motioned for me to undress.

"Boris won't come back, if that's what you're worried about," she said, eyeing me.

That didn't top the list of my worries, but it was kind of her to tell me.

"He said I might meet Clarys." He hadn't promised that, hustling me in here, but she didn't need to know the details.

"A bath first, surely." She tutted at me, wrinkling her nose.

My eyes darted around the room. It was just us, and a bath would be so nice.

I gave in. She turned around so I could slide out of my dress and slip into the water. It was easy to sink in, and I was immediately so relaxed that I hardly noticed when she pulled a stool up to the edge of my tub, allowing her to scrub my shoulders and oil my arms. In fact, my eyes only cracked open when she addressed me by name.

"It's nice to finally meet you, Regula."

She fixed me with a bright hazel gaze. A trickster's gaze, I thought.

"Your lad's been half out of his mind searching for you, you know," she said, as if it were common knowledge. "And you! Braver than the sailors themselves, taking on what you did for your friend, and that ship."

I sat up. She should not know so much about me.

Her hand came to rest on my shoulder with just enough pressure to keep me in the tub.

"Don't worry, love, you'll soon be reunited." *If only.* She spoke as if she had absolute say in such things. She didn't know where I'd left him.

I ducked under her hand, levering myself up and out of the water.

"I don't think so."

He's lying just as still as Earnest.

"I don't mean you any harm. I owe Connor a favor."

"He won't appreciate it," I muttered under my breath, trying not to show her too much as I climbed out. She was between me and the wall of expertly rolled towels.

"He will."

I glared at her. I should never have come here, and I certainly shouldn't have gotten in her bath.

"Connor's not... I don't think he's coming back." It was all I could say.

She rolled her pretty eyes and tossed me a towel.

"Don't be dramatic. He's only sleeping."

What was she talking about?

"I saw him—" I had to get out of here.

"Yes, yes, he got a little roughed up. A scuffle is hardly anything to worry about."

"He's here?" I was starting to believe her, against my better judgment. He'd still been struggling when I ran. Maybe…

She cocked her head, her cherry lips hinting at a devilish smile.

"How sweet." She chewed on the words. "Yes, love. You did a fabulous job of losing yourself to the city, so he's worn some holes in his boots, but he's no worse for wear. In fact, I think he deserves a treat. Will you indulge me?" she purred.

"Me?"

"It's the first night of winter, and I'd like to finally clear my debt to the *Wretched Lady*."

I blinked. What was she talking about?

"You need my help for that?"

"Yes, of course!" she exclaimed. "I've been waiting for you. Say yes." I got the feeling this woman didn't beg unless the mood was right, but her eyes urged me on.

"If Connor is here, then I'll see him." I'd agree to nothing much beyond that. I didn't trust her, and I wouldn't until I had my eyes on him.

"That's the heart of my plan, lady."

47

CONNOR

C annonballs startled me from my sleep. No, not cannonballs. A pounding on the door. I scrambled up. Not on the ship. In a bed. In the channel city.

Regula. Ah seas, I'd lost Regula.

I heard laughter through the door. My unease drained away with the last dregs of sleep. More than once I'd been called to witness some parlor trick or assist in a hand of cards. Bobbin's girls had no way of knowing I was an inch or two from true despair, and those who did might be willing to rouse me from my depths in an attempt to help. Or on a whim. Or at Rory's say-so.

When I opened the door, I did not immediately encounter my right-hand man. A Bobbin's girl stood there instead.

I hadn't had the pleasure of her acquaintance, I didn't think, but she looked familiar.

"You're the pirate, right? I'm Clarys." I nodded. "The mistress has a surprise for you," she said, her eyes flicking over my rumpled clothes.

"I don't—" I started, having a good idea what sort of surprise Bobby might go all in for.

"Either you accept or you're out on your ass." She pursed her lips, and one of her light brown curls sprang from its careful pinning. It wasn't unlike Bobby to extend some generosity to her guests, but I had poured my heart out to her only this afternoon. She knew I wanted no one but Regula.

If she was back in residence, rather than in the council's luxurious apartments with her wife, she had no doubt been caught up on the success of our plan, and all my personal failures. Rory would have made sure of it.

How long had I slept?

At any other time, I would have indulged Clarys's mistress. As it was, I was hardly fit company for anyone. Whatever gift she had to show me, I didn't want it. I had mistakes to make up for and there was no reason to wait.

"The seat of my pants, then."

I didn't have a thing to gather, and I never should have retired for the night. Regula was out there.

"You can't! Come on, you'll like it!" Clarys propped her hands on her hips.

"No doubt, no doubt. Give your mistress my apologies. I'll see myself out."

"She said you'd say something like that. Lovestruck, you are."

"Sorry, Clarys, I got caught up. Is he giving you trouble?" Rory rounded the far end of the hall, calling out to my visitor.

"Walking out is what he is!" Clarys waved him over. She was almost as tall as Rory, now that I bothered to notice.

I scowled at my friend. There were roses in his cheeks and a gleam in his eye that usually meant trouble.

"He won't accept our gift." She shrugged.

"That's a shame." Rory made short work of the hall, stopping just in front of me. "It's just the thing to get him out of his mood." Clarys nodded at him, her eyes darting between us.

"Seas, Rory, you can't be—"

"Oh, chin up, Connor." He grinned at me, unsettling me further. "You won't mind this, I promise. Not one bit."

If the bastard would only tell me what to expect, I might believe him. But it wasn't his way. We were siblings of a sort, with

Griffin as our much-maligned older brother, and he'd take any opening to needle me. I hoped just a little, because I couldn't stand a sizable blow at the moment.

I sighed, and Clarys's smile crept back onto her face.

Curse it. No one was stopping me from leaving this overbearing establishment the moment after they revealed whatever conspiracy I'd become the center of.

I prepared to bow out gracefully as I followed them back down the hall. Clarys's pinned skirts swished as we traced a line toward the suites that usually meant heavier purses or more permanent stays.

Whatever lay ahead, I could always tell Bobby to stuff it. I settled behind that certainty.

Rory's glee was apparent even with his back to me. I groaned and set my face into a captain's unreadable mug. No surprise could ruffle me.

"Ah, here we are," Rory said, slipping into a teasing, posh voice and exaggerating the sweep of his hand to a handsome door. I felt Clarys's eyes on my face.

I wouldn't give them a show.

48

CONNOR

F or once, Rory had been right.

The instant I laid my eyes on Bobby's surprise, I dropped all pretense and sank to my knees in the doorway.

Regula.

Radiant.

On a luxurious couch. Dressed like a present.

I crawled to her.

If there was laughter or a whistle or two behind me, I could not hear it over the stark, chest-pounding gratitude I felt at seeing her again. Alive. Well.

It was only when Bobby swished up and caught my face in her hands that I remembered we were far from alone. The mistress of the house was clad in subtle browns and creams, so it was no wonder I'd missed her.

"Tell Griffin my debts are cleared," she said, looking down at me.

"Tell him yourself. You'll see him again, I swear it."

She laughed and dropped my chin.

"I'll hold you to that. He's a particular favorite of mine." I couldn't help my blush. "Not like that, lad. He introduced me to both of my lovers. I never thought I'd be able to pay him back."

"Paying me back, more like." I grinned at her.

"He'll take it."

She was right. Griffin would understand if—*when* he met Regula.

"Now," Bobby addressed the room, "let us leave these two to their reunion."

"Yes, do be gone." Regula was laughing, her attention fixed on the small crowd that had gathered in the doorway. "We've had enough of your meddling. Especially you, you brute."

I did not have to turn to know whom she addressed. Not when Rory trotted up to escort Bobby out on his arm, nudging me with his knee in the process. I pinched him back. He'd pay for subjecting me to this torment one day.

Right now I was busy with a more alluring opponent.

They left us just as Coisume's bells tolled in the distance.

One... two... three.

I was hit with a wave of wonder that was wholly unlike me. In years past, I'd taken pleasure where I could, but I did not make a habit of losing myself to anything or, truly, anyone. I'd traded favors and leaped from partner to partner for so long that I hardly knew what to do with the corner of my chest I'd carved out for this woman.

Four... five.

I was choking on the feeling. It would be easier to bury myself in Regula and forget it, but my soul cried out for release. If I placed it between us, if I spoke it aloud, I might free myself from the ache.

"Would you get off your knees? There's no one to impress."

How wrong she was. I acceded to her request, mostly due to my growing desire to remain an equal in her eyes, no matter the cost.

"Was I ever good enough for you, Connor?" She waited until

I was settled on the same couch, my knee arranged so I might face her on it as she railed at me.

"I—I don't—" I'd made so many mistakes, it was hard to pinpoint just one.

"I would not have imagined myself a pirate if you had not dangled the possibility in my face." She scowled at me, a sharp line between her brows. "You made me want things… Made me want to save you," she muttered at me.

Her care was hidden in fury. I was of half a mind to work her up further. The other half wanted to stop her worrying with my lips. I'd doomed myself by betraying her, because I could do neither.

I had to explain myself first.

"Regula, I've given up the captaincy." This shocked her, her fists bunching up in her skirts. "I was muddled, before. I was… I am desperate to liberate Griffin, and I find I cannot leave you alone." I had no idea what played upon my face as I spoke, rushing as I was to free myself from the feeling of her.

"It's clearer now. There is no war between my desires. Delivering you into the hands of that Vestal nearly broke me. Seeing you with the pirate hunter cut through all my confusion. I could never give you up, not willingly, not unless you wished it. I'd sooner die than see a pirate hunter hurt you. I'd fight him again if I could. Sanctuary is not worthy of your life."

She did not seem convinced, and started in again.

"All this fuss for the blond one? He could hardly stand. Well, he did get the best of you, I guess." She looked puzzled.

"He spared me. I'd made my peace with death."

She raised a dark brow, ready to ask me more.

"You don't have to forgive me. I took your choice from you because I thought I knew better."

Regula scoffed. "I'm so unused to holding the reins of my own life that I let you decide for me." She reached up and ran a thumb over my lips, the softest touch startling me into silence. "Never again."

I dared not hope, only echoed her. "I will no longer stand in the way of your future, I swear it."

She watched me, her fingers stroking down the join of my jaw, tracing over my fresh bruises. I was a hopeless beggar for her touch, and I might very well lose it.

"I need you, Regula." I was scared to look at her. "Everything I question about myself, and every fear I have, drops away in your company. When you left... To see you walk away with someone else... I felt the loss of you in my own body, as acutely as the clip of a musket ball."

"That's flattering." She was slow to tease me.

"No, lady, I mean it. I crave you. Nothing has ever moved me as you do. I cannot leave you in a strange city." I ventured a glance at her. She was frowning slightly, but at least she hadn't dropped her hand from my neck.

Would she quit me? I had to be sure.

"Join me on the *Wretched Lady*. Be mine, so that I will not be subjected to losing you again."

"Losing me? You sent me off, Captain," she said, hope flickering in my gut. Her eyes, when they met mine, were shining. My heart began to hammer.

"My mistake." I grinned.

"My former husband was there... At the pheasants' ball."

Her words slammed into me, though the brightness did not disappear from her eyes. *What? How?*

"Did he recognize you? Hurt you?" I searched her face for a hint of what I'd missed. I'd been so focused on Rillen.

"He saw me, and he would have... He didn't have a chance." Was that a tear in the corner of her eye?

"Where is he? I will make short work of him."

She started sobbing. I waited a moment, threading my fingers into the hair at her temple.

"You were fighting... I... I think I killed him," she said, under the cover of her tears. "He was going to hurt you, after you revealed yourself, while you were distracted with your pirate hunter."

Ah, now I knew who she was talking about. The older man who'd mistaken me for Forewell. It would be insensitive to shrug, but what did I care for Sanctuarians? Except that I would have killed him myself if I'd known he was standing right there.

The man who'd tied her up. Who'd led her away for questioning.

He deserved a slower death.

But I was a pirate, and she wasn't. Yet.

I pressed my nose to her wet cheek. Her breathing was only a little uneven now.

"Is that all?" I kissed her forehead, then her chin, then the hollows of her eyes.

"Oh, Connor... I am not the same as I was. I don't know—" She was on the verge of tears again.

"You are perfect. You're mine, if you'll have me. The blood on your hands, if there is any, suits you, I swear it."

I tricked her into a smile, even as her shoulders heaved a little.

"I'm not sure... The Regula you met on the *Wretched Lady* feels leagues different from the Regula I am now."

"So, never stop. Change as much as you like, however you like." I sat back and looked at her. There was a tremble to her lip and a wariness in her eyes that I could not stand. "There's no scaring me away, no matter how you try."

She peered at me, then wiped away the remains of her tears.

Our fears put to rest for the moment.

I cupped her jaw, prompting her to bite at me.

"I almost ran down the dock to take you back."

"I missed you too, I think, even when I believed you were only with me because you pitied me." she pressed a hand to her chest. "It hurt to see the hunter's hands about your neck."

She missed me.

A smile crept across my face. I wasn't alone in this. I wasn't the only one in shambles. I wasn't some pirate she'd tumbled and would soon forget.

No, she, perhaps, was more the pirate now, because she did not hesitate to lean in, searching out my lips with hers, waiting not a moment more to plunder.

Now this, I had not had the courage to ask her. I wanted to claim her. I was not thinking clearly as we came together, lips and teeth and tongue, drowning in each other. I wanted it, I wanted her, for as long as I could keep her.

I pulled away, bracing myself on my arms, though it pained me to do so.

"Is that a yes?"

She gaped at me, her lips glistening in the warm light of Bobby's lamps.

"Sail with me, Regula. Stay by my side until fate is done with us." It was the sort of plea a pirate, caught on deck during a storm without a rope to anchor him, made of the sea.

I watched her think about it. Very nearly shut my eyes rather than read the answer in hers. I might not recover from her honesty.

"I'd be honored," she finally replied, her face going fiendish with delight.

I could taste my relief. "Regula, I believe you've stolen my heart."

"Pirated it, you mean. And I didn't. We traded. You've been walking around with mine."

"My pirate queen." I marveled at her. "My Eagle."

I reached out, desperate to close the space I'd put between us. Seas, I could barely believe my luck. Look at her, blush touched and freshly kissed. All unbound dark hair in a newly rumpled dress.

It was a gift to touch her, to hold her, to keep her with me. One I wouldn't ever take for granted.

I kissed her with unhurried reverence. She answered me in a rush, one hand firmly in my hair as she pulled my head back, and said, "Is this a bad time to inquire after your bed?"

I looked at her, and then at the strange couch in the lovely room in the second best brothel in a city where I'd never bothered to spend much time.

"Now?" I croaked, startling a laugh from her, the wind of it brushing against my cheek.

"No," she said, catching her breath. "No, I guess not, but I've been very curious about it. Seems unlikely you even have one, much less the time to introduce a lover to it." She smirked, twisting her fingers in my hair.

"If my lady wishes to acquaint herself with my bed, she has only to ask." I wound my arms around her, anchoring myself in her soft skin and sumptuous scent. "Though, I recommend she set aside a sizable chunk of her day for the visit." I froze, teasing her, until she clasped me to her bosom.

"I don't recall any such errand taking much time in the recent past," she said, as I nosed at the swell of her breast where it peeked from the collar of her dress.

"That is—" I bit her, lightly. "—because I have had to steal every taste of you." I bit again, a little harder, a little higher, and she arched under me. "Now that I know you've missed me, and only me, I intend to take my time, should we visit my bed."

The red tracks of my teeth traced the veins beneath her skin. I could get used to that.

"Mm, you'd better not be lying to me, Captain." I freed a knee from beneath her and slid up to take her lips.

"Never, Eagle," I whispered. "Seems a waste to save such things for my bed…" I pretended uncertainty. "In truth, I'm not sure I even have one anymore, as I'm no longer the captain."

She shifted, rucking up her skirts so that the silk of her thighs rested over mine.

"That's too bad. A regular sailor might use a serviceable couch instead… and one does not always have to linger." Her eyes flashed over the scenery before daring me to deny her.

"He might," I murmured as I went searching up her skirts, finding her slick to the touch.

Her fingers trailed over my buttons, deftly undoing them. Her haste was intoxicating, and I stopped short of reminding her that we had the rest of the night—no, the rest of our lives to explore each other. If she wanted me fast, I would not convince her otherwise.

She fitted herself to me, brushing off my hardworking fingers, and bid me to fuck her with all the politeness of a pirate.

I obliged her. I was beginning to think I'd forgotten how to refuse, as I slid slowly into her heat.

"I'd really rather not wait." She baited me, wrapping a hand around my neck and drawing me down to her.

"No, never again," I tried to say, but it was lost as I thrust. Seas, she felt so good. I was surprised at my own hunger. How had I lasted the whole of my captaincy without this? How had I waited my whole life for her?

She urged me on. The dizzy collision of our bodies provoked a sentiment softer and more serious than I'd ever known. I wanted to meet her step for step, to drink the dew that collected against her curls and set my teeth into every inch of her. To think that I would have the opportunity to do just that, over and over, was intoxicating. I was close to forgetting myself in her already, spurred on by my thoughts.

The sight of her spread beneath me, still stitched into her bodice and only halfway to unraveling, made me hitch her hips higher on mine. I pressed a foot down to the floor and bent my knee. There. That was what I was looking for. The sweet swell of her belly and splay of her ribcage would finish the job the pirate hunter had started. I was in danger of dying from the slight rock of her head every time I thrust. It would be worth it for the tight, rapturous squeeze of her. It echoed all the way to her eyelids and the clench of her jaw, and would soon bring me to begging myself.

I'd always known love would come to me, in the way people

often say it does, pounding at my door, but I had not guessed it would drench even the smallest of things. I wanted to make a map of her freckles and collect her sighs. I shut my eyes against her, trying to center myself, pulling myself back and out and down and in. But there was only so much I could handle when she was working herself against me, all the while muttering my name, half in curse and half in praise.

Her nails found the flesh of my arms and I felt the first shimmer of her release.

My own desire knocked against my ribcage, shouting frenzied down my body. Selfish. Unrelenting.

She shuddered around me, crying "Captain" loud enough to guide me to my own satisfaction. I rushed after her, and found myself undone, exquisitely spent, and utterly under her power when I came back to my senses.

I collapsed against her, twisting to fit into the cavern of her side, where it seemed she was more than willing to let me stay.

49

REGULA

The morning's docks were only as impenetrable as the men guarding them. Odette's note had been found and a search laid out by the council, headed up by their emissaries from Sanctuary. I wanted to run when I first woke to their squabbling outside, despite being cradled in Connor's arms. The group was louder than the rest of the festive city, standing around in the street as they sent a few men into every building.

My pirate captain didn't let me bolt, holding tight to my middle.

"This is Coisume, Eagle, not Sanctuary," he said. "There's too much money at stake to let strangers bust open every door. The council won't piss off the madams in the middle of a festival week, no matter how hard your countrymen push them."

That explained the noise. They weren't arguing with Bobby, but with each other.

I finally broke away and peered down from the window, hidden by lush curtains. None of the party bore the black uniform of the Ocuis. That was a small relief. If Valentin wanted me punished for what he'd seen, his men would be among the searchers, and there was no telling whether they'd found Earnest's body.

They were looking for Odette, but they might also be looking for me.

Connor was right. The men eventually moved away, continuing with their search. No one broke down our door, or, at least, no stranger.

We had only a few precious moments before Rory came barreling in, anxious to get back to the *Wretched Lady*.

"And what if we were busy, you lout?" Connor snapped at him, still reclining on the divan.

"You? Busy? Before midday? I don't think so." Rory grinned. I eyed the two of them from the safety of my curtain.

Connor relented, patting the seat beside him in invitation.

"Bobby and Clarys should—" Rory was interrupted by the arrival of the two women, bursting with ideas for our escape. I was beginning to think Connor and I were the only ones who'd gotten any sleep. There was a brightness to their eyes and a tightness to their plotting that suggested they'd stayed up much of the night.

Bobby wanted us to sneak out under the noses of the council and Sanctuary. The docks would be heavily guarded, and there was no veil of darkness or guise of celebration to hide us. Bobby took this as a challenge, and after hearing her plan, I was willing to risk it.

We'd all had a long night. Especially the men on the docks, with their new supervision and extra work. Bobby proposed their favorite sort of distraction. A group of Bobbin's sewists, sent in the spirit of the winter festivities, to take a load off the poor workers. If there were a few new girls mixed in, who'd notice?

In fact, the hardest part of our escape was concealing Rory. The man was built like a city gate, and the water was too cold to send him swimming to the ship.

Connor made a tidy prostitute after a close shave, some powder and paint, and a bit of padding under his dress. Rory, on the other hand, was too big of a risk to hide in the background and hope. There were a handful of girls in the city who had similar shoulders or as much height, some even with jaws to match. But they were few, and popular, and would certainly be sought after in a party of this type.

It was Clarys who came up with a disguise for the redheaded giant.

And it was I who was asked to sacrifice.

"Looks a bit like Boris, doesn't he?" She said, after wiping our attempt at rouge from his cheeks.

"Not when his head gleams like that," Connor said, halfway into a dress the color of cornflowers. I stuck a blossom, stolen from a dried winter wreath, into his newly curled locks.

"He might not have the hair, but she does," Clarys said, pointing at me with her brush, caked in red. She'd quickly settled in with the rest of us, not minding the pirate way of things.

"You can't possibly mean…" I held up a hank of my dark hair. I hadn't bothered pinning it up yet, and it hung to the bottom of my back.

"How would he wear it?" I bit my lip, considering her proposal. Sure, there was some similarity to the men, with their bulk and commanding height, but it would be a stretch.

"Tuck it under a scarf. He wears one sometimes, when it's too cold or sweaty out." The girl waved me off. "They'd expect to see him there, if we really were coming from Bobbin's. He's always with the girls. Be stranger without him."

"They don't look enough alike," Connor said.

"No one looks at Boris if they can help it!" Clarys cackled. "Besides us, that is. Take away all that metal." She squinted up at his piercings. "Give him a couple of scars and her hair. Dress him up in white. They'll jump out of his way."

"I don't know…" It *was* my hair they'd be chopping off to complete the fakery.

"Love, you're about to head off on a ship. Do you really want to keep all that?" Bobby asked. "In the wind and the rain and the like? I'd be ready to cut it off."

Perhaps she was right. I was on the precipice of a new life, one that would take some getting used to, no matter the state of my hair. I thought back to the pirates I'd seen aboard. Some had longer hair, oiled or braided or tucked under a cap. Others kept it sharp-blade short. Connor's poked out under his ears, and he surely hacked it off whenever it threatened his shoulders.

"There's sense to that," I agreed. "Is there no other way?"

"I don't think he'll make it as one of the ladies," Connor said.

"And I won't be swimming, not unless my life depends on it." Rory weighed in for the first time. He'd long since thrown his hands up and relinquished all responsibility in the matter, saying he'd be happy to stay in the channel city a season until things cooled off. I didn't believe him for an instant.

So it was decided.

A girl was sent to scare up some of Boris' signature clothing, and I was spun around and plied with a shot of whiskey to ease my loss. Clarys took great pleasure in shearing me. There was no sadness when it was done, only the wind kissing my neck and whispering promises.

More than one of the sewists sported short, flirtatious locks, so I didn't worry too much for my own disguise.

It was remarkable. Cutting my hair. Leaving on the *Wretched Lady*. *Living* on the *Wretched Lady*. So far off from the Regula of a week ago, and yet somehow right. It had been a long, long time since I'd had a heaping of joy or any reason to hope for more. Now, I had my boot heels firmly planted in a whole new life.

If my outer transformation stood in for my inner one, Rory's could not have been more inspired. Clarys had borrowed some eyebrow gum and applied it like snakes to his skin, dusting it with equal parts white and red powder, which at a glance, did absolutely ape Boris's famous scars. My hair was a passable match, though it kept slipping off his shaved head.

It was Bobby who grabbed it out of Clarys's hands. A few

forceful stitches later, she had all my hair affixed to the scarf, hanging down just as her husband's did.

"Never seen a sewist before?" she said when she saw my surprise.

Apparently not.

We left Bobbin's transformed.

Connor was pretty and forgettable. Rory was just as scary as the usual minder. I was good enough to blend in, and the women who'd offered to come with us were excited to show off. In fact, they bet on who'd lure the guards farthest from their post. I didn't have a purse, much less coin to lay on anyone, so I was spared from choosing among them.

I would have to come back to find out who won.

We only ran across one hiccup. There was a Sanctuarian assigned to our dock. A real stick-in-the-mud. He hemmed and hawed over the necessity of such a gift, with his nose set firmly in the air. When his fellows did not appreciate his dismissal of their surprise, he switched over to an argument of morality, which drew just about every channeler in the area to defend the honor of our sewists.

He quickly decided he was needed elsewhere when his fellows asked him if he'd like to search the freezing waters of Coisume's port. Rory didn't even have to affect Boris's clipped Vestine accent or raise a meaty fist.

Trenna, seemingly, had full faith in us, and the ship was ready the moment we were spotted down dock. If there was surprise over our costumes, none of it reached my ears.

Odette, Robin, and Jack had managed their own escape, and were hiding in the cooperage.

We were quietly swarmed by pirates, checked over, and declared good enough while Trenna made her way down to the deck beside us.

She held a beaten-up spyglass in her hands.

"I believe this is yours," she said, her voice carrying across the deck, and held it out to Connor.

He shook his head, his eyes glued somewhere below his skirts.

"Come on, Captain. We couldn't leave you." She jabbed the spyglass at his chest with no heed for his bodice, and added, "We voted. The *Wretched Lady* missed you."

He jerked his chin up at that, his eyes a little wide where they met the navigator's. I resisted the urge to twine his hand with mine.

"Will you lead us?"

Connor opened his mouth. Closed it.

"Until Griffin—"

Trenna held a hand up.

"Your crew voted for you, Connor. In truth. Not as a placeholder."

He finally snagged the spyglass from her grip, his mouth hard and hands steady. He looked around, the faces of the pirates reflected in his eyes. His crew.

They waited on his word. Nodding the truth of Trenna's words.

Rory was a little too quiet beside me.

The whole ship held its breath.

"It would be my honor," Connor said. He couldn't argue with his crew. Not in this. There was no great cheer, since we could not draw attention to ourselves just yet, but everyone began to buzz. Trenna slung an arm over Silver's shoulders and let out a dramatic sigh of relief.

Rory slapped Connor's back, and I pressed myself to his side, where he did not hesitate to gather me closer.

"What? Did you lot forget what it means to have a captain?" Connor's solemn manner dissolved into that of the careless captain I'd first met. "Here's my first order of business. Get us out of here!" He flung the flowers from his hair.

The crew cast us off.

It was only after the ropes were coiled aboard and Connor pulled away by his pirates that I noticed Clarys still standing on the deck, staring at Coisume receding in the distance. She wasn't going back.

I joined her, unable to stifle my smile, neither of us needing to say a word.

50

REGULA

Connor found me a while later, still at the rail. He'd changed out of his dress, but hadn't managed to clean off all of his paint. He nuzzled against the back of my neck, pressing his words against my skin.

"And for my second order of business—"

We were tackled into the railing.

The *Wretched Lady* was finally out of the range of Coisume's guns, and Odette was her own sort of cannonball, flying across the deck the moment she was cleared to come up.

Connor was swiftly banished, though I did not miss her eyes running wild over the both of us, and was sure I would be answering a myriad of questions as soon as she confirmed I was in one piece. It seemed, for the first time, that she would be caring for me.

I wanted to remind her that it was her own safety she should worry about, as she ran her fingers through my newly shorn hair, muttering her shock. But I couldn't. I wasn't her minder any longer. If she wanted to trot herself out in front of foreign governments or climb up to the crow's nest, I wouldn't be the one to stop her.

It was bittersweet. My path was clear before me for the first time, and hers… hers was out of my hands.

I had no doubt she would shape it to her liking. Things tended to go her way. She was adored. Her family would be so happy to have her back that they'd never question her multiple kidnappings. Or so she assured me.

I swatted at her. It wasn't me she would have to convince.

We danced around the particulars of our escapes. There was enough to both our stories that it would be better to wait and tell them before the whole of the ship rather than over and over again. I found myself instead burdening her with my deepest discomfort—the moments on the council's steps after I'd been dragged away. The satisfying heft of Earnest's body. His stillness in the distance.

Odette was silent, the wheels in her head turning. Her night had probably been just as blurry as mine, except that it had been full of dancing and feasting and at least one soaking in wine.

After a while, she shook her head. There had been no word of his death while she sat with the council. She knew nothing that might set my mind at ease.

Dread raced through me, tightening my fingers on the side of the ship.

Whether he was alive or dead, Earnest would haunt me.

I stared out at the ocean, regretting my past, but not the last few days. I would push him again if it meant he could not hurt Connor, or anyone, ever again.

Odette let the captain back into our orbit, the sight of him chasing away my morbid thoughts. I was here, on the deck of the *Wretched Lady*, with two of the people I cherished most in the world. I could not ruminate on dark thoughts with such a bounty before me.

Connor tugged on my wrist, glaring at Odette all the while. "Before we were so rudely interrupted…"

She flashed him a sweet but deadly smile.

"Promise you'll find me later?" Odette said. I swore it, and she melted into the crew, leaving me all to Connor. He marched me under the deck where Trenna held the helm, and into a familiar hallway.

"Surely the captain is too busy to be dragging me to his cabin?" I teased, for his intention was clear.

He turned on me, his boots half in and half out of the shadows.

"There is nothing more important than you."

I could think of a few things.

I rolled my eyes and found myself instantly pressed up against the planks just outside his door.

"Nothing," he repeated, deadly serious. His fingers tightened around my wrists, trapping them above my head on the cool wood.

Then he kissed me. Convincing me. Devouring me in the dark of the hall.

"You promised me your bed, Captain," I said when we broke apart for air. It was impossible to keep the plea from my voice.

"Is that what you want?"

I did, desperately. But there was something else I could no longer put off.

"No," I said, and his face went carefully blank. He dropped my wrists, but I caught one of his hands and laced our fingers together. He raised a brow.

By the time I'd guided him back out into the light, he was near to grinning. My partner in this, and perhaps all things.

To truly to become a pirate, I needed to whisper my name to the sea. It wouldn't do to test her goodwill any further.

I had Connor's strong hands on my hips and his encouragement in my ear while I leaned over the railing, casting my voice toward the attentive waves.

Safety had always been my priority. Boring, quiet, polite. These had been the hallmarks of my being, and it was a relief to relinquish them, even to so powerful a mistress.

I would take whatever the Far Flung threw at me now,

knowing myself to be part of a greater whole. Be it a crew, or with Connor, I was not going to simply drag myself toward my end, but reach out and grab life where I found it. I would take the risk with the wonder.

I was the one in the ropes, now.

I'd been Regula for a long time, and while I'd changed everything else, I decided to keep my name. I was finally proud of it.

I was sure the sea, which had spared me a watery grave more than once already, would not mind that she wasn't the only one to use it.

Though, if a nickname came along, or a descriptor was tacked on, I wouldn't fight it. Regula the Great sounded fair lovely to my ear. Red Regula too, maybe, if I spent too much time above decks without a hat for shade. The Eagle, maybe, to those who came to know me well enough.

The possibilities were endless and through it all the *Wretched Lady* would sail on.

John Baptista Tavernier, 1678

ACKNOWLEDGMENTS

What a strange pleasure to release *Shiver Me* into the world.

I could not have written this book without the help of my first readers: Elise, Jan, Jaskeerat, Jean, Jeanne, Jess, Natalie, and Sarko. You're all welcome on the *Wretched Lady* for life.

I wrote a novel in part because it meant commissioning pirate art. I never guessed I'd have amazing work from Camille Kolo, Jess Klier, Nafisah Tung, Squisite Art, and Zlue to obsess over! (Many more on the way, of course). Without my friend, Chynna, the book would not look this good.

Without Jess Klier, Connor & Regula would never have come to life, and without Camille Kolo, the world of the *Wretched Lady* would be a lot duller.

Huge thanks to my editor, Kate Wood of Kate Wood Proofreading. She's responsible for the polished, lovely story you've just read. She banished all my debut author fears with her cool & precise edits. All mistakes in the text are mine and mine alone.

It was a dream to work with my proofreader, Jaskeerat K. Malik. Stay tuned for her amazing book sometime in the future.

My creative (sometimes) mentor, Luna Shadows, is definitely to blame for *Shiver Me*. She made sure I never stopped writing.

I never thought my mother would read EVERY draft of my pirate romance novel, but she did, and it made all the difference. She birthed me and midwifed this book.

To my partner who said I should write, and then carved out the time and space for me to do so. Without your love and care there would have been no book at all.

And to you, dear reader. I'd like to thank you. Your thoughts & excitement are the very best part!

ABOUT THE AUTHOR

Vermillion would be far happier on the deck of the *Wretched Lady* than in Los Angeles sitting in front of her laptop. *Shiver Me* is her debut novel, but she has plenty of fantastical tales with charming bisexual characters up her sleeve. When she's not scheming over a story, you're just as likely to find her on a walk in a gnarled wood as in a dark bar with a book in her hand.

Sign up for her author newsletter at
READVERMILLION.COM

www.ingramcontent.com/pod-product-compliance
Lightning Source LLC
Chambersburg PA
CBHW030240120726
47903CB00005B/1555